John Law Media

NIGHT-SCENTED

David Barrie was born in Scotland.
He lives in Paris, where he works as a management consultant.

www.nightscented.com

Also by David Barrie

Wasp-Waisted

David Barrie

NIGHT-SCENTED

John Law Media

Published by John Law Media Ltd.
P.O. Box 26515, Glasgow G74 9EF
www.johnlawmedia.com
contact@johnlawmedia.com
First published in Great Britain 2010.

ISBN 978 0 9562518 1 7

Printed in Scotland by Thomson Litho, East Kilbride.

Il est dans Paris certaines rues déshonorées autant que peut l'être un homme coupable d'infamie; puis il existe des rues nobles, puis des rues simplement honnêtes, puis de jeunes rues sur la moralité desquelles le public ne s'est pas encore formé d'opinion ...

Certain streets in Paris are as disreputable as a man who has committed the worst of crimes. There are others whose nobility is uncontested; others honest in their modesty; and then there are those whose moral standing has yet to be determined.

Honoré de Balzac, *Ferragus*

A glossary of French terms can be found at the end of the book (the very last page inside the back cover).

"Captain, there's a stain on my dress."

That's what she said.

Not, hello.

Not, how are you?

Not, remember me?

It took Franck Guerin no more than a few seconds to place her voice, even though he had not heard it for about six months. He then quickly sifted his options. He could point out that the Brigade Criminelle did not run a dry-cleaning service out of the quai des Orfèvres. He could recommend dabbing – not rubbing – with vinegar or a solution of baking soda. Or he could tell her he had other things on his mind than the state of whatever she happened to be wearing.

But he did not.

In as calm and as pleasant a tone as he could muster on a morning when the coffee machine in the corridor was once more out of order he said, "Good morning, Sonia. That's a terrible shame."

"No it's not," she countered. "It's not a terrible shame. It's a crime."

"I doubt that," he objected, albeit diffidently, as she sounded perfectly serious. This was unusual for Sonia Delemazure, a young model – although she would instantly have corrected him with not-so-young, for she was all of twenty-eight – whom Franck had met while investigating the Du Bellay murders. And not heard from since, although it was now clear that she had hung onto his mobile number. "Still, I'm prepared to admit that crimes against fashion aren't really my speciality," he continued, wondering how expensive a dress she could be wearing at this time in the morning. Unless, of course, for her the previous night had not yet ended.

"I wouldn't be so sure of that. I seem to remember you committing them on a regular basis."

That was more like the Sonia he remembered.

"Point taken," he conceded. "Tell me about the dress."

"It's an Ephémère evening dress. Dark-blue with a fantastic cut. Makes me look two metres tall. A real scene-stealer. That's why I'm supposed to be last down the catwalk. A knockout blow right at the end. Fix their vision of the entire collection."

"So you're working?"

"Ephémère's Spring/Summer *haute couture* show. You don't get much more serious than that."

"At eleven forty in the morning?" asked Franck, having checked his watch.

"It's Fashion Week. Shows are on round the clock. Craveri's got this notion that early is the new late, so she chose a morning slot. Seems to have worked. Everyone's here, and most of them seem conscious."

Fashion Week. Four days in the winter cold when the big names in high fashion dictated what would be next summer's styles and colours for the ultra-rich and thereby, through osmosis, for everyone else. When every journalist and photographer in the world assigned to the fashion beat was to be found in Paris, or back home complaining about not having been allowed to go to Paris. When self-proclaimed fashion-loving celebrities took possession of every luxury suite in the capital and did their tricks for the paparazzi camped outside. When *défilés* were scheduled back-to-back from morning to night and designers measured their power by the minutes or hours they could run late. When improbably tall and impossibly thin young women were rushed from venue to venue to parade unbelievably expensive outfits on elevated platforms to the accompaniment of deafening music. When Paris took fleeting delight in feeling that it was once again the centre of the world.

"So what about this stain?"

"White splotches all over the back of the dress where it trails on the ground. I might get away with walking down the catwalk, but I couldn't turn around."

"Maybe they're not that big. Maybe no one will see them," he said, trying to sound encouraging.

"These people can see the thread count in a piece of fabric from across a room. They'll see them."

"Can't you get it out?" Still trying to be helpful.

"I think it's bleach, captain. Bleach doesn't come out."

"What makes you think it's bleach?"

"From the smell."

A thought struck Franck. Sonia was a tall girl, and surely very supple, but her dress would have to have a very long train indeed for her to be able to crouch down, pull it round and bring it to her nose.

"Does this dress look like something from the eighteenth century?"

"Of course not. This is the Ephémère show. Lacroix was yesterday."

"You can smell this stuff from a few spots down around your feet?"

"No, I caught the scent from the murdered guy in the corner of the room who stinks of chlorine."

Franck briefly nurtured the hope that this was just a sarcastic aside. Fifteen seconds of resolute silence from Sonia taught him otherwise.

"I'm on my way. Where are you?"

*

She had said she was in the André Citroen park, tucked into the south-western corner of the fifteenth arrondissement where the Seine met the city's ring road. It took Franck about twenty minutes to get there, siren wailing on the car he had snatched from the Brigade's pool. He called the incident in as he went, asking for a forensic team and backup from the local uniforms.

One of Paris' larger green spaces, the André Citroen park had colonised land that had once been home to Citroen's design office and assembly line. It now boasted several expanses of trees, flowers and grass, all regulated with geometric precision. Standing proudly at its head, much like the chateau looming over the gardens of Versailles, were two imposing glass structures. Easily fifteen metres tall and perched on sloping ground, they oversaw a vast lawn running down to the Seine. One was full – nobody was quite sure why – of Australian flora. The other was nominally home to a collection of fruit trees rooted in individual wooden caissons but had become such a popular venue for corporate events that they spent most of their time huddled together in a heated tent set up outside while lights were hung, hors d'oeuvres served, and speeches delivered in their place.

Today was no exception, although the transformation that had been effected upon the emptied glasshouse was particularly elaborate. All the exterior walls, with the exception of the one that held the entrance, were hung with what appeared to be massive transparent columns filled with water. An incessant stream of bubbles jostled inside the plastic cylinders, generated by small boxy pump units that sat beneath them. The resulting current gave life to the glittering light-blue star shapes and fantastically coloured plastic fish that had been placed inside them. The aquarium theme was echoed by a wide border of blond sand which encircled the glasshouse. It had been sculpted into tiny dunes, except at the entrance, where it respectfully drew itself back from a long ribbon of blue carpet leading up to the main door.

The only people visible outside were two young black men with shaven heads and tight dark suits which clung to their muscles. Everyone else seemed to be inside, behind the glass walls and the colourful tubes of turbulent liquid. Flashing lights bounced off the interior of the glasshouse and a rapidly pounding beat seeped from it. It did not look like a crime scene.

Franck walked swiftly towards the entrance, his parka open and a leather briefcase which had been restitched more than once in its life clutched in one hand. As he neared the glasshouse the music and lights inside reached a climax, after which silence momentarily intervened, only to be broken by a muffled wave of applause and cheers.

One of the black men extended an arm, palm out, as Franck drew closer.

"Show's nearly over, sir," he said, without budging from where he stood. "I'd stand well clear of the door."

It proved good advice. The door to the glasshouse pushed open and a stream of people shot out, most of them stylishly dressed women clutching hastily snatched coats, bags jammed under one arm and mobiles pressed against their ears. Dowdily dressed photographers sprinted after them like faithful dogs running to heel. There was less than an hour to go before the next *défilé* and the race was on for the best seats. Since the local uniforms had yet to turn up, Franck had no means to hold them at the scene – if that indeed was what it was. Even assuming that fashion reporters were no less blasé than journalists in general, there would surely have been some sign of agitation or trouble had they been privy to a murder.

Franck stepped backwards off the blue carpet, his shoes sinking into the light-coloured sand, and let them pass. He listened as best he could, but caught only snatches of conversation concerning colours, fabric layering, stylistic audacity and something about a deconstructive assault on marine stereotypes that nonetheless respected their mythic foundations.

When the flood had spent itself he moved back towards the entrance.

"I assume you do have an invitation?" asked one of the black guys, managing to be both polite and menacing at the same time.

"Perfect timing, captain!" cried Sonia Delemazure, who had just appeared behind the two security men. Although they had probably received strict instructions to keep their eyes front, both turned to look at her.

She had not been joking. She was a show-stopper.

From her eyelids to her toes, she was a portrait in shades of blue. Her dress clung precariously to the edge of her right shoulder before evolving in a series of folds to a tightly clenched waist. From there the pleats billowed out once more, having changed direction, and descended in a series of overhanging waves before expiring around her left foot. The fabric was a dark, almost bruised, blue, reminiscent of the sea at night, a notion reinforced by a mottled pattern of white and off-white that spread across it as if sprinkled from above, like reflected starlight. The effect was enhanced by a second layer that hovered above the dress itself. A thin screen of muslin, teased to such near-transparency that it seemed on the verge of disintegration, had settled on her otherwise naked left shoulder, veiling a colourful tattoo that stood guard over Sonia's famously sculpted collarbone. The layer of gauze mirrored the diagonal cut of her dress, only in reverse, terminating by her right ankle. When Sonia moved – her feet were perched on tapering stilettos, her toes and heels held in a lattice of delicate light-blue leather straps, ensuring that she was in constant, albeit almost imperceptible, motion in order to maintain her equilibrium – it shifted, as if borne by a night-time breeze, giving the impression that the white speckles beneath were winking in a distant sky.

As Franck observed her, Sonia turned complacently from side to side, beaming at him.

"If I don't make the cover of *Vogue* in this there's no justice in the world," she pronounced. "And since justice is your department, you're the one I'll call to complain to."

"How about we start with this morning's call," suggested Franck. "Where's the corpse?"

The two security men snapped their eyes back to him, perplexed frowns gathering on their foreheads. Apparently it was the first they had heard about a dead body.

"All work and no play," complained Sonia. "First of all, tell me how good I look."

"You look good," he stated. "Now can we get on with it?"

"Good?" came a new voice. "I'm sure your vocabulary runs to a little more than that, captain. I take it this is the captain you told me about?"

Sonia stepped hurriedly aside, clearing the entrance and turning to answer the question. Although he had to be mistaken, Franck had the fleeting impression that she had curtsied.

"This is captain Franck Guerin of the Brigade Criminelle, madame Craveri," said Sonia.

"Francesca," corrected the woman who was now the centre of everyone's attention, the slight Italian accent that been hiding behind her French bursting to the fore as she said her own name. She stepped out of the glasshouse. "Indulge me with Francesca. Madame Craveri just reminds me of how many years separate me from your youth and beauty. You wore the dress magnificently, Sonia. Marco is greatly indebted to you, as am I."

"It was a privilege to wear it," insisted Sonia. This time she definitely did curtsey.

Franck had encountered enough top executives in his time to recognise the air of command that Francesca Craveri projected. Probably in her late fifties, she was dressed with restraint in a knee-length skirt, a starched white blouse, and a jacket cut expertly to her size. Her shoulder-length hair was tucked neatly behind her ears, her jewellery was discreet – two rings bearing single gems, a pearl necklace, and tiny gold hoops in her ears – and her heels modest. She showed none of the studied, or slightly desperate, desire to make a sartorial statement that had characterised those who had poured out at the end of the show. Nor of the expensive extravagance embodied by Sonia and some of the other figures Franck could now glimpse moving about behind her in the glasshouse.

"Captain Guerin," she said, stepping towards him, her right hand held out, palm upwards, at shoulder height. For a brief moment – he could not have said why – Franck momentarily wondered whether he was expected to respectfully capture and kiss it. However, as he lifted his own hand hers gracefully arced down to shake it.

"I am Francesca Craveri," she said in a low voice, as if he alone was to be privilege to this information. "I have the good fortune to sit at the head of Ephémère."

No connoisseur, Franck nonetheless was well aware of Ephémère's status and activities. Whenever Chanel was mentioned, Ephémère would be named in the same breath. Both laid claim to the title of the country's, if not the world's, most emblematic fashion house. Like haughty and envious Arab princes, they jealously groomed and indulged *couture* designers in order to send their collections forth to battle for critical applause. A second front was provided by their relentlessly promoted rival perfumes, Eternal and Numéro Cinq having tussled for the laurels of the world's top upmarket scent for over eighty years.

"I, of course, know who you are," continued Craveri. "You sought justice for Laure Sarraute."

Laure, a young model who had unwittingly precipitated her own death by signing a contract with Ephémère, had been Franck's first criminal case. Seven months ago, though it seemed a lot longer.

She released his hand, saying, "It is a pity we could not meet in more auspicious circumstances. Today we revealed the result of four months' ceaseless work by our *haute couture* team. Right now we should be caught up in relief and celebration. But something dark and terrible happened here today and, though we had nothing to do with it, its shadow falls upon us. In any case, I'm indebted to you for not having interfered with the end of the *défilé*."

"Thank the traffic," he said, although not ungraciously. "I can't say I'm entirely happy at having let several hundred potential witnesses rush past me."

"They saw nothing," she assured him. "Or, at least, it is most unlikely that they could have seen anything. In any case, we will supply you with all their details. No one gets into a *défilé* without an invitation. We know who they are and how to reach them."

"I'll happily take all you've got," said Franck. "Maybe you can show me whatever it is they could not see?"

"Of course," said Craveri. "Perhaps we should wait for your colleagues?"

Her eyes switched to a point in the distance behind him.

Franck turned to see two technicians from the forensic squad coming towards them, each carrying two large black holdalls. He recognised one as Georges Sternberg, with whom he'd worked before. The other was so young he assumed she was a trainee.

Franck raised a hand and motioned them on.

"Let's go. They'll catch up."

"Perhaps you gentlemen could help them with their bags," suggested Craveri, addressing the two doorkeepers before she extended a hand to Franck, inviting him to cross the entrance.

"After you, madame," he insisted.

She smiled at him.

"In a public space you would be quite right, but not here. This is my domain. I am the one who should stand aside and invite you in. Please, proceed."

He bowed to her superior knowledge of the rules of courtesy and stepped into the glasshouse. Sonia was ushered in after him, and Craveri brought up the rear. Outside the security men sprinted towards the technicians, who ignored their offer of help and hung stubbornly onto the bags containing their equipment.

"This way," said Craveri, guiding Franck through the debris of the *défilé*.

There were several hundred seats that, although displaced in the recent rush for the exit, had clearly once been arranged in neat rows on either side of a catwalk which ran from a distant stage down most of the length of the building. Spotlights hung heavily from steel rods suspended on chains from the ceiling. Banks of speakers that could have handled a small rock concert were piled on either side of the stage. Figures milled about. Young men dressed in black t-shirts and canvas trousers were hauling cables, clutching clipboards or beginning to pile up the seats. Long-legged models in flimsy dresses which probably cost more than their weight in gold were lounging around or talking excitedly to their agents and minders. A man in his late thirties, barefoot in worn jeans and an open-necked shirt, sat on the catwalk with his knees drawn up to his chin, his hair tousled and his eyes bloodshot.

"That's Marco Chiriotti, the designer," whispered Sonia. "Hasn't slept for three days."

He raised a weary hand as they swept past, everyone stepping smartly out of Francesca Craveri's way.

Craveri broke her pace momentarily to call out to the designer, "It was a triumph Marco. They loved everything. Time to stop worrying and celebrate. You can rest afterwards."

He mouthed a silent *grazia* and blew her a kiss.

They continued round the edge of the stage and through a door behind it set into one of the lateral glass walls. This led into a temporary structure which had been erected outside the glasshouse for the *défilé*. A corridor ran ahead of them. To the left were three sets of double doors, all of which opened onto the same space – a vast room packed with dressing tables, full-sized mirrors and clothes rails under oppressively bright industrial lighting. To the right were three evenly spaced doors, all shut. One was marked 'Toilets', one 'Technical', and the furthest away 'Catering'. At the end was a fire escape which, despite the outside temperature, was propped open.

A young man who appeared to have been cloned from the two sentinels at the main entrance stood in front of the door marked 'Catering'. He moved aside as Craveri advanced towards him, opening the door inwards but staying in the corridor.

"It's all yours, captain," said Craveri. "You'll be the first person in since Sonia here came rushing out."

"Screaming?" asked Franck.

"Quiet and determined would be a better description. Would that be fair, Sonia?"

Sonia blushed slightly, delighting in the compliment.

A hand tapped on Franck's shoulder. It was Georges Sternberg, who handed him a pair of elasticated plastic bags to go over his shoes. As Franck slipped them on Sternberg did the same. He then handed over a pair of disposable gloves.

"Got my own," said Franck, tapping his briefcase.

"Mine are better," declared Sternberg. "They've come straight from the box, rather than lying about in your grubby briefcase for weeks."

Franck pulled on Sternberg's gloves.

"Me first?"

"You're the one with the gun."

"Ever known a corpse to start shooting?"

"We'll know it's a corpse when I say it is."

Franck went through the entrance and stepped to one side of the door. The room was surprisingly large, some fifteen metres long. Overall, the temporary structure erected for the *défilé* probably had as large a footprint as the glasshouse itself. Long tables piled with glasses, bottles of water and juice, platters of fruit, and largely untouched baskets of *viennoiseries* lined the walls on both sides. At the midpoint of each series of tables were three coffee machines surrounded by hundreds of empty capsules and countless abandoned espresso cups. The centre of the floor was occupied by high-perched round tables and accompanying bar stools. A few metres short of the end wall a screen with a single opening had been drawn across the room.

Sternberg followed Franck's example, taking up position on the opposite side of the door.

"Sonia," said Franck. "Talk me through what happened."

"I'd been made up and dressed for ages. Unlike everyone else, I was only to go on once. A new face for the last dress in the show, just to heighten the effect. Problem was, I was starving. I arrived a little late this morning, and didn't get a chance to grab anything before they started on my hair. Then straight on with the make-up. Then the dress. I was done long before the *défilé* even started, because Marco wanted to make sure I was perfect. But once you're dressed, you're not allowed to eat or drink anything. House rules, in case something gets spilled. And once the *défilé* starts, absolutely nobody's allowed into Catering – not the make-up girls, not the hairdressers, not the seamstresses, not the technical crew. There's too much chaos backstage, something's bound to get knocked over."

"But you were starving," prompted Franck.

"So I slipped off my shoes – to move quicker – and snuck in here to get a banana. Then I figured I might as well have a coffee, so I made an espresso and took it over to one of the tables to drink it. I was just standing there dreamily when I looked down and noticed a white patch on the bottom of my dress near my right foot. I checked more closely and found there were several of them. You don't want to know what I said then, but I was not happy. I'd been so careful! I'd avoided everything that was flaky or could have left the odd crumb. I'd treated the coffee machine like it was an explosive device. It was so unfair! So I looked at the floor and noticed a trail of clear drops that ran from the bin underneath the three coffee machines over there to the screen back there." Her arm extended over Franck's shoulder to point to the right-hand side and the far end of the room. "So I hitched up my dress and followed it. Do the same and look to your left."

Franck motioned to Sternberg, who slipped a digital SLR from his shoulder and moved over to the coffee machines, crouching down to photograph the bin beneath them and the surrounding floor area.

Franck gave him a wide berth and walked through the clumps of tables and stools towards the far end of the room.

"Definite bleach smell from here," he observed, even before reaching the opening in the screen.

He stepped delicately through it, keeping his feet off any trace of liquid on the floor. To his right shrink-wrapped packs of bottled water were stacked up, alongside large boxes marked

'Nespresso' and others containing glassware. To his left two cleaner's trolleys were parked against the wall, each with brushes, mops, a frame to hold a large bin bag and a deep tray containing all sorts of cleaning products.

Beyond them a man lay on his back, his legs extended towards Franck, both slightly bent at the knee. He wore what had once been a midnight-blue wool suit with a thin pinstripe, black shoes, a navy-blue tie, and a white shirt with folded-back cuffs. Understated elegance and impeccable tailoring, although the effect was somewhat spoiled by the large and irregular red patch that discoloured his shirt just above his trouser belt. The bullet hole in his forehead did not help either. Nor the fact that his suit exhibited slowly spreading patches of colour loss. The final indignity was provided by the fact that he lay, his hair soaking, in a clear puddle that stank of chlorine.

Franck stood stock-still, taking in every detail.

Sternberg came round the screen behind him, looked over his shoulder, and made his pronouncement. "OK. It's a corpse."

"I'm glad you cleared that up," said Franck. "It's all yours."

He stepped back outside the screen while Sternberg took a series of photos before summoning his assistant over and delving into one of their bags of tricks.

"Did you recognise him?" Franck's question was for Sonia, who remained outside the door.

"No," she replied. "Nicely cut suit. Not so keen on the new colour scheme, though. Didn't work as well as on my dress. Too heavy-handed with the bleach, I suspect."

"Can I borrow that?" Franck asked Sternberg's assistant, who had been handed the SLR camera.

She nodded and passed it over. Franck walked back to the corridor. He held the camera up so that the screen on the back was at eye level for Francesca Craveri. Sonia hung back, looking chastised. Franck felt sure he had missed some observation by Craveri about Sonia's flippant remarks.

"Can you identify him?"

Craveri took the camera from him without hesitation and flicked back through several images.

"Alain Perrin," she said.

"As in Perrin Industries?" asked Franck.

"The very same."

An arms manufacturer shot in the forehead. All the bleach in the world could not stop this from getting messy.

*

Franck was about to leave when he remembered something.

There were now only a few dozen people around. Three uniformed policeman had finally arrived from the fifteenth arrondissement commissariat and had helped to take statements from the backstage team and the few guests who had the misfortune to still be around when Franck announced that no one could leave without talking to the police. It was now after five. He wanted to think over what he had and talk to his boss. Georges Sternberg had left two hours before, after the medical examiner had breezed through, providing a quick briefing on the body and authorising its removal.

Franck sought out Sonia. She was sitting in the dressing room in the extension listening with uncharacteristic seriousness to Francesca Craveri. She had changed into black jeans and a baggy, wide-necked red sweater. The dress she had been wearing hung in state on a nearby rack.

"Sorry to disturb you, but this should be the last time for today," he said as he approached them.

Craveri beckoned him forward.

"If that means we can all go, you can disturb us all you like, captain," she said. "Valentino's last show is due to start at the Rodin museum in less than an hour. Despite what has happened here today, I am honour-bound to go and pay homage to him."

Franck pointed to the dress on its hanger.

"Can you show me the stain that started all this?"

"Only approximately," said Sonia, getting to her feet. She lifted the dress by its hanger and turned it around. She pointed vaguely to an area of mottled fabric near the hem.

"I can't see any difference between that spot and the rest," said Franck.

"That's because you're looking at Marco's handiwork." Craveri said this with a proud smile, taking obvious delight in her designer's talents.

Sonia jumped in with the explanation. "I knew I couldn't go down the catwalk with a stain, so I rushed to find Marco. I showed him what had happened. He didn't even blow up. Just held the hem in his hands for a few seconds, sniffed at it, and then knew what to do. Utter genius."

"Which was?" prompted Franck.

"Shot off and grabbed a container of bleach."

"From where?" interrupted Franck. So much for the sanctity of his crime scene.

"From a storage area in the toilets. We're frivolous but we're not completely irresponsible," Sonia shot back. "He dismantled one of the sprays the wardrobe mistresses use if they have to dampen fabric, filled it full of bleach, threw a plastic bag over my head, and sprayed the entire dress. Then he dug out a muslin shawl – God knows from where – and draped it over me. What was sombre and stately became exciting and enigmatic."

"He did a Jackson Pollock," murmured Franck.

"Indeed he did," agreed Craveri, looking at him approvingly. "Just wait till you see the photos."

*

Yves de Chaumont, *juge d'instruction*, drummed his fingertips on the folder that lay before him on his otherwise unencumbered desk. The cover was marked 'CHANTREAU, Regis', who was suspected of running a network that raided isolated country churches for paintings and liturgical objects by obscure eighteenth- and nineteenth-century artists, feeding them to antiquarians and collectors abroad. A subject dear to Yves' heart. A folder he had presented with a flourish to Franck two days previously.

"I'm going to have to find someone else for this, am I not?" he conceded.

"Or keep it on hold for a while," suggested Franck.

"And let another few village chapels lose their triptychs in the meantime?" asked Yves, shaking his head. "I'll find another solution."

With one resolute finger he pushed it aside.

"The fatal shooting of Alain Perrin," announced Yves. "Your new case. One to the stomach, one to the head."

"First shot incapacitates," said Franck, one hand moving unconsciously to place itself protectively across his stomach. He knew what he was talking about. "Second shot kills."

"Sort of rules the amateurs out, doesn't it?" observed Yves. "Although the bleach thing is rather strange."

"It was found on site. There were three empty bleach containers in a bin under one of the food tables. They probably came from the cleaning trolleys parked behind the screen."

"That was very considerate of our killer. Not one to leave rubbish lying around. Unfortunately, that makes it unlikely he left his prints on them."

"Carried them a bit haphazardly, though. That's where the trail of spots on the floor came from."

"And the tell-tale stain on mademoiselle Delemazure's dress?"

"Exactly," said Franck.

"So was this a symbolic or practical gesture?"

"Bleach does a pretty good job of destroying any trace of foreign DNA. It doesn't look like there was a struggle, but given the use of bleach there must have been some kind of physical contact. Otherwise, why bother? You can shoot a man from a metre away and not leave a shred of biological evidence. Maybe they shook hands. Maybe the killer spat on his victim after he was dead. Or kissed him. Or even licked him."

"Stranger things have happened," conceded Yves. "But this was a lot of bleach, was it not?"

"Three 1.5 litre bottles. His clothes were soaked in it, and it was leaching all around the body."

"Sounds a bit excessive. And what is excessive is sometimes symbolic. So what does bleach do?"

"Removes colour and kills bacteria," replied Franck. "Whitens and cleans."

"Purification through destruction," observed Yves. "Worth keeping in mind. What else have we got?"

"Remarkably little – for a murder that took place at an event with nearly four hundred guests and about eighty backstage."

"If you want no one to see you, head for a crowd. Don't tell me you managed to process almost five hundred witnesses in the course of a single afternoon? Stakhanov would be proud."

"Just the backstage lot. There were a handful of guests still hanging around, but most were on their way out as I arrived on the scene. We've got contact details for them all, so we can still chase them down. A lot are from overseas, though, and will probably leave at the end of Fashion Week."

"Which is?"

"Tomorrow night."

"Forget it. You'll never catch them," said Yves. "We'll have to wait and see if someone comes forward once the news about Perrin comes out. Anything from the witnesses you talked to?"

"The team from the fifteenth arrondissement took most of the statements, but based on what I heard nobody remembers seeing the victim go backstage. Nobody remembers hearing a shot either. That said, if it was fired during the *défilé*, that's no surprise. They had concert-level amplification in the glasshouse and had piped the music through to the extension outside. There were speakers in the dressing area, the main corridor and the catering section where the shooting took place

– small ones, but loud enough."

"Didn't you say there was a technical section right next door to where the body was found?"

"Yes, but it was used only for storage. The sound and lighting crew were all in the glasshouse."

"And there was only one means of access to the extension?"

"Only one door from the glasshouse. However, there were fire doors in every room in the extension, and at the end of the corridor that ran through it. They all opened onto short flights of steps."

"One-way doors?"

"In theory, yes. Panic bars on the inside and nothing on the outside. But at least three were jammed open when I got there. Smokers nipping in and out, I imagine."

"Including the one in the catering section?"

"I'm afraid so."

"Several access points, then. And nobody watched over them?"

"Apparently not. There was no surveillance of the extension from the outside. Just to make things worse, they'd erected a sight screen all around it to stop any passers-by gawking."

"How convenient. What about the door between the extension and the glasshouse?"

"Constant movement during the *défilé* and before it started. And not just backstage traffic either. The only toilets in the place were in the extension, so guests got mixed up in it too."

"And nobody saw Perrin?"

"Sure, several remember him arriving. He got there relatively early, it seems. Just after nine."

"On his own?"

"Yes. Was wearing a long black cashmere coat, which we found over the back of a chair out front. And carrying a hard-bodied briefcase. A wide one, like the sample cases sales reps use."

"Was the briefcase left with the coat?"

"No. We found it in the catering section."

"With the body?"

"No. On the floor in the main part of the room at the foot of one of the stools. He had been in there before the *défilé* started. He was seen eating a croissant – which is apparently the kind of thing people remark at fashion events."

"Jealously, I suppose," observed Yves. "He didn't just stay there and sit out the show?"

"Couldn't have done. The catering section was closed just before eleven, although it wasn't locked. And, more to the point, one of the wardrobe team remembers seeing him going back into the glasshouse. Complimented him on his suit."

"He may simply have forgotten his briefcase and gone back to find it," suggested Yves. "Contents?"

"Very little. A sheaf of business documents. Today's copy of *Les Echos*. That's it."

"How thick?"

"*Les Echos*?" Franck knew the question was stupid as it left his lips. It had been a tiring day, but that was a pretty poor excuse. Then again, he had refused to allow anyone – including himself – access to the coffee machines in the catering section.

"The documents," Yves clarified.

"No more than a dozen sheets in all."

"Nothing he couldn't have carried in a folder or in an inside pocket of his coat, then. Was there a combination on the briefcase?"

"I don't remember one. I'll check. You think there was something else in it?"

Yves shrugged. "Nobody – present company excepted – likes carrying a briefcase. Particularly to what was basically a social occasion. Gets in the way if you carry it about. Gets in everyone else's way if you leave it propped against your chair. Wasn't there a coat check?"

Franck thought back to the layout of the glasshouse. "Yes there was, but given the speed at which they poured out at the end, I don't think many used it."

"In any case, Alain Perrin chose not to. He also chose not to leave his briefcase in his car, assuming he had a car. Did you find one?"

"A chauffeur turned up looking for him around one. Had been waiting outside the park since dropping him off that morning."

"He could have looked after it for Perrin, but he wasn't asked to. Curious. Maybe I'm making too much of this briefcase ..."

"But I'll check it out," Franck assured him.

"So Perrin arrives, goes into the extension at some point, eats his croissant, comes out again. The *défilé* starts. Then what?"

"Then it's all eyes on the show and pandemonium backstage."

"So the next recorded sighting is when mademoiselle Delemazure gets a little peckish?"

"I'm afraid so."

"I suppose we should be thankful that at least one model still has an appetite."

Thursday, 24th January

"Sorry to have kept you waiting. As you can imagine, this is not proving the easiest of days."

Franck shook Benoît Nallard's outstretched hand. They were on the seventeenth floor of one of the towers of La Défense, looking out across the low-rise tedium of neighbouring Puteaux. It was ten thirty-five. Franck had been waiting for about three quarters of an hour in Perrin Industries' main reception area. The day's copy of *Les Echos* lay open on a nearby coffee table. The murder of Alain Perrin was on page three. A brief article accompanied by a photo announced his death at the hands of an unknown party and named the firm's Financial Director as interim CEO. Nothing else. News that it was an execution-style shooting had not leaked out.

"Short, isn't it?" observed Nallard, glancing down at the paper. "One of the advantages of not being publicly listed. No shareholders to reassure."

"Someone's been asking you questions, though," said Franck. "Otherwise you wouldn't be running so late."

"You can't imagine. And now I suspect it's your turn, captain. I trust you're a little better at it than those I've been fobbing off since yesterday afternoon. Let me take you to my office."

He led Franck down a corridor and through a door marked 'Benoît Nallard. Financial Director'. It led into a generously sized office with a large desk in one corner, a round table that could seat eight in another, and two paperboards covered with scribbled figures and stranded words. Nallard gestured to the table and sat one chair away from Franck.

"Coffee? Tea? Water?"

"I'm fine," said Franck, who had already drained two coffees provided by the firm's attentive receptionist. He extracted a business card from his briefcase and pushed it across the tabletop to Nallard, who reciprocated instantly.

"As you can see, it's no longer entirely accurate," said

Nallard, referring to the title printed upon his card. "I only wish it still was." It sounded like genuine regret.

"I'm sorry for the circumstances that bring me here," offered Franck.

"They are not of your making, captain Guerin. How can I help you?"

"Do you know of any reason why someone would kill Alain Perrin?"

"This may surprise you, but no, I don't. No reason whatsoever."

"You're right. It does surprise me. You're in the arms business, after all. It's not the most angelic of industries."

Nallard raised a finger, a prelude to clarification. "We are gunsmiths. It's not quite the same thing."

Franck delved into his briefcase and pulled out a glossy booklet he had picked up from one of the display racks in the reception area. The front cover showed an infantryman in full camouflage gear holding a scope-equipped rifle across his body. Beside him, reaching no higher than his waist, was a squat device with two sets of caterpillar tracks, a number of antennae, camera units and sensor panels, and a telescopic arm supporting a single-barrelled gun. The booklet bore the title 'Perrin Industries. Precision Munitions.'.

"Not quite your sporting aristocrats out for a day's game-shooting," he observed.

"Granted," said Nallard. "But it's not a pile of anti-personnel mines either, nor a container-load of AK-47s or something similarly cheap and cheerful on its way to an African conflict zone. Sure, we're in the arms trade, but not the market segment where you get shot in the head when a deal goes awry."

"So what segment are you in?"

Nallard pointed to the booklet Franck had produced. "Like it says. Precision munitions. Ever since Hervé Perrin crafted his first set of hunting rifles for Napoleon III in 1853 and drove James Purdey and his shotguns back across the Channel. We still have a sporting range, which is used by the national Olympic squad and those of six other countries. Today, however, most of our activity is devoted to military and security uses. What you have here is a bolt-action PI54 with an effective range of 1300 metres if you use the right ammunition. Beside it is an APS, or Automated Precision Shooter, basically a remote-controlled sniper robot. We make the rifle mechanism. Since an APS only does what it's told and is unable to adjust its shot instinctively the way a human marksman can, its ballistic performance must be entirely predictable and reliable. Our weapon on the APS delivers 0.3 MOA, if that means anything to you."

"That it's very good at what it's supposed to do?" hazarded Franck. It was a guess, but not a very difficult one.

Nallard nodded.

"What you're saying," continued Franck, "is that you make very elaborate weapons with a price tag to match. Low volumes, high prices and plenty of legitimate acquirers."

"Precisely. Without exception, all our military and security business is carried out with NATO countries. Our sporting range is sold the world over, but I doubt Alain Perrin was murdered because somebody failed to bag a fourteen-pointer with one of our guns."

"Fair enough. If it had nothing to do with Perrin Industries' business activities, were you close enough to Alain Perrin to know if he had any major problems in his private life?"

"Alain inherited the controlling stake in Perrin Industries from his father two years ago. I've been in charge of Finances here for the past eleven years. We worked together very closely ever since he took over the reins. Honestly, I don't think he had much time for a private life."

"He wasn't married," Franck stated. "Was he seeing someone?"

"Not that I know of. I'm over twenty years older than him ... than he was. It's not as if we spent a lot of time on the town together, but I'm sure that if he'd had a steady girlfriend, he'd have mentioned something about her."

"A thirty year old multi-millionaire, and all he did was work?"

"When you own the firm you run, work and play are not necessarily distinct categories," insisted Nallard. "Alain had been raised with a strong entrepreneurial spirit. He really wanted to see how far he could develop Perrin Industries. And when he wasn't doing that, he had other projects. The ownership stake here was only part of his wealth."

"A hands-on company director, an active investor, a young man with many responsibilities and demands on his time," recited Franck. Nallard nodded along. "Then he takes the morning off to go to a fashion show?"

Nallard's head stopped bobbing. "I don't know what to say. An unusual choice, I grant you that."

"He never mentioned it to you?"

"No. He was originally scheduled to chair the quarterly TQR yesterday morning..."

"TQR?"

"Total Quality Review. A presentation of performance indicators charting the quality of our design and manufacturing processes."

"Sounds irresistible," said Franck. "I'd choose that over a *haute couture défilé* any day."

Nallard smiled politely. "Alain was committed to our Total Quality system. He reinforced it within months of taking over. He'd never missed a quarterly review before."

"So how did he explain his absence?"

"He didn't. He called our Production Director at home on Saturday afternoon and asked him to take his place. Said he had to make good on a commitment elsewhere."

"Did he call in at the office before the show yesterday?"

"Not as far as I'm aware. According to his schedule, he was to be picked up at home at eight ten and driven to the André Citroen park. The driver was to wait in the vicinity and then take him to lunch at le Grand Véfour. Afterwards he was due back here at three to interview a candidate for one of our top posts in sales."

"Lunch with whom?"

"Myself and two Americans from a robotics company in New Mexico. There's talk from the Pentagon about a stealth version of the APS. We're thinking of collaborating."

"Was he to bring anything to this meeting?"

"Like?"

"Technical plans. Samples. Anything that a competitor might be interested in stealing."

"No. Nothing like that."

Franck leaned back in his chair. This was going nowhere.

"Can you send me a copy of his agenda?"

"Digital?"

"Yes. My email's on my card."

"Of course. What period?"

"The last six months should do."

"I'm sorry I've not been more useful," said Nallard. He sounded genuine, but at the same time his eyes glanced at his watch.

Which was fair enough. He had a company with a 400 million euro turnover to get to grips with.

Nallard steered Franck back down the corridor to the reception area.

As they shook hands, he grimaced slightly before leaning close to Franck and saying, in an embarrassed undertone, "We were told Alain was killed. That's all."

"That's right," said Franck, keeping his own voice low. "No other details have been released."

"It's just – you know – I don't want the staff getting carried away and imagining some horror story."

"He was shot."

"A clean shot?"

Franck's eyes widened momentarily, but he managed to say nothing.

Nallard did work in precision munitions, after all.

*

"A perfectionist," muttered Franck, sharing his thoughts with a keyboard, a screen and the four featureless walls of his office. "Wonder how long he'll last."

He had an email from lieutenant Blanchard, who had turned up the day before in the André Citroen park at the head of the two *gardiens de paix* despatched by the fifteenth arrondissement commissariat. He had a vague recollection of a young, serious face, and of the care with which he had set up neat rows of chairs on one side of the glasshouse for those waiting to be interviewed while spacing his men out on the other so that statements could be taken out of earshot. They had all debriefed before Franck left the scene but Blanchard had promised to collate the information his team had gathered.

And collate he had. Having provided a concise summary for each person interviewed, appending the phone numbers gathered and the initials of the policeman who took the statement, Blanchard went on to extract the salient details. Not exactly gripping stuff. Alain Perrin was definitely on site by nine ten or nine fifteen. Some of the witnesses noted the quality of his suit, but none seemed to be aware of who he was. He had been seen in the catering section before the *défilé*, where he had courteously made coffee for three make-up girls before taking his own. No one had any recollection of seeing Perrin moving about during the *défilé* – however, as Blanchard took pains to point out, as most of the guests had escaped questioning, they had not been able to identify anyone who had been sitting close to him. No one remembered hearing a sound that might have been that of a gunshot. No one had been standing outside the extension during the *défilé*. A total of four of the backstage staff recalled rapidly smoking a cigarette beside an open fire door during that time, but they had seen nothing out of the ordinary.

Just when it was beginning to look as if Blanchard's efforts had served only to assuage his own professional conscience, Franck stumbled upon something new. It came from the doormen, or security detail, as apparently they had insisted on being called. They had been on site since five in the morning. Although the temporary structure outside the glasshouse had been set up and equipped over the previous two days, the racks of clothes, the cosmetics, the gift bags for guests, and the traiteur's spread for the catering section had arrived in a fleet of vans before dawn. The doormen reported having repeatedly warned off a homeless man who hovered like a vulture around the traiteur's vehicle. He was still in the immediate vicinity when the guests began to pour in, sitting amongst some nearby trees, watching them intently.

Franck had no recollection of having seen such a figure when he arrived. And yet the homeless were nothing if not persistent in the presence of a potential free meal. Whoever it was, he must have known he had a better chance of running off with pocketfuls of croissants and brioches if he waited until after the event. At that point the traiteur would have been happy to give him what remained to save having to haul it away. He must have hung around during the *défilé* – which made him the one potential observer of any goings-on outside the extension. And if he had not, then something may have happened to scare him off.

The meticulous Blanchard had noted the number of the agency that had provided the security detail, and the doormen's individual mobile numbers. Franck started calling and within half an hour had succeeded in questioning all three of the men who had been present the previous morning. He wanted a description.

He got it: the homeless man had been dirty and smelly. Nobody could tell him whether he had been young or old, bearded or clean-shaven, dressed in rags or in normal clothes. It was as if their eyes had proved as reluctant to rest upon him as their noses to catch his odour or their bodies to be anywhere near him.

Being homeless was as near as you could get to being invisible.

*

Franck stood outside the Westin hotel on the rue de Castiglione. It was almost four o'clock. The world's fashion press was streaming past him, heading through its revolving doors. The same hurried, exuberant crowd as yesterday. He felt that he ought to be pulling them aside, asking questions, hoping that someone had let their eyes slip from the catwalk during the Ephémère *défilé* and noticed Alain Perrin on the move.

He glanced at his watch. He had been told to wait here for Francesca Craveri. Her personal assistant had expressed polite disbelief when he had phoned to ask to talk to her, having set aside lieutenant Blanchard's exemplary report. The assistant had pointed out that Fashion Week was still in full swing and that the line of people currently waiting to have a word with madame Craveri now bordered on the infinite. However, when he pointed out in return that he was in charge of the Alain Perrin murder investigation, she said she would see what she could do. An hour later Craveri's assistant phoned back, interrupting his late lunch to offer him a four o'clock spot outside the Westin. She was very specific about the outside part.

Some insistent horn blowing broke out. Franck surveyed the scrum of taxis disgorging a strange mix of chic, sober, and outrageous profiles at the curb before him. Although there was a lot of jostling for position going on, that was not where the sound had come from. He looked further. On the far side of the street a silver-grey BMW with tinted glass sat alone, its engine running and its rear passenger window half open. Francesca Craveri waved her fingers at him.

Franck jogged across, weaving through the slow-moving traffic heading down the street from place Vendôme. He skirted round behind the car and slid into the back seat opposite

Craveri.

"Drive us around, Richard," she said to the driver. "Don't leave the neighbourhood, though."

She then turned to Franck and shook his hand.

"I must apologise for receiving you like this," she said. "But if I'd joined you at the Westin, we would not have been able to talk."

"This is fine," insisted Franck. "Thanks for making the time for me."

Craveri nodded to acknowledge his thanks then waved a hand to dismiss them. "Ephémère will do anything it can to help you solve this crime, captain. This may be one of the busiest times of our year, but you have priority. And I invite you to remind me of that if you ever feel that it is necessary."

"I'll try not to be a pest, but I do have a question about Alain Perrin."

"Go ahead."

"What was he doing at the *défilé*?"

"I would like to think he was admiring the dresses, but even I have to face the fact that he might just have been staring at the girls." They shared a complicit smile.

"That's entirely possible," said Franck, "I suspect his reading of choice was more *Les Echos* than *Vogue* or *L'Officiel de la Mode.*"

"You're not really an avid follower of fashion yourself, are you captain? Just so you know, the true equivalent of *Les Echos* in our world is *WWD*, so long as you're happy to read in English. You, however, should at least be reading *L'Officiel* – the *de la Mode* bit isn't *à la mode* anymore. It needs every reader it can get. If *L'Officiel* ever folds, then we will finally have to accept that New York really has won."

"I'll give it a try. But it's true, I have other centres of interest. So did Alain Perrin. Precision rifles. Industrial processes. Business issues."

"Is fashion not a business?"

"Sure, but it wasn't his business."

"I think you'll find you're wrong about that," she said.

"Enlighten me."

"There were 408 places for our show. The first draft invitation list had over a thousand names. It took a lot of whittling down. Few friendships are formed at fashion shows, but it's easy to acquire an enemy for life by withholding an invitation. Given that his was – as you point out – an unusual, if not unlikely, presence, Perrin was only there because someone really wanted him to be there."

"And that someone was you?"

"Not at all. I had never met Alain Perrin. I knew vaguely who he was, but like you, I would have assumed that our worlds were quite separate."

"So who got him onto the list?"

"Another of our guests."

"Guests get to invite other guests?"

"Not normally. But this was someone whose presence was very important to me, for symbolic reasons. So when she asked that Perrin be invited too, I scored someone else off the list and made room for him."

"Who was this indispensible guest?"

"Isabelle Arbaud," she stated. Craveri sat back in her seat and momentarily took her eyes off Franck's to glance outside at the buildings and the people they were gliding by. "*Ma petite* Isabelle."

Franck said nothing. He watched the side of Craveri's face. It took no more than an instant for her to come back to him, smiling apologetically.

"But then you don't read *L'Officiel*, so you don't know who she is, do you?"

"I'm afraid not."

"Isabelle used to work for Ephémère. She was with us for seven years. She was so good we had to create a board-level position for her. Brand Strategy Director at the age of twenty-nine. She pulled everything tighter together – perfumes, *haute couture*, accessories, licensing deals. She was fierce, fearless and focused. I began to think I'd found my successor."

"But?" asked Franck, because this tale was clearly heading towards one.

"But she proved a little too fierce. Ruffling feathers inside a fashion house is rarely a good idea. There's a lot of delicate plumage, particularly on those who have the most talent. I tried to teach her the virtues of patience and restraint. She wasn't interested. So she left. The day after our Autumn/Winter show in 2006."

"To go where?"

"Where do you go after Ephémère? Normally it's either across – to Chanel – or down. Or you invent a completely new direction. That's what Isabelle decided to attempt. So she created her own fashion house."

"Called what?"

"Chanel, Dior, Lacroix, Gaultier, Valentino, Armani, ... Ephémère is a rare exception in our field. Fashion houses normally bear their founder's name. So when Isabelle created one she called it Arbaud."

"Should I have heard of it?"

"Not really," said Craveri, looking at Franck indulgently. "One, because you don't read *L'Officiel*, or anything similar. And two, because Arbaud hasn't yet produced anything."

"What's the link with Perrin?"

"I can't tell you for sure, but I know that running a fashion house is a very expensive business. Creating one from scratch all the more so. Particularly as Isabelle had no intention of starting small."

"You think Perrin put up the money?"

"Somebody must have. Isabelle does not come from money. Her father is in the army, and although there may be great honour in serving your country, there's little wealth to be gained. It would make sense to bring an investor to a Fashion Week event. A way to help him understand the nature of the horse on which he's placed his bet."

"You don't think there was a personal connection between

them?"

"A romantic connection? I doubt it. I saw a lot of Isabelle's ambition while she was with us, but her heart was not much in evidence. Anyhow, if they were involved that way, somebody would have found out, and it would certainly have got back to me. In the fashion world there may be secret deals, secret sketches, and secret ad campaigns, but never secret affairs."

The BMW had just fought its way across place de la Concorde and was heading up rue Royale towards the pillared facade of the Madeleine church.

"Take a right into rue Saint Honoré," said Craveri, switching her attention to the driver. "When you reach rue de Castiglione this time you can drop me off."

"Would you like to come in?" she asked Franck. "It's Stéphane Rolland. He's very good. Very theatrical."

"I'm not invited," Franck pointed out.

"You're with me. You'll get in."

"I also have a murder investigation to get on with."

She raised her hands, conceding the point.

"It seems I'm proving as frivolous as your charming young friend Sonia Delemazure."

"Acquaintance might be a more accurate description," insisted Franck.

"In which case, the loss is yours. She may not be the most demure of young women, but from what I've seen Sonia has many qualities." Craveri raised a finger to stop the reply that was forming on Franck's lips. "But it's not my place to meddle."

The car turned into rue de Castiglione and stopped a good twenty metres short of the Westin. The huddle of interlocked vehicles in front of the entrance had grown even larger. While Craveri thanked her driver and asked him to come back in ninety minutes, Franck got out and walked round to her side of the car, opening the door. She extended her right hand and he took it as she slid her legs out of the car and rose majestically to the pavement.

"I've known very few policemen in my time," she remarked. "If they are all as courteous as you, I have clearly been moving in the wrong circles."

Franck found himself bowing slightly, and suddenly remembered a similar gesture coming from Sonia the day before. There was definitely something effortlessly regal about Craveri.

"Before I lose you to the mob," Franck nodded towards the many faces that had turned to focus on Craveri as soon as she emerged from the car, "can I ask one thing?"

"Of course."

"Why did you invite her?"

"Isabelle?"

"Yes. Isn't she a competitor now?"

"Oh, she's more than that. Isabelle is my nemesis."

*

Had he known who she was, Franck's first reaction on encountering Isabelle Arbaud would have been to wonder what she was doing in his office. As it was, he allowed himself to concentrate for a few seconds on how good she smelled. Only then did he ask the question that brought his brief idyll to an end.

"Who are you?"

It was meant as a friendly enquiry. It was five thirty. He had walked back to 36 quai des Orfèvres through the Tuileries gardens and across the Pont Neuf, pausing for a while to watch the effects of the declining sun on the surface of the Seine. He was in a relatively good mood. There were documents lying in open view on his desk, but he knew that none of them were sensitive or confidential. All in all, he could afford to be pleasantly surprised upon discovering an attractive woman maybe three or four years younger than him sitting impatiently on the second chair in his office. The one that had uneven legs and rocked back and forwards if you were not sitting perfectly still. Which she was.

"Who are you?" she retorted, managing to make the question sound quite different. As if he was some kind of imposter, or was now so late for an appointment that he was no longer expected.

"Captain Franck Guerin. Brigade Criminelle. At your service."

He shifted his parka from his shoulders and deposited it on the coat rack to his right, alongside a garment that was not his. It was a black short-haired fur coat with a smooth silky lining. It cried out to be stroked both inside and out. He could imagine it bristling at the proximity of his scuffed and stained parka. Looking at them side by side, he suddenly realised that he had just inflicted his coat on Francesca Craveri during their circuitous ride in her BMW. To her credit, Craveri had not batted an eyelid. Not visibly, anyhow.

His visitor continued to ignore his question. She sat sideways on the chair, one leg folded over the other in semi-transparent dark stockings. By her feet, propped against a chair leg, was a sizeable handbag, wider than it was tall, a mix of textured and smooth leather with two sturdily fixed straps that could as easily drape across the shoulder as hang from the hands. She wore a dark-grey skirt that stopped short of her knees, a cream-coloured top knitted from very fine but wiry-looking wool and a short jacket cut from the same cloth as her skirt. She had thin, pale-red lips, prominent cheekbones, and light-chestnut hair cut short at the base of her neck. A trio of delicate silver chains lay just inside her collarbone. Her eyes were unblinking, which made it impossible to miss the fact that one of them was half hazel and half green, split vertically.

Without shifting her gaze, she raised a hand and pointed to his side of the desk.

He shut the door behind him and sat down opposite her. She swivelled to face him.

"My name is Isabelle Arbaud," she finally announced.

Franck nodded, but only as a means of hiding the fact that it was the last name he expected to hear.

"Can I ask how you ended up in here waiting for me?"

"I said we had an appointment. That you'd told me to wait for you if you were held up. So they let me through the little side door all the policemen go in and out, and one of your colleagues led me here and invited me to make myself comfortable."

"We had an appointment? My memory's clearly not what it used to be," said Franck.

Arbaud shrugged. "I optimised the situation."

First she had directed him to his chair. Now she was playing linguistic games with him. Maybe it was time to snarl – just a little – to show he did, after all, have a few teeth.

"I'm not a great fan of euphemisms, mademoiselle Arbaud – or is it madame?"

"Mademoiselle," was her curt response.

"What you meant to say is that you used deceit to get in here," he continued.

"Of course I did. I lied. It was important that I see you and I wasn't going to sit down there." She gestured behind her with her head. Down there. The Brigade Criminelle's public waiting area. He could not blame her. It was not the most salubrious of spaces. Franck began to wonder whether he was not being a little ungracious.

"To tell the truth, I'm delighted to see you," he said. "I was about to try to hunt you down."

"So you've worked it out?"

"Worked what out?"

"That somebody is trying to destroy my firm." This ought to have sounded melodramatic, but given the way she said it, it came out as a simple statement of fact.

"No, I must admit, I hadn't quite reached that point. All I know is that you were instrumental in getting Alain Perrin an invitation to yesterday's Ephémère fashion show. His presence proved fatal to him and you were no longer around when we arrived on the scene. That's it."

"You're not very good at this, are you?"

"Good at what?" asked Franck, choosing to be amused.

"Putting two and two together."

"Give me the two twos and I'll see what I can do with them. Let me try some questions. Did you and Alain Perrin arrive together at the *défilé* yesterday?"

"No. He had his own invitation. He didn't need me."

"How did he get it?"

"I asked Ephémère to have it delivered to his home address. Since I requested that he be included on the guest list last Friday, I assume they did it over the weekend."

"Did he know you were behind it?"

"Yes."

"So how much did you see of him yesterday?"

"He was already there when I arrived. I hadn't asked that we be given reserved seating, so he'd chosen a spot and tried to keep a place for me beside him, but some pushy South American magazine editor snatched it. I had a chat with him before the show started and then left him to enjoy it."

"Left him?" quizzed Franck.

"I ended up sitting on the other side of the glasshouse. I didn't see him after that."

"You didn't see him get up during the show?"

"No. I was watching the *défilé*, like everyone else. Ever been to one? Apart from the music and constant movement, there are photographers setting off flashes all along both sides of the catwalk. Not an easy environment in which to keep your eye on someone."

"When it was over, you didn't try to find him to ask him what he thought of it, or to say goodbye? Even if the invitation came from Ephémère, he was basically your guest."

"I did. But I was in a hurry, like most of those present. I looked around, couldn't see Alain, and assumed he'd left. So I did the same."

"You didn't think it odd that he didn't come over to thank you?"

"Not really. He is – or he was – a busy man. We would have been in touch soon enough, he'd have had his chance."

"How soon? How close were you?"

"How close?" She frowned, and looked at him askance. "You mean, were we sleeping together?"

"I mean, it would help if I knew the nature of your relationship – business acquaintances, friends, lovers?"

She blew some air sharply from between her lips in an exasperated fashion. "I cannot believe this. Is this the best the police can do?" She placed her elbows on his desk, made fists of her hands and lowered her brow to them. "You don't have any of the twos, do you? It's not surprising you can't put them together."

"You were a potential witness at a crime scene," said Franck, his patience straining. "I have to start with that. The wider picture – why it is that you think someone is trying to destroy your firm – will come later."

"When?" she demanded, looking up again. "Right now we're wasting time. You know nothing, and you're not letting me resolve your ignorance."

"OK," he shot back. "Tell me your story, mademoiselle Arbaud. You can start with your decision to leave Ephémère, if you like."

She raised her eyebrows, a pair of thin curving lines.

"I don't have the all the twos," said Franck. "But I may have a one, or a one and a half."

"Let me be the judge of that. Listen and learn."

She paused, waiting for something.

When he did not react she said, "You might want to write this down."

"I might. Let me be the judge of that."

Her lips twitched, but she began all the same. "On the 8th of July the year before last I told Francesca Craveri – who runs Ephémère, has done so since the late eighties, and clearly intends to continue doing so until she reaches her own late eighties, if not beyond – that I was leaving."

"At that point, how long had you held the post of Brand Strategy Director?" Franck cut in.

Arbaud stopped again, this time allowing herself the ghost of a smile.

"Are you playing with me, captain?"

"If I am, that was my last card." Hoping he had succeeded in taking the edge off her disdain, he tried to steer them both into calmer waters. "I'll stop trying to show off now."

"You find me too aggressive, don't you?" she said, sitting back in her chair. Her hand came up to touch the silver chains where they ran past a prominent vein in the side of her neck. "You wouldn't be the first."

"A little intense, perhaps," he suggested. "I wouldn't say aggressive."

"Intense," she echoed, laughing to herself. "Now there's a word that's rarely used as a compliment. Hear my story, captain. Then judge me."

"Is it a long story?" asked Franck.

"That depends on your attention span."

"Would you like some coffee before you begin?"

"I take it that means that you need some before I begin."

"Stay there," he instructed, and set off down the corridor.

He was in luck – in the sense that a wanderer in the desert feels lucky when he encounters a stagnant pond – as the coffee machine had been repaired. He brought back two half-cups. Black, no sugar. It was a test. Not of her, but of him. If he instinctively understood her taste in coffee, it ought to be possible at some stage to read the rest of her.

She took one sip and tossed the cup dead-centre into his wastepaper basket.

"Disgusting," she declared. "How do you drink that?"

"Were I a heroin addict, I probably wouldn't blanch at a dirty needle. You want to pick up where I interrupted you?"

"I'd held the post for three years. I'd been there for seven. It took them four years to realise what I could do for them."

"Sounds quite quick to me," said Franck.

"You work in the public sector, captain. We don't have the same notion of time."

"Point taken."

"In the three years I ran brand strategy, both sales and profit margins improved significantly. I made sure prices were raised across the board. I convinced them to move into jewellery and got some of the best of the Swiss to work on a range of Ephémère wristwear. Chanel had inched ahead and reached five billion annual turnover first. Thanks to me, Ephémère caught up."

"So why leave?"

"I'm not a creature of the shadows. I had no desire to spend the next twenty years as Francesca Craveri's sidekick. I have an unparalleled understanding of the luxury goods market."

"Unparalleled?"

Arbaud nodded.

"Add arrogance to aggression in your list of my failings, if you must. But yes, I know what unparalleled means, and I have an unparalleled understanding of the luxury goods market."

"So why not knock on Chanel's door?"

"And run into the same problem? I'd just turned thirty-three. Too young to be considered for the top job in any major fashion house. Too old to let others profit from my talents while promising me great things at some unspecified date in the distant future."

"So you set up your own firm."

"You make it sound so banal, like I opened a corner shop, or rented a workshop and proudly set up my hand-drawn sign in some dingy alley. I founded an international fashion house. I created a brand that will redefine what luxury means. I threw down a gauntlet before Ephémère and Chanel. They didn't have the foresight to tremble then, but they soon will."

Her upper body was now bent across the desk that separated them. She held Franck with her gaze, especially with her left eye, whose two half-spheres of colour gave it the portentous aura of a previously undiscovered planet.

"And Alain Perrin in all this?" he asked, breaking the spell.

"I had a business plan. I had been perfecting it for some time. It called for initial financing of 150 million euros. All I could bring to the table was my reputation and my unique vision. Someone else had to bring the chequebook."

"Was this about the time that Alain inherited control of Perrin Industries?"

"Shortly afterwards. Alain inherited both his father's business and his considerable personal wealth. I provided him with a highly promising, albeit risky, investment for some of the latter."

"So he is – was – your source of capital."

"No. Not capital," she said, wagging a chastising finger. "I insisted on a convertible debenture. I didn't want to create a company only to share control of it. Alain Perrin lent me fifty million euros and I promised to pay him back in ten years at a very reasonable interest rate. If I didn't meet the deadline, then he could convert his loan into stock. He took some persuading, but I can be very persuasive when I know I'm right."

It was the first time Franck had ever heard of a convertible debenture, but he let it pass. It must have made sense to the two parties involved, and that was good enough for him.

"If his only contribution was his money, why drag him to the Ephémère *défilé*?" he asked.

"I wanted him to have a better understanding of what we were aiming at."

"Because you didn't yet have a show of your own? Because Arbaud has not yet produced anything?" Franck suggested, borrowing Craveri's words.

"That's right. We're not starting with *haute couture*. It'll come, but it's not my priority."

"So what is?"

"Perfume. That's where the margins are. That's what underwrites the *haute couture* collections of all the big players. Far more women will buy or be given an outrageously expensive bottle of perfume than acquire a hand-stitched dress.

In time, we will do *couture*, but we will start with perfume. Once our product has become the very scent of luxury, the rest will follow."

"It costs 150 million euros to develop a new perfume?"

"It costs 150 million euros to infiltrate the imagination of the world's big spenders and make them covet a new-born brand."

Franck could only take her word for it. "So Perrin stumped up fifty, what about the other hundred?"

"I made a very clear decision when I set out – I didn't want to get involved with any institutions, be they investment banks, venture funds or sovereign wealth funds. The only thing that interested me was private wealth. People who understand what it is to build an empire."

"There are a lot of them around?" asked Franck. Napoleon and Charlemagne came to mind, but they were unlikely to be in the contemporary investing game.

"Oh, there are many of them. But they are hard to approach and harder to convince. With the help of a very talented private banker, however, I found the three that I needed."

"Perrin, and?"

"Guillaume Thèves," she cited.

Franck gave her a blank look.

"IPS?" she prompted. "International Paper Supplies?"

Franck's expression did not change.

"IPS is number one in office equipment and stationary in France, Germany, Scandinavia and Holland. Number two almost everywhere else in Europe. Has a minority stake in two of the most important North American players, which one day will be forced together. IPS belongs in its entirety to Guillaume Thèves."

"Never heard of him."

"I think that's how he likes it," she said.

"And the third?"

"Nathalie Chautard."

Franck frowned. This time the name vaguely meant

something to him.

"CWM," continued Arbaud. "Chautard Waste Management. Industrial and domestic waste treatment. Holds all of southern Europe in the palm of its hand – with the exception of southern Italy, of course, which is too toxic even for it."

Franck was still frowning, still searching.

"If she sounds familiar," said Arbaud, "it's because she was murdered two months ago."

She let her statement hang in the air for a moment.

"Do you believe in coincidences, captain?"

"They make me uneasy."

She sighed. "At last we agree on something. I cannot believe this is accidental. I'm convinced someone is trying to destroy Arbaud by cutting off its lifeblood. Someone who knows that I can do great things in this business – but not without money."

Franck shook his head, grimacing a little.

"I said coincidences make me uneasy. They don't make me paranoid."

"Look into it. That's all I ask."

"I will. That I promise."

"In which case, I will leave you to get on with it."

She pushed back her chair and rose to her feet. Franck did the same, going to the door and opening it. She recovered her coat and folded it neatly over her arm. Franck offered her one of his cards.

"I'll see you out," he said.

"I think I remember the way."

Franck stepped aside and she moved through the doorway. With her back to him she brought up her bag and quickly dipped a hand into it. She then turned to face him once more, presenting him with her card. It was easily twice as thick as his, its edges precision-cut and its glossy surface pristine.

As they shook hands she said, "Thank you for receiving me."

"Thank you for helping with the enquiry."

"You'll be in touch," she declared, then walked briskly away down the corridor.

He watched her go. She soon turned out of sight.

Franck stepped back into his office and closed the door. It was still there. A faint presence, but unmistakeable. Her scent.

Isabelle Arbaud was not the most ingratiating of women, but her scent was hypnotic.

*

No known handgun was used to kill Alain Perrin.

Franck's brow was creased as he puzzled over the preliminary forensic report attached to an email Georges Sternberg had sent him that afternoon. Everything else in it corresponded to his expectations: Perrin had been shot twice in quick succession and had died instantly when the second bullet entered his brain; no cartridges had been found on the scene, suggesting that the killer had picked them up or used a revolver; the victim's stomach indicated that his last meal had been a croissant with coffee; he had been killed where he was found, in the narrow space behind the screen in the catering room; there were no traces of foreign DNA on his body or on his clothes, although a detailed footnote explained that both had been in contact with a sufficient quantity of bleach for long enough to destroy any such evidence; the prints on his briefcase were his own, his chauffeur's and his secretary's; the empty bottles of bleach found on the site had been wiped down, leaving only partial prints which had been matched to employees of the cleaning company hired for the event; the bleach itself was a standard industrial solution generally sold in 1.5 litre containers on the business-to-business market. Page after page of description of a crime scene that refused to tell any of its secrets.

But was happy to provide an enigma.

Franck looked at his watch. It was after nine thirty. Not a reasonable time to call an overworked forensic specialist no doubt enjoying an evening in the company of the living.

He dialled Sternberg's mobile number.

"Yes?" There was a lot of background noise.

"Georges? This is Franck Guerin."

"Good evening, Franck. Another quiet evening in with the case files?"

"This is not a good time, is it?"

"Do you want my opinion on that, or that of my wife, her two sisters, their husbands, or the people at the tables around us looking daggers at me for answering my phone?"

"What's the *plat du jour*?"

"Honey and spice duck *pastilla* with a *gratin dauphinois*."

He could hear Sternberg moving.

"Unusual combination," observed Franck. "Any good?"

"Not bad, but I expect it won't taste the same half-cold once I'm through with you."

"I'll be quick."

"You'd better be. I'm outside now and I don't have my coat."

"6.5mm slugs?" It came out sounding more like a challenge than a question. Franck knew enough about handguns to know that they fired fatter rounds than that. Like the 9mm bullets that had been dug out of him the previous year.

"Absolutely. A lightweight 6.5mm diameter bullet. Fast, low recoil, and digs in deep," confirmed Sternberg. "Looks like the Vikings are up to their old tricks again, sailing down the Seine and raising havoc."

"Care to explain that?" requested Franck.

"6.5mm calibre rifles are a Scandinavian peculiarity. All other Western forces prefer a 7.62mm cartridge, but the Swedes and Norwegians swear by their narrow rounds."

"Right now it's not so much the nationality of the guy behind the trigger that worries me, as what the trigger was attached to," insisted Franck. "Are you telling me Perrin was shot with a rifle?"

"Looks like it."

"What, somebody carried a rifle into and out of an Ephémère fashion show, and nobody noticed?"

"Maybe everybody thought it was a prop," suggested Sternberg.

"The collection embodied the profound serenity of the endless ocean and the elegant extravagance of its inhabitants," declared Franck, quoting a phrase he'd read from the press notes distributed at the event. "Not much call for rifles."

"Fair point. Want to know the rest?"

"Go ahead."

"The rifling marks on the bullets are very strange."

"Isn't it too early to be looking at the rifling?" asked Franck. "Don't we have to have the gun first to be able to match its barrel to the bullets?"

"Sure, for an exact match. But the bullet from the stomach was in very good condition and it was probably fired from a weapon with a twist rate somewhere around 130mm."

"Which is?"

"Very unusual. Could be a custom-bored barrel."

"When will we know?"

"When you find the murder weapon, captain."

Nathalie Chautard was not murdered; she died in suspicious circumstances.

That was what the file entry on the national police network said.

On the 22nd of November 2007, Nathalie Chautard had hosted a meeting in an airport hotel at Marignane. Although it served as Marseille's airport, Marignane sat on the edge of the Etang de Berre, an inland sea with an eighty kilometre shoreline which was home to over a dozen chemical plants and oil refineries. The most important industrial site on the Mediterranean coast, the Etang de Berre had a long history of accidental spills, fatal accidents, and legal but devastating discharges of a wide range of pollutants. It was also a cherished source of much-needed jobs for the inhabitants of Marseille, generating a love-hate relationship between the local community and the companies implanted on its shores.

Nathalie Chautard had come to explain to those very companies – in a conference suite filled with their Production Managers, Safety Executives and Financial Directors – that their individual efforts at pollution control were costly and inefficient. That handing over the entire problem to a single operator would generate significant economies of scale and, just as importantly, free them of the need to interact with environmental watchdogs, pressure groups and local politicians. Chautard Waste Management would take total responsibility for every waste product – liquids, solids, and sludges – at the point of production. It was an unprecedented opportunity for those present to wash their hands of the most irritating, not to mention unprofitable, aspect of their business. A lot of interested scribbling went on around the table during her presentation and spirits were high during the ensuing lunch.

The meeting finally broke up at just before three in the afternoon. Chautard's next meeting was at six in Toulon with the CWM regional logistics team. She left Marignane in a rented Mercedes E350. Although alone, it was not difficult to reconstruct her itinerary, as she spent much of it on her mobile phone. She headed east on the A50 but abandoned the motorway after Aubagne, preferring the more modest D8n that ran up through the dry and fragrant inland hills. She headed through the Font Blanche forest, came down into the small town of Le Beausset and was on the route des Gorges, a few kilometres from the outskirts of Toulon, when her car left the road.

A passing motorist called in the accident. Dark, malodorous skid marks showed the path the E350 had taken across the tarmac, through an inadequately robust side rail, and into a rocky ravine about six metres deep, turning as it fell. Although Chautard had been held more or less in place in the driver's seat by the front and side air bags, her head lay at an impossible angle on her neck.

The first patrol car on the scene had instantly remarked the fact that, although the E350 had entered the ravine nose first, its rear left corner looked like it had been crushed by a blow from a giant's fist. Forensics quickly established the presence of foreign paint at this impact point. It took all of fifteen minutes to identify its origin – a heavy goods vehicle abandoned in a lay-by five hundred metres further down the road. The only fingerprints upon the steering wheel were those of its regular driver, who had reported the truck's disappearance the previous day.

Not your average traffic accident, thought Franck. Just like Alain Perrin's death was not your average shooting.

However, interviews with other executives in CWM had revealed no known threats to Chautard. Her ex-husband and the rest of her family, including her children, were equally perplexed when asked who might have wished her harm. Like any very successful businesswoman, she had as many detractors as admirers, but none of them were known for their homicidal tendencies.

Franck called the contact number given on the file. Eric

Bonifay was noted as a *commandant* with the Police Judiciaire in Toulon, and as such should have been difficult to get on the line. But, as ever, announcing that the call came from the Brigade Criminelle in Paris worked wonders. Everyone in the force was always curious to know what Maigret's successors were up to.

"*Commandant*, good morning. This is captain Franck Guerin. I'm calling from the quai des Orfèvres. Hope I'm not disturbing you."

"Worried about interrupting our regular mid-morning game of *pétanque*?" suggested Bonifay.

Franck laughed, as he was expected to, before responding with, "That's what you get for having too many law-abiding citizens."

Toulon was home to the French navy's Mediterranean fleet. It was also caught in the crossfire between Nice and Marseille, the two principal centres of organised crime on the south coast. Not the quietest of postings.

"What can I do for you captain? Freezing your balls off in Paris? Looking for an excuse to come down south for a little winter sun?"

"I was just wondering if you could give me an update on Nathalie Chautard. Whether you've got any further with discovering who stole the truck that bounced her off the road."

"I'd love to," said Bonifay, although his tone had changed. The joviality had gone, and a hint of righteous indignation had taken its place. "But the case is no longer ours."

"Who's got it?"

"The DST. Not the Marseille office. Your lot, in Paris. The real bastards."

His lot. Bonifay could not know how close he was to the truth. Although he no longer bore its badge, the DST was still paying Franck's salary, since administratively he was only on loan to the Brigade Criminelle. For an indeterminate period of time.

"Any idea why?" asked Franck.

"Chautard Waste Management. Sensitive industrial dossier. Too big for us, apparently."

"Good way to make sure her killer never gets caught," offered Franck, as balm to Bonifay's pride. "You don't think they believe this was an accident? That the truck driver just got scared and ran away?"

"If they do, they're the only ones."

Isabelle Arbaud would agree with him on that.

Franck thanked the *commandant* and hung up.

Time to call the real bastards.

It was the 25th. She would not be expecting a call for another week at the earliest, since the last one had been on the 3rd of January, but enough time had gone by for her to pick up when she saw his name.

He turned once again to the phone on his desk. Whether he called with his mobile, or from here, or from home, she always knew it was him. He dialled the confidential number of Catherine Vautrin, who – habit being a stubborn creature – he had difficulty not thinking of as his commanding officer.

She picked up. But said nothing.

"Catherine?"

"Have you ever known anyone else to answer my phone?"

"Good morning. I hope I'm not disturbing you."

"Last time I checked, it was still January. You're getting impatient, Franck. It's not a good sign. A good agent knows how to bide his time."

"Yes, well, I'm not such a good agent, am I?"

"That we don't know yet," said Catherine, dispassionately. "We have to wait to see what the report says."

She was referring to the Corsican incident. The reason why Franck had been sent off to cool his heels at the quai des Orfèvres under the supervision of Yves de Chaumont. The reason why he knew how debilitating a shot to the stomach could be. The reason why – as agreed with Catherine, and despite the formal instructions with which he had been issued at the close of the internal enquiry the previous summer – he phoned her every month to be updated on the progress of the official report into the operation.

"Five months," Franck pointed out. "Soon be six. It's a report, not *A la recherche du temps perdu*. Somebody better remind whoever's in charge of drafting this masterpiece that Proust died before he got to the end of his."

"If there was someone in charge, it would have been bound and distributed long ago. But there happen to be several interested parties fighting over it. You're an unlucky man, Franck. You had the misfortune to run a failed operation in the dying days of the DST as an independent outfit."

On the 13th of September the previous year the Minister of the Interior had announced that the Direction de la Surveillance du Territoire would be merged with the Renseignements Généraux. A new era of seamless cooperation between the two arms of the domestic intelligence apparatus would be ushered in. The DST would stop despising the RG for its obsession with minutiae and its insistence that patient compilation of encyclopaedic dossiers was the only true path to actionable intelligence. The RG would accept that the DST's penchant for striking before the iron got too hot was a valuable proactive approach to managing national security. All would live happily ever after, and the nation would sleep more securely in its bed. Fat chance. At least if Catherine Vautrin had anything to do with it.

"It's become abundantly clear," she pursued, "that the truth of what did or did not happen in Corsica matters a lot less now than what it can be made to symbolise."

"How much longer will all this take?" asked Franck. The new service – the Direction Centrale du Renseignement Intérieur – was supposed to be up and running by next June. The winners and losers would have to be identified some time before then. The internal tussling could not last forever.

"Maybe not much longer," she offered. "It looks as if the DST will take two of the three top jobs. Of course, that doesn't mean you won't be offered up as a scapegoat to make the result easier to swallow for our disappointed friends in the RG."

"That's what I love about talking to you, Catherine. You're so supportive."

"Go cry on Yves de Chaumont's shoulder, if you like," she suggested. "Are we finished here? Can I go back to maintaining a safe environment in which you can continue to play policeman?"

"Just one thing. Can you tell me anything about the investigation into the death of Nathalie Chautard?"

Catherine tutted. "Don't go there Franck. If there's anybody who shouldn't go there, it's you."

"Care to explain that?"

"No."

"What if I had a theory that Chautard's death had nothing to do with her, or with CWM?" he ventured.

"I'd tell you that you were wrong."

"What if I said that I can see a potential link between Chautard's death and a murder case I'm currently handling?"

"I'd tell you that you were wrong," she repeated.

"What if I told you that I'm going to pursue this line of investigation, whatever you say?"

"I'd tell you that you were a fool."

With that, she hung up.

*

It was midday. Were it summer, Franck imagined that the André Citroen park would be full of employees from the neighbouring glass-fronted office blocks and massive hospital – the Georges Pompidou European Hospital, the city's largest and newest, and perhaps most mocked, since it was rumoured that when it had opened it was discovered that the interior doorways were too narrow to wheel the beds through.

However, as it was a chilly Friday in January, Franck was one of the few people to be seen. The temporary structure built for the Ephémère *défilé* had almost all gone. Only the steel frame that had supported it – a giant children's toy of interlocking beams and adjustable feet – was still present. The fruit trees that had shivered outside as models paraded in their place had regained their muggy abode. When Franck tried to join them, the door to the glasshouse would not open.

"It's shut," came a voice behind him.

Franck turned to find a North African man in his forties bearing the uniform of the city's parks service.

"The other one's open," he offered, motioning to its twin. "A little bit of Australia. Nice and warm this time of year."

"Any kangaroos?" asked Franck.

The park-keeper laughed. "We've got plenty of ducks, and the odd seagull, but that's as far as our wildlife collection goes."

"Any interesting human specimens?"

"You should have been here Wednesday. Big fashion show. Some very interesting specimens. Not that any of us got in."

"Didn't end so well, though, did it?" Franck pulled out his ID and showed it to the man, who studied it attentively.

"You involved in the case?"

Frank nodded. "You see anything?"

"No. I watched them arrive, but once they were inside you couldn't make anything out. They had all these weird tubes of water and stuff strapped to the side of the glasshouse. I soon got fed up and wandered off on my rounds."

He nodded towards to the rest of the park.

A rectangular swathe of grass framed by a shallow canal swept down to an elevated railway line that marked the official limit of the park. From that point onwards cobbles took over until the edge of the Seine, where a series of river-going cruisers were strapped to bollards. This was the port of Javel, the first of a series of ports along the river within the boundaries of the city. To a remarkable extent for a major European capital the Seine remained a working river.

To the left of the vast lawn was a raised concrete walkway, complete with fountains and an elevated pond. To the right was a wall of dense vegetation penetrated by walkways which led to an area of elaborately sunk or cantilevered walled gardens. It was a determinedly modern park, shaped by architects rather than by gardeners.

"Were there many people around?" asked Franck.

"Not really. Much like today. Most of the morning joggers had been through by the time they started blasting their music. Just the retired and the unemployed, out for a morning walk."

"Get many homeless?"

"Sure, we get our share. We have toilets over there." He gestured to the right. "Clean. Running water. Paper most of the time. We have our regulars. Nobody sleeps here, though. The gates are shut every evening and we throw everyone out."

"Doesn't mean they don't sneak back in," Franck pointed out.

"You seen our fences? You could break your neck climbing over them."

This was true. André Citroen's railings stood higher than those of any other park in Paris, not to mention the fact that one side of the park was lined with a forbidding-looking moat. With its sheltered grassy expanse and numerous tree-enclosed niches, it would otherwise have been too tempting a camping spot.

"You see any of the regulars Wednesday morning?"

He thought for a moment.

"I saw Adeline with her trolley. She's here most days. And Michel said hello. He was already inside when I started my shift. Must have got through the supplier's gate when they were setting up the fashion show."

"Can you describe this Michel?"

The park-keeper whistled softly, as if Franck had just asked him to name every president of the Fifth Republic.

"Beard. Long hair. Long coat. Nice enough bloke."

"About your age? Older? Younger?" quizzed Franck.

"Hard to say. They age fast. Course, that's the drink. Never seen Michel drunk, but I only ever see him in the morning.

Probably comes here to take a shit."

"You see him this morning?"

"Actually, no."

"Yesterday?"

He thought about it. "No."

"Not since Wednesday then?"

"That's right."

"That strike you as strange?"

"Not really. He comes and goes. That's true of most of them – Paul, Jean-François, Blanche,... They disappear and they reappear. Or they don't, and you never know what happened to them."

"How long has Michel been a regular?"

"I've been here two years. At least as long as me."

"Do you know where he sleeps?"

"No. But I don't suppose it's far."

Neither did Franck.

"How would I recognise Adeline?"

"If you see a supermarket trolley filled with old newspapers and magazines and hung around with plastic bags, then look behind it. If she's fat with crinkly red hair and lots of rings, that's Adeline. But you won't find her today."

"I'm too late?"

"No, it's just that she never comes on Fridays. Says it's her day for taking tea with the queen."

Another coincidence. For today Franck could have said the same thing.

*

Place François Premier was one of the better-kept secrets of the eighth arrondissement. Hiding inside the triangle formed by the constant traffic of cours Albert along the right bank of the Seine, the tourist bustle around the Grand and Petit Palais and the clicking of designer heels on avenue Montaigne, it saw few cars and fewer pedestrians. The network of short streets that radiated out from the place held diverse bedfellows: the commercial radio station RTL; the piously serious Bayard Press, publishers of *La Croix*, which had once bayed for Dreyfus' blood and was the only daily newspaper to dedicate several pages to the goings-on in the Vatican; various firms of corporate lawyers; and an Armenian cathedral. The stately buildings that stood on the much-prized plots around the circular place itself provided an anchor to the heterogeneous neighbourhood. One of these had seen the creation of Ephémère as a fledgling fashion house in the 1920s and had remained its headquarters to this day, albeit the workshops, not to mention the back-office functions that had grown with its expansion, had all long since migrated elsewhere. Nowadays 3 place François Premier provided offices for the firm's seven top executives, an ornate conference suite for board meetings, and a series of ground floor salons for corporate events.

This afternoon it was playing host to captain Franck Guerin of the Brigade Criminelle (temporary assignment). That is what the Japanese receptionist intoned, reading from Franck's police ID with a perfect French accent, as she informed madame Craveri's personal assistant of Franck's arrival a few minutes ahead of his three o'clock appointment. She was wearing a simply cut one-piece sky-blue dress with a narrow embroidered border around the neck and sleeves. The embroidered motif looked vaguely familiar, probably from Wednesday's *défilé*, which left Franck wondering whether he was looking at the first signs of the trickle-down from *haute couture* to *prêt-à-porter* that allowed the major fashion houses to turn a profit from indulging the expensive impulses of their designers.

Craveri's personal assistant rapidly materialised, walking briskly down a curving flight of stairs with an elaborately scrolled wrought-iron banister. Her dress was identical to that of the receptionist.

"New corporate uniform?" asked Franck as she led him back up the stairs, affording him ample opportunity to admire the way her dress had been trimmed exactly to her size.

She paused to beam a smile down at him.

"It's a house tradition. After the last party on the last night of Fashion Week, the design team work up an outfit as a present for those who ensured the week went smoothly. They only have a few hours to do it, so it's always something very simple. Terribly chic, though, don't you think?"

"It suits you very well," observed Franck.

"Thank you," she replied, with practised ease. Compliments were clearly nothing new in this young woman's life.

Once on the first floor she led him to a pair of doors, tapped lightly upon one of them, opened it without waiting for a reply, and ushered Franck in.

Francesca Craveri stood waiting for him in a sizeable room looking out over place François Premier. It was furnished with six Louis XV armchairs drawn in a wide circle around a low walnut table with delicate, curving feet. The walls on both sides of the entrance were hung with tapestries illustrating tales from La Fontaine's *Fables*. One featured a fox apparently conversing with a crow while the bird struggled to maintain a hefty circular block of cheese in its beak. The other showed an army of over-sized frogs gathered in puzzlement around a decaying log. Franck felt safe to assume that these, along with the furniture, were originals.

"Good afternoon, captain Guerin," she greeted him. "Thank you for coming."

"Thank you for inviting me. I'm sorry to have given you so little notice. Once again."

He had phoned that morning upon closing the Chautard dossier.

"Today is an easier day. The maelstrom of Fashion Week is finally behind us and it looks as if we're still afloat. I hate to say it, but Alain Perrin's tragic death does not seem to have overshadowed coverage of our collection."

"I see you've been judged part of the team that contributed to the week's success."

For, to his surprise, Craveri's dress was identical to that of her assistant.

"Marco's little joke," she explained good-humouredly, glancing down at her simple blue dress, to which she had added a light-green skein of silk, cast negligently around her neck and shoulders. "He likes to think of himself as the lord of Misrule, turning hierarchy on its head. After all he's done over the past weeks, he deserves his day of fun."

"It suits you," offered Franck, conscious that he was repeating himself.

"Not as well as it suits Marilyn, who brought you to me" she countered, with a slight smile, before gesturing to the armchairs. "Please sit. I hope you have nothing against the rococo?"

"I'm a bit wary about sitting on something I imagine has survived since the eighteenth century. Isn't this the kind of stuff you normally see in museums with little warning notices and velvet cords draped across the armrests to keep you off?"

"Nonsense," said Francesca. "Furniture is to be used, as dresses are to be worn. I have no doubt these chairs have been restored many times since they left Heurtaut's workshop and I'm sure they're happy to render service in their old age. Make yourself comfortable, captain. I insist."

Franck lowered himself gently into the over-stuffed cushioning of one of the chairs. Francesca waited until he was in place before seating herself to his left.

"Coffee?" she asked.

"Yes please. Black."

On the table lay a silver platter bearing two delicate china cups, a porcelain coffee pot, a dainty sugar holder and a plate of madeleines. Francesca poured coffee into the two cups and placed one, with its painted saucer, before Franck.

"Eighteenth-century too?" he asked, grasping the thin bow of the cup's handle between finger and thumb.

"Nineteenth-century German porcelain," said Francesca. "Rummage around in any junk shop, you'll find much the same."

Franck kept his doubts about the latter to himself. He sipped his coffee, which proved surprisingly robust for such elegant surroundings.

"Are you making progress with Alain Perrin?" asked Francesca.

"I can't say much about it, but I certainly know more than I did two days ago. You were right about his connection to Isabelle Arbaud."

"That he invested in her project?"

"Yes. But he wasn't the only one."

"That's not surprising. She's running a very expensive operation. Have you visited her offices yet?"

"No," said Franck.

"So you haven't seen her?"

"Yes, I have. She came to my office."

Francesca raised her eyebrows and tipped her head to one side.

"Isabelle came to you? She did not summon you to come to her?"

Franck nodded.

"Had I known such power came with a card marked 'Brigade Criminelle (temporary assignment)' I might have sought one myself," mused Francesca. "If Isabelle came to you, you must have something she wants very badly."

"All she wants is to see me clear up Perrin's death, which seems to have created a big problem for her."

"Has she burned through her money already, and needs some more? I recall her being very good with her spreadsheets. I'd be surprised if she had underestimated how much she would need."

"Which would be?" asked Franck.

Francesca raised her hands and let them open, like a flower, in the air.

"Create a new global brand in high-end perfume and a platform for expansion into all other luxury markets? Snatch what was the most prestigious site available in Paris for your headquarters? Sign an exclusive agreement with the best Nose in the business? Tease the fashion media non-stop so that every weekly editorial conference in New York, Tokyo or Milan ends with speculation about the release date for Night-Scented? Convince the members of the Comité Colbert that your rightful place is amongst them? I can't see it happening for less than a hundred million."

"Sounds about right," conceded Franck.

"That must represent a fair chunk of the Perrin family fortune."

"Perrin wasn't alone," Franck informed her. "That's where things get tricky. Ever heard of CWM?"

"I'm afraid not."

"Chautard Waste Management."

"Waste management? Not really my field, captain."

"Big business, or so it seems. Nathalie Chautard, who ran and owned CWM, also provided funds for Arbaud."

"That's *ma petite* Isabelle for you – a very far-sighted girl. When she wants a lot of eggs, she looks for a lot of baskets."

"Nathalie Chautard died in unexplained circumstances last November. I think it highly likely she was killed."

A silence hung in the room. Craveri suddenly noticed that Franck's cup was empty. Her own had not once been raised to her lips. She reached for the coffee pot and poured her guest a second cup. Franck took it and emptied half of it. He waited.

"Which makes you think someone is crushing Isabelle's baskets, one after the other?" Francesca eventually enquired.

"It's what she thinks. Given the circumstances, it's not difficult to understand how she came to such a conclusion."

"And you are wondering who might be inclined to do such a thing?"

Franck nodded. "She worked closely with you until relatively recently. You probably know her as well as anyone. You also know the market she's trying to break into. Whose nose might she have put out of joint?"

Francesca shook her head and looked forgivingly at Franck.

"Whose nose indeed? I do admire how delicate you are. However, there's no need to tiptoe around me. Arbaud, if Isabelle pulls it off – which I think unlikely, but not impossible, and if anyone can do it, she can – will hurt both Ephémère and Chanel. Of the two, Ephémère is by far the most vulnerable, because Isabelle knows everything about us, and has already caused us immeasurable harm."

"By leaving?"

"That was a significant loss, but no, I'm not talking about that. What is it they say? Graveyards are full of those once judged indispensible. Fortunately, Ephémère rests on more solid foundations than the individuals who manage it at any one time. Myself included. We are just the storekeepers, or bookkeepers."

"So what did she do?" prompted Franck.

"She poached some of the real talent. Some think I am the genius behind Ephémère's current success. They are wrong. At most, I am like Julius Rovere, who may have held the keys to heaven, but whose real significance lay in his ability to recognise the gifts of Raphael, Michelangelo and Bramante. People wouldn't queue up from dawn to visit the Sistine Chapel if Julius had decided to paint it himself."

For a moment Francesca seemed lost in her thoughts.

"So?" prompted Franck.

"My Michelangelo was Louis Halphen. Louis is the greatest Nose of his generation."

Before going further Craveri glanced at Franck to ensure that she had not lost him. He nodded to reassure her. He knew what a Nose was: someone possessed of a highly sensitive sense of smell who had transformed his gift into a precise analytical tool by training himself to distinguish and classify the many odours the world could offer. Thus equipped, a Nose could mix and match scents in order to produce new combinations. Franck's knowledge, however, was theoretical. He had never actually met a Nose, let alone the apparently legendary Louis Halphen, whose tale Francesca resumed.

"I turned to him when Eternal had slipped far behind Numéro Cinq, when we were about to lose what the vulgar call the Perfume Wars. What we had always believed to be a timeless classic was now perceived as an outmoded scent. Tastes had changed and Eternal, which since its inception had always had a rather more distinctive character than Numéro Cinq, had drifted dangerously out of alignment."

"And this Louis Halphen saved the day?"

Francesca nodded emphatically. "Louis insisted that we do the unthinkable. That we change the formula."

"Launch a new perfume?"

"Ah, no. That would have been the end. Eternal had held a cherished place in women's imagination for three generations. It meant something. Rebellious daughters who spurned it in their teens turned to it in their late twenties. Eternal was a form of pole star in the ever-changing seas of fashion and society. Tearing it down and setting something in its place would have been incredibly risky. It's what Isabelle has set out to do, and the only thing that allows her to make such an attempt is that she has nothing to lose."

"So what did you do?"

"You mean, what did Louis do? He set out to renew Eternal – almost subliminally. To allow it to evolve without betraying its fundamental nature. To nudge it back into the spirit of the times. And once we had started to do so, we realised that we had to continue. Every year Louis would work his magic, slightly adjusting a note here or there. Every year we won new converts without losing any of the faithful. Thanks to him, we even overtook Chanel at one point."

"So Eternal is not – eternal?"

"Eternal is not immutable, but it remains essentially the same. Think of a great wine. Each year leaves its individual trace on a Château d'Yquem, but the name still represents something that connoisseurs will fight for."

"And Isabelle Arbaud snatched this Louis Halphen from you?"

She chastised him with a raised finger. "Ours is not such a violent world – despite whatever your hypothesis about Perrin's death might be. Isabelle did not snatch Louis, she seduced him, much like the serpent in the garden of Eden."

"With the promise of infinite knowledge?"

"With the promise of infinite liberty. That he would have the resources of a Chanel or an Ephémère, but be held to no brief. Rather than tinker with one of the world's greatest perfumes, he could create one."

"When did he join her?"

"A year ago."

"So who is keeping Eternal alive?"

"Not who – what. Inertia is keeping Eternal alive for the moment. But we created an expectation when we allowed it to evolve under Louis' guidance. If we cannot meet it, then it will once more begin to decline. Eternal must have a new custodian."

"A replacement for Louis Halphen," said Franck.

"A once-in-a-generation talent? Not an easy challenge. Where do you think I would have to look to find such a thing?"

"No idea," said Franck.

He could, however, think of an alternative. If Craveri was faced with a fruitless quest, she might be tempted to cut off Halphen's oxygen and force him back. Kicking and screaming if need be.

*

Paris had known its fair share of queens. Although the monarchy had at times preferred other locations – the Valois kings the comfort of the Loire valley, and Louis XIV the regimented pomp of Versailles – rare indeed were the royal spouses who had not at some stage graced the streets of the capital. Few, however, had left any trace of their passage which might catch the attention of a homeless woman.

Franck was betting on Marie de Medicis, Henri IV's strong-willed second wife, regent after his death, and occasional conspirator against her own son in the troubled decades of the early seventeenth century. Before being driven into exile in 1631 she had acquired a plot of land belonging to the duke of Luxembourg to the south of the Latin Quarter and called into being a stately palace and extensive gardens for herself and her son, Louis XIII. Now home to the Senate, the upper house of the French parliament, and the capital's most prized public park, it bore the name of its original owner – the Jardin du Luxembourg – rather than that of the queen who had given it its definitive form.

Adeline, however, clearly had not forgotten her.

Franck found the woman he assumed to be Adeline in an elevated section that overlooked the south-western corner of the Jardin du Luxembourg's central flower beds and boating pond. She had taken possession of two of the park's many cast iron chairs, propping her feet on one and her bulk on the other, with a supermarket trolley drawn up alongside her. Her back was turned to the passers-by so that she could face one of the park's hundred or so notoriously mediocre marble statues. Carved to order in the 1840s as part of a series of the nation's royal, noble and saintly heroines, it presented a richly costumed but stiffly posed Marie de Medicis.

As he approached Franck could see that his prey wore several torn woollen jumpers above a long ragged skirt and, of all things, stained and torn purple ballet shoes on swollen feet. Matted curls protruded from beneath a brightly coloured ski hat. From what he could see of her face Franck guessed she was in her sixties. He was astonished that the Luxembourg park-keepers, whose attachment to order and discipline had made the park the epitome of bourgeois respectability, left her undisturbed. Perhaps she had proven herself as formidable as the queen whose company she sought. Add to that the fact that she apparently visited only once a week, and they may simply have come to the conclusion that it was a battle not worth fighting.

Franck approached her from her right-hand side, the supermarket trolley forming a barrier to her left. She was reading *Le Monde* and kept her eyes fixed on its black type as he drew up alongside her.

"I hope I'm not disturbing you," he began.

"You are," she shot back. "I'm reading."

But not about current events. Judging by the headlines he could see, including a few references to François Mitterrand, Franck guessed she was reading a paper from the early 1980s. A glance at the trolley showed that it was packed with newspapers and magazines, each one tightly rolled into a scroll and jammed amongst the others.

"The library of Alexandria," he said, pointing to the trolley.

She looked up at him. "Alexandria had around half a million scrolls. I couldn't push that many trolleys."

"But you're doing what you can," Franck suggested.

She folded up the paper she had been reading, laid it flat upon her extended legs, and rolled it up into a slim tube. She drew an elastic band from her right wrist and bound it up. Every single one of her fingers, thumbs included, bore one or two rings – some gold, some silver, some plain, some with gems. A large reddish-coloured wooden box sitting in her lap probably contained even more of them, judging by the sounds that came from it as she shifted in her seat.

"17th of July 1984," she announced, tapping the now-cylindrical copy of *Le Monde*. "Mitterrand tosses Mauroy aside and turns to Fabius, a young puppet for an ageing master."

"You've got the 10th of May 1981?" he asked. Mitterrand's triumphant election, when the Pantheon was besieged by elated rose-waving supporters.

"Of course," she snorted.

"9th of November 1970?" The death of De Gaulle.

She nodded warily. "Before you ask, I don't go much further back than that. That's about when I started archiving."

"How do you keep them dry?" asked Franck.

"Plastic's easy to find, if you know where to look. Why are

you so interested?" Her initial delight at being quizzed on her treasures was ebbing away, leaving suspicion in its place. "You can't have them."

"I've no intention of stealing them," he assured her. "I'm with the police."

Her eyes narrowed. Franck assumed that she was waiting for him to attempt to move her on. He was wrong. Having studied his face for a minute or two she smiled crookedly and relaxed again.

"I've got you," she declared.

"You have?"

Her left hand stretched out over the trolley by her side and wandered over the mass of tightly packed scrolls. On two occasions she began to tug one out only to tap it back in. Then she triumphantly pulled out and unbound a glossy magazine.

"27th of June 2007," she stated, quickly flipping through it before holding up a two-page spread. "It's you, isn't it?"

Franck saw several photos of himself in different locations in Paris. It was the issue of *Exposé* which recounted the investigation into the Du Bellay murders. It had briefly made a celebrity of him before the enquiry into the Corsican incident had muddied the waters and the beginning of the long summer holiday season had thrust him thankfully back into obscurity.

"It's me," he conceded. "I'm not sure it deserves to sit alongside the events of Mitterrand's reign and the death of De Gaulle, though."

"Times have changed," she observed. "It's all trivia now."

"I haven't introduced myself properly," said Franck. "My name is Franck Guerin and I'm with the Brigade Criminelle."

"Adeline," she murmured, as if it was some time since she had been called upon to name herself.

"I came here today to consult you, Adeline," continued Franck. "I'm hoping you can help me."

"If it's in here, I can help you," she declared, enthusiastically sweeping her hand over the contents of her trolley.

"Unfortunately, I don't think it is. I'm trying to get in touch with Michel. Michel from the André Citroen park."

Suspicion clouded her features again.

"Why?"

"I need his help, that's all. I think he can help me with a new enquiry. I think he may have seen something in the park this week."

"The death at the fashion show?"

"That's right. He's talked to you about it?"

She shook her head. "Read about it in the papers, where else?"

"Do you know where I can find him?"

"Why should I tell you? We can't trust people like you."

"You can trust me, Adeline. You know about me." He indicated the copy of *Exposé* which she still held in her hands. "You've read about me. I may not be the best *flic* in the business, but I'm one of the good guys."

She looked down at the printed photos and then gave Franck an appraising look from head to toe.

"Still carrying the same briefcase," she observed.

Franck held it high. "Wouldn't go anywhere without it."

"Take it to the Alexandre III bridge. That's where he sleeps."

*

Alexander III never got to see the bridge named in his honour. One of the surviving relics of the 1900 Universal Exhibition, its foundation stone was solemnly laid by his son Nicolas II, before his own unceremonious end at the hands of the Bolsheviks. All in all, the Franco-Russian alliance, which the bridge was intended to symbolise, did not seem to have brought much luck to the Russian Emperors. Nor indeed to the people of France, since during the alliance they assiduously subscribed to a series of massive loans intended to encourage industrial development in Russia, only to lose everything when the Revolution came.

If the alliance had been cursed, at least the bridge itself was not. Wide and flat, it linked the majestic sweep of the Invalides esplanade with the self-assured splendour of the Grand and Petit Palais, creating the only spot in Paris where the left and right banks of the Seine joined in harmonious unity. True to the spirit of progress that the Universal Exhibition sought to illustrate, it was built of steel, a lattice of beams forming a single shallow arch massively buttressed on each shore. The bridge was profusely decorated, with blindingly gilded triumphant statues at each end and elaborately forged lamps illuminating its entire length. It was an obligatory stop for any tourist equipped with a half-decent guidebook.

All of which made it an unlikely location for a homeless man to sleep. Although tourists made a major contribution towards keeping the city's homeless fed and watered, the latter generally preferred to bed down where there was no one around, since the less attention they attracted the better chance they had of sleeping undisturbed.

It was now just after six. The sun had set about a quarter of an hour before but the bridge was still populated with couples and families wrapped up against the chill of the evening, taking in the illuminated sights of the Eiffel Tower downstream and the golden dome of the Invalides to the south. Franck wandered the length of both sides of the bridge without once being solicited for some change, a cigarette or a luncheon voucher. He stopped near the southern end, leaning against the parapet, his eyes resting on the slight bend in the Seine as it flowed down from the heart of the city. Bulky tourist boats, casting light outwards from the glassed-in shells that held their passengers, moved sluggishly up and down its now-dark surface. Faster-moving traffic shot along the roads that ran level with the river on either bank, hurtling underneath him.

It did not look like he was going to find Michel tonight. It was time to go home, given that he at least had a home to go to.

"You've never played. Not once, not ever?"

Fontainebleau forest had once been accustomed to the horns and padded hoofs of royal hunting parties. It still supported a healthy population of wild deer and boars, which in turn attracted an annual influx of camouflaged men clutching arms, including the odd scoped rifle from Perrin Industries.

The prosperous and upmarket streets of the town of Fontainebleau ran right to the forest's edge, preventing suburban sprawl and maintaining the property value of its existing stock of houses. There was a general consensus that allowing any incursion into the woods was in no one's interest, and the only exceptions made over the past century had been the construction of INSEAD, an MBA factory which drained ambitious executives from all corners of the world, and the laying out of one of France's first and most select golf courses. Membership of the Fontainebleau golf club, founded in 1909, was doled out parsimoniously to the rich and successful, creating a closed world where deals could be struck, a sense of privilege cultivated, and marriages made and unmade.

Needless to say, Franck had never set foot in the golf club before. He had caught a train from Paris that morning, shuffled dutifully onto a bus that took him from the station to the heart of the town, and walked to the club's entrance at its southern extremity. As he passed through the car park, overwhelmingly populated by examples of German automotive engineering, he wondered whether he was the only person in the club's history to approach it on foot.

He now sat in what he assumed to be some kind of committee room. Its centre was occupied by a baize-covered table surrounded by upright chairs, but two leather sofas had been squashed comfortably into a corner for less formal discussions. Guillaume Thèves, who must have played well that morning as he was visibly in a good mood, sat across from him on one of them. A low table between them offered a bottle of cognac and two fat-bellied glasses.

Thèves seemed incredulous, refusing to accept what Franck had just told him.

"Not once, not ever," confirmed Franck.

"How is that possible?"

"Not many golf courses in my arrondissement." As an excuse it seemed more diplomatic than to admit that he just did not see the point of golf, puttering around a landscape as artificial as the grounds of a château in pursuit of a tiny ball with a bagful of expensive irons and woods. Its advocates argued for its zen-like properties, but Franck remained unconvinced. For him it stood alongside cricket as one of the mysteries of the Anglo-Saxon universe. He took solace from the fact that even Yves de Chaumont, unlike many of his fellow magistrates, showed no interest in the game.

"You want to whack a few balls once we've finished?" suggested Thèves.

"Unfortunately I won't have the time."

"I wouldn't have your job," commented Thèves. "My wife thinks I work all the time, but at least I don't spend my weekends worrying about who's been murdered, and who's next in line."

Franck had briefly explained the reason for the interview when he'd phoned International Paper Supplies the previous day. He had been obliged to insist heavily on the serious nature of his enquiry in order to get past mademoiselle Montfort, Thèves' stonewalling secretary, and to convince the man himself to accept to see him over the weekend.

"You knew Alain Perrin well?" Franck asked. Thèves had already filled both glasses and taken a good gulp from one of them. The preliminaries were over.

"The way you do. Which is to say, not really. Alain was about the same age as one of my sons. Our paths might have crossed a few times before, but it was only after I got involved in Arbaud that I really had any opportunity or reason to talk to him. We'd meet up at Isabelle Arbaud's occasional briefings, but they never lasted long, and Isabelle never wasted her time wining or dining us."

"Just as well. It would have been with your own money," Franck pointed out. "You, Perrin and Chautard brought all the money to the table, if I've understood correctly."

"Good point," conceded Thèves. "But it was more than that. Isabelle Arbaud is all business and no pleasure. Makes you wonder how she ever made it in her chosen field. A lot of drinking and eating goes on in office supplies. I can't imagine there's any less in the fashion world. And yet she just doesn't seem interested."

"But you didn't hesitate to lend her fifty million euros?"

"I checked her out. There are only two ways to make a lot of money in this world. You either do it with your own hands – that's how I built up International Paper Supplies – or you back the right horse long before it reaches the starting gate. Isabelle has a very audacious plan, and is probably the only person in her field capable of pulling it off."

"Because she has an unparalleled understanding of the luxury goods market?" offered Franck.

Thèves smiled in recognition of the phrase.

"She's very convincing, isn't she?" he said. "Be wary, captain, she'll soon have you signing over your life savings if you don't watch out."

"I don't think she'd waste her time. They wouldn't cover one of her handbags. So you're saying you only encountered Alain Perrin at business meetings, and never socialised with him?"

"That's right."

"What about Nathalie Chautard?"

"Nathalie was different," said Thèves. "Nathalie was a self-made woman, not a trust-fund baby. I knew Nathalie. I wouldn't say we were friends, but we moved in similar circles. She played a good game of golf."

"Were you surprised by her death?"

"Honestly?" said Thèves, leaning forward, as if they were in a crowded room and he did not want anyone else to hear him. "Not entirely. Nathalie loved fast cars. I've even heard her ex-husband say that one of the reasons for their divorce was that she terrified him with her driving."

"So you believe it was an accident?"

Thèves shrugged. "It might have been. She could have overtaken the truck, pulled in too quickly to avoid oncoming traffic and been rear-ended."

"So why would the truck driver disappear?"

"The truck was stolen, wasn't it? Kind of hard to explain that the accident wasn't your fault if you've already demonstrated your criminal tendencies."

"So you just shrugged it off?"

Thèves frowned. "I didn't say that. Nathalie was a good businesswoman and I know people who liked her a lot. She shouldn't have gone that way, nor so soon. But life's a risky business."

"I'm sure Alain Perrin would agree," said Franck.

"Perrin is different," insisted Thèves. "His was a clear case of murder – at least, that's what you lot said and the press and television repeated."

"It was pretty clear-cut," confirmed Franck.

"But nobody has reported anything that suggests it had anything to do with his involvement with Arbaud," continued Thèves. "So unless you're about to reveal some new information to me, I don't see why I should be especially worried."

"What if I said I could prove that Chautard was murdered? Two out of three – wouldn't that make you wonder?"

"Can you?"

Franck waved aside his question. "Imagine I could. Would you begin to see things differently?"

Thèves did not spend very long thinking about it.

"A little," he conceded. "But not much. Assume the Arbaud connection is the common link. Well, if someone wanted to stop Arbaud in its tracks, all they'd have to do is kill Isabelle

Arbaud. We just brought the money. Money's banal. You can find it anywhere. She brought the vision and the talent."

"It can't be that easy to pull together so many millions. But what I need to understand is whether killing those who put up the money – Chautard and Perrin ..."

"Not to mention me," added Thèves.

"Not to mention you. Would doing so make the money that had already been put up disappear?"

"It all depends. We signed ten year indentures, but in each of them there's a clause allowing the lender to pull out his money with four month's notice. If Chautard's inheritors, or Perrin's, want to abandon the venture, they can. But Chautard had a very bitter divorce and two of her three children sided with her ex-husband. Rumour has it that there are two teams of very expensive lawyers fighting over CWM, her houses, her cars, her jewellery and everything else she left. Perrin was single, so we can assume that all he has will go to his two sisters, one of whom works for a NGO campaigning against the arms trade. Since the future of Perrin Industries is at stake, I can't see that going smoothly either. Neither estate will be taking any financial decisions any time soon. So, as far as Chautard and Perrin are concerned, their deaths will probably have no immediate impact on Arbaud. All in all, it doesn't make your conspiracy theory look good."

Thèves patted Franck consolingly on the shoulder and drained his glass. He motioned to the one that sat before Franck, as yet untouched.

"Not interested?"

"Not really."

"Well, here's an object lesson in the difference between a self-made man and someone who has inherited his wealth," announced Thèves, swooping Franck's glass up in his hand and carrying it to his lips. "I never let anything go to waste."

"Thanks for your time, monsieur Thèves," said Franck.

Thèves smiled sympathetically. "You came all the way out here and didn't get what you wanted, did you?"

"I wasn't looking for anything in particular," Franck stated. "I'm just pursuing all relevant lines of enquiry."

"Can't have you leaving empty-handed," insisted Thèves. "If you're really convinced that Arbaud is the key to all this, then I've got a good suspect for you. Have you ever met Louis Halphen?"

"The Nose?"

"The very same. I take it you haven't. You would have said something. It's not an experience you easily forget. Well, if anyone hated us – us being the money-grubbing financiers – then it was Louis Halphen."

"Why? You were bankrolling his work."

Thèves laughed heartily. "You definitely haven't meet Louis Halphen. We were privileged to be granted the opportunity to contribute to the creation of his greatest masterpiece. A perfume that would be unlike any other the world had ever seen. A perfume that would last as long as Mozart's operas, or the Mona Lisa, or ... I forget the rest."

"So? Aren't creative types always a little eccentric?"

"God preserve us from the creative types," declared Thèves. "You should see some of the crap advertising agencies have tried to get me to swallow down the years. As if there's a better way of selling boxes of envelopes than a six-for-four offer, or a free gift that will sit nicely in the kitchen."

"I'd be surprised if that's how Arbaud is planning to market its wares."

"When or if Arbaud has something to sell. That's the problem. In the initial business plan Halphen had six months to come up with his perfume. He's now been at it for twelve months, and we're picking up the tab. In October last year the three of us had a rather stormy meeting with Isabelle and insisted she bring Halphen to heel. Smart girl that she is, she arranged an encounter with him, just to show us that we were asking for the moon. We sat through a two-hour tirade in the course of which he threatened to destroy his work rather than allow us to force him to botch it."

"Did you back off?"

"Guillaume Thèves back off? Nathalie Chautard back off? Alain was a little more circumspect, but we stuck to our guns. A project without a firm completion date is just a black hole into which money endlessly disappears. We told him the perfume had to be ready within three months or we'd pull out our funds. Nathalie thought we were being too soft. She wanted to pull the plug right away. We talked her round on the day, but I could tell she wasn't really convinced."

"What did Halphen say?"

"Nothing. He gave us a hate-filled stare and walked out of the room," explained Thèves.

"Three months," mused Franck.

Thèves spelled it out for him, "November, December, January. The day Alain Perrin was killed, Halphen had about a week left to make the deadline. Or to find a way to make it disappear."

Sunday, 27th January

"Fuck you and your fucking taxi!"

Franck had left his apartment at around six thirty that morning, when the skies were still dark. It had taken him less than ten minutes to stumble into his clothes and reheat an old carafe of coffee in his microwave. He had not bothered to wash or shave. Given his prey, it scarcely mattered.

He reached the Invalides esplanade just after seven. The day had still not arrived, obliging the elegant lamps on the deserted Alexandre III bridge to continue their vigil. A chill wind followed the river as it flowed downstream, causing him to zip his parka right up to his throat. He wished he had brought a scarf. Gloves would have been nice too.

An hour and half later the sun finally put in an appearance. Franck had kept moving, strolling from one end of the bridge to the other, hands deep in his pockets. Eight individuals had crossed the bridge during that time. Five had been in evening wear. Although they seemed to have forgotten their coats somewhere, they appeared sufficiently fortified by champagne to ignore the ambient temperature. Franck had declined to take a swig from the bottle one of them tendered to him. The other three had been isolated pedestrians walking quickly, heads down, well-wrapped up in layers of clean clothes and wearing sensible shoes. They were of no interest to him.

Of the few cars that had passed him, almost all had been taxis. The same thing was true of the traffic he had seen on the roads running alongside the river under the bridge. The night shift carrying their last fares home. He knew these would be the younger or more desperate taxi drivers. Although business was brisk, and tips could be good, Saturday nights were not for the faint of heart. Most of the attacks that took place on taxi drivers occurred as Saturday shaded into Sunday, as did a lot of fare-skipping and in-car spills of bodily or other fluids. Not to mention a fair number of bumps and scrapes, which came directly out of the takings of the majority of drivers who rented, rather than owned, their vehicle.

A sudden screech of brakes and an angry yell seemed to indicate that something of this nature had just, or almost, occurred. Franck idled over to the parapet facing upstream where the bridge touched the left bank. Sufficient light had now conquered the sky for him to study the scene below. A taxi was immobile on one of the two lanes that ran along the river bank. The driver had lowered his window and was shouting obscenities at a ragged figure who stood defiantly a metre or so in front of his bumper, offering his own stream of abuse in return. No doubt realising the futility of the exchange, the taxi driver soon pulled his head back in, skirted round the still immobile figure in the right-hand lane, and shot off.

"You OK?" Franck yelled.

"Fuck off!" came the reply. "You and your fucking sympathy! Fuck the fuck off and leave me in peace."

It sounded promising.

Franck left the parapet and headed for a flight of stairs that led down to the road at the riverside level and a little-used entrance to the nearby Invalides RER station.

The man was still on the road, now standing on the white line that separated its two lanes. A car passed, swerving slightly to avoid him and angrily blowing its horn. Another, right behind it, did the same. The man just laughed at them. If two were to arrive running parallel on both lanes the scene might suddenly cease to seem so comical. It was time to intervene.

Franck let another vehicle pass, glanced up the road to make sure it was clear, and strode forward.

"Get your fucking hands off me!" he was told, in no uncertain terms.

Franck ignored the request and half-pulled, half-carried the man back to the entrance to the RER station. It was not a pleasant experience. His clothes were greasy to the touch and a soiled smell enveloped him. Franck propped him against a wall and stepped back.

"It's too early to get run over," he said. "The ambulance crews are still having breakfast. Wait a little. Don't be so selfish."

"Fuck off!" he was told, once more.

"Don't worry, I will," said Franck, pulling a pack of paper tissues from one of the rear pockets of his jeans. He extracted one and wiped his hands. "You sleep here?"

"Fuck off." There was less energy to it this time. "Look behind you, you stupid fuck."

Franck turned and looked back across the road. The underside of the bridge curved up from massive foundations sunk deep into the river bank. A series of steel girders traced an identical arc up to the mid-point of the bridge. About a metre apart, each was bound to its neighbours at regular intervals by robust horizontal struts. The resulting fretwork of metal suspended over the dark waters of the Seine was home to well over a dozen improvised nests. Sheets of plywood had been jammed between the supports, both horizontally and vertically, to form fragile-looking open boxes. Most held a muffled figure, twisted uncomfortably to fit into insufficient space and buried inside a stained sleeping bag or grimy collection of blankets. Rucksacks and plastic bags were stuffed into the available corners or hung on improvised wire hooks from the struts. This aerial shantytown looked cold and miserable, offering little shelter from the wind but at least cut off from the rain by the surface of the bridge above. Its one great advantage, Franck surmised, was its relative inaccessibility. During the day, when traffic thundered non-stop along the river bank, it was about as secure as a castle behind a deep moat. In return for putting up with the noise and the exhaust fumes, its inhabitants and their few possessions must have felt relatively secure.

"I'm looking for Michel," Franck stated. "And if you tell me to fuck off again, I'll push you back out into that road. Only I'll wait for a car first."

"What do you want with Michel?" The man eyed him with

p.77

deep distrust, presumably weighing the menace Franck represented against some feeling of solidarity with his homeless fellows.

"I need his help. He's not in any trouble."

"That one there." He pointed to a platform high up under the bridge.

Franck crossed the road and carefully swung himself up onto one of the steel beams that rose from the bank. It was wide enough for him to rest both feet upon it, but its surface was studded with round-headed bolts. He stepped forward carefully, leaning out to grasp a vertical shaft that ran from the beam up to the underside of the bridge. He kept his eyes from the uninviting water beneath him and concentrated on not dislodging any of the wooden planks that supported a still-sleeping figure to his right.

It took three minutes of careful manoeuvring to reach his destination, one of the highest-perched nests under the bridge. As he neared, two eyes followed his progress from the depths of a khaki sleeping bag. When he finally reached the platform, his knees and back bent into a crouch to cope with the diminishing headroom, a hand came out to help him steady himself.

"If you're Michel," said Franck, "I'm here to offer you some breakfast."

"You don't care much about being popular, do you?" the man called Michel observed.

Franck kept his eyes on the manager of the café as he walked away between the tables. He paused beside a waiter, uttered a few words with a scowl, and disappeared round a corner. Franck slipped his police ID back into his pocket. It looked like they were going to be served after all.

The Alexandre III bridge was one of the few spots in Paris that did not have a café or bistrot in line of sight. All it had to offer was the open expanse of the Invalides esplanade and the public gardens around the Grand and Petit Palais, which were better suited for summer picnics than winter snacks. Franck had led Michel across the esplanade, heading south and then west into the rue Saint Dominique. He pushed open the door of the first street-corner café they came across and ushered Michel through.

There was only a scattering of customers, most catching a coffee before heading towards the market in nearby rue Cler. As Franck steered Michel to a table in a quiet corner he could not fail to catch the looks coming their way. Dressed in dark-brown corduroy trousers with fraying cuffs, a massive knitted green jumper which reached almost to his knees, a mackintosh whose original colour was now difficult to determine, surprisingly well cared for hiking boots and a loden green felt Homburg which had lost its ribbon, Michel certainly did not look like he belonged in this affluent corner of the seventh arrondissement. The tangled hair that tumbled to his shoulders when he took off his hat and the long, cracked nails which he ran approvingly across the table top when he sat down, did nothing to help convince the staff that his was a desirable presence in their establishment. However, it was probably the smell – not one of unsanitary squalor, as with the man Franck had wrestled from the roadway that morning, but one of organic matter, like a damp barn – that brought the manager to them with a peremptory invitation to leave.

That was when Franck had slipped him his ID and pointed out, in a low and calm voice, that he would personally see to it that the café's kitchen, toilets, employment records and accounts would suffer stringent inspection within the next seven days if their custom was refused. A few minutes later he ordered two coffees – a double for Michel, plus a bowl of warm milk – and a basket of croissants, *pains au chocolat* and *pains aux raisins* from the waiter despatched to serve them.

When their order arrived, Franck suggested to Michel that they eat first and talk afterwards. Michel nodded his acceptance. He cradled the bowl of milk in his hands and lowered his face over it as if staring into its depths. The inspection over, he brought it to his lips and emptied it in one long, slow motion.

"Childhood," he said. "Breakfast before hurrying off to school."

"I always had chocolate powder in mine," offered Franck.

"Chocolate is headier, a whiff of distant lands. Milk on its own exudes the pastoral innocence of a Norman plain or an Alpine valley."

Michel then took a *pain aux raisins* and held it vertically before his eyes, turning it on its axis.

"Caramelised sugar, raisins holding jealously onto what remains of their sweet moisture." He bit into it. "Butter and eggs reaching out from the flour into which they have been whipped." He finished it slowly, gathering up the crumbs that fell to the table and swallowing them too.

He turned his attention to his coffee, holding the cup parallel to his lips, allowing the steam to waft up over his face.

"Kenya," he uttered, as if greeting an old friend. "The high plateaus, the sun and the rain. The sturdy bean, hugging its aroma to itself until crushed."

And then, once more, he drained it at a steady pace.

"I can get you another," offered Franck, suddenly no longer sure of what he had fished from beneath the bridge. Walking over, Michel had said nothing, mutely following Franck's directions. Now he seemed to be revealing himself as a vagabond poet. Too clichéd to be true, it was nonetheless an impressive act.

"I don't want to abuse your hospitality, captain," said Michel. "But may I take the rest of the *viennoiseries* with me?"

"Feel free."

With one hand Michel held open a side pocket of his mackintosh, which he had not taken off, and ferried the rest of the pastries into it, one at a time. He then licked his fingertips and nodded appreciatively towards Franck.

"I'm ready to be interrogated."

"Thank you," said Franck. "Just a few questions, that's all."

"It says Brigade Criminelle on your ID. Interrogations are more the house style, I would have thought."

Franck wondered how he would have reacted to his old DST card, but did not pursue the point.

"Your name is Michel?"

"That's correct."

"Just Michel?"

"Just Michel."

"No family name?"

"None I'm using for the time being."

"I could ask to see your identity card," Franck pointed out.

"You would then be obliged – if I refused – to conduct me to the nearest police station and hold me until such time as my identity was established. Which would put an end to our nice little chat."

"We'll stick with Michel for the time being," Franck conceded. "I've been told you're a frequent visitor to the André Citroen park."

"That's true."

"Every morning?"

Michel chuckled. "I'm a homeless man. My life is somewhat unpredictable. I don't have a routine cast in concrete."

"But you do go there regularly?" insisted Franck.

"Yes, I do. It's a well-tended park. A good place to get washed. And they've got a lot of interesting plants and shrubs."

"Were you there last Wednesday morning?"

"You mean the morning of the murder at the Ephémère *défilé*?" asked Michel calmly, inviting Franck not to take him for a fool.

"Yes, that morning. The security personnel at the site say they saw a homeless man in the vicinity when the traiteur was bringing in refreshments for the show. Could that have been you?"

"That was almost certainly me. They were using Fauchon. That was a fine *pain aux raisins*," – he indicated the now-empty basket on the table – "but Fauchon's are quite a few notches above. I thought I'd try my luck."

"When did you get there?"

"I was hanging about outside from about five thirty. I hadn't slept well that night and thought I might as well go for a walk. I knew the Ephémère show was scheduled for the park that day, so I wandered over."

"When did you leave?"

"I had originally intended to stay until they started packing everything away, once the whole thing was over. But after the guests had gone, I saw three uniformed policeman arrive, and realised that everybody else seemed to be being held inside. So I figured something bad had happened and decided it wasn't such a good idea to hang around any longer."

"Why something bad?"

"One or two policemen wandering by is a normal enough occurrence. Three of them marching in unison and looking grim is never a good omen."

"So you were in the vicinity of the glasshouse and the temporary structure behind it from the moment the supplier's entrance was opened before sunrise till sometime after midday?"

"Sounds right," confirmed Michel.

"Did you see anything suspicious during that time?"

"No. I saw the food arrive, and the clothes, and the models, and all the rest of the backstage staff. I saw the fashionistas and the photographers come in the front door. I saw the lights and heard the music. And then I watched everyone leave."

"Did you hear anything strange?"

"Like what?"

"Like a gunshot."

"I can't say I'm familiar with the sound of gunfire, but I didn't hear anything strange. Don't forget that it was a noisy show, even if it was muffled by the glass."

"Did you see this man at any stage?"

Franck laid a photograph of Alain Perrin on the table.

Michel glanced at it.

"That's Alain Perrin, isn't it? They used the same photo in one of the papers."

Franck bit back a question, but Michel went on to answer it anyway.

"We're great readers of the papers," he explained. "We, the homeless. We pick up whatever's lying around, and since that's the fate of most papers, we eventually get round to reading them all. We're often a day or too late, but we're pretty well informed."

Having met Adeline, Franck had no reason to doubt what he was being told.

"Do you remember seeing him on the day?" he asked.

"No, I can't say I do." Michel seemed genuinely to regret the fact. "I get the feeling you bought me breakfast for nothing."

Franck sighed. A shadowy armed assassin spotted slipping into the extension outside the glasshouse in the middle of the show would not have made the enquiry any easier, but it would have made it less mysterious.

"Keep thinking about that morning over the next few days," he said. "If something comes to you, call me."

He slipped Michel his business card and a ten-euro note.

"What's that for?" asked Michel.

"Buy a phone card and use it to call me."

Michel pushed the money back towards Franck.

"I'll find a way to get in touch with you if need be. You've shown enough generosity this morning, captain Guerin."

"Call me Franck. After all, I'm obliged to call you Michel."

"OK, Franck. If you've got other questions, you know where to find me."

They shook hands and then Michel got up to leave. On his way out he nodded amicably at the waiter and the manager, who eyed him coldly from behind the bar.

Franck paid the bill and made his way to the door. He fancied another coffee, but not here. With its scrubbed tables, painstakingly swept floor and clients outfitted in variants of the same strictly prescribed casual Sunday fashions, the place had all the charm of a church hall packed with sanctimonious parishioners. Stained and odorous as he was, Michel possessed far more vitality than the café's staff and clientele put together.

It was always heartening to find someone truly alive in the midst of a murder enquiry.

*

"Thank you for coming, captain."

Franck shook Benoît Nallard's outstretched hand. They were both dressed in black, although Nallard's suit and coat bespoke a level of tailoring far beyond that of those Franck was wearing. He had, however, visited his shower and reacquainted himself with his razor since his early morning outing.

It was mid-afternoon and the day was proving chilly, but dry. Which was just as well. Rain might strike the poetic as evidence of heaven's tears, but Franck always felt it interfered with the dignity and purpose of a funeral. Few minds were sufficiently resolute at the best of times to focus on the contents of a coffin and what they represented; wrestling with umbrellas and stepping cautiously around puddles provided too welcome a distraction.

A vast, well-disciplined city of the dead, the Montparnasse cemetery could easily absorb the largest of funeral parties. It had taken the burial of Alain Perrin in its stride, even though there must have been nearly a hundred people in attendance.

They were all dispersing now, heading slowly towards the main gate, discussing in low voices. The two Perrin sisters had been easy to spot, given their place in the procession. They stood together at the graveside, but drifted apart once the ceremony was over. Franck noticed that one of them was receiving a disproportionate share of the attention of the older, more dispassionate mourners. He assumed the latter represented the Perrin Industries business connections: the merchants of death. Which meant that the other sister, her head bowed under a long mantle of golden hair, was the black sheep of the family. The rebel whose proclaimed intention was to bite the hand that fed her.

"A sad day for a proud family firm," continued Nallard. "I'm the first non-Perrin to be in charge, and I'll probably not be the last."

"You're sure all the members of the family are that proud of it?" asked Franck.

"You mean Marie-Chantal? That's going to be an interesting problem to resolve." He shook his head and took a deep breath. "Any progress on your front?"

"I need your help." Franck slipped a hand into one of the pockets of his slightly worn merino wool coat, one of the few items of formal outerwear he possessed, and pulled out two clear plastic bags. Each contained a single bullet head. "I need to talk to someone who knows about barrel rifling."

Nallard reached out and pushed Franck's hand down.

"You really think this is the best place to be waving those about?"

"Probably not," Franck conceded, putting them back in his pocket. "But I assumed that whoever your expert is, he has to be here."

"It's important for the investigation?"

"Very."

"You want to talk to Jean-Charles Velasque. He's our head gunsmith. Come with me."

Franck followed Nallard as he moved steadily through the crowd heading out of the cemetery. Nallard nodded or waved discreetly at those he passed, but never stopped until he grabbed the elbow of a grey-haired man in his early sixties.

"Jean-Charles, can I take you aside for a moment?" asked Nallard.

Velasque assented and moved to the side of the cobbled path in order not to obstruct the flow of those behind him.

"This is captain Franck Guerin of the Brigade Criminelle.

He's handling the investigation into Alain's death."

"Good afternoon, captain," said Velasque, shaking hands with Franck.

"Can I talk to you in private?" asked Franck.

"Of course."

Nallard left them and Franck steered Velasque out of the cemetery and down a side street to where boulevard Raspail met the boulevard de Montparnasse.

"La Coupole?" he suggested. A legendary brasserie that had nourished the neighbourhood's bohemian tribe in the early decades of the twentieth century, its vast dining area was crowded on this, as on every other, Sunday afternoon. However, a narrow space was set apart for the café trade in a glass veranda between the main room and the street. They managed to grab a table there.

Velasque ordered a beer. Franck stuck to coffee.

"I'm afraid I don't know what a head gunsmith is," Franck confessed.

"I'm in charge of the design team," Velasque explained. "We come up with ideas for new guns, make experimental versions, test them, perfect them, and then draw up the specifications for industrialisation."

"You've been with Perrin Industries for a long time?"

"Since I was an apprentice. When I started Alain's grandfather was still around."

"I'd like to show you these, see what you can tell me about them."

Franck brought out the bags with the bullets and placed them on the table.

"These are what killed Alain?" asked Velasque, who did not seem at all disturbed by their presence.

"Yes."

Velasque pulled a small leather case from the inside pocket of his coat. It unzipped at the side to reveal a thin steel ruler about 10 centimetres long, two pairs of callipers, a magnifying glass and a jeweller's eyepiece.

"May I?" He gestured towards the bags with one of the callipers.

"Go ahead."

Velasque removed each bullet in turn, measured their width with the callipers, laid them down beside the ruler while he studied them with the magnifying glass, and then held them in the air, turning them before the eyepiece which he had fixed to his right eye.

"6.5mm bullet shot with a very high spin from a precision-rifled barrel," he said.

"Does Perrin Industries make 6.5mm calibre rifles?"

"Most of what we do is 7.62mm. NATO's our biggest customer, so we have to stick to their standard calibre. But we make two 6.5mm hunting rifles. Extra-long barrels with progressive rifling. Long distance, head or heart. Not for your casual weekend hunter. They're for marksmen who can shoot up to a kilometre away with ammunition that only kills if you hit the right spot. If you fumble you've got a wounded animal that's probably too far away to track down and put out of its misery."

"There are that many good shooters out there?"

"Probably not. They're very expensive rifles. Unfortunately, that tends to attract the wrong kind of buyer. The rich are rarely aware of their own limitations."

"These bullets could have come from one of these rifles?"

Velasque gently rocked one of the bullets from side to side on the tabletop with the edge of the callipers.

"I don't think so. I'd need better magnification to be sure, but with an extra-long barrel the bullet stays inside longer, so you've got more time to spin it. A tightly packed groove for a high spin is tricky to cut and difficult to keep clean. It's not the kind of thing you do if you can avoid it. Particularly since you can easily overtwist. Over very long distances excessive spin might throw the trajectory off. We've never bored a barrel for a hunting rifle with a twist rate below 160mm."

"And you reckon these were fired from a weapon with

narrower rifling?"

"Looks like it. As I said, I'd have to check to be certain, but I've been at this a long time. I'm not often wrong."

Franck nodded to himself. "It's probably just as well. Had Alain been killed with a Perrin Industries rifle, you can imagine the fallout the firm would have had to handle. In any case, there's no way the murderer could have got a rifle into the crime scene without being spotted."

"Perhaps we can move on from the rifles then," suggested Velasque.

"Sorry?"

Velasque delved once more into his coat and brought out a mechanical pencil and a small bound notebook with unlined pages. He made a rapid sketch and then turned it to face Franck.

"The PI87. A long-barrelled automatic pistol, same dimensions as a Borchardt-Luger, more or less. But a smaller calibre – 6.5mm rather than 7.65mm – to get a longer range, a smoother flight and neater penetration. Which means you need more spin. Since we had a 130mm barrel length we set ourselves the challenge of a 130mm twist rate. It took us some time to get the bore right. We couldn't do it with a broaching bit, so we ended up flow-forming."

Franck realised he should have brought Georges Sternberg along. This was way above his head. He decided to simplify things.

"So you do make a gun that could have fired this?"

"Yes we do. It's for the hunter who likes to make things difficult for himself. And who's confident he's got a very steady hand."

"Easy to conceal?"

"It's not the smallest of handguns. I assume you're armed, captain, but it's completely inconspicuous. If you had a PI87 I'd probably have seen the bulge."

"You wouldn't want to stick a PI87 in your pocket or shove it down the back of your trousers?"

"Not really," said Velasque. "You'd be better taking a briefcase."

Monday, 28th January

"Can I ask you to remove your shoes, captain?"

Franck complied with the request and was handed a pair of immaculate white Japanese house slippers. The young man assisting him was dressed in a white shirt and a pair of white canvas trousers, making the blue handkerchief neatly folded in the breast pocket of his shirt difficult to miss.

White seemed to be the colour of the day.

He found himself on the fifth floor of 26 rue Vavin. It was the first time he had set foot inside the building, although he had walked past it many times when heading from Montparnasse to the Jardin du Luxembourg. In a city characterised by pale-pastel stone-built apartment buildings, the complex at 26 rue Vavin was impossible to ignore. Designed by the architect Henri Sauvage in 1913 it took the form of a ziggurat, presenting a facade that took an extra step back from the street with each floor. Its reinforced concrete core was overlaid with brilliantly white rectangular tiles interspersed occasionally with touches of marine blue. Washed clean by every shower that passed, it caught whatever light the weather afforded and shone in an otherwise undistinguished street, a beacon of hygiene and modernity. The effect was remarkable, and had been achieved at surprisingly little expense, as Sauvage had simply appropriated a consignment of the ceramic tiles that were being used at the time for the decoration of the ever-expanding metro.

"You may wish to wash your hands," the young man suggested.

In the hallway where they stood there was a polished steel coat rack, on which Franck's parka now hung, a bare wooden bench, a block of wooden cubbyholes in which his shoes now sat, another one which held countless pairs of slippers, and three square ceramic basins bolted to a wall under a marble shelf on which neatly folded hand towels had been piled. The floor was tiled. White, needless to say.

p.90

Franck stepped over to one of the basins and washed his hands with an odourless liquid soap. The young man followed his example. When Franck had dried his hands with a small towel taken from the shelf above and was looking around for a hook or rail on which to leave it, the young man took it gently from him and deposited it in a pedal-operated bin under the basin.

"If you will follow me. Do bear in mind that monsieur Halphen was not expecting visitors this morning. Mademoiselle Arbaud's assistant only called us a few hours ago. We are not used to receiving people at such short notice. If you find monsieur Halphen a little tense, please make allowances."

Halphen's assistant, who had introduced himself as Justin, seemed quite accustomed to issuing such warnings. He led Franck, who found himself shuffling in his new footwear, through an unfurnished room, also paved with ceramic tiles, and into another. A good fifteen metres wide, its tiled floor ran up to three wall-to-ceiling windows which looked out onto a generous, but empty, terrace. Two teak benches faced each other across a low wooden table. That aside, the room was bare.

On the farthest bench a very tall man – almost two metres – sat with his back to the windows. His hands were folded in his lap and his long, gaunt face observed his visitor. He wore wooden-soled sandals and a wide-sleeved kimono. To Franck's relief, the latter was light blue.

"Captain Franck Guerin of the Brigade Criminelle," announced Justin. He then turned to Franck and added, "Monsieur Louis Halphen".

Franck walked, making a conscious effort to lift rather than drag his feet, across to Halphen, who stood to meet him.

Halphen glanced quickly at Justin, who stood off to one side. When the latter nodded slightly Halphen offered Franck his hand. After a brief handshake, he indicated that Franck should sit on the bench across from him.

"Thank you for making yourself available," said Franck. "I'm sure my visit must surprise you."

"It both surprises and inconveniences me," declared Halphen. He spoke quietly, but there was steel in his tone. "Mademoiselle Arbaud is responsible for your presence here. She will have to deal with the consequences."

"I wouldn't blame Isabelle Arbaud. I asked for this meeting and insisted that it be arranged so quickly. It's not easy to refuse a request from the Brigade Criminelle." She had tried, insisting that Halphen had nothing to do with the case, and that distracting him could provoke delays and complications that would cost Arbaud dearly. Franck had persisted and in the end she had capitulated. He had sensed, as he hung up, that one day she would have her revenge.

"If you had started with me, I might have proved better at it," stated Halphen. "Still, no matter – you are here, so do what you came to do."

"You were not at the Ephémère fashion show on the 23rd of January?"

"Why would I waste my time at such an event? *Défilés* are a form of circus thrown for the press and the retailers. They provide the worst possible conditions in which to study a new outfit, and the best in which to be influenced by manipulative publicists and become the object of gossip for the small-minded."

"I'll take that as a 'no'," said Franck.

"You may."

"Where were you on the morning of the 23rd of January?"

"In my laboratory."

"Which is here?"

Halphen looked at Franck strangely, as if suddenly uncertain of the captain's intelligence.

"This is my home," he said. "I could not work here. There are too many distractions."

Distractions? It was Franck's turn to be assailed by doubt, but he kept it to himself.

"Where is your laboratory then?"

"Rue Boileau."

"Where's that?" Franck knew Paris well, but did not have the encyclopaedic knowledge of a taxi driver. Indeed, with the arrival of GPS, fewer and fewer taxi drivers had it either.

"In the sixteenth arrondissement. Auteuil. Off boulevard Exelmans."

Franck rarely had cause to set foot in the southern half of the sixteenth, but he had a vague idea of the neighbourhood Halphen was talking about: one where entire streets of individual houses could still be found, rather than the apartment buildings which dominated the rest of the city.

"Others were there with you?" asked Franck.

"Justin." Justin nodded from where he stood, hovering between the benches and the door. "And the technicians who work there for me."

"When did you last see Alain Perrin?"

"I honestly cannot remember. I did not seek out young monsieur Perrin's company, and I do not think he appreciated mine. I am not what you would call a worldly man, captain Guerin. I live a simple life between my home, my lab, and my sources of inspiration."

"And the Arbaud offices?" prompted Franck.

Halphen sighed. "Isabelle forces me to go there from time to time. To talk to journalists, to pretend to be amused by simpering celebrities, to do my bit for the burgeoning fame of Arbaud."

"Never to meet the investors?"

"Oh, once or twice. But it never went well. You know your Oscar Wilde, captain?"

"I know where he's buried," offered Franck. "He's a big attraction at Père Lachaise."

"With good reason. I would feel privileged to lie in the same ground as him," said Halphen. "Wilde declared that a cynic was someone who knows the price of everything and the value of nothing. Had he had the misfortune to frequent many investors I'm sure he would have said much the same of them."

"You didn't see eye to eye?"

"If only they had eyes to see. Isabelle's investors can think of only one thing – getting their money back, and a lot more besides, as quickly as possible. They have been putting insufferable pressure on her – and thereby on me – for months now. I have tried explaining to them how short-sighted they are, but it seems their problems are not just ocular. They do not have ears to listen either."

"Why short-sighted?"

"Because what I am creating for Arbaud – Night-Scented – is an alchemist's dream. I am taking simple ingredients – things that Nature makes and tosses aside without a second thought – and purifying, combining and transforming them to make a perfume which women will embrace for the rest of this century. It will ensure my lasting fame. It will be the foundation of Arbaud's future success. And if the investors are patient, it will provide them with a generous return on their stakes."

"They didn't believe you?"

"They have no beliefs. That's the problem with financial types. They have their spreadsheets, their risk assessments and their constant, anxious fear of the future – that's all. They want their money back now, or tomorrow at the latest, for fear it will all have disappeared by next week. I despise them."

"But Arbaud can't happen without them," Franck pointed out.

"That is an unfortunate truth. Unfortunate truths are not my field. That's what I kept telling Isabelle and, I'm glad to say, she finally listened to me. I don't have to go to business meetings anymore."

"But you didn't win the argument, did you?"

"What do you mean?"

"Didn't the investors impose a deadline for the development of the perfume?" asked Franck. "A deadline that runs out in a few days?"

Halphen's lips twisted, as if he had just swallowed something unpleasant.

"Yes they did. And in doing so, they put everything in danger. If I am to create the perfect perfume I need to work in perfect conditions. For the past three months I have had to discipline myself to thrust aside all thought of this stupid deadline. Whenever it intrudes on my thoughts, panic and irritation seep in and I begin to lose my way."

"What will happen if you don't deliver on time?"

Halphen winced. "Presumably they will carry out their threat, demand their money back – or what's left of it – and leave Night-Scented and Arbaud stillborn," he said.

"Except there's no longer a 'they'," said Franck.

"I don't follow you, captain."

"Alain Perrin and Nathalie Chautard are dead. Both their estates are in a state of turmoil and are in no situation to take any important decisions. Guillaume Thèves is the only one who could really pull out at this point."

A spectral smile flitted across Halphen's face.

"I like your analysis, captain. Without Thèves' money, we'd have to be a little less ambitious, but I imagine we could still go ahead."

"I'm always happy to be the bearer of good tidings. Pity a man and a woman had to die to make it possible."

"God works in mysterious ways," observed Halphen.

"I don't think God pulled the trigger on Perrin, or drove Chautard off the road."

"In which case, who did?" asked Halphen. "And how exactly am I supposed to be of assistance in helping you find out? Ah, thank you Justin."

At some point Justin had left the room, for he now returned carrying a flat-edged wooden tray which he laid on the table between them. It bore two palm-sized white china bowls containing a clear liquid which let off a faint cloud of steam. Halphen bent forward and brought both hands round to cup one of the bowls before resuming his former position.

"A star anise infusion. Chinese of course," he explained, smirking at a joke Franck did not get. He took a gentle sip. "Purges the system."

More through curiosity than thirst, Franck took the other bowl. At the bottom of what he assumed was recently boiled water lay two seed pods shaped like eight-pointed stars. He took a little of the liquid into his mouth. At first he registered nothing, and then became aware of a bitter liquorice taste spreading across his tongue. He did not pursue the experiment.

He had to wait a few minutes while Halphen slowly emptied his bowl, having apparently lost all interest in their conversation, and maybe even all consciousness of Franck's presence.

Finally, Halphen returned his bowl to the tray.

"I hope you have concluded that I am not a serious candidate for the part of Alain Perrin's murderer," he said.

"You have a very solid alibi," said Franck. "Out of curiosity, though, have you ever handled a firearm?"

"I'm glad to say I have not."

"Never? If I check your past, I'll not come up with any trace of firearms experience? Not even during your military service?"

"Military service? What a quaint idea. I was declared unfit for service *in absentia*. My mother took care of it."

"In which case, I'll let you get on with things," said Franck, rising to his feet. "You only have a few days left, after all."

"Justin, see captain Guerin out, will you?" instructed Halphen.

Franck waited an instant to see if Halphen would shake his hand once more.

"Captain?" prompted Justin.

He followed the young man out of the room and back to the entrance hall.

"Don't think badly of him," murmured Justin. "He is under tremendous pressure."

"He doesn't have a murder to solve," countered Franck.

Justin grimaced and raised an apologetic hand, but Franck cut him off. "Don't worry. We don't lock people away just for being self-absorbed."

He stepped out of his slippers and handed them over. Justin laid them on top of the others and retrieved Franck's shoes from the other set of cubbyholes. As he was about to pass them to Franck, he froze. Wrinkling his nose, he turned them over. There was a trace of dogshit on one of the soles.

"Paris," commented Franck. He spent a lot of time walking the streets of the capital. His stoicism was born of experience. "I'll put them on outside."

"If you would."

Franck took his shoes from Justin, who held them as far from his body as possible.

"Do you remember where you put your feet when you came in?" asked Justin. "Before I gave you the slippers."

"Around about there," said Franck, indicating a rough circle about two metres in diameter.

Wordlessly, Justin opened a cupboard door set flush into one of the walls. An interior light came on automatically, allowing Franck to study the collection of brushes, mops, buckets, and cleaning products that it contained. Justin grasped a large blue plastic container, screwed off its bright-red top, and began pouring a pool of transparent liquid in the centre of the area Franck had sketched out.

"Bleach," explained Justin. "If you want something really clean, really fast, it's the only solution."

*

"Here you are Franck!"

Yves de Chaumont came forward to shake his hand, adding an extra squeeze at the end.

"Catherine said you'd soon be dropping in."

A car had been waiting for him outside 26 rue Vavin. Unaware of its presence, Franck had paused upon leaving the building to scrape the sole of his left shoe on the edge of the kerb where the pavement met the road. The car's occupants had waited until he had finished before starting their engine and pulling up alongside him. That way they did not have to worry about cleaning the interior.

"Hope you didn't mind me sending a car, Franck," said Catherine Vautrin.

She sat on the visitor's side of Yves' baize-covered desk. Untidy hair, an unadorned long-sleeved cotton top, dark trousers, flat shoes, a leather jacket on the back of her chair, a bulky shoulder bag on the floor, the fingers of one hand turning a mobile phone in a slow, constant motion to compensate for the absence of a cigarette: Catherine Vautrin in all her neglected splendour, head of section C3 of the Direction de la Surveillance du Territoire, come to pay an unannounced visit.

"I'm impressed you knew where I was," said Franck, taking the seat beside her as Yves regained his own place behind his desk. Franck's appointment with Halphen had been set up that morning. The DST had either been listening to his calls or had tailed him when he left the quai des Orfèvres to go to rue Vavin.

"You know us. We like to keep tabs on our own."

"And here was me thinking Franck was mine," said Yves, smiling broadly at Catherine as he did so.

"A loan doesn't transfer ownership," Catherine observed. "But I trust he's giving satisfaction?"

"Abundantly so," declared Yves.

"Would you like to check my teeth while you're at it?" asked Franck, wondering if this was what it had felt like standing on a podium at a slave auction in the French Caribbean.

"I'm sure monsieur *le juge* has been taking care of you."

"I believe I have," said Yves. "To the best of my knowledge, Franck hasn't caught any bullets while marching under my colours."

"He probably will, sooner or later," countered Catherine.

"He has a propensity for it."

Yves brought his palms together with a sharp clap and then posed his hands on the desktop.

"This is fun," he declared. "But if we don't hold ourselves in check, we could go on like this all day. Let's get down to business."

Catherine nodded her assent.

Yves turned to Franck and explained, "Catherine – whom I don't see often enough – paid me a surprise visit three quarters of an hour ago to make a somewhat unusual request. We have been discussing it ever since, but as you are directly concerned I am delighted to see that she had already arranged for you to be present to give us your opinion on the matter."

"What do you want?" asked Franck, eyeing his old boss warily.

"The Alain Perrin case. I want it transferred to the DST."

"Why? Why's it even on your radar? Perrin Industries are scarcely a major player in the arms industry. They can't sell more than a couple of hundred sniper rifles to the army each year."

"Tens of thousands, actually," Catherine informed him. "That's if you take into account all the NATO countries. And their automated weapons program is closely followed in high places. But no, you're right, Perrin Industries aren't really big enough for anything that happens to them to start ringing our alarm bells."

"So? Why the interest?"

"It's on my radar because you put it there, Franck," she said, reaching out to pat his arm. "As ever, you found something out that puts the case in a completely different light."

"Which is?"

"The PI87," said Catherine. "The weapon you've identified as the most probable source of the bullets lodged in Perrin's stomach and skull. Manipulated by an expert shooter whose hand remained steady as he stared his victim in the eye."

Yves de Chaumont, whose hands were now clasped under his chin, raised his eyebrows.

"Since both of you seem to know something I don't, maybe someone would like to explain it to me?" he suggested.

"Perrin was killed with a 6.5mm calibre weapon," said Franck. "That's pretty unusual. The markings on the bullets suggested a barrel precision-engineered for long-distance accuracy."

"A sniper's weapon?" said Yves. "Wouldn't a sniper have taken the head shot straight away rather than hit the stomach and make the target double over?"

Franck paused. He had not thought of that. Yves' insights never failed to impress him. "You're right. In any case, the shooting took place in a confined space where a rifle would have been completely unnecessary and very hard to conceal. It had the forensic team stumped."

"Until you found the solution, I assume," prompted Yves.

"I talked with Perrin Industries' head gunsmith yesterday. He told me about the PI87, which is some kind of fancy handgun they make for people who like a challenge – like using a pistol that thinks it's a sniper's rifle. He's pretty sure the bullets we found were fired from one of them."

"You talked to him yesterday?"

"Yes, just after Alain Perrin's funeral."

"And I imagine that at some point afterwards you wandered by the office to update your case notes on your PC and verify a few things?" continued Yves.

Franck nodded. The quai des Orfèvres was about as central as you could get in Paris. He never thought twice about popping in, weekend or not. DST discipline: always keep your case notes up to date in case something unforeseen happens and another agent has to step in and take your place.

"The DST hasn't been hacking into Franck's files, by any chance?" Yves asked Catherine.

"As if we would," she replied, smiling. Showing all her irregular, slightly nicotine-stained teeth.

They observed each other for a while.

"One day it will all blow up in your faces," Yves warned her.

"I sincerely doubt it," Catherine declared. "The tide is moving in our favour. The *juges d'instruction* are not long for this world."

"You may be right, Catherine, but it'll be a sad day for the Republic if it comes to pass."

Catherine shrugged. Yves shook his head, silently.

Franck broke the stalemate.

"So why does the PI87 theory make a banal homicide an internal security matter?" he asked.

"Because of how Nathalie Chautard died," Catherine stated, switching her eyes back to him.

"Run off the road with a truck," said Franck. "What's the connection?"

Catherine smiled to herself. "He didn't tell you, did he? The file on the network has been doctored, so you couldn't have seen it there, but *commandant* Bonifay knows all the details. He's more disciplined – or more interested in his career – than I thought. We told him in no uncertain terms to keep it to himself, but I didn't imagine he'd hide it from you. Not from the quai des Orfèvres."

Franck sighed. "I'm not a mouse, and you're not a cat, Catherine. So just tell me."

"As you said, Nathalie Chautard was run off the road with a truck. Quite deliberately, of course. It had shadowed her since she left the airport at Marignane, having been stolen for that very purpose the previous day."

"And the link to the PI87?"

"It was a CWM truck. Full of the gunk they discharge through a sub-sea pipe that runs offshore from Port de Bouc where the Etang de Berre meets with the sea. It was left inside the abandoned truck. Personally, I would have dumped it on her car after the accident. Maybe that was the plan, but at the point where Chautard went off the road it wasn't possible to back a large vehicle up against the ravine. In the end, it didn't matter that much. What had been done was enough. Chautard had been killed with a symbol of her own making."

"And two months later you have Alain Perrin shot with a weapon that is a perfect example of what his firm is famous for," said Franck. "Precision munitions."

"Poetic justice," pronounced Yves from behind his desk.

"Exactly," said Catherine. "And who is interested in poetic justice?"

"Poets?" suggested Yves, offering his long-practised impersonation of perfect credulity.

Catherine obligingly rolled her eyes.

"Only those with a cause are interested in the symbolism of the acts they commit," she said.

"You have anyone in particular in mind?" asked Yves.

"Appoghiu Terra Corsa," said Catherine, turning to face Franck as she said it.

An armed Corsican nationalist group, Appoghiu Terra Corsa had appeared, apparently out of nowhere, four years previously. They were held responsible for three assassinations on the island, including that of a prominent German industrialist who had managed to obtain planning permission to build a massive villa on a previously protected inlet on the island's south coast. The group was run, and by all accounts had been created, by a man called Gabriel Agostini, who had escaped capture by the DST the previous year. The failed operation had left two agents and a German hiker seriously injured. The next day a government spokesman had prudently held the whole thing at arm's length by referring to it as the Corsican incident and declaring that it would be the object of an official, albeit largely confidential, enquiry. The name had stuck. It still hung over the head of the operation's principal field officer, a certain Franck Guerin.

"Chautard had a link with Corsica?" demanded Franck, instantly sceptical. Agostini had never before intervened on the mainland.

"She did business all across the Mediterranean. CWM has contracts for garbage collection in Ajaccio, Corte and Bonifacio. In time, they'll have the whole island."

"What about Perrin Industries?"

"That's less obvious," she conceded. "But we'll find it. Once we have the case."

"I think you're wrong, Catherine," declared Franck. "You're deliberately ignoring the more obvious connection between Perrin and Chautard."

"You think they're all being killed over a bottle of perfume?" Catherine asked scornfully.

"If you're looking for poets, then Arbaud and the universe it's part of is a pretty good bet," insisted Franck. "Pursue a parallel investigation if you like, but I'm not giving up mine."

"Franck, use your head," said Catherine, wearily. "This is a case that could be linked with Gabriel Agostini. You really think I can leave it in your hands? You're already under investigation for letting him get away the last time."

Yves quickly intervened, while maintaining his preternatural calm.

"That's an unfortunate choice of words, Catherine. Agostini got away and Franck was there – those are the only established facts of the situation. You and I both know full well that Franck did the right thing, otherwise you would have had him sacked and I would not have requested his assistance."

"It's not about truth, Yves," she muttered. "It's about politics."

Yves sighed. "With the DST, it's always about politics. That's why you're not the easiest of organisations to deal with. However, I understand that you find yourself in a difficult situation, Catherine, so I'm going to make things easy for you."

Catherine snorted and shook her head, no doubt because she could see what was coming.

"I officially take note of your request to recover the case of the murder of Alain Perrin," announced Yves. "After careful consideration, and with the freedom of action that is mine as a *juge d'instruction*, I refuse to allow the matter to be taken out of the hands of this office. Captain Franck Guerin remains in charge of the enquiry."

"Yves, you are a very intelligent man, and undoubtedly the finest *juge* in this building ..." commenced Catherine.

"I am honoured you think so," he interjected.

"... but this time you're wrong. It's Agostini, and it will all end in tears."

With that she swept from his office.

"She really misses you, Franck," observed Yves.

"Chautard slain by one of her own trucks. Perrin shot with one of his own guns. She could be right about the symbolic nature of the killings," said Franck.

"So what's it to be for Guillaume Thèves?" asked Yves. "Death by a thousand paper cuts?"

*

"You've got to stop doing this," said Franck, at once serious and amused.

His amusement was not destined to last for long.

The door to his office had swung open violently, hitting the inside of the wall and rebounding slightly. She stood glowering at him in a light-grey dress with a cherry-coloured jacket. Her right hand clutched the straps of her handbag, which were looped over her shoulder. Her grip was vicelike, turning her knuckles white. Poised on heels, she looked as if she was about to lunge forward and devour him. Her eyes were flashing, particularly the green and hazel one. Isabelle Arbaud. The second unannounced visitor of the day.

"What the hell were you up to this morning?" she demanded, stalking up to his desk.

Franck shook his head.

"If that's the way we're going to talk to each other, what the hell are you doing in my office?"

Her lips, thin by nature, were tightly compressed, a slash of red – the same shade as her jacket and bag – across the fine features of her face. She remained standing, her shoulders raised and tugged backwards, her hand now directing an accusing finger at him.

"I should have known," she said bitterly. "It's not a homicidal plot that's going to stop me, it's an incompetent, ignorant and idiotic policeman."

Franck pointed towards the chair alongside her. She ignored him.

"When you called me this morning and begged me to set up an interview with Louis Halphen, you could have warned me you were about to accuse him of murder."

"Don't be ridiculous," he began, but got no further.

"It wasn't easy for me to get Louis to change his schedule and agree to see you," she continued. "He's in the final straight. He's been working on Night-Scented night and day for over a week. He says he has a few notes to adjust, a final harmony to find, and then it will be ready. Asking him to take a few hours out was already taking a risk. A few hours! Break the rhythm at this stage and you can lose days, weeks, or even months. But you said it was important and I trusted you."

"It was important," insisted Franck. "And I didn't accuse him."

"So you had a nice, cosy chat and left each other the best of friends. That'll be why Louis hasn't left his apartment all day. Why he's locked away in his bedroom. Why the staff in his lab are turning their thumbs. Why he refuses to speak to Justin, let alone to me."

"We talked about his animosity towards the investors, that's all."

"And you asked him if he knew how to use a gun. Louis Halphen! Use a gun! Do you have any idea who you're dealing with?"

Franck sat back in his seat, putting a few extra centimetres between himself and Isabelle's menacing presence. He bit back the phrase that was on his tongue, forcing himself to think about what she was saying.

"No," he conceded. "I don't. Why don't you tell me?"

Her eyes left his face for the first time since she had entered the room. They glanced at the empty chair beside her. When she looked back at him, most of the fire had gone. She sat down, propping her bag against the leg of the chair.

"A Nose is like a composer who uses odours instead of notes. A perfume is like a score whose notes can be many or few and key changes simple or complex, depending on the desired effect. As with a piece of music, it can and should change through time – themes are presented and then replaced by others, subtle effects slowly come to the surface, and each sensation is influenced by the memory of those which went before. To create a perfect perfume you have to have a vision of the beginning, the middle and the end before you even set foot in the lab. That means you not only have to safeguard in your olfactory memory every odour that can conceivably be integrated into a perfume, you also have to have the ability to predict the effect of different combinations and concentrations. A Nose spends half his life cataloguing and distinguishing the scents of the real world, and the other half imagining new and unforeseen harmonies, like a jazz musician predicting the effect of a note not yet played. Halphen's gift is his exquisite sensitivity. His achievement is the way he has developed it, both in range and depth. His genius is his creative imagination."

"And his Achilles' heel is his temper?" suggested Franck.

"Do not be distracted by what is superficial," admonished Isabelle. "His temper is a symptom. He is cursed to the same extent that he is gifted. His acute sensitivity leaves him acutely vulnerable. A smell, or taste, or sight that might repulse, irritate or offend you or me is a torment to him. And if his creativity takes a dark turn, his ability to conjure the highest of sensual delights out of nothing becomes an inability to avert his mind from the worst of imagined horrors."

"Which is why he lives in an empty apartment kept

scrupulously clean and consumes only the most tasteless of nourishments?"

"Which is why he has chosen an ascetic path. He protects his senses and disciplines his mind so that nothing can interfere with his true vocation."

"Creating works of art for the nose?" Franck knew there was a hint of mockery in his voice. He was unable to keep it at bay.

"Were he to do it for the eyes with paint or for the ears with an orchestra, you would be more inclined to find him worthy of your respect. But he does it for the nose, and he does it for women who wish to seduce, and therefore you dismiss him as a frivolous fool. But ask a woman what it is like to move with a halo of enchanted scent around her, to sense herself more alluring and to have this belief confirmed by the reaction of all those she walks past. You will quickly learn that great art is not necessarily high art, and that a tiny vial sold in a boutique for hundreds of euros can change lives."

"OK. Let's say Halphen is a great artist. So what? You think a fanatical artist won't kill for his art?" It was Franck's turn to display a little fire. He was speaking from recent, and bitter, experience.

"I don't doubt that Louis has imagined us all dead a hundred times – me for my impositions and crass commercialism, my investors for their impatience and cupidity, you for your clumsy and distasteful suppositions. But between imagination and action lies a gap that – for him – is unbridgeable. Louis cannot soil his hands. Physically, psychologically and even metaphorically, it is beyond him. He must be pure. If he is tainted in any way, he can no longer exercise his calling."

She paused for breath. She had spoken rapidly, suggesting both deep conviction and a desperate need to convince him.

"You have to understand," she concluded, both hands flat on the surface of his desk and her face thrust towards him. "Louis cannot be a suspect. Even to think of him as such is to disturb his equilibrium and to prevent Night-Scented from being born."

"Which would mean 150 million euros down the drain."

"Which would mean shattering Louis' dream of completing his life's work. And that, I fear, would kill him. Those who aim highest fall the furthest when they fail. Ask Icarus. If that were to happen, you would be as guilty as whoever pulled the trigger on Alain Perrin."

"But it would also mean 150 million euros down the drain," repeated Franck.

"Indeed it would," conceded Isabelle. "Which would mean that Louis' ghost would be the least of your problems. I would sue without a moment's hesitation. And I know some very expensive lawyers."

With that, she stood up brusquely, snatching her handbag and levelling a warning finger at Franck.

"Leave him alone. From now on, you deal only with me."

"I'm not in the habit of taking orders from parties of interest in a murder case," Franck informed her.

"That's your pride speaking, captain. It is of no great concern to me."

She turned from him and walked resolutely out of the door. Franck made no attempt to stop her. He sat listening as her heels echoed down the corridor and then disappeared.

She was gone. And yet part of her was still there. A lingering scent that talked of another, different Isabelle Arbaud. Of a carefree, warm, and enticing woman.

Franck wondered when he would get to meet her.

Franck was prepared to concede that he might be stubborn, but he drew the line at obtuse.

Catherine's theory that some kind of poetic justice might have been visited upon Chautard and Perrin was as credible a working hypothesis as Isabelle Arbaud's paranoia about Ephémère – or Chanel for that matter – committing dark deeds to preserve market share. The only way to dismiss it would be to disprove it. A couple of hours surfing the web had been enough to demonstrate that Chautard Waste Management was above neither criticism nor suspicion. The very nature of its activity – taking waste products off the hands of polluters and then making them disappear, as far from public sight as possible – was enough to ensure that it was one of the corporate giants environmental activists loved to hate. Beyond that, down the years it had been the object of so many rumours and accusations about corruption, flaunting of norms, and aggressive industrial practices that even in the absence of proof there was reason to doubt that Nathalie Chautard's hands were entirely clean.

Perrin Industries, however, had no such sulphurous reputation, at least as far as Franck could determine. To ensure this was the case, he had decided to seek out the person he hoped would prove the firm's most critical and best-informed observer.

The fact that she was an attractive woman in her late twenties did not hurt either.

When she welcomed him to her tiny, ill-appointed office that morning she was dressed entirely in black: tailored black jeans, black knee-length boots, and a finely woven black sweater. Even her blonde hair was held in place by a black plastic claw poised on the top of her head. It was not clear whether this was simply a fashion choice or a deliberate sign of mourning.

"Mademoiselle Perrin, I'm very sorry for your brother."

Marie-Chantal Perrin bit her lips. "It's been six days now," she said. "I've still not got used to the idea that he's dead. Part of me hopes that I never will."

"I've come to ask some questions that you might find strange or rather upsetting," Franck warned her. "I'd just like to say in advance that I wouldn't be asking them if I didn't think they'd help in trying to bring your brother's killer to justice."

"I understand," she said. "Or at least I think I do."

"There are three possible ways to explain your brother's murder. The first is that he was unlucky – he was in the wrong place at the wrong time, and was killed for reasons that had nothing to do with him."

Marie-Chantal recoiled slightly in her chair. This was not what she wanted to hear. Yves had once warned Franck about this phenomenon: most relatives of murder victims preferred to deal with the thought of deliberate malice rather than the notion of random misfortune.

"The circumstances of the case make such a possibility highly unlikely," stressed Franck. "The second explanation is that he was killed for personal reasons. Somebody, either on the spur of the moment or by premeditation wanted to kill him because of something that he had done, or said, or believed, or whatever. The third is that he was killed because of something he represented. That Alain Perrin the man was of no interest to the killer, only Alain Perrin the symbol."

"You mean that if he had not been my father's son, if he had not inherited control of Perrin Industries, he would not have been killed?"

"Something like that," Franck said. "If the third theory is the correct one."

"That's what you believe?"

"To be quite frank, no, it's not what I believe. But maybe I should. Maybe I'm missing something. Something you can tell me."

"Why me?"

Franck cast a hand at the walls around them. They were

hung with posters denouncing the arms trade, both for its effect on Third World countries and for the way it led to a creeping militarisation of the domestic economy. All bore the same logo in their bottom right-hand corner: 'Swords into Ploughshares'.

"You campaign against those who profit through sales of arms and munitions," he pointed out. "For years your organisation has highlighted the way in which Western arms companies deal with corrupt officials and criminal organisations. How they refuse to concern themselves with the origins of the payments they accept or the uses to which their weapons are put. How quickly and efficiently crates of grenades, bullets and machine guns appear in regions where UN food convoys can never get through. You're the best-known and best-informed anti-arms lobby in Europe, and maybe in the world. Your organisation knows things most people don't. Add to that the fact that you – Marie-Chantal Perrin – grew up with Perrin Industries, I can't think of anyone better placed to tell me whether I should be pursing the third hypothesis."

"You want to know whether Perrin Industries has been involved in some dirty deals?"

"Benoît Nallard has assured me that it hasn't," Franck stated. "Then again, it's scarcely conceivable that he could ever say anything else."

"He told you the truth," she said, without hesitation. "My father, whatever the nature of his trade, was an honourable man. He raised Alain in his own image. Anyhow, all you have to do is look at their client list. I don't think they had a single client east of Berlin or west of Washington."

"OK," said Franck. "Could someone nonetheless have objected to the very existence of Perrin Industries, and sought to punish Alain for that?"

"I objected to the very existence of Perrin Industries," she said flatly. "I still do. If I have my way, when the estate is settled I will use my half stake in the firm to block every initiative proposed by the new management team. I will veto every investment plan and question every contract. I will also stop any attempt to sell it to another industrialist. I will paralyse it from within until, through time, thanks to the unforgiving laws of the marketplace, it withers and dies."

Franck was silent, momentarily unsure of how to continue.

"I sense your unease, captain," she said. "So let me say it – I did not kill my brother so as to bring about this situation. I loved Alain. Just as I loved my father. Our philosophical differences were exactly that – philosophical."

"And yet the end result is that Perrin Industries may perish. It's not inconceivable that someone might have killed Alain knowing how you would react in the situation thus created."

"You're saying that indirectly I could be responsible for Alain's death?" Her tone was not indignant. She seemed to be thinking through his suggestion.

"If somebody else wanted Perrin Industries to disappear badly enough, you could be an unwitting means to their end."

"But why would someone else want it so badly? For me it's personal – I have to be coherent in my beliefs, otherwise what I'm doing here makes no sense. If you're a member of Greenpeace you don't wear your grandmother's ivory broach, no matter how beautiful it might be. But that doesn't mean you break into other people's houses to destroy their grandmothers' ivory broaches. You go after the poachers and traders who are still out there."

Franck repeated his early gesture, designating at random a number of the posters around them. "Some people might," he insisted.

Marie-Chantal shook her head.

"Perrin Industries is a sideshow," she stated. "In the context of all the suffering and evil fomented by the world's arms manufacturers, it is utterly insignificant. Get rid of Perrin Industries and you'd have a few less snipers and a few less hunters. You'd probably end up saving more stags than people. Someone as motivated and as determined as you suggest would pick a bigger target."

"So for you, the most probable explanation is that Alain was killed because of something he did, not because of who he was?"

A tear appeared. Then another. She shut her eyes and breathed slowly, reining them in. She then shook her head before a brief laugh, both bitter and sad, escaped her.

"Yes. I believe – I want to believe – that Alain must have had a part to play in his own death. How cruel and absurd is that?"

*

He missed.

Franck knew he was not the best shot in the world, but at thirty metres he ought to have punched a hole in at least one of the concentric circles on the target.

He slid the ear protectors down around his neck and turned to Georges Sternberg, who seemed rather amused.

"Try it," said Franck. "You'll see. It's not that easy."

Sternberg folded his arms and slowly shook his head.

"If I never fire another one in my life, it won't be too soon. I've seen what they do too many times. That said, in your hands, the PI87 seems a remarkably innocuous weapon."

Franck looked down at the pistol. Unlike most firearms, which proclaimed their modernity through smooth surfaces and simple ergonomics, the PI87 looked deliberately archaic, like something destined for a collector's cabinet. Its maple-carved, brass-reinforced wooden stock, hollowed-out to take a five-cartridge magazine, was too wide to be squeezed tightly, and forced the shooter to adopt a more relaxed grip. Its long barrel culminated in a high and thin sight, which seemed to him more distracting than useful. Its breech section seemed unusually thick, with moulding swelling out on both sides to accommodate – so he had been told – a sophisticated device for dispersing recoil. The sweeping curves of its metal components – which had the dull, bruised shine of high-carbon steel – had patently been cast with more than simple utility in mind.

"You need to handle it less roughly," he was told.

Franck stepped to one side and handed the weapon over to Jean-Charles Velasque. As Perrin Industries' head gunsmith, it was safe to assume he knew what he was talking about.

Velasque put his own ear protectors in place and stepped up to the firing line. He held the weapon in one hand, rather than the two Franck had used, and made no attempt to crouch. The fingers of his right hand curved almost negligently around the stock, the tip of his index stroking the trigger.

"Trust it," he explained. "It balances perfectly and it will not jump out of your hands. Hold it high and let the centre of the target drift into the middle of the sight. Pause." His extended arm was immobile, a feat Franck could only admire in a man in his sixties. "And as you breathe out, squeeze."

When the shot rang out, the pistol barely moved, other than to eject a cartridge, which dropped lazily out of one side and rebounded on the concrete floor.

The target now bore a hole dead-centre.

Velasque stepped back, lowering the gun and thumbing on the safety catch.

"Try again?" he offered.

Franck took his place. He emptied what remained of the magazine, coming closer each time. It did not feel like any handgun he had ever used. There was no sensation of exploding power in his hands. But the holes in the target did not lie.

"Use a PI87 in a hurry," said Velasque, "and you'll certainly hit something, but it's unlikely to be your target."

"Even at a close quarters?" asked Sternberg.

"If it's a man-sized target, at close quarters you'll no doubt hit him somewhere."

"But probably not right between the eyes," said Franck.

Velasque, suddenly solemn, nodded.

Franck passed him the weapon. Velasque extracted the now empty magazine and packed the PI87 away in a wooden presentation box. While he was doing so, Georges Sternberg jogged down to the far end of the firing range and carefully prised the bullets from the target.

The three of them then proceeded down a short corridor to Velasque's office, where they sat around a small circular table in one corner.

"You have the sales information?" Franck asked.

Velasque passed him a manila folder.

"The PI87 has been in production for five years. We make them in small batches since they're slow sellers."

"How many are in circulation?"

"A hundred and four. A hundred and seven have been sold, but we have three of them in the workshop right now undergoing repairs."

"And in stock?"

"Fourteen, including this one." He tapped the cherrywood presentation box he had carried back from the range. "However, it turns out that ten days ago we had fifteen."

"A recent sale?"

"One was signed out by Alain Perrin. On Tuesday the 22nd."

"Why?" asked Franck.

"The stock register doesn't say."

"He didn't talk to you about this?"

"No."

"He could just walk into the armoury and take anything he liked?"

"It was his firm. He owned it all," Velasque pointed out.

"He knew how to handle a PI87?"

"Of course," said Velasque. "He grew up surrounded by guns. Alain was a very good shot."

"Suggests he thought he needed a little extra protection," suggested Sternberg.

"Not the most obvious of choices, though," said Franck. "You must have weapons here that are easier to carry, not to mention easier to fire."

"It's the only handgun we make," Velasque pointed out.

"The PI87 may not fit in the palm of your hand, but it's a lot more discreet than a long-barrelled sniper's rifle."

Franck reached out to the box that sat in the middle of the table. He held it up and turned it in front of his eyes, admiring the fine grain of the red-stained wood and the precision of the dovetail joints that held it together.

"They all come in these?" he asked.

Velasque nodded. "We buy them in from a local cabinetmaker. The foam mould inside we make ourselves."

Franck moved his chair back so as to swing his legs up and place his heels on the edge of the table. He then placed the box on his lap.

"Alain Perrin took one of these to the Ephémère show," he said.

"There wasn't one on the crime scene inventory," Sternberg objected.

"You telling me we noted every single glass, plate, container, and bottle in the catering section?"

"No," admitted Sternberg. "Only the stuff behind the partition. And the contents of the bins. And Perrin's briefcase, of course."

"There was a box just like this left in there."

"How can you be so sure?"

"I know who's got it."

*

Having made a detour, it was late afternoon by the time Franck reached the André Citroen park. The sun would soon be setting, but for the moment it lay resplendently low in the sky to the west, allowing the park's two giant glass-walled structures to bathe in its rays.

Franck walked across the wide paved area that separated the glasshouses from the vast lawn that ran to the Seine. It had been a chilly day, and although the sun had finally slipped out from beneath the clouds that had hidden it since morning, he still felt the need to have his parka closed tightly around him. He wished he had brought his gloves, as the fingers holding the handle of his briefcase were numb. So were those on his other hand, which clutched at a plastic shopping bag. The only place in the park that could offer any semblance of warmth was the glasshouse that held the collection of Australian flora. It seemed the obvious place to start. Particularly as he could see a supermarket trolley pulled up outside it.

He walked over to the trolley. Aside from half a dozen or so bulging plastic bags tied to its sides, it was full of tightly rolled newspapers and magazines. Suddenly a furious hammering came from above him. He looked up to see Adeline in a long skirt and a ripped jumper, her curly red hair hanging heavily from her head, her face enraged, her lips mouthing obscenities, and her fists banging against thick panes of industrial glass. Defending her archives.

Franck stepped back from the trolley and waved at her. She frowned at him, unsure of who he was or what he was up to. He unzipped his parka and unrolled the scarf from around his neck, all the while smiling up at her. Recognition finally came. She returned his smile and motioned to him to join her.

On the left-hand side of the glasshouse, directly inside its transparent front wall, was a bench that looked out across the park. An ideal suntrap. Although the temperature inside was not quite Australian, it had allowed Adeline to shed three of her jumpers, which she had spread across the wooden slats of the bench, either to make it more comfortable or to ward others off.

She was sitting at one end of the bench beside a small pile of her scrolls. Franck lowered himself gingerly onto the layer of stained and torn knitted wool alongside her. He glanced at the newspaper she had in her hands. A copy of *Libération* whose cover bore a photo of Pierre Beregovoy, a former prime minister who had been found shot dead alongside a canal five weeks after the fall of the government he had led.

"May 93?" asked Franck.

"2nd of May," she confirmed. "Day after his assassination."

"The police report concluded he had shot himself," Franck reminded her. "So did the RG after all the rumours started flying."

"The RG!" scoffed Adeline. "What do they ever know?"

Franck did not pursue the subject. He had heard Catherine Vautrin voice similar sentiments several times.

Adeline closed the newspaper, rolled it up, and encircled it with an elastic band. Franck attempted to count the number of rings on her fingers as she did so: somewhere between fifteen and eighteen.

"You have a remarkable collection of rings," he commented.

She raised her hands and waved her fingers in the air so that they could both admire them.

"Every one a broken heart," she declared.

"How so?" asked Franck.

"Women don't lose rings, captain, not outside their homes anyway. They throw them away."

She mimed the gesture of slipping a ring from her finger and casting it over her shoulder.

"They toss them in anger when betrayed or abandoned, or light-heartedly when they're the ones saying good riddance. Rings embody emotions. If the feelings they recall suddenly seem too painful, too burdensome or too ridiculous, a slip of the finger makes them disappear. A lot easier to handle than the ones we keep in here." She tapped her chest.

"And you gather them up?"

"I save papers that capture the reality of a single day," she said, motioning with her chin towards the trolley below them on the other side of the glass. "I save rings that capture a moment of happiness or promise. Everybody thinks that when you toss things aside their meaning disappears. I know better."

"You have more?" asked Franck. "It happens that often? I've never seen a woman deliberately throw a ring away."

Adeline looked at him as an adult would an innocent child.

"You've led a very sheltered life, captain."

She turned to the side, leaning awkwardly over the end of the bench, her right arm searching beneath it. When she righted herself, she had a red-tinged wooden box in her hand.

"May I?" asked Franck.

She passed the box to him. Franck ran his fingers over its carefully sanded and varnished surface, noting how the joints that bound its corners together were almost imperceptible to the touch. It was identical to the one he had held that morning. He gently folded back the top to reveal a jumble of rings.

"How many?"

"Over fifty, if you include these" said Adeline proudly, once more waving her fingers.

"It's a pity they're all mixed up together," commented Franck. "Must make it difficult to pick out the ones you want to wear each day."

Adeline shrugged. "I make do with what I've got."

"Maybe this would help," said Franck, diving into the plastic bag that he had deposited alongside his briefcase and pulling out a black fake-leather jewellery box. He opened it up to reveal a set of trays that folded out with the lid, with others lying stacked below them. He had made a lucky guess. This one had compartments for seventy small- to medium-sized items of jewellery, or so he had been informed in the run-down jewellers where he had bought it.

Adeline caught her breath and her hands flew to her mouth.

"It's a present," said Franck. "For you."

"The homeless don't get presents," she eventually said. "We get handouts."

"Well this is a present," insisted Franck. "You can't eat it, you can't drink it and won't keep you warm or dry. So what else could it be?"

She took it from him and laid it on the bench between them.

"I like things to be orderly," she confessed.

Franck pointed towards her trolley, with its collection of tightly packed scrolls. "I noticed."

"Will you help me?"

He did. Together they transferred her collection to the plastic trays of the new jewellery box. When they had finished Franck picked up the cherrywood box and shook it beside his head.

"Nothing left in here," he declared. "What are you going to do with it? It's a nicely made box."

"You like it, captain?"

"I must admit, I do."

"Then it's yours. Not a handout. A present."

"Thank you, Adeline. I'll certainly put it to good use. And if you ever come across any others like it, let me know."

"You'd have to talk to Michel about that. He gave it to me."

*

"Remember we agreed we'd no longer talk about my cases or your deals?"

It was Franck who brought it up. He had waited until their coffee had come, along with a small dish of handmade chocolate truffles which he nudged towards the other side of the table.

"Indeed I do," said Sylvie Thomas. She turned her wine glass in the air, looking at Franck through it. She wore a high-necked top of crushed silk that almost matched the colour of the Burgundy in the glass. "I still think it's a terrible pity. Where's the fun in frequenting a *flic* who won't tell you about the dark deeds that our fair city so elegantly hides?"

It was now after midnight. She had arrived late, as ever, coming by chauffeur-driven car from the offices of Lasry Frères at La Défense. Having being nominated senior partner as 2007 drew to a close, a Peugeot 607 with driver was now at her disposal night and day, but this had done nothing to improve her punctuality. They were now the only couple left in the restaurant.

"Not to mention not revealing any more excellent

investment opportunities," she continued, since she always seemed to enjoy prodding Franck where he felt most sensitive.

He refused to rise to the bait. Last November Sylvie had overseen the sale of the Du Bellay lingerie business on behalf of the consortium she had pulled together to acquire it a mere five months previously. She had never told him how much she had made by flipping it – by that point the embargo on talking shop was already in place – but made no secret of the fact that the deal had clinched her end-of-year promotion.

"I'd like to temporarily set aside all restrictions," Franck announced.

"Really? What do I stand to gain by agreeing?" she asked.

"The satisfaction of doing a good deed."

"Is that all?"

"What would you prefer?"

She winked at him slowly and extended a foot under the table to nudge his left calf. Going from excessively to outrageously wealthy had changed Sylvie somewhat. The concept of restraint seemed to have become totally alien to her.

"I'd prefer to have captain Franck Guerin in my debt," she said. "Something I can cash in whenever I like."

Franck raised his eyes to the ceiling. They had played this game before. She always won.

"Deal?" she asked, still stroking the side of his leg.

"Deal."

Sylvie retracted her foot and slid it back into her round-toed Patrick Cox black patent pump.

"Go ahead," she invited.

"Nathalie Chautard, Chautard Waste Management. Alain Perrin, Perrin Industries," Franck reeled off. "Familiar?"

"You could say so. We've worked with CWM on the corporate side, and both Nathalie and Alain are – were – private wealth clients. With any luck their inheritors will follow their example, once we know who they are." She sipped from her wine glass and then set it aside. She reached for her coffee, and then noticed that Franck had finished his. She pushed hers towards him. "You have it. With my guilty conscience, I have enough trouble sleeping as it is."

Franck's right hand moved automatically towards the small china cup and he drained its contents

"You know about all the rumours and accusations about CWM's business practices?" he asked.

"All completely unfounded of course, otherwise Lasry Frères would never have had anything to do with them," she replied.

"Of course. Have you ever heard anything similar about Perrin Industries? Everybody says their hands are clean. Even Marie-Chantal Perrin ..."

"You've met Marie-Chantal?"

"This morning."

"A very attractive young woman, Franck," observed Sylvie. "A crusader for a better world. I bet she sleeps the deep, contented sleep of the pure at heart. She could fall for you. It would solve your financial problems in one fell swoop."

"I don't have any financial problems," stated Franck.

"That's because you think you have to have finances to have financial problems. Nobody ever explained to you that being penniless is in itself a problem."

Franck ignored this comment. If there was one subject not worth discussing with Sylvie, it was the question of his personal finances.

"I'm sure Marie-Chantal Perrin can find herself someone far more suitable than me."

"It's not what I hear ..."

"Stop it, Sylvie," he insisted.

She bit her lips.

"Perrin Industries," he continued. "That's what I want to know about."

"Perrin Industries is as above-board as you can get in the arms business. What everybody has been telling you is true."

"OK. Thanks." He toyed with the two empty coffee cups before him. "We can go back to the old rules now."

"Wait a minute," said Sylvie. "I take it from your question that the suspicious circumstances in which Nathalie Chautard died were very suspicious indeed."

Franck waved a hand dismissively. "I can't say."

Sylvie raised an eyebrow and twirled her own hand in the air, mocking him. "So much for reciprocity."

"If I answer your question, are we quits?"

Sylvie seemed to consider his proposal, and then shook her head.

"No, I'm keeping my chips for later in the game."

Franck glanced over at the waiters who were hovering in a far corner of the restaurant.

"Maybe we should get the bill and go."

He sensed Sylvie's foot, which had returned to teasing his leg.

"Sure you don't want to know anything else about Chautard and Perrin?" she asked playfully.

"Sure."

"Fuck off, you fucking fuckers!"

Franck seemed to have stumbled across the same suicidal ritual, only this time it was a weekday morning, which meant there was far more traffic under the Alexandre III bridge. It was half seven in the morning and the capital's commuters were hurtling in.

Franck waited for a quiet moment and sprinted across the road, grabbing the homeless traffic-baiter as he did so and dragging him to the traffic barrier that ran alongside the Seine.

"Stop doing that, or I'll have you arrested," Franck told him.

The man eyed him blearily, then made to walk around him back out onto the road. Franck caught the sleeve of his coat and swung him back to the kerb.

"Take this," he said, shoving a ten-euro note into his pocket. "Go and get something to drink. And stay out of trouble."

The man extracted the banknote and looked at it uncertainly. The sun had not yet risen and the road lamps under the bridge provided a shifting, watery light.

"It's real," Franck assured him. "Now go."

This time his advice was taken. The man surged across the road, narrowly missed by a speeding car, and disappeared up the steps that led to the Invalides esplanade.

Franck had brought a small Maglite torch which he held in his teeth as he climbed up the steel fretwork of the bridge to Michel's distant nest. Once there, he crouched over the bundled form. Only Michel's face was visible, quietly snoring. His features were at peace, despite a bruise on his left cheek which had not been there the last time they had talked. Franck felt momentarily guilty about robbing him of the balm of sleep, given what he assumed to be the unforgiving reality of his days, but it did not hold him back for long.

"Michel, it's Franck Guerin," he said, bending over and shaking him gently.

Michel's eyes opened and focused on him. Franck shone the torch on himself to compensate for the lack of light high up under the bridge.

"Isn't that what kids do to scare each other?" asked Michel.

"Is it working?"

"Your eyes aren't menacing enough," said Michel, yawning. "This is room service, I take it?"

"Afraid not. Take your time. I'll wait for you down there."

Franck gripped the torch in his teeth once more and began his descent.

Michel caught up with him about five minutes later. As well as his voluminous coat, he had a duffle bag slung over one shoulder.

"This time it's my treat," he said. "Follow me."

He led Franck up onto the bridge and across to the right bank. Once there they crossed cours la Reine, packed with traffic heading west, and walked up to the rear of the Petit Palais, which was surrounded by grass and numerous trees.

Michel invited Franck to sit down on a park bench.

"Feeling the cold?" he asked, as Franck blew into his hands.

"I keep forgetting my gloves," Franck explained.

"Never mind. I'll soon warm you up."

Michel began to unpack some of the contents of his bag onto the ground before the bench. He quickly set up a lightweight camping stove, filled an aluminium cooking pot from a large, bashed plastic water bottle, and set out two enamelled mugs. As the water heated up, he dug out a leather pouch and undid the drawstring that pinched it closed at one end. He passed it to Franck.

"Smell that."

Franck did as he was told.

"Thyme?" he suggested.

"Very good," said Michel. "Thyme with sage and rosemary. Keeps bronchitis at bay. Should dry up your mucous membranes too. Very important at this time of the year. Picked it and mixed it myself last summer."

"Here in Paris?"

"Of course not," laughed Michel. "Although if you know where to look, you can find most of the herbs you need here in the capital. But I don't stay here during the summer. Around about April I set off for the south when the land begins to heat up and the flowers and trees feel that it's safe to blossom once again. Paris is a wonderful place, captain, but it hides all that from you – Nature flexing its limbs after its winter captivity, recreating paradise with selfless abandon, forgetting that it'll have to make exactly the same effort twelve months later."

He turned back to the stove. He threw a pinch of dried herbs into each cup and filled them up with boiling water.

"Five minutes," he announced while he busied himself extracting a semi-circular chunk of rustic bread from his bag, along with a twist of greased paper which soon revealed several misshapen lumps of butter. He pulled a folding knife from his pocket, opened it up, locked the blade into position, and began cutting the loaf into thick slices.

"The bread was baked for La Tour d'Argent. Michelin may have stripped them down to one star, but they've still got an excellent *boulanger*. Of course, it's not as fresh as it once was, but quality keeps."

"The butter?"

"Organic. Gathered up when the Raspail *marché* was closing yesterday."

He passed a buttered slice to Franck, who bit into it without hesitating. He had never dined at La Tour d'Argent. This might be the closest he would ever get.

A few minutes later Michel allowed him to sip from one of the enamel cups. He found the herbal tea almost tasteless and sadly lacking the punch of coffee. Michel, judging by the rapt attention with which he held the other cup beneath his nose and sipped at it gently, did not share his opinion.

When they had finished, Michel gathered everything up and was repacking his duffle bag when a dog came wandering past, its nose pressed to the ground, its master some distance off.

"Here boy," said Michel, holding out a piece of bread in his hand.

The dog, an impeccably groomed golden retriever, came over quickly. It ignored the bread, preferring to press itself against Michel's knees and surrender its ears to his caresses.

Its owner called out its name. When he did so a second time with more insistence, the retriever looked at Michel apologetically, withdrew itself from his hands, and gambolled off.

"Ever wished you were a dog?" asked Michel.

"Can't say I have. Too much running after fatuous snobs," said Franck, watching the retriever's owner grab it by the collar and scold it while casting disapproving glances in their direction.

"If I thought I'd reincarnate as a dog, I'd probably throw myself into the Seine tomorrow," said Michel.

"You'd see that as a promotion? Going from man to dog?"

"Absolutely." He said it without hesitation, and then cocked his head at Franck. "You going to tell me why you got up so early this morning?"

"To show you this," said Franck. He pulled up a small backpack that he had brought in the place of his customary briefcase. Opening it, he carefully extracted the cherrywood box he had recovered the previous day.

"That's Adeline's," said Michel. "She keeps her rings in it."

"Not any more. I gave her a new jewellery box and she let me take this one."

Michel reached out for the box and Franck handed it over. He ran the palm of one hand over the lid and then opened it up, delving his nose inside as he inspected it.

"I suspect you got the best of the bargain, captain. Cherry lightly rubbed with linseed oil. Cut with patience and assembled with care."

"She told me you gave it to her."

"So I did."

"Would you mind telling me where you got it?"

"Not at all. Just outside the André Citroen park. Last Friday, I think. In the skip they brought when they were taking down the extension built around the glasshouse. Anything they didn't want to take away they tossed in there. There was a lot of junk. Clothes racks, broken chairs, a burnt-out hairdryer, bits and pieces of make-up, that sort of thing. I had a rummage around and found this. It always saddens me to see fine craftsmanship thrown away, so I rescued it."

"Was there anything inside the box?"

"Some bits of foam with holes cut in it. Looked like it had been used to store a drill, or something like that."

"You threw them away?"

"Yes. Just left them in the skip. They were no use to anyone."

"Did you see anyone else around this skip while you were there?"

"No, just the workmen who were dismantling the extension. They chased me away soon enough."

"And you didn't see anything that looked like a firearm?"

"No. Should I have?"

"Probably not. I can see this box being left in the extension for two days and being ignored by everybody, but not a pistol."

"There's a connection between this box and the killing of Alain Perrin?"

"Not with the box. With what it once held."

Franck placed the wooden box back in his rucksack and stood up.

"Thanks for breakfast, Michel. I have to be going now."

They shook hands.

"I'm a bit of a disappointment as a witness, aren't I?" said Michel.

"It's me," replied Franck, as he began to walk off. "I'm just not asking the right questions."

*

Lost in the isolation of the black hood, Franck forced himself to memorise and put into sequence the events of the past few minutes: a delivery van stopped on the outside lane of the quai des Tuileries, halfway down the uniform facade of the Louvre; angry drivers blowing their horns and fighting to get into the middle lane in order to get around it; a burly man with an absurd-looking black beret kneeling alongside the rear tyre at the kerbside; the sound of the van's side door sliding open as Franck walked past; muscular arms grabbing him from behind, squashing his backpack and its contents into his spine and pinning his arms to his side; a hood dropping down over his head, cutting off his sight; two men throwing him into the back of the van, pinning him down with their bodies; plastic snap cuffs biting into his wrists and ankles; the motor starting up and the van pulling away; the noise of traffic outside and of heavy breathing inside, his own; their refusal to engage him in conversation.

He had been snatched. By pros. Like those who had drawn a bead on Alain Perrin and tracked Nathalie Chautard.

*

Franck was doing his best to remain calm. If he concentrated on the job at hand – deducing as much as possible about his current situation – he would be able to ignore the fact that fear was circling him, gnawing at his defences.

The hood had come off a little more than four hours ago. This he knew because he could see his watch, even though his wrists were taped to the chair that supported his weight. For some reason his captors had deliberately avoided covering the face of his watch when circling his left wrist with duct tape. His chest and his legs were also bound to the chair. He reckoned it had taken an hour or so to bring him from the quai des Tuileries to here, install him and leave him. So he had been missing for five hours. Too little time for anyone to have noticed.

He seemed to be in a large underground parking garage. There were no cars in sight but before him and on either side he could see paint-marked parking bays, tyre tracks and oil stains. Fluorescent strip-lighting hung at regular intervals from the ceiling. He knew he had been brought here in a lift, and assumed its entrance was directly behind him because he could not see it. Bolts attached the legs of his chair to the concrete floor. They looked temporary, but tug as he might, he could not displace them.

Before disappearing, one of his captors had folded back the hood above his mouth and made him drink a small bottle of Evian, holding it to his lips. He had then taken up position behind him, tugged the hood off completely, and walked away. Once he was felt he was alone, Franck had tried yelling, but had grown tired of hearing his voice echoing around him.

His gun, his telephone and his backpack had not been the only things taken from him. His shoes, his trousers and his underwear sat within his field of vision, off to the left, on top of a solid metal chair identical to the one on which he sat. A large coarse towel had been wrapped repeatedly around his waist before he had been strapped in. At first this had puzzled and alarmed Franck but now, four hours later, he understood why. The towel was damp but not uncomfortably so. It absorbed well.

You do not kidnap a *flic*. Everybody knew that. Kidnapping and hostage-taking were rare enough events anyway, and never ended well, but to kidnap a *flic* was to humiliate and challenge the entire police force. It was not a recipe for a long and healthy life.

Which meant that whoever had ordered him snatched had a very serious, and assuredly dark, purpose in mind. None of the cases he had handled in his eight months spent with the Brigade Criminelle could have provoked this. It had to come from his time in the DST, which was scarcely encouraging. The DST's prey were not known for their clemency towards those who tracked them.

He heard the lift come to life and took a deep breath, steeling himself. The doors opened behind him and footsteps approached where he sat. A single pair of footsteps. This was to be a tête-à-tête.

"Good afternoon, captain. I apologise for the circumstances of this encounter. I also apologise for the time it took me to get here. Once you'd been installed we had to wait a few hours to make sure the site was still secure before I could come in. Sorry about the towel, and all that. We couldn't do it any other way."

The speaker of these words had waited until he was standing directly in front of Franck before addressing him. He then bowed slightly, presumably because they could not shake hands. He had brought Franck's backpack with him and placed it flat on the floor. He then carefully took the trousers, underwear and shoes from the nearby chair and laid them gently on top of the pack. This done, he took possession of the chair and positioned himself about a metre away from Franck.

He was in his early thirties, tall and athletic. His hair was dark, wavy and somewhat undisciplined, but stopped short of the collar of his black shirt. He was wearing worn but clean jeans and a pair of relatively new running shoes. He had the permanent tan of a sailor, dark-chestnut eyes and what looked like a carefully maintained three-day stubble. He had the physical ease of a man who knows himself to be particularly attractive. This had often been commented upon during briefing sessions where his photo had been projected, particularly by Catherine Vautrin.

"How's the abdomen?" asked Gabriel Agostini.

"Fine," said Franck. Now that the threat had a face, fear was no longer a concern. He had switched to operational mode. "Healing better on the inside than the outside, though."

"Ugly scars?"

"I try to think of them as interesting rather than ugly."

"But everything else is working?" pursued Agostini. "I was aiming away from your vital organs but I worried afterwards that I might have shot too low."

"That's very considerate of you. I hope you haven't been losing sleep over it."

Agostini studied Franck's face silently for a while before asking, "You do know I did it deliberately?"

"Not take the killshot? Yes, I figured that out. So – unfortunately – did several other people, which is why I'm no longer with the DST."

"They would have preferred it if you'd died?"

"They would have preferred it if it hadn't been you who called the shooting in and requested immediate medical aid."

"You work for some very strange people, captain," commented Agostini. "They'd rather I was a bloodthirsty psychopath and you a dead hero."

"And you aren't?"

"A bloodthirsty psychopath? I do hope not."

"Me too." Franck nodded towards his restraints. "I'm not in the best of positions to defend myself."

"You're in no danger, Franck. Can I call you Franck, or do you prefer captain?"

"Franck's fine."

"In which case, please call me Gabriel."

The last time their paths had crossed there had been no time for introductions. During the two hours it had taken them to half-carry, half-drag Gerhart Lange from the refuge at Ortu de Piobbu down to Bonifatu all their energy had been focused on the task at hand. Once they had reached the forest road at Bonifatu and laid down the German hiker, who had been caught in their crossfire up on the ridge, Agostini did not bother to ask Franck's name before stepping back and shooting him. He then picked up Franck's radio and called for immediate assistance, providing the exact coordinates of their location. Doubled over with pain, Franck's last glimpse of Agostini was an uncertain memory. He could not say for sure whether Agostini really had saluted him before slipping into the trees.

"OK, Gabriel, why am I here?" asked Franck.

"I need to talk to you."

"You could have popped into the quai des Orfèvres."

Gabriel smiled. "Actually, I probably could have. The security's appalling." As Isabelle Arbaud had recently demonstrated this twice in quick succession, waltzing through the staff entrance on the basis of her good looks and air of authority, probably showing no ID and avoiding the metal detector through which members of the public were normally forced to troop, Franck was inclined to accept his assessment. "However, someone might have disturbed us, which is far less likely here."

"Here being?"

"A parking garage in the thirteenth arrondissement," Gabriel explained. "We've never used it before, and won't be using it again, so when your colleagues arrive tell them not to waste their time going over the floors with a toothcomb and knocking holes in the walls."

"This time I get to walk away without a scratch?" asked Franck.

"Yes you do. I owe you that. When you were hunting me in Corsica, you had authorisation to shoot on sight. One of your agents was already on life-support by the time you tracked me to the refuge. When you caught me trying to save Lange you had the opportunity to take me down. But you didn't do it. You holstered your weapon and helped me bring him out. You did the right thing – the humane thing. You put the life of someone you didn't even know over and above your orders and the loyalty you owed to an organisation where you'd spent the best part of your adult life. You're too good a man to kill, Franck."

"I'm not sure I feel the same way about you."

"I don't expect you to," Gabriel assured him. "That's why I took the precaution of having you immobilised. If you throw yourself back on my trail the moment I step out of here, I won't blame you."

"You didn't bring me here to sing my praises. What am I

here to hear?"

"You're investigating the murder of Alain Perrin. You've begun to wonder whether his death is linked to that of Nathalie Chautard of Chautard Waste Management – a case that was snatched from the Toulon police by the DST. The DST is thinking along the same lines and has made at least one attempt to take the Perrin case from you." Gabriel paused. "Am I right so far?"

"You're telling me you have sources inside the DST?"

Franck's question made Gabriel chuckle. "How should I answer that? If I did, I wouldn't tell you. If I didn't, I'd say I did so as to sow the seeds of distrust. Of course, if I did, I might also be tempted to say that I did, so that you'd think I was bluffing and conclude that I didn't. And so on. In a world of mendacity, your question is senseless."

"Do you?" insisted Franck.

Gabriel smiled and shook his head, as if confirming something to himself.

"I want to make a pact with you, Franck. One for the long term. If I tell you something, now or in the future, I promise you it will be the truth. The 'if' is, of course, important. I reserve the right to remain silent – we've got to learn something from the Americans, after all. Depending on the circumstances, I may not be frank – no joke intended – but I will always be honest. In return, I'd like you to do the same for me. Are you interested?"

Franck paused, but not for long. Like Faust, he thought he was strong enough to survive a pact with the devil.

"Agreed."

"Thank you," said Gabriel, beaming at him. "As for your question – no, I don't have any sources within the DST. The tussling about the Perrin and Chautard cases is common knowledge in the upper echelons of the Ministry of the Interior."

"That's where your mole is?"

Gabriel chuckled again. "We don't have any moles, Franck.

We don't need any. Once a piece of information has come to the attention of a dozen people in the innermost circles of the Ministry it's out in the open for anyone who has ears. There's nothing more gratifying to an official's ego than to share a secret he possesses with someone who does not. He tells someone, who tells someone else, who tells someone else, and so it goes. Somewhere along the line, it falls into the hands of someone who knows us. It's human nature. There's not much you can do about it."

"Discipline," suggested Franck.

"Discipline only works with a sense of vocation. That's the secret of the DST. But at the Ministry they're just politicians and careerist civil servants. It's just a job, not a calling."

"So what about these cases? As far as the DST is concerned Appoghiu Terra Corsa is written all over Chautard's death."

"They're quite right," said Gabriel.

Franck frowned at him.

"The pact, Franck," Gabriel reminded him. "If I say we did it, then we did it."

"You've never struck outside of Corsica before."

"That's true. But things have changed. More to the point, I've changed. After our last encounter, I've spent a lot of time in hiding. Which meant a lot of time thinking things over. Appoghui was never your average Corsican separatist organisation – I take it you lot had worked that out, at least?"

"All the others boil down to Corsica for the Corsicans. Your claim was to protect Corsica itself, probably against other Corsicans if necessary."

"It's reassuring to know that someone was reading our tracts closely."

"Since we're trading confidences, you might like to know that the Ideology section loved your pamphlets. In briefings they'd always slip in a remark about the elegance and rhythm of the prose."

Under the harsh fluorescent light, Franck could have sworn he saw a hint of crimson in Gabriel's cheeks.

"I'm flattered."

"Well, you did go to Ulm," Franck pointed out. Rue d'Ulm in the fifth arrondissement had been home since 1794 to the Ecole Normale Supérieure, a legendary institution that harvested the nation's most gifted students. Agostini was perhaps not the first intellectual terrorist it had produced – Sartre was a Normalien, after all – but he was probably the first to take the term so literally.

"You're well-placed to know that," observed Gabriel, but did not pursue the point. "Appoghui was my attempt to think global and act local. But I came to realise that our localism was a mistake. We can't save Corsica if the Mediterranean becomes a poisonous soup. We can't save the Mediterranean if the rivers that run into it and the skies that move above it carry heavy metals or acid rain."

"So you're going to take on the entire industrialised world?"

Gabriel bit his lip, looking slightly embarrassed, and then nodded his head.

"Exactly."

"How?"

"By killing those who sit at the head of corporations whose actions harm the earth."

"It's been tried before. It didn't work then. It won't work now. Ask the Red Army Faction, ask the Revolutionary Cells, ask the Red Brigades – hundreds of bombings, dozens of assassinations, and for what? Capitalism has never looked stronger."

"You're right. But theirs was a political program – a revolutionary vanguard preparing the way for a mass uprising. Society had to follow them for victory to be theirs. Our approach is much more modest, much more personal – our sole objective is to convince a relatively small number of individuals that it's not worth the risk taking on the post of Chief Executive Officer of a certain number of companies."

"Which companies? There's a list?"

"No, there's not a list. There's a simple criterion. If the

company is endangering the long-term health of the planet, then the man or woman at the top shouldn't expect to reach retirement."

"Who decides that it's endangering the planet?"

"We do. Or those who will be inspired by our example to start their own group. It really doesn't matter. What does is that the top executives in those firms stop spending their time calculating how likely it is that their noxious practices get found out and how many points of margin they may lose to fines, and start worrying about their own life expectancy."

"So what? They'll just buy more security. A handful of Corsicans can't beat the world's largest corporations."

"Are you so sure? Most executives want to live normal lives – financially privileged, sure, but normal all the same. They don't want to live in fortresses and be shadowed by armed guards night and day. I think we have the potential to drain the talent pool to a considerable extent. And, like I said, it won't always just be a handful of Corsicans."

"Everyone will turn against you. You can't assassinate people just for doing their jobs and expect to be applauded for it. All of the Green parties will rush to denounce you. You will be pariahs within your own movement."

"Indeed we will. You'll notice that we've not sought to draw attention to our role in Nathalie Chautard's death. I've got bad news for the Ideology section – there'll be no more tracts. We're not looking to win hearts and minds. You're right – we cannot win the public battle. A fringe of hot-headed youth will worship us, but everyone else, from Right to Left, will line up against us. And you know why? When Rome's foundations were crumbling and the savage hordes were pouring in, what were the barbarians seeking to do? Destroy all trace of the Empire that had kept its foot on their necks for so long? Not at all. They came to become the next generation of emperors. Why did the class war grind to a halt, Franck? Because the top-hatted cigar-smoking barons of capitalism succeeded in rebranding themselves. They became business celebrities –

smart and sexy winners whose only crime was to be more talented and try harder than everyone else. So now, that's what ninety-nine percent of the population aspires to be. The sad truth is that our enemy – the planet's enemy – is not a select few. It's almost everybody."

"So what's the point?"

"We won't fight battles we can't win. We're not interested in political propaganda. We don't believe we can persuade the world's executive and managerial staff that their desires and dreams are morally contemptible. But we might be able to persuade them that they are dangerous for their health. In which case, they might rethink their priorities and adjust their ambitions. They might even go off and get a job where they'll do less harm."

"This is something you think you can achieve by running Nathalie Chautard off the road and not publicising the fact that Appoghiu was behind it?"

"We don't need our campaign to become public knowledge. We don't even want it to – because then the vast might of the media will be thrown against us. We want it to be a dirty little secret, something that's whispered in the corridors of corporate power. The kind of thing that is brought to the attention of a talented young executive as he rises to board level. A word in the ear just to make him know what he's letting himself in for. A source of constant unease that will become more compelling with every victim that we notch up. Terrorism has come to mean striking fear into the greatest number. We're going to try something different. We're going to focus on a few at a time, and their anxiety will reach out to us, desperate to know if the rumours of assassinations are true. We won't have to go to them. We're going to become terrorism's equivalent of an exclusive luxury brand reserved for the cognoscenti."

"Why tell me, Gabriel?" demanded Franck. "All it means is that as soon as you let me go, I'll go looking for my gun and come after you."

"No you won't," stated Gabriel. "The DST will, but they'll

keep you at arm's length. If you were already suspect, imagine what this meeting will inspire in your critics' minds."

"So all this is just to take me out of the game?"

"In and of itself, that would have been a worthwhile objective. After all, you're the only one who ever came close to catching me. But no, all this is for something else."

"Which is?"

"Appoghui Terra – because that's what we're calling ourselves now – had nothing ...."

"You're dropping the 'Corsa'?" interrupted Franck.

"Yes. I hate to admit it, but branding is important, and the shorter name is better aligned with our new goals."

"The shorter name is better aligned with your new goals?" repeated Franck, his voice thick with irony. "And you say you're fighting against the system?"

"Marketing has become a science powerful enough to threaten to destroy all life on this planet," stated Gabriel. "We'd be fools not to learn the odd lesson from it. As I was going to say, Appoghui Terra is about to become the nightmare of the world's CEOs, but it's essential that our message remain clear and simple. If there's any confusion about our goals or methods, then people will start to dismiss us and the level of fear will fall."

"Where's the confusion going to come from?" asked Franck.

"From people attributing our actions to others, or attributing others' actions to us. That's where you come in Franck. From now on, whenever there's any risk of doubt or ambiguity, we will clarify the situation through you. If I tell you we did it, then we did it. If I tell you we didn't, then we didn't. Our pact."

"No way," said Franck. "I'm not about to become your spokesman."

"I'm not asking you to become our spokesman. I'm asking you to become our connoisseur – in the strictest sense of the term."

"You're proposing to communicate with me

systematically?"

"No. Like I said, only when there's a risk of doubt or ambiguity. To do so systematically would be too dangerous for me, and too burdensome for you. I don't want to get between you and your cases. You're a policeman, Franck. You've got an important job to do."

"You are my case."

"No, I'm the DST's case," insisted Gabriel. "Alain Perrin is your case."

They both went silent for a moment.

"So that's why we're talking here and now?" asked Franck.

"That's right."

"That's what you were about to say when I interrupted you – that Alain Perrin's death has nothing to do with you or Appoghiu Terra?"

"Correct. Alain Perrin's death has nothing to do with me or Appoghiu Terra."

*

"And you believe him?" Catherine was incredulous.

Franck nodded his head. He believed him.

He had finally been cut loose about three hours after Agostini had left. A call had come through on Catherine Vautrin's direct line informing her that Franck Guerin had been taken into custody by Appoghiu Terra but was now available for collection on level four of a subterranean parking garage in the rue du Château des Rentiers. Within thirty minutes of the call the garage, which had closed for refurbishment two weeks previously, had been cordoned off and was surrounded by sharpshooters. Twenty minutes later a bomb squad arrived with a radio-controlled buggy equipped with lights, video cameras, and a sniffer apparatus. It worked its way down, clearing floor after floor. It took it an hour and forty minutes to reach Franck, who was tempted to pat it gratefully, but whose wrists were still immobilised by duct tape. Twenty minutes later four members of the GIGN, the gendarmerie's elite hostage rescue squad, entered the fourth floor by a stairwell which fed into a far corner. In black fatigues over body armour, they moved cautiously from pillar to pillar. Franck did not bother explaining to them that it was not a trap. They had no reason to trust him. Once they had signalled that all was clear the lift doors opened and footsteps clicked towards Franck. He knew who it would be, so did not bother craning his head. When Catherine Vautrin came round in front of him she had her revolver in one hand, a cigarette in the other, and an oversized bulletproof vest that made her look even smaller than she was. Franck told her how ridiculous she looked. She told him how badly he smelled. The GIGN troops looked on passively.

A shower later, having recovered his trousers, underwear, shoes and backpack – which turned out to contain his gun and mobile phone – Franck was once more pinned to a chair. The surroundings – one of the DST interrogation rooms – were not much more congenial, but at least there was a pot of coffee and toilets just down the corridor.

Catherine had visibly got over whatever relief she might have felt at finding him alive.

"You're prepared to believe that Agostini risked getting caught – here, in the centre of Paris – just to ensure that your little murder investigation didn't take a wrong turn?"

"No, he wanted to make sure that Appoghiu Terra didn't get blamed for a murder that wasn't theirs. Why lie about that? He'd already confessed to the killing of Nathalie Chautard."

"In the absence of any corroborating witnesses."

"What do you care about witnesses?" Franck snorted. "You're not looking to put Agostini on trial. There's been a shoot-to-kill mandate on him for at least a year now."

"He's trying to manipulate you, Franck. And through you, he's trying to manipulate us."

"What makes you so sure?"

"Because that's what these people do. Particularly when they're as smart as Agostini. 'I may not be frank but I will always be honest' – sounds a lot like strings being pulled to me."

Franck raised both hands in the air like a marionette, and then let them fall to the tabletop before him. "I'm not saying Agostini has changed. He was a dangerous terrorist before, he's even more so now. He used to limit himself to policing nine thousand square kilometres – now he's given himself the whole planet as his beat. But it doesn't mean he doesn't have a sense of honour. He saved Gerhart Lange, after all."

"After shooting him three times," Catherine scoffed.

"By mistake. He thought he was one of us."

"Well that's reassuring."

"Look, I don't know what else to tell you, Catherine. He gave me his word."

"And you gave him yours. Your little pact. Our future colleagues from the RG are going to love that. Not only are the DST a bunch of cowboys, they fraternise with enemies of the state."

She got up and paced unhappily around the room.

"I think you've spent too long in the company of Yves de Chaumont. His sense of chivalry is rubbing off on you."

"You want to take me back?"

She laughed bitterly, almost a cackle. "Everything you do makes it less and less likely that you'll ever get back here. First the Du Bellay spectacle – eight pages in *Exposé*! – and now this – Franck Guerin, personal friend and confident to Gabriel Agostini."

"Friends?" Franck shot back, allowing himself to show a little anger. "Ask my scars down there." He nodded towards his abdomen.

Catherine came back to the table, placed her palms upon it, and leant towards him.

"You've started to admire him, Franck," she said softly, with a hint of pity. "He's hooked you."

Franck bridled at this and his tongue prepared to lash out back at her. But he stopped himself. He knew that there was some truth in what she had said.

"So what do we do?" he eventually asked.

Catherine regained her seat.

"You go back to the Perrin case. You tell Yves de Chaumont from me that he was right, although it pains me to admit it. And we tell no one – no one – not even Yves – about your arrangement with Agostini."

"I have to tell Yves."

"OK. But nobody else."

"Are you going to put me under surveillance? Assuming that you'd actually stopped after our last chat."

"If I keep a detail on you I'll be admitting that you're still involved with the hunt for Agostini, or that I don't think you can be trusted. The boys and girls from the RG would have a field day with that. For the moment, we'll leave you alone. Provided you behave yourself. Anyhow, if Agostini's to be believed you're not in any danger."

"So it seems," agreed Franck.

"But if he ever contacts you again – and he will – you report to me, and only to me. Got that?"

"Of course. In any case, I imagine that's exactly what Gabriel wants."

"One more thing."

"Yes?"

"Agostini might be honey-tongued, but he's got icy veins and he's a practised killer. Don't forget it. If you get a chance the next time you see him, you might want to try shooting him – but only to kill. We don't want him getting away. Again."

"You probably have nothing to worry about."

Isabelle Arbaud did not look convinced.

"You cannot tell me how you know that the killing of Nathalie Chautard had nothing to do with Arbaud, but you ask me to believe it all the same?"

"Yes."

"So can you tell me why Alain Perrin was killed," continued Isabelle, disdainfully, "while we wait for you to find out who did it?"

"We're no further forward on that point," Franck conceded.

"And yet you dare to walk in here, present me with not a single piece of information, and tell me not to bother my pretty little head about what's going on?"

All of a sudden Franck had the feeling that this was going to prove a short meeting.

He was not wrong.

But at least he had found an excuse to visit the Arbaud headquarters, a mere ten minute stroll from his own office on the quai des Orfèvres – which made it easier to understand Isabelle's recently acquired habit of bursting in on him.

Isabelle Arbaud had sunk what must have been a substantial portion of her start-up funds into purchasing the hôtel Lambert, an imposing seventeenth-century mansion on the Ile Saint Louis which had previously belonged to the Rothschilds. Given its stately central courtyard, its three floors of panelled rooms and galleries, its extensive enclosed garden, and the names of those who had created or helped to conserve its beauty – Le Vau, Le Sueur, Le Brun, Viollet-le-Duc, and Delacroix – its acquisition was an unambiguous statement of Arbaud's ambition to embody a very specific form of refined, elegant, and virtually unobtainable luxury. Rumour had it that she had outbid a Qatari prince to obtain the title deeds.

The hôtel's famed Hercules gallery had become her private office. On the second floor, twenty-five metres long, overlooking a walled garden on one side and the Seine from its gracefully rounded tip, its gilded walls recounted the life of antiquity's most celebrated hero in a series of round and octagonal medallions supported by elaborate stucco plinths. She had received Franck enthroned behind a vast desk at its far end, her back to the river. From there she only had to raise her eyes to contemplate a painted ceiling dating from the 1650s which showed Hercules subduing centaurs, saving a princess from a sea monster, and finally receiving his due when allowed to join the ranks of the immortals of Olympus. Francesca Craveri had chosen to work under the sceptical but good-humoured eye of La Fontaine; Isabelle had chosen to keep company with a demi-god. Little wonder she gave him such short shrift.

Once she had summarily expelled Franck, her assistant bustled forward to offer him his parka. She stood guard in an oval vestibule just off the hôtel's grand central staircase where suitors awaited an audience with Arbaud's presiding genius. The firm already seemed to have a significant and bustling workforce, despite the fact that it had as yet nothing to sell – except, as Franck was now beginning to appreciate – its notion of itself.

As he slipped his parka on, a voice he had heard before reached him.

"You really should get that thing cleaned, captain."

Sitting on one of the eight armchairs disposed against the room's curving walls was a young man dressed in a dark-blue suit with a pale-pink shirt worn without a tie. He got to his feet and came forward to shake Franck's hand.

"Justin, isn't it?" said Franck.

Justin nodded.

"I hope you've been paying more attention to where you put your feet," he said.

"There's one dog for every fifteen humans in Paris," said Franck. "It's a losing battle."

"Not if you keep scanning the pavement."

"It's a beautiful city. Pity to miss it just so that you can keep your eyes peeled for dogshit."

It came to Franck that this was probably one of the things Justin did for Louis Halphen. He decided to change the subject.

"If you're here to see Isabelle Arbaud, she's not in the best of moods. Just returning the favour."

Justin smiled, catching Franck's reference to their last encounter. "I'm used to it, captain. When you deal with the gifted – and mademoiselle Arbaud is no less so in her field of expertise than monsieur Halphen in his – you make allowances."

"Is he here?"

"Monsieur Halphen? No, he tends not to come here unless he absolutely has to."

"Shut up in the lab, then? Or locked away in rue Vavin?"

"Actually, no. He's gone to church."

"Louis Halphen in a public place?"

Justin frowned at Franck. "Do not mock him, captain. He has good reason to protect himself from the outside world. But, whatever you might think, he is not a recluse. Not totally, anyway."

"I bet it's a really clean church, though."

"I wouldn't know. He never asks me to accompany him there. I just pick him up in the car afterwards."

"Not really the metro type, is he?" asked Franck.

"Monsieur Halphen? The crowds, the noises, the smells? Not really, no. Arbaud provides a BMW."

"With a driver?"

"I take charge of the driving while monsieur Halphen relaxes in the back. I think he rather likes watching the buildings as we drift by. Like you said, it's a beautiful city. Pity to miss it by travelling underground."

"Where is this church?"

"It's inside the Institut Catholique."

"Saint Joseph des Carmes?"

Justin shrugged, not recognising the name.

"If it is, it's a curious choice," continued Franck.

"Why?"

"It was once bathed in blood. Over a hundred priests were massacred there in 1792 by a revolutionary mob."

"It's also in the rue d'Assas, a short stroll from his apartment," Justin pointed out.

"Maybe," Franck conceded, although he was pretty sure that churches were not in short supply in the immediate neighbourhood of Halphen's place in rue Vavin. "If he's out and about, I assume that means he's got over the aftershock of our little discussion?"

"I'm glad to say he has."

"I hope not to have to disturb monsieur Halphen again," said Franck.

"That would be preferable. He's getting close. Any distraction now could set us back months."

"So you're here to give the boss an update?" asked Franck, pointing over his shoulder with his thumb.

"You could say that."

Justin raised a small rigid briefcase. It was slim, black, and closed with a lock that required two keys. It bore the Arbaud logo: the company's name in an elegant calligraphic script superimposed on a field of colour that evolved from hazel to green.

"Is that it?" asked Franck. "The perfume that's worth 150 million euros?"

"Not yet," said Justin. "But every time we have a stable version – something monsieur Halphen thinks he will keep and build upon – he makes a tiny sample for mademoiselle Arbaud. For the past five months she has worn every version he has produced. She has become monsieur Halphen's touchstone. He is, in a sense, making a perfume specifically for her, and she will in turn present it as a gift to the world."

"I'm not quite sure she intends to just give it away."

"I said a gift, captain. Not a handout."

"Still, you've just cleared up one of the things I never

understood about this case," said Franck.

"Which is?"

"Why Isabelle Arbaud always smells so good."

*

"You really should do something about the security in this place," she said. "All I had to do was smile to get in here."

This was a technique he suspected Isabelle Arbaud had never tried.

"You've got a nice smile, Sonia, but I suspect the rest helps too," said Franck, looking down at her where she sat behind his desk.

She was still in her coat, a waist-length garment with bell-shaped sleeves that stopped halfway down her forearms, allowing her to exhibit very long black leather gloves. Under it she wore a one-piece, wide-necked, black-and-white houndstooth dress that stopped well above her knees, revealing a generous stretch of leg above wide-cuffed ankle boots. A beret hung jauntily off the side of her head. Franck suspected that more thought had gone into her outfit than into some of the investigations currently being handled in the offices around them.

She rose so that they could kiss each other's cheeks. Franck sat opposite her in the chair normally reserved for visitors.

"I recently met a man with one of those," he said, pointing to her beret.

"A man in a beret? Chances are he was either over seventy, a tourist, or gay."

"I didn't get a good look at him. He blindfolded me, tied me up and threw me in a van," said Franck.

"Definitely gay. I'm impressed. I never suspected you had such an exciting sex life."

"Me neither. So what can I do for you, Sonia? Come to ask me out to lunch?"

"Lunch?" she cried, in mock-horror. "Lunch is for fatties.

p.148

No, I've come to show you this."

She picked up a sizeable handbag of unblemished leather with looping handles. Opening it involved undoing a clutch on a strap which ran horizontally across one side. This released a flap which then had to be folded backwards to gain access to the interior. Franck watched the process with bemusement. He could get into his briefcase in a quarter of the time. Given that he was in the habit of carrying his MR73 revolver inside it, this was not a superfluous consideration.

What Sonia tugged out triumphantly, however, was not a weapon but a thick copy of *Vogue*.

She tossed it onto the surface of his desk.

"The February issue. Hit the kiosks last Tuesday. I figured you'd have missed it."

"I've been a bit busy," said Franck, reaching out for the magazine.

There she was. On the cover, as promised, her dress shot in such a fashion that it seemed to embody the shifting surface of the sea. 'Ephémère plumbs the mysteries of the deep' was printed in large type across the lower half of the photo, dominating tags for other articles inside.

"Well done," he said.

"It's only French Vogue," cautioned Sonia, "but all the same. Marco's over the moon."

"Francesca Craveri too, I imagine."

"Over the moon? Not her style. She's the other reason I'm here."

"Really?"

"There's an Ephémère reception this evening. Since I'm the heroine of the hour, I am of course invited. And you are to be my partner."

"What about Luc?" asked Franck. "Won't he be a little jealous?"

Sonia tutted. "You're completely out of touch, captain. Luc and I didn't make it through Christmas."

"I'm sorry to hear that."

"So was he."

"What went wrong?"

"Work," said Sonia, twisting her lips. "Work, work, work. Believe me, Luc's reputation as a playboy is greatly exaggerated. It was all meetings, sales trips, visits to suppliers, presentations to the new investors – he never took his mind off Du Bellay. We didn't go out on dates, we reserved empty slots in his schedule. So I ditched him."

"How did he take it?"

"He said he was very upset. Didn't stop him flying to Milan for a meeting the next day, though. If his heart had really been broken, he'd have cancelled everything and begged me to stay."

"How about your heart? Is it broken?" asked Franck.

Sonia sagged languorously in her seat, dropped her chin and looked up at Franck from beneath her eyelids.

"Do I look like I'm pining away?" she asked.

"Less a lovelorn maiden than an artful vamp," he offered.

"No one gives a compliment like you," she declared, winking at him. "So are you coming with me this evening?"

"Wouldn't I be a little out of place? I don't think I'm the stuff of Ephémère receptions."

"I would agree with you on that. Although it would be a great honour for me to be accompanied by the famous Franck Guerin of the Brigade Criminelle, I have to admit you weren't the first name I thought of."

"What, everyone else turned you down?"

"Of course not. It took me five minutes to get a partner. But two hours ago I had to call the guy and tell him he couldn't come any more."

"Why?"

"Because Francesca Craveri phoned me. She said she hoped I'd be bringing that nice captain Guerin with me this evening. And since no one in their right mind ever says no to Francesca Craveri, that means you're coming."

"I suppose it does," conceded Franck.

Sonia sprung to her feet.

"I'm off. It's at the Ephémère headquarters, place François Premier. In the eighth."

"I know the address."

"I'll meet you there at eight thirty. Outside. But don't you dare come in that appalling parka."

Franck had not yet got round to taking it off, and as a result was now feeling a little too warm. As he got up to say goodbye to Sonia he unzipped it and reached out to place it on the nearby coat stand.

Sonia stopped short of the door and spun to face him. She reached out and tugged him towards her, burying her nose in his neck. Franck froze, but she kept moving, jabbing her nose at his hair, his shoulders and his chest. She brought her face up to his, her hands still clamped on his elbows.

"What on earth is that?" she asked.

"What?" asked Franck, utterly perplexed.

"You don't smell like a man. Is this from your adventures in the van?"

Franck raised his eyes and shrugged his arms free.

"Seriously," she pursued. "You actually smell quite alluring. Whatever it is, get me some as soon as you can."

"I was with Isabelle Arbaud an hour ago," he explained.

"You're sleeping with Isabelle Arbaud!" she exclaimed. "Wow! You're a sly one, captain. Nobody knows!"

He sighed and shook his head. "I was in her office. Talking about the Perrin investigation."

"Ah," said Sonia. "The trace effect."

"The what?"

"Isabelle Arbaud has been wearing test versions of her future perfume for months now. It's been creating quite a buzz."

"I know," said Franck. "Well, not about the buzz – about the perfume."

"It smells like heaven. Everyone says so. But there's also a trace effect. It lingers. Anybody Isabelle comes close to is haunted by the ghost of her scent for hours afterwards. Nobody knows how it's done. They say it's a new technique that Louis Halphen has come up with."

"What's so great about that?" asked Franck.

"What's so great about that?" echoed Sonia. "It's not the smell of the perfume that's transferred – that would be stupid and clumsy. Imagine Numéro Cinq or Eternal on you. It just wouldn't smell right. You're a man, your chemistry's wrong, all that stuff. No, it's the smell of Isabelle Arbaud wearing the perfume that stays behind. She marks every man – and every woman, for that matter – who comes within her intimate sphere."

"Her what?"

"Within a metre of her," explained Sonia. "They don't teach you much in detective school, do they?"

"Not much about perfume, that's for sure."

"It's an incredible trick. They're going to bring out a product that will sell the world over but react in a distinct fashion to every woman who wears it, and then allow her to leave that unique result behind her. To mark her man, or her prey or her territory."

"Like a dog peeing on lampposts," suggested Franck.

Sonia snorted and stepped out the door, shaking her head at him.

"It's a waste of time talking to you about the finer things in life," she declared. "Eight thirty. Try to look half decent."

Off she stalked, leaving Franck not entirely comfortable with the notion that Isabelle Arbaud had somehow left her mark on him.

*

"Was this your father's?"

Sonia was only twenty minutes late, which surprised him. Sylvie Thomas had accustomed him to far worse.

She emerged from a taxi and skipped up the steps of the

Ephémère building. She posed for the handful of paparazzi who were there and then grabbed Franck's arm. She swept him through the main entrance, passing unchallenged through a line of uniformed hostesses, and directed him to a cloakroom. He helped her off with her coat – a different, longer, model from the one he had seen earlier – and laid his own alongside it on the counter. He had traded his parka for the coat he had worn to Perrin's funeral.

Sonia's comment was directed at his suit. Franck pretended not to have heard her. Even he did not feel too comfortable about what he was wearing. When he had gone home to change, he discovered that the few respectable suits he owned were either at the drycleaners or in urgent need of a visit to it. Digging around at the back of his wardrobe produced a suit he probably hadn't worn since his mid-twenties. The waist was tight, the jacket was double-breasted, and the light-grey cloth from which it was cut made him look pale and unsubstantial. Bowing to necessity, he had thrown it on with a white shirt and a thin red tie.

"Still, it means less competition for me," she conceded.

She wore a black flapper-style dress with multiple fringes sewn in successive waves from shoulder to knee onto a shift of largely transparent gauze. Ballet pumps, a clutch purse, and a sequinned headband completed her outfit.

"Delighted to be of service, mademoiselle," said Franck, offering her his arm. Together they walked into the main reception room, where a crowd of eighty or so were mingling, drinks in hand. A white-coated waiter presented himself before them with a tray full of champagne glasses. They each took one.

"Great look, Sonia," said Marco Chiriotti, Ephémère's resident prince of *haute couture*, pecking her on each cheek. He smiled and tipped his head at Franck, whose face clearly meant nothing to him. "That's a nice retro touch you've got there. Double-breasted will come back with a vengeance, just you wait and see."

"Captain Franck Guerin," said Sonia. "From the *défilé*."

"Of course," said Marco, lightly slapping his forehead. "So while you were interrogating Sonia, she was busy winkling your phone number from you?"

"We'd already met," said Franck. "We're old ..."

"Don't get carried away, Marco," insisted Sonia, cutting across Franck. "He's not my date. I'm chaperoning him for someone else."

"In which case, maybe you can cut him loose to have some fun on his own," suggested Marco. "That way you can chaperone me and make sure I don't eat too much. You don't mind, captain, do you?"

He minded greatly, but was not about to say so. Marco and Sonia waltzed away, laughing and whispering to each other, leaving him stranded in what he feared would prove a roomful of alien beings.

"Captain Guerin?" said a young voice.

Franck turned to face a girl in her early twenties with close-cut ash-brown hair and a dark-blue strapless dress that commenced on the slope of her breasts, hugged her ribs, puffed out from her waist, and curved back in halfway down her thighs. Her face was vaguely familiar.

"Marilyn," she said. "Madame Craveri's assistant."

"Of course," said Franck. "How are you?"

"I'm very well, captain. I hope you're enjoying the reception?"

"I've only just arrived, but ..."

"And only just been cut adrift," she observed. "May I take you in hand, captain? Madame Craveri is tied up at the moment, but would like to speak with you a little later."

Without waiting for a reply she gestured to the heart of the crowd and led Franck into the thick of the bespoke suits, cocktail dresses, dandified outfits, and party gowns. For the next hour she introduced him to guest after guest, watched over his champagne glass, ensured that he got to taste the many exquisite varieties of finger-food on offer, and kept him company with a combination of professional courtesy and personal charm.

He was in the middle of explaining the impact of DNA testing on homicide investigations to a man from Piaget when Marilyn raised her index finger and stroked the tip of her nose, magically causing both men to turn to her.

"I'm very sorry monsieur Kreyenbühl, I'm afraid I have to tear the captain from you."

She led Franck away, out of the reception area and back into the hall. They walked together up the massive curving staircase that led to the upper floor.

"If you could wait here, madame Craveri will not be a moment."

He found himself in the same room as the last time with the Louis XV armchairs and the wall-hangings. Left to his own devices, he wandered over to one of the walls and glanced behind the tapestry that hid it, studying the chaos of threads that made possible its detailed recounting of La Fontaine's fable of the Crow and the Fox.

Francesca Craveri's voice came from behind him.

"Sire Crow, perched high in the trees,
held in his beak a wondrous cheese.
Sire Fox, whom its odour did please,
let these words float up on the breeze.
Sire Crow, good day,
how your beauty makes me stay.
Were your voice of such note
as the feathers of your coat,
you would be the phoenix of this forest."

Franck turned to her as she closed the door. She wore a long teal-green evening dress with a draped neckline. Her décolleté framed a necklace strung together from tesserae of Venetian glass in varying shades of blue. Her hair was bound up in a chignon, exposing her neck. She grasped a small purse in her left hand.

She raised her other hand towards him, palm upwards,

fingers spread. A clear invitation.

"The Crow, who had long thought he was the best,
instantly proposed to vocalise
and opened his beak, only to lose his prize.
The Fox seized it and said, dear sir,
learn from this that every flatterer
steals from whomsoever lends him his ear.
A cheese, for such wisdom, is a price not too dear."

Francesca clapped with lightly cupped hands. Franck bowed and then returned the applause.

"Never trust a man who doesn't know his La Fontaine," she said, coming towards him.

"Never trust a fox who sings your praises," offered Franck in return, shaking her graciously extended hand.

"Of which there are many in the world of fashion," she said, inviting him to sit and then joining him in an adjacent armchair. "Praise is the universal currency with which many seek to pay their way in our industry."

"We don't have that problem in the police. I don't think we're even aware that praise exists."

"In which case, I will now attempt to make up for that," said Francesca. "I wanted you to know how appreciative I am of the discretion you have shown in investigating the murder of Alain Perrin. It could so easily have become a scandal overshadowing all the work Marco had put into his collection. We are on the cover of *Vogue* with a dress spattered with bleach. We could so easily have found ourselves depicted by some less forgiving publications with one drenched in blood."

"I'm not sure it's all our doing – or my doing, for that matter. Alain Perrin was a very serious young man, so his death hasn't attracted the attention other potential victims of his wealth and status might have done. There's also the fact that we haven't made much progress. A murder case with no suspect and no clear motive doesn't give the press much to cover."

"I was surprised to see so little speculation about motive in the press. I had feared, I admit, that *ma petite* Isabelle might broadcast her paranoid theories to all and sundry. It seems she has chosen you as her sole confident. If you knew her better, you would realise that this is quite a compliment. Her mother died when she was a toddler. Having met him, I doubt very much her father was someone in whom it was safe to confide. As a result Isabelle rarely opens up to anyone. She must have seen something special in you."

"I don't think she's that impressed with me anymore. I told her this morning we're treating Perrin's death as an isolated homicide. I don't think she was too pleased."

"You don't believe it had anything to do with his involvement in Arbaud?"

"I have no idea what it had to do with. But I'm sure that Nathalie Chautard's death had nothing to do with Arbaud, which makes the conspiracy theory hard to sustain."

Francesca placed her hands together and held them against her lips, her thumbs hooked beneath her chin. She seemed to be turning a thought in her head.

"Do you think she's having problems?" she finally asked.

"Isabelle Arbaud?" Franck found it hard to conceive of her as someone who had problems.

"Yes, Isabelle. If she wants to believe – or to make you believe, and through you, eventually, the rest of the world – that someone is trying to derail her project, could it be that things are not going well? She's not very good at admitting that she's wrong, you see. Not, of course, that she often is. But it can happen to anyone, and maybe it's happening to Isabelle. She's already months behind her original schedule for Night-Scented. Maybe she needs someone or something to blame. What better than a dark conspiracy?"

"I don't think it's that," said Franck. "If anything, I believe they're making good progress."

"Well, that would explain why everyone was raving after all the shows she went to last week. Apparently her scent was hypnotic. The beauty editors were falling over each other inventing questions just so that they could stick close to her."

"*Sire Fox, whom its odour did please, let these words float up on the breeze. Sire Crow, good day, how your beauty makes me stay,*" cited Franck.

"Isabelle won't let slip her cheese, you needn't worry about that. In any case, Isabelle doesn't have the cheese. It's Louis who has it. He's the true crow in this tale, and Isabelle the cunning fox. But if you say there's been progress, does this mean you know something I don't? Has there been a sudden breakthrough? Has Louis leapt from his bathtub crying 'Eureka' and run naked through the streets?"

"Louis Halphen in the street without a biohazard protection suit? Somehow, I don't see it."

Francesca tutted. "That is cruel, and needlessly so to boot. Louis lives like an anchorite for a reason. It has allowed him to perform incredible feats for over twenty-five years. Why change now? Change is full of dread, a destroyer of the certainties of the past and an inexhaustible source of anxiety – read your Proust if you have any doubt about that."

"He's not that allergic to change. He left Ephémère for Arbaud, after all," Franck pointed out.

"To be fair, that was as much my doing as Isabelle's. She promised him endless freedom while I sought to confine him to the essential task of keeping Eternal alive."

"Still no solution for that?" he asked.

Francesca's head bobbed from side to side. "Perhaps," she said, her eyes twinkling. "But I'm certainly not going to tell someone who shares secrets with Isabelle Arbaud."

"Your nemesis."

"That's right, my nemesis, to whom I should be grateful for keeping me on my toes." She clapped her hands. "But let me return to my gratitude. I have something for you."

"You have information about Perrin?" asked Franck, sitting up and leaning forward.

"No, I have something for you. Forget about the case for a minute."

She slipped a hand into the slim purse that lay in her lap and pulled out a mobile phone. She tapped one key and held it to her ear.

"You can bring it in," she said.

Franck was about to ask something when she held a finger up to her lips and shushed him. They sat in companionable silence for the next three minutes.

The door opened and Marilyn stepped in. Her arms were held out horizontally. Draped over them was a long sable coat.

"It's a full length top-coat," explained Francesca. "Worsted wool and cashmere from an English mill, with a silk lining of course. Marco cut it for you – which explains the rather thin lapels and ever-so-slightly pinched waist. He felt you should have an aerodynamic look – just right for chasing hoodlums. And I believe there's a specially counterweighted pocket on the inside left for your little gun."

"It's for me?" said Franck. He stood as Marilyn let it slip from her arms to his.

"We couldn't help noticing that you needed a new coat," said Francesca. "Don't be offended captain – that's the kind of people we are. These things matter to us."

"I'm flattered," he said. "But a little embarrassed. I'm afraid I can't accept this, madame Craveri."

"Francesca," she insisted.

"Francesca, I can't. Really. It's not that I don't appreciate the gesture, but there's an investigation under way. I can't accept gifts, not from ..."

"A party of interest to the investigation?"

He nodded, mutely.

"In which case, captain – Franck – Marilyn will set it aside for you. When you have Alain Perrin's murderer behind bars, we will send it on. Would that be acceptable?"

"Yes," said Franck, who could not help feeling slightly churlish.

"Try it on first, though. We've been dying to see you in it."

He stood and allowed Marilyn to help him on with the coat.

She slipped round in front of him to do up four of its buttons, tug it down on his shoulders, and step aside to allow Francesca to admire him.

"It makes you look very distinguished," she announced.

Franck smiled, somewhat uncomfortably, and bowed slightly. His determination to leave without it remained undiminished.

He cast a glance at the tapestry, wondering if he too had a cheese in his beak and – if so – what it could possibly be.

Friday, 1st February

The Mirabeau bridge was a contemporary of the Alexandre III. Completed in 1897, it too was a product of the spell that forged steel cast upon French engineers at the end of the nineteenth century. Easily as elegant in its form, its decoration was less ostentatious but just as portentous, with four massive female statues adorning two stone pillars sunk midstream to support its weight. Allegories of the river's role in sustaining Paris' fortunes, they suggested that its construction was motivated by more down-to-earth considerations than that of paying tribute to the tsar of all the Russians. Although it had not escaped celebration at the hands of at least one poet – Apollinaire, in 1913 – it was rarely troubled by tourists. Frequented and ignored by Parisians, it was a practical, businesslike bridge.

From that point of view, it was a fitting resting place for Guillaume Thèves.

Franck stared at its span overhead. Had Thèves been killed directly underneath it there was next to no chance that anyone might have seen the deed. Immediately upstream was a large parking space, beyond which sat the offices of a couple of rent-a-cruise firms, none of which were likely to have been in operation on a cold Thursday evening in January. Downstream was a cement works, complete with a facility for loading sand and limestone from barges, and another parking area, this one reserved for a fleet of hulking mixer trucks. Thèves' car, a Renault Laguna, had been left in splendid isolation in the upstream car park. Two technicians were approaching it, ready to dust, photograph, and search for any trace material. Another was looking for tyre tracks in the immediate vicinity. He was finding far too many, since the cement trucks were not averse to pulling over there while waiting to move into the downstream charging area.

It was now half ten, and the sun had come out in a cloudless sky to make their job easier. It was still cold, though, and Franck kept his hands deep in the pockets of his parka whenever he could. He had once again left his gloves at home.

The body had been found by a pair of early morning runners who called the fifteenth arrondissement commissariat, sending the ever-eager lieutenant Blanchard into action. When the lieutenant saw the pool of liquid around the victim, the patches of fading colour on his clothes, his bloodied stomach and the entry wound in the centre of his forehead, he knew immediately whom to call. Franck, in turn, had alerted Georges Sternberg.

While his team fussed over the car, and a medical examiner fiddled with the body, Sternberg discussed the scene with Franck. They had got rid of Blanchard by sending him off to interview the staff of the cement works to check at what time everyone had left the previous day.

"Good choice of location," said Sternberg. "Easy access from the ring road, lots of parking, no lowlife hanging around. If I was a busy executive and somebody wanted to meet me for a quick, confidential chat, I'd think this was an ideal spot."

"Two cars pull up, they get out and wander under the bridge while they talk ..." mused Franck.

"Or," Sternberg broke in, "Thèves parks upstream, the killer parks downstream amongst the cement trucks, where no one's going to see his car, and they walk towards each other, meeting under the bridge."

"You'd park next to the cement trucks? What about the risk of catching dust inside your wheel rims and in all those sneaky places you forensic types just love to probe?"

"Not as much of a risk as you might think. The trucks are hosed down every evening. It stops the city authorities complaining about the mess they make when they go through the streets. Anyhow, the state of his wheel rims scarcely matters. He'll have ditched his car by now. Five minutes after the shooting he would have been back on the ring road. In ten he could have been on the motorway to Normandy, Brittany or to the south. The car could be parked in a suburb of Rennes and he could be stepping off the TGV in Montparnasse as we speak."

"OK, let's say they meet under the bridge," said Franck. "There's not much light – just those lampposts there and there – but it's enough to recognise each other. The killer pulls out his PI87."

"Conjecture," interjected Sternberg. "We haven't seen the bullets yet."

"Want to bet on it?"

"No."

"The killer pulls out his PI87. Shoots Thèves in the stomach, perhaps from some distance, then comes close and finishes him off. Pockets the cartridges and walks off."

"There won't have been enough light for a distant shot. He must have fired at close range both times. They may even have talked for a while first. Maybe Thèves wasn't already condemned when he agreed to come here. Maybe he just said the wrong thing, or made the wrong choice. That's when the PI87 came out."

"Out from where?" asked Franck. "It would take a really deep pocket to hold one of those."

"One of those nice cherrywood boxes?" suggested Sternberg.

"Our killer doesn't have it anymore. We do."

"Out of a briefcase, then. A meeting with the head of a major corporation, what else do you bring but a briefcase?"

"Late at night under a bridge on a deserted quai?"

"We're not international executives, Franck. What do we know?"

"How about – the two cars pull up, more or less side by side. Thèves gets into the killer's car, or vice versa, and they talk. At some stage Thèves gets out and walks under the bridge."

"Why?"

"Wants to smoke? Wants to pee? Wants to think something over on his own."

"It might make sense," said Sternberg. "He's not wearing a

coat. If he'd planned on standing outside for half an hour or so on a winter's night, he'd surely have brought one."

"The killer turns on the headlights full-beam and steps out of the car."

"And suddenly we've enough light for a distant shot," conceded Sternberg.

"Then once Thèves is down on the ground and can't go anywhere, the killer walks over and finishes him off."

The medical examiner came over.

"Sorry to interrupt all this speculation," he said. "I've done all I can here. I'll have the body moved now, if you've no objection."

"We're fine," said Sternberg. His team had started with the corpse and its immediate vicinity when they arrived. They were now working their way outwards. They could well be at it for the rest of the day.

"Does the fact that he's drenched in bleach mean anything to you?" asked the examiner.

"I wish it did," said Franck. "Can you give us a time of death?"

"Between nine and eleven last night, I'd say."

"Thanks."

By that time it would have been pitch-dark.

By that time this part of the riverfront would have been deserted.

By that time the drivers on the bridge overhead would have been too busy hurrying home and listening to their car radios to hear two gunshots.

By that time he would have been reciting La Fontaine to Francesca Craveri.

One of Sternberg's technicians came running over from Thèves' car. It was the trainee from the André Citroen crime scene.

"Can you come over, Georges? We've got something strange."

The three of them walked to the Laguna. The technician

handed them plastic gloves and directed them towards the driver's side door.

"Look inside. What do you see?" she asked.

"The leather looks wet," said Sternberg.

"Not just the leather. The floor carpets too."

"Petrol? Spirits?" asked Sternberg. "The car was meant to be torched, but something happened to scare the killer away?"

"Set a car on fire down here and you'll see it from up there," said Franck, pointing up to the bridge, which was carrying its customary heavy traffic. "Not a good idea if you want to slip away quietly."

"A timer device that failed to go off?" suggested Sternberg.

The technician sighed and shook her head. "Stop trying to guess – just open the door."

They did.

"No mistaking that," said Sternberg.

Nor was there. It was an odour of which they were fast becoming connoisseurs.

The aggressive and corrosive scent of bleach.

*

"Where did the bleach come from?"

Franck and Georges Sternberg had broken for lunch at midday, eating in a brasserie right next to the bridge. Afterwards Sternberg had gone back to the crime scene and Franck had caught the RER to Saint Michel, hoping to negotiate his way around madame Alba, Yves de Chaumont's guardian angel, and intercept the *juge* before he got caught up in his afternoon appointments. He had succeeded.

"First time around it just happened to be there, lying in a cleaner's cart," continued Yves. "That suggests it was an afterthought."

"Or a means to solve a problem the killer hadn't expected," suggested Franck. "Contact when none was foreseen."

"You think he learned his lesson, and deliberately brought it this time?" asked Yves. "Where are the empty containers?"

"That we don't know," replied Franck. "They could still be in the boot of the killer's car."

"Assuming he came in a car. You've got no evidence of that."

"Sternberg reckons that four or five litres of liquid were poured into Thèves' Laguna. That's a lot of bleach to be carrying by hand."

"Good point. So he drove it there and drove the empty bottles away?"

"He could have thrown them into the river once he was finished."

"*Beneath the Mirabeau bridge flows the Seine*," said Yves, quoting Apollinaire. "At a steady pace. By the time you lot got there a plastic bottle tossed into the river at the time of death could have been ten kilometres downstream. That said, there are a fair number of obstacles in the port of Javel, so if the containers hugged the banks they could still be there."

"You think I should check the riverside for any empty bottles of bleach?"

"Sounds like the kind of thing this lieutenant from the fifteenth – what was his name?"

"Blanchard," supplied Franck.

"Sounds like the kind of thing he'd love to do."

"Bit pointless though, since any prints will have been washed off."

"True, but we'd know if the killer has a favourite brand."

"You think there's a firm manufacturing concentrated bleach specifically for the homicide market?"

"It would make sense. Hasn't it become rather popular for destroying biological evidence?"

"So it seems, but it's a complicated issue. If you like I can ask Georges Sternberg to come in and give you his lecture on the difference between destroying and concealing evidence. Bleach does destroy DNA, that's certainly true. It's not so good at making bloodstains disappear, though. If you clean a surface with bleach, the blood will not be visible to the naked eye but you can make latent stains positive with luminal if you wait long enough, since the hypochlorite in the bleach deteriorates through time."

Yves complimented Franck with a raised eyebrow. "Contemplating a transfer to the forensic division, are we? You're forgetting that concealment doesn't seem to be a high priority for our assassin. He's not got a problem about leaving his victims where they fall. He's happy for us to know there's a killer. But he doesn't want us to know who he is, and thinks that if he didn't clean up behind himself with bleach we might work it out."

"Maybe he knows he's in the national DNA database," suggested Franck.

"That's a big help. Thanks to the zeal with which we've been filling it up I'm told there are now a million records in it. All we have to do is call them all up and ask them where they were on Thursday evening."

"Wonder how many lieutenant Blanchards they've got in the fifteenth?" mused Franck.

*

It made a pleasant change to visit a corporate headquarters that eschewed the prestigious neighbourhoods of the inner arrondissements and the herd instinct that prevailed at La Défense. Or it would have, had Guillaume Thèves not installed International Paper Supplies in La Courneuve, a hinterland of crumbling warehouses, scrap heaps, and small factories, relics of a now-lost industrial past. The IPS headquarters and the surrounding buildings sat on the wrong side of the Saint-Denis canal, gazing across it with bitter jealousy at the sight of the National Stadium constructed for the 1998 World Cup and the bright, shiny office and retail units that it had spawned in its shadow. Suburban development was as cruel and precise in its demarcations as any apartheid regime: one moment Franck was sitting in the RER train looking out at the futuristic architecture of an elevated station that marked the beginning of a wide landscaped avenue leading to the stadium entrance; the next he was facing the tired brickwork and torn posters of the Courneuve-Aubervilliers RER stop. Three minutes were enough to transport you from a playpark dedicated to media-fuelled spectacles to an oppressive warren of decaying industry.

Although by far the biggest – and certainly the most prosperous – undertaking in the area, International Paper Supplies had made no effort to shrug off the prevailing local style. Surrounded by high brick walls topped with broken glass, the grounds it possessed were covered in split and pock-marked tarmac, stained by the oil and tyres of the fleet of delivery vehicles which rumbled constantly in and out of its gates. Guillaume Thèves could not have been accused of wasting his money on appearances.

Even his office edged on the tawdry. Brown carpeting that had seen too many feet, wallpaper that had been assaulted by too many drawing pins, vertical blinds that had lost their colour to a war of attrition waged by tired sunlight: Thèves had worked in surroundings that would have depressed even a *fonctionnaire* used to the dusty and neglected corridors of the French bureaucratic machine.

"He did it deliberately," said Jeanine Montfort, his secretary – IPS was not the kind of firm that had any truck with the notion of personal assistants – when she observed the way Franck took in his surroundings. Jeanine herself was anything but tawdry. In her late twenties, in an open-necked blouse and tight, straight-cut jeans, she allowed her long ash-blond hair to tumble in waves down her back and her chunky black glasses to perch coquettishly halfway down her nose. Franck felt sure that she was in the habit of dressing for her boss.

"This is where he negotiated with our major suppliers," she explained. "When you're out to add a few extra centimes to your resale margin, you make them as uncomfortable as possible."

She seemed less upset about her boss' death than intent on demonstrating her grasp of the way he had operated. Franck was tempted to remind her that she was not interviewing to hang on to her place. But he preferred to keep her talking.

Not that he had learned much thus far. She had noticed no change in Thèves' demeanour over the past few days or weeks. There had been no unusual meetings, phone calls or emails. All had been normal in the vast bulk-buying, order-taking and palette-shipping enterprise that was IPS.

She was now explaining to him in detail Thèves' schedule for that week, naming and identifying those with whom he had met, made scheduled calls, lunched, and dined. Thèves was relentlessly active, negotiating and manoeuvring from seven or so in the morning until evening. He liked to close the day's toil with a late dinner in a Parisian restaurant. That was when the penny-pinching mask was tossed aside and the man Franck had briefly encountered at the Fontainebleau golf club emerged once more: his favourite tables included Gagnaire, Robuchon, le Grand Véfour, Savoy, Ducasse, and Rostang. His miserly demeanour clearly vanished with the setting sun.

"Yesterday?" prompted Franck.

"Spent the morning here. Met a delegation from Clairefontaine, then one from M-Real. Had a conference call with the heads of our European subsidiaries. Had lunch with the Sales Director."

"Where?"

"Here. A boxed lunch."

"Then?"

"Dealt with his emails. Took a walk around the loading docks. Went out and chased away some demonstrators who've been hanging about the gates for the past few weeks."

"Don't you have security to deal with that?" asked Franck.

"Of course. Security kept them outside the gates. Guillaume wanted them out of the street. He went out and gave them a piece of his mind. He liked doing things like that."

"I'm sure he did. Then?"

"A meeting with some Chinese who want to supply us with magnetic boards and flipcharts. A call with a major client about a contract that's just been put out to tender."

"Which client?"

"A major client," she repeated. "Is it relevant to the murder investigation?"

"Probably not," conceded Franck. "Then?"

"A meeting with our call centre outsourcer. A private call with his financial adviser. A long meeting with some local officials about a plan to buy over and clear one of the scrap yards along the canal. That's when I left."

"Which was when?"

"Just after seven."

"He had anything scheduled afterwards?"

"No. He tends to read reports and answer emails in the evening, before going off to dinner."

"He had a reservation last night?"

"Of course. L'Arpège."

"Rue de Varenne?" asked Franck. Although he had eaten in none of the capital's three-star restaurants, like a fair number of Parisians Franck could identify them all.

She nodded, adding, "Table for two, nine thirty."

Rue de Varenne was just off the Invalides esplanade, and as such no more than ten minutes by car from where Thèves' body had been found.

"Who was he due to meet?" asked Franck. With a time of death from nine to eleven, it seemed safe to assume that Thèves had never made it to the restaurant.

"A bitch by the name of Isabelle Arbaud," said Montfort.

"Isabelle Arbaud," echoed Franck. "Why do you say a bitch? You knew her?"

"No, but she called yesterday morning. Insisted she get to speak with Guillaume. Treated me like shit. After I'd put her through, Guillaume told me to change his dinner plans and make a reservation for two at L'Arpège."

"He told you explicitly it was to see her?"

"I told him I hoped it wasn't to see that ill-tempered bitch, and he said it was."

"He defended her?" asked Franck. Not that ill-tempered seemed particularly unjust, given his own experience.

"No."

"You think he shared your opinion?"

"We shared a lot, captain."

Franck left by the main entrance about thirty minutes later. His briefcase held several documents concerning Thèves' recent movements and deals. It was after five. The day was waning.

Having gone through the massive, rusting iron gates that allowed both vehicular and foot passage into the IPS premises, he turned to the left, dodged between two student types who were standing there, and headed for the RER station. A hand thrust something at him as he passed and he took it without thinking. Just as automatically, having glanced down and seen that it was some kind of flyer printed on thin, off-white paper, he folded it in two and began scanning for a bin where he could deposit it.

"If you're not interested, can we have it back?" came a voice behind him.

Franck stopped and turned. One of the pamphleteers, a girl who might not have been out of her teens, in a long patchwork skirt, a hand-knitted jumper, and several scarves, stepped towards him with her hand out.

"You give them away and then you ask for them back?"

"If you're just going to chuck it away, yes," she said. "That's a tree you've got in your hand. We don't want it to have died for nothing."

Franck unfolded the flyer and scanned the contents. It called upon IPS to exclude from its catalogue all non WFPA-certified manufacturers of paper products.

"What does WFPA mean?" he asked.

"World Forest Protection Agency," she explained. "It's a NGO dedicated to preserving the world's forests from destructive practices. If paper is WFPA-certified that means the manufacturer isn't devastating natural forests, or destroying native communities, or using dangerous pesticides, or in general screwing with the planet."

"And if it's not?"

"Then he is. Even if he says he's not."

"IPS isn't a manufacturer," Franck pointed out.

"No, but they're the principal supplier of paper to the corporate sector and government agencies in France. And they're key players in several other European markets too. Over sixty percent of their paper sales involve non-WFPA products. If they refused to distribute them, they could force both consumers and manufacturers to face up to their responsibilities."

"I take it Guillaume Thèves wasn't amenable to your arguments?"

"Who?" she asked.

"Thèves. Runs this place. Or ran it," explained Franck. "He came out to chase you off yesterday, so I'm told."

"The big boss," she said, her lip curling. "Typical free market Pontius Pilate, washing his hands and saying the customers decide, he only supplies."

"Have you heard that he's dead?"

"Who?"

"Thèves. The big boss. Pontius Pilate. He was shot dead yesterday evening."

She seemed momentarily stunned, and then observed, "So there is some justice in the world."

Franck folded the leaflet once more and slid it into a pocket.

"Think I'll keep this after all."

*

You had to hand it to the café waiters: they certainly had an extraordinary sense of equilibrium. Even though the once-traditional race in which they ran several kilometres through Paris carrying trays loaded with glasses and bottles had disappeared a few years back, their ability to navigate a shifting crowd of customers, chair legs and undisciplined pets all day long with next to no spillage was a testimony to their hard-won dexterity. As for Franck, he was having a hard enough time holding a tray with two hands as he ascended one of the narrow staircases of the quai des Orfèvres.

He had stopped off at a café round the corner and asked if he could carry out two coffees complete with cups and saucers. Given that he was a regular, and was a significant source of revenue for its owner, his request was granted.

Although his sense of balance was not all it might be – his decision to place the saucers over the top of the cups as a means of reducing heat loss was not making things any easier – his instincts told him that the effort would not be wasted.

He was not mistaken.

Isabelle Arbaud had installed herself in his office. She wore a dark-blue pleated skirt whose narrow folds ran all the way up to the thin belt clutching her waist. A silver-grey silky top, a high-cut jacket and a thin silver neck chain completed her outfit. She was thumbing at a Blackberry with her elbows propped on his desk. Her handbag sat on the floor. She did not look round at him.

"Good evening, mademoiselle Arbaud," said Franck. He placed the tray on the table. "I can offer you some decent coffee this time."

She finished what she was doing and looked at him as he sat across from her. Franck immediately sensed a difference.

"Thank you," she said, reaching out to rearrange the cups so that they were sitting on the saucers. She took one from the tray and placed it before Franck. The other she lifted to her lips and drained in one smooth motion.

"You're here about Guillaume Thèves," said Franck.

She nodded. "I sat in a restaurant for an hour yesterday

evening waiting for a dead man. I'm hoping you'll take me a little more seriously now."

"Tell me about yesterday. Why this last-minute appointment with Thèves?"

She raised an eyebrow. "So you know about that? You work fast, captain."

"Call me Franck. I've just come back from talking to Thèves' secretary."

"What's she like?"

"What do you mean?"

"She sounds very young, rather vulgar, and a little too sure of her hold over her boss," said Isabelle.

"Never mind her. You don't want to know what she thinks you sound like."

"Oh, I can well imagine, Franck. Thèves liked his women ballsy and cheeky. She must think I'm a stuck-up irritating bitch."

"Something like that," conceded Franck. "You were frequently in contact?"

"No. But she managed Thèves' schedule like a jealous mistress. Since mine was always at least as tightly packed as his, my assistant had some memorable battles with her."

"But you fought one yourself yesterday. And won."

"Some victory, for all the good it did me."

"What did you have to talk to him about so urgently?"

"I wanted to change the funding schedule. The three founding loans were not paid in their entirety when they were granted. The money was to come in on fixed dates tied to the requirements of the original business plan. Since that plan has changed..."

"Because the perfume is running late," interjected Franck.

"Yes," confirmed Isabelle, glaring at him momentarily. He decided not to interrupt again. "When I announced that we could not hold to the original development plan, the investors insisted on modifying the funding schedule, pushing back the cash injections. Now that I have some good news, I wanted to bring them forward, but since both Chautard's and Perrin's estates are frozen, Thèves was the only person I could ask."

"What's the good news?"

"We're nearly there. Night-Scented is almost ready."

"This has something to do with the sample Justin brought you yesterday?"

She frowned, her eyes narrowing. "He told you? Justin should know better than that. There's too much at stake for him to be offering information to our competitors and enemies."

"I'm neither," Franck reminded her.

"Maybe not, but the best way to keep a secret – indeed, the only way to keep a secret – is never to utter it." This was a DST mantra, but he did not point it out to her.

"And that's the only reason you wanted to see Thèves yesterday?"

"Yes."

"Did anyone else know you'd made the appointment?"

"His secretary. My assistant. My Financial Director. Some of the rest of my staff. Whoever Thèves told. The front of house people at l'Arpège. In other words, all of Paris."

"Yes, but did anyone else know why you'd made the appointment?"

"I had discussed our funding requirements with my Financial Director and a few others inside Arbaud. I naturally informed Thèves of the purpose of the meeting. I don't know who he talked to." She paused, eyeing Franck. "Still, I'm glad to see you're finally thinking like me."

"I am?"

"You're wondering whether Thèves was killed to stop him agreeing to my request. After all, that's what's happened. His estate will now fall into the hands of his executors, and that'll take forever to work out. I bet even his secretary's waiting for a slice."

"So what are your options?" asked Franck.

"Financially?"

"Yes."

"We'll have to make do with what we've got. I have neither the time nor the inclination to seek out additional investors."

"Will it be enough?"

Isabelle allowed herself a short, bitter laugh. "I appreciate your concern for the success of my business, Franck. I would, though, rather see you showing a little more for my life."

"You think it's in danger?"

She took a deep breath and looked straight at him. Her chin did not tremble, her eyes remained steady, her breathing held calm, but Franck felt that she was allowing him to see something she was determined to hide from the rest of the world. He had the impression that her ears were pricked and her senses alert. That fear may have begun to stalk Isabelle Arbaud.

"There are no investors left. The only person left to come after is me."

*

"Nice place."

"I'm glad you like it."

Franck returned his gun to his briefcase. He had only taken it out to reassure her. It was a form of pantomime, but he hoped it would allow her to sleep more easily.

"Next time you might want to take off the safety catch," she observed, sweeping past him into the salon. He had forgotten that her father was a military man.

He had offered to escort her home. Her first reaction was to scoff at the suggestion that she was ready to go home, but she then surprised him by accepting his offer, providing they could nip back to the hôtel Lambert first. Franck walked her across the bridge that linked the Ile de la Cité to the Ile Saint Louis. They soon arrived at the hôtel Lambert, where she ensconced herself in her office for the next two hours.

Left to himself, Franck called Georges Sternberg to get some feedback on the forensics. To nobody's surprise, two

6.5mm calibre bullets had been found lodged in Guillaume Thèves. The rifling patterns recalled those from the Perrin hit. Thèves' car had been towed to a lab where they were waiting for the bleach to dry out. Sternberg's team would then check to see if any blood or other traces of biological material had survived or escaped its attention. The bleach had tested at twelve percent hypochlorite: industrial-strength, not for sale to the general public but readily available from a whole host of professional suppliers.

Franck spent the rest of the time reading his way through the abundant corporate propaganda to be found in the vestibule where he had been abandoned. Flicking through heavy glossy pages full of sumptuous photographs of beautiful women in striking surroundings, of interior and exterior shots of the hôtel Lambert, of Isabelle Arbaud speaking at industry events, and of the cadaverous profile of Louis Halphen, it was easy to forget that Arbaud was for the moment no more than an extraordinarily ambitious start-up and not a long-established fashion house. Franck found himself yielding grudgingly to admiration at the way Isabelle's communications strategy conjured up an as-yet hypothetical future state. That was when the memory of Gabriel Agostini, and the way he had talked of Appoghiu Terra as a potential global brand, came back to him. He stopped reading at that point, suddenly unwilling to trust his mind to the hands of marketeers of any persuasion.

When Isabelle emerged from her office the reception staff were long gone, although there were still people working in other areas of the hôtel. Franck was standing at a window that looked out onto the main courtyard, watching soberly dressed men and women peer into screens and conduct animated discussions in the building's opposite wing. Isabelle tapped him on the shoulder and told him she was ready to go.

They walked out the main entrance and round the corner to an underground parking garage. Isabelle took the wheel of a silver Alfa Romeo Spider, whose top was thankfully up to protect them against the chill of the evening. She drove them to the southern half of the sixteenth arrondissement, plunging into another subterranean garage beneath an apartment building on avenue Mozart. Franck forbore from pointing out that they could have made it in almost the same time by picking up the metro at Maubert Mutualité and getting off at Michel-Ange Auteuil. Taking the metro was no doubt not an Arbaud thing to do.

A lift took them from the garage to the fourth floor, where Isabelle unlocked the door to one of the four apartments accessible from the landing. She then nodded Franck ahead of her and he swept the place, gun in hand.

Her apartment had a small entrance hall, a large salon overlooking the street, a fitted kitchen which was large enough to accommodate a table for six, a bedroom holding a king-sized bed and a wide mirrored dressing table, a second bedroom which had been converted into a home office, a walk-in closet, a well-appointed bathroom and a separate toilet. A far cry from the seventeenth-century majesty of the hôtel Lambert, it was nonetheless three times bigger than Franck's one-bedroomed place in the fourteenth. Its front door was reinforced with steel and had a four-point locking system. It would take a professional to get through it. Unfortunately – given the precision with which Perrin and Thèves had been shot, and the care taken to clean both crime scenes – they were probably dealing with one.

Franck shrugged off his parka and hung it, and his briefcase, on an empty hat stand in the entrance hall. He then stepped into the salon.

Isabelle was sitting on the edge of one of two matching canapés. Her handbag lay on its side on a nearby low table. She had slipped off her shoes and folded her legs beneath her. Her pleated skirt was spread in a perfect half circle alongside her. Franck reckoned it could not have done so unaided.

"Thank you for accompanying me, captain," she said. So much for his first name. "But you ought to try harder to conceal the fact that you do not take my fears seriously. Not unless you are deliberately seeking to make me feel like a foolish young girl."

"You're wrong. I don't blame you for feeling concerned about your safety, Isabelle," he said, pausing to see if she would react to the use of her name. She did not seem to notice. "Yesterday you spoke with someone who was then shot dead on his way to see you. Nine days ago you invited someone to a fashion show only for him to be killed while he was there. It would be surprising if you didn't feel at least a little anxious for yourself."

"And several months ago I lost an investor in an incident no one has ever satisfactorily explained," she insisted.

Franck shook his head. "I've told you before. That was mere coincidence."

"So you did. But you also failed to provide any proof to back up your assertion."

Franck sighed. "Look, Chautard was not killed in the same way as the two others."

"In the same way?" she repeated. "You mean the fact that she wasn't shot, like Alain and Guillaume?"

"They weren't just shot. They were shot in a very distinctive fashion. In all probability, the killer used the same weapon both times."

"So the two cases are definitely linked," she stated.

"Yes," conceded Franck. "But don't assume that the link is necessarily Arbaud. Or, if it is, that it then extends to you."

"I am Arbaud," she declared. "Of course it extends to me."

"You're setting up a fashion house," exclaimed Franck, impatiently. "It's not an industry known for its fistfights, let alone its gunfights."

"You don't know what I know," she said, darkly. "You didn't run Ephémère's brand strategy for three years."

"You're telling me Francesca Craveri is in the habit of hiring hitmen? She might be Italian, but she's not from Sicily to the best of my knowledge."

"What do you know about Francesca Craveri!" exploded

Isabelle. "You have no idea what she's capable of."

"I've talked to her," said Franck, keeping his voice level. "More than once. I didn't get the impression I was conversing with a corporate killer, red in tooth and claw."

There was a pause. Isabelle ran the palm of her hand over the surface of the canapé on the opposite side from her skirt.

"Sit down, Franck," she said.

His first name was back. He did as he was told.

"Francesca Craveri has kept Ephémère in the struggle for the number one spot for twenty years." She spoke quietly, but intently. "She has poured her entire life into the firm. She has no children. She has no husband. She has no lovers. She has her success and her power, and that's all. She also knows that one day she will lose both. Do not underestimate what she will do to push that day as far into the future as she can."

Franck borrowed her tone. "Isabelle Arbaud has been preparing to set foot on the very same battleground for the last eighteen months, if not longer. She is pouring her entire life into the endeavour. She has no children. She has no husband. And nothing in this spotless apartment with its neatly tucked bed and strictly aligned towels suggests she has any lovers. Does that make her a homicidal maniac?"

"You dare to compare me with Francesca Craveri?" The question was one of wonderment, but tinged with anger. "Some would see that as the highest compliment you could pay me. But they would be wrong." Her tongue sharpened, her brow tipping to present a more menacing profile. "I am better than Craveri, and I will soon prove it. As for your deep understanding of female psychology, it might sound convincing when you're propped up against the counter of a café, but excuse me if I hold it in contempt."

Franck did not point out that he had simply played her portrait of Craveri back at her.

"I'm not judging you, Isabelle," he said, in as pacific a tone as he could manage. "I'm just cautioning against judging others. Give me one piece of information that makes Craveri look like a credible murder suspect and I'll pursue it relentlessly."

"Otherwise I just have to wait until the day she spits on my corpse?"

Even then she would not necessarily be caught. The bleach would just wash it off.

Saturday, 2nd February

"Fucking rich bastards with your fucking homes and fucking cars."

Franck heard him before he saw him. This time he would not intervene. Let him get run over. That way the others would get a little more sleep every morning.

Sleep was one thing he too could have done with a little more of. He had set his alarm for six, and could no longer remember when he had finally gone to bed last night. He had spent too much time trying to understand how Isabelle Arbaud could mutely appeal to him one moment and treat him with disdain the next.

Now he was hoping for another little chat with Michel. The André Citroen park-keeper had told him Michel was a regular morning visitor. The easiest way to get from the Alexandre III bridge to the Citroen park on foot was to follow the Seine. Michel might well know if there were any homeless people who frequented the banks of the river around the Mirabeau bridge. Given the current lack of witnesses to the Thèves shooting, Franck would take anything he could get.

He ignored the lunatic in the middle of the roadway playing torero with the passing cars. He clambered up onto the bridge's supporting girders and, helped once more by a torch, followed his now customary route up to Michel's nest.

It was empty. Or rather, Michel was not there, whereas his sleeping bag, his rucksack, his duffle bag with his cooking gear, his small store of food, and what Franck assumed were the rest of his worldly possessions were all there, neatly stored. It looked like he had chosen, or been forced, to spend the night elsewhere. Assuming that Michel would make his way back to his gear as soon as he could, Franck decided to wait for him. Squatting in the limited space available underneath the roadway that ran overhead quickly proved very uncomfortable, so Franck lay down on the wooden board that served as a floor. The pre-dawn chill, accentuated by the river passing below him, soon had him shivering, despite his parka. Although he hesitated to do so, he finally unrolled Michel's sleeping bag and burrowed inside it, having first removed his shoes. He did his best not to dwell on its lived-in smell, and listened instead to the irregular symphony of snores and muttering around him, underscored by the rumbling of the traffic on the bridge above. He wondered how anyone could sleep other than fitfully in such circumstances.

The first thing he noticed when he woke up was that day had finally dawned. The second thing he noticed was that something was tickling the side of his neck. The third was that a scrawny man with matted hair was leaning over him. His hand was holding a knife near Franck's jugular vein. Its tip shook.

"This is Michel's stuff," the man said. "It's not for taking."

As Franck tried to edge away from the blade it followed him, oscillating dangerously close to his skin.

"I'm a friend of Michel's," he said.

"If you were his friend, you wouldn't be touching his gear."

"I was waiting for him," Franck explained. "I must have fallen asleep."

"Sure." The man did not sound convinced.

"Let me show you something," said Franck. Very slowly he located the zip on the inside of the sleeping bag and tugged it down to his waist. He then opened his parka.

The man watched him warily.

"You're not homeless," he said.

"No," Franck confirmed, digging into an inner pocket of his parka and pulling out his ID.

The man glanced at it.

"Not every day I get to pull a knife on a *flic*."

He let a few seconds go by and then removed the blade, shifting back to sit on the nearest steel strut. This let Franck sit up.

"You're a *flic* and you say you're a friend of Michel's?"

Franck nodded. "Franck Guerin. Brigade Criminelle.

Michel and I have had a few chats recently."

"Well, Michel does have some strange friends," the man observed, slipping the knife into his belt under the heavy workman's jacket he was wearing. "I'm Paul, Paul Rosolin."

They shook hands.

"When you say strange friends, you mean stranger than me?" asked Franck, as casually as he could manage.

Rosolin snorted. "Michel talks to everybody. To the hopeless alcoholics, to the runaways turning tricks, to the road sweepers, to the rich folk in polished cars, and now to the *flics*."

"Do you know where he slept last night?"

"Not here, that's for sure. But if he told you to meet him here, he'll come. He's reliable, Michel. He's probably the only one of us who is."

"So where'd he go? Off on a bender? Give the road sweepers a hand?"

"You won't catch Michel drinking. Not anymore. He'll eat anything – even things most of us wouldn't touch – but he's sworn off the drink."

"But not off rich folk in fast cars?" asked Franck.

"I didn't say fast. I said polished. I know my cars."

"So we're not talking about a Spider, for instance?"

Rosolin shook his head. "More your BMW 5 Series."

Franck nodded appreciatively. "Expensive. Man or a woman?"

"Who?"

"Whoever's in the BMW."

"A young guy drives it. Well-dressed. Handsome. He gets out and opens the back door for Michel, like he was the President of the Republic."

"Anyone else in it? In the back seat?"

"Couldn't say. The windows are tinted black."

"He gets picked up here?"

"Yeah."

"This a regular thing?"

"Getting to be. Started two, three weeks ago. Has happened three times when I've been around."

"You remember when?"

"Day before yesterday, about a week before, and maybe another week before that."

"You can't be more precise?"

"Hey, I'm not his secretary."

"What about the last time?"

"What about it?"

"You say it was the day before yesterday. That means it was Thursday. Do you remember when the car came by?"

"Early in the morning, before sunrise."

"Seven thirty, eight, something like that?"

"Yeah, probably."

"Has he been back since?"

"No."

"Is that unusual?"

"We all disappear from time to time. Michel's no different from the rest of us when it comes to that."

"But when he goes off in this car, does he always stay away for two days?"

"Sometimes he doesn't come back that night. But he always comes back. Always brings food too. Fancy stuff. From traiteurs. Shares it out."

"He ever talk about who's behind the wheel? What goes on while he's away?"

"No."

"You've never asked him?"

"We joke about it, but he won't talk. Hey, it's up to him. You don't steal someone's gear, and you leave him his secrets."

Franck pulled out one of his cards and a ten-euro note.

"Next time this happens, call me, will you?"

Rosolin shook his head.

"Can't do that."

Franck sighed. "Will you tell Michel I came looking for

him?"

"I can do that."

"Fair enough," said Franck.

He climbed down from the bridge, thinking about well-groomed young men in the habit of chauffeuring expensive cars.

He had, perhaps, left Michel his secrets a little too long. And not just Michel.

*

"How do I get to see Louis Halphen again?"

"You don't."

Isabelle Arbaud's statement was flat and unequivocal.

"There has to be a way," insisted Franck, holding his mobile phone tight against his ear. He was walking along quai Anatole France, heading up the Seine towards his office, and there was a lot of traffic. "He can't be working round the clock."

"I don't think you understand me, captain." So today it was 'captain', not 'Franck'. "You don't get to see Louis Halphen." The emphasis was firmly on the 'you'.

"Says who?"

"I say so. The news about Thèves' death has done enough to destabilise him. I don't want you making things worse. This is a critical time for Night-Scented."

"I'm surprised he's upset. I didn't think he liked Guillaume Thèves," observed Franck.

"He didn't. But there are days when Louis doesn't particularly like me. Despite which, I doubt he's ever wished me dead. Anyhow, it's not the loss of Thèves that has disturbed him. It's the ring of death that seems to be closing in around Arbaud. Aren't you supposed to be doing something about that?"

"That's why I need to see him," said Franck, exercising his patience.

"Forget it. I forbid you to go anywhere near him. You

understand?"

"I hear you."

"That I do not doubt," said Isabelle. "But do you understand what I'm saying."

"I understand," said Franck.

"Good." She rang off.

Heard. Understood. But not acknowledged. She had forgotten the last of the three steps required to ensure a command is carried out.

There were, it seems, some things that her father had not taught her.

*

"I have an appointment with Louis Halphen."

It was a lie, but it could not be helped.

Having got nowhere on the phone with Isabelle Arbaud, Franck had considered two options. One was to sit in Saint Julien des Carmes, the church inside the Institut Catholique, and hope Halphen popped in for a little quiet contemplation. The other was to try rue Boileau in the sixteenth arrondissement, where he had said his lab was located. Although it was a Saturday, if Halphen was working against a deadline – assuming that it still held – Franck decided that the latter was probably the likeliest place to find him.

He veered up boulevard Saint Germain, switched to boulevard Raspail, and plunged into the metro at Sèvres-Babylone. A little over half an hour later he emerged at Michel-Ange Molitor, helping an old lady up the steps as he did so. He abandoned her politely and walked a hundred metres down rue Molitor to where it cut across rue Boileau. Not knowing the number of Halphen's laboratory, he chose at random to follow the southern branch of the street.

One side of rue Boileau was monopolised by individual houses hiding behind high walls, tall railings or overgrown trellises. The other side had been taken over by apartment buildings whose plunging viewpoints must have annoyed the owners of the houses no end.

Franck advanced slowly, reading the nameplates outside of each house. He discovered the existence of an international school run by the Algerian Embassy in a building whose brickwork had been enhanced by coloured tiles and a host of elegant touches. He was less impressed by the Vietnamese Embassy a little further on, a hideous concrete structure whose all-white facade clashed brutally with the colour scheme of the rest of the street. He felt sure that this must be a source of irritation to Louis Halphen, for the Embassy stood right next to a substantial three-storied house set back from the street behind a large gate which sported the number 54 and a discreet plaque bearing the perfumer's name.

He had found Halphen's lair. All that remained was to get inside. He tried his luck with the interphone to the right of the gate.

"Monsieur Halphen has no appointments today," he was told by a female voice.

"Ask Justin. He knows about it."

The intercom went dead. It remained that way for a quarter of an hour. Franck leant against the gate. A few minutes later he started pacing back and forwards. Normally he was good at waiting. Patience was one of his virtues, albeit less so on days when the only coffee he had tasted had been hastily gulped down four hours before.

The intercom came back. With a new voice this time. One he recognised.

"Who is this?"

"Good morning, Justin. It's captain Franck Guerin."

"I didn't know you had an appointment, captain."

"And if I had one, you would know, correct?"

"I'm afraid so."

"I need to see Louis Halphen."

"Believe me, captain. This is not the day for it."

"Justin, as of yesterday I'm investigating a double

homicide. I really don't care what is or is not convenient for you two."

"I have strict orders not to let you in."

"I don't give a damn what Halphen's told you."

"They don't come from monsieur Halphen," said Justin.

Franck blew the air from his lungs in frustration.

"She called?"

"Mademoiselle Arbaud called. About forty minutes ago. She had a feeling you might come over."

Clearly he was wrong to have doubted the quality of her instruction at her father's hands.

"You're obstructing the enquiry," stated Franck. "All I have to do is come back with a warrant."

A short pause followed.

"You say nothing about this to her," insisted Justin.

There was a buzzing sound. The gate opened, allowing him to step onto a wide expanse of gravel. A large black BMW was parked in the middle of it, its pristine bodywork gleaming in the cold morning sun. Franck paused alongside it, looking at his own reflection in the tinted windows.

The house stood to his right, a building that probably dated from the last years of the nineteenth century. Behind it he could see a glass-walled structure, and beyond that a smaller building which was probably once a carriage house. Franck walked across the gravel to the main house and opened the door. Upon stepping inside he discovered that the building's facade was its only remaining link to its past.

It had been gutted. Circular pillars sheathed in a form of opaque plastic had taken the place of the interior walls. The flooring was some of kind of synthetic stone that had been poured in place before being sealed and polished. He could see right through to the back of the building, where windows in aluminium frames looked out onto a massive conservatory full of plants. Off to his left a wide staircase of bright stainless steel led to the floor above. Desks and workbenches were positioned at regular intervals throughout the available space. Several computers were in evidence, as were a host of lab machines. Some seemed designed to spin, dry, or mix; others had purposes that were impossible to deduce. Many had extractor hoods hooked up to a network of gleaming pipes which snaked across the ceiling.

There were six white-coated figures in the room. With one exception, they did little more than glance at Franck before returning to their tasks in hand. The exception was Justin, who strode towards him. Underneath his white lab coat he was wearing a light-blue shirt, khaki chinos and spotless white tennis shoes. He had an elasticated polythene cap over his hair.

He shook Franck's hand.

"I'm afraid some of this has to come off," he said.

Following his instructions, Franck took off his parka, sweater, and shoes, depositing them, along with his briefcase, in a locker that sat in a row of its fellows to the side of the door he had just come through. He was given a lab coat and a pair of tennis shoes that were slightly too large for him. Justin helped him fit a transparent cap over his head, looping the elastic behind his ears. They then washed their hands in concert, with Justin instructing him on the proper circular motion to use to clean the area between his knuckles and the tips of his fingers.

"So this is it," declared Franck, once the ritual cleansing was completed. "The wizard's lair."

"Actually, no. That's upstairs. Sometimes it's even upstairs from upstairs, since there are two floors above us. Down here we prep things and develop ways to industrialise what monsieur Halphen comes up with."

"And these are all Noses?" asked Franck, sweeping his hand to take in the other five people.

"No, these are all chemical engineers. There's only one Nose here."

"Where is he?"

"Two flights up," said Justin, pointing to the ceiling.

"Should I go up, or can we call him down?"

"I let you in, captain, but that doesn't mean you can see him immediately. He's occupied. You'll have to wait until he takes a break."

"When will that be?"

"I have no idea."

"While we're waiting, and so as not to upset monsieur Halphen's delicate temperament, I'll ask you – where were both of you on Thursday evening?"

"Here," said Justin.

"Until when?"

"Till about one in the morning, I think."

"Just the two of you?"

"No. The entire lab crew was here."

"What about Thursday morning? Before I ran into you at the hôtel Lambert."

"Let me think." Justin paused momentarily. "I went to monsieur Halphen's apartment, expecting to run him to the lab. He told me to go on my own, to collect the sample we'd been working on the previous evening and take it to Isabelle Arbaud. While I did that he went to church and I picked him up afterwards."

"When did you get to his apartment?"

"Just after eight, probably."

"You already had the car by then?"

"Yes. I'd dropped him off the previous evening and kept the car."

"Pick anything up on the way to rue Vavin that morning?"

"Like what?" asked Justin.

"Anything at all."

"No, I don't believe I did." Justin frowned at Franck. "Is something the matter, captain?"

"I don't know," said Franck. "That's why I have to talk to your boss."

"I'll let you know when he is free."

"So what do I do? Take a seat and fiddle with one of your strange machines?"

"You can wait in the conservatory," suggested Justin. "It's a little less ... sterile ... than here."

He led Franck across the building to what looked like an airlock with two sets of sliding doors. On the other side stood the conservatory, which had a vast white-painted steel frame that curved away from the rear of the house and rose to a point four or five metres above them. Seen from outside it must have looked like the hull of an overturned ship. They went through the double doors, which opened and shut alternately.

The air was temperate and very slightly humid. Plants grew from aluminium trays set on low benches alongside a fair number of bushes and small trees kept in individual wooden caissons. Given the variety of forms, Franck suspected that he was looking at species from all around the world. One thing was clear: they had been chosen as much for their scent as for their beauty.

In the centre of the conservatory, where the roof swelled to its highest point, was a circular wooden deck that stood slightly above the tiled floor. It bore six wooden chairs gathered in a circle around two low-lying tables. Franck took a seat and succumbed to Justin's offer of coffee.

Justin returned ten minutes later with a tray carrying a brushed aluminium flask, a white porcelain cup and saucer and a selection of reading material, running from the previous day's *Le Monde* to the copy of *Vogue* with Sonia Delemazure on the cover.

"Try to be patient," Justin advised him as he left.

Franck tried, but by the time he had read through *Le Monde*, flicked through a copy of *Cahiers du Cinéma*, and begun listlessly browsing *Vogue*, he was beginning to wish he had just barged upstairs when he arrived.

"I didn't take you for a *Vogue* reader, captain," said Louis Halphen.

Franck looked around. Halphen was gently stroking the wide fronds of a nearby clump of ferns.

"It's a world which I know very little about," said Franck. "But it keeps dragging me in."

"Well, if you are immune to its blandishments, you are probably better placed than most to deal with it," said Halphen, skirting the table bearing the ferns and stepping up onto the deck. He chose a chair opposite Franck. "You wanted to see me?"

"Yes. I know you're very busy, so I'm grateful that you've taken some time out to talk to me."

"Rest assured, captain, I have done nothing of the sort. I cannot work all day non-stop. I have to pause to let my mind settle, refresh my senses, and renew my instincts. That is why I have descended from my laboratory and come out here. I did so despite knowing of your presence, not because of it."

"Where's Justin?"

"Sorry?"

"Is Justin still inside?"

"I expect so," said Halphen. "He didn't follow me out. Do you want me to call him? Would you like some more coffee?"

"No. I want to ask you some questions about him. I'd prefer him not to be around while I'm doing so."

Halphen shrugged. "Ask your questions, captain. Although I give you no guarantee that I will not repeat them to him afterwards."

"That's up to you. How long have you known Justin?"

"He has been working for me since I left Ephémère. My former assistant elected to stay behind when I accepted Isabelle Arbaud's offer to work exclusively for her. I am sure he rues the day he made that decision."

"You didn't know Justin before then?"

"No."

"So how did he get the job?"

"Isabelle found him for me. He had all the right qualifications – he is intelligent, industrious, loyal, and has the highest regard for my work and my gifts. He is also rather handsome, as I trust you have noticed."

"I suppose he is," conceded Franck. "You've never regretted your choice?"

"Never."

"Even after he let me in here today, despite Isabelle Arbaud forbidding him to do so?"

"His job is to do my bidding, not that of Isabelle Arbaud – even if she is the one who pays his salary. In any case, I prize his sense of initiative. I need someone who can anticipate, who knows the right thing to do without waiting for me to instruct him."

"Letting me in was the right thing to do?"

"Of course. That way I could see you at my convenience. If he had turned you away, you would have found some way to force yourself upon us at yours. Is that not so?"

"I suppose it is," admitted Franck. "So he's the perfect employee?"

"Perfection is a lot to ask for, captain. You can aim for it in a perfume, but to seek it in a human being is a sure path to deception. However, to answer your question another way, I am very glad I offered him the job."

"Whatever you ask him to do, he does?"

Halphen frowned and fixed Franck with a long, silent stare.

"You are clearly a man who likes lifting rocks in the hope of finding squirming insects beneath them. It is a most distasteful habit," he said, rising to his feet. "I must return to my work now, captain. I suggest you do the same. I believe you have a few murders to solve – Nathalie Chautard, Alain Perrin, and now the boorish Guillaume Thèves. I wish you luck."

He began to move through the conservatory. Franck left his seat and caught up with him as he entered the outer door of the airlock.

"There are a lot of rocks in the world. When I choose one in particular to turn over, I generally have a good reason for doing so," said Franck.

Halphen looked at him blankly. The inner door opened and he strode out.

"I'm going back upstairs," he announced. "Justin, I want

you to come with me."

"Your lack of cooperation may return to haunt you," Franck called out as Halphen and his assistant began to ascend the stairs. "Other lives may be at stake."

"You think so?" replied Halphen. "Whoever it is has three out of three. His collection is complete."

For a man supposedly terrorised by the ring of death closing in around him, Louis Halphen seemed remarkably serene.

*

"I'm looking for Paul Rosolin."

All he got in return was an uncomprehending stare. A couple of cars had gone past while he was speaking, the sound of their rapid passage reverberating under the bridge. It was half ten in the evening and the Saturday night traffic was flowing recklessly along the riverside.

Franck repeated himself. The man he had addressed turned his head and shouted Paul's name. Others picked it up and did the same, a wave of cries spreading out across the steel fretwork of the Alexandre III bridge. Most of the improvised nests it sheltered were occupied, although few of the inhabitants seemed to be asleep. Huddled bodies in blankets or sleeping bags sat in ones or twos, some content with the fitful light produced by the nearby road lights, others equipped with lanterns screwed to small gas canisters. A number were heating meals or drinks over camping stoves in dangerous proximity to a host of inflammable material.

A figure came down one of the bridge's beams, moving confidently. When he got closer Franck recognised Rosolin, who this time greeted him without a knife in his hand.

"Is that you again, captain?"

"I'm afraid it is."

Rosolin hopped down to stand on the roadside beside Franck. They shook hands and bowed their heads alongside each other to overcome the noise of the traffic.

"Two visits in the same day? You really do need to see Michel, don't you?"

"Has he been back?"

"No. Nobody's seen him."

"I'd like to wait for him," said Franck.

"You'll probably end up standing there all night for nothing," Rosolin warned him.

"I thought I'd sleep in his place. Wait for him like that. Would that be OK? I've brought my own sleeping bag." He turned slightly to show Rosolin the rucksack on his back.

"Well, normally we don't let strangers in. But since you're a friend of Michel's. And you won't be touching his gear..."

"And I've brought some beers," added Franck.

"I wouldn't say that too loud," cautioned Rosolin. "There're over twenty people up there."

"I've brought a dozen cans. They can pass them around."

"In which case, you are officially our guest."

"Thank you," said Franck.

"Just one thing, though."

"Yes?"

"When Vincent starts yelling at the cars tomorrow morning, could you shut him up?"

"Is that possible?"

"You could try shooting the bastard. Between the eyes should do it."

Sunday, 3rd February

"Fucking cars going so fucking fast! Think I can't catch you?"

Vincent the torero was certainly an early riser. Franck first became aware of him just before seven. Nobody else seemed to be paying him any attention, presumably having learned to filter him out. Franck was actually surprised to find that he had been asleep when the shouting started. The night had been long, cold and uncomfortable. He felt sure he had spent most of it shifting in place to subdue the complaints from his back and his sides and to attempt to generate a little warmth inside his sleeping bag. If in the end he had got beyond fitful dozing it must have been utter exhaustion that did the trick.

He wished he could go back to sleep now, but knew it would be impossible. His spine was stiff and his legs ached from having been hunched up against him all night in a desperate attempt to conserve body heat. He unzipped his sleeping bag and rolled up onto his knees. He was already in his parka, having taken it off before bedding down and then retrieved it at some point in the middle of the night.

A number of sounds came in quick succession. A car horn blaring, rubber squealing as it was dragged at high speed across an unyielding surface, and then the sound of metal crumpling against stone.

Vincent himself made no noise. The front of the car caught him side-on, folding him violently down onto the hood, then up against the windshield, before tossing him onto the road. The car carried on for another twenty metres, sliding into and along the crash barrier that separated it from the waters of the Seine.

Franck was the first to come down from the beams supporting the bridge. Vincent lay on his back, his legs skewed at an unnatural angle, his arms splayed out, his face covered in torn skin. His eyes were blinking rapidly, fighting against the blood welling into them from cuts across his forehead. Franck gently laid his left hand across Vincent's eyebrows, taking care not to move his head, and dug into the pockets of his parka in the hope of finding something he could use to staunch the flow of blood. Vincent's lips were moving, but in the noise that now enveloped them – shouting, other cars braking, feet running – Franck could not hear him. He bent his head to lay his ear directly above Vincent's mouth.

"Fucking bastards in their fucking cars," whispered Vincent, over and over again.

"You're right about that," murmured Franck.

His other hand had found his mobile phone. He turned it on, waited for a signal, and tapped in 15 to call for an ambulance.

Others were now crowding around them, kneeling down and reaching out to Vincent.

"Don't move him!" Franck warned them. "Stand back until the ambulance comes."

A hand appeared before him, palm open, bearing a white packet whose top had been ripped off. Inside was a surgical dressing. Franck extracted it, lifted his now-bloody palm, and placed the bandage delicately above Vincent's eyes, where it immediately became a vivid red.

"You got more?" asked Franck.

"Lots." It was Paul Rosolin. "I can take over if you like, captain. I've some medical training. Basic combat stuff."

Franck stepped back, yielding to the other's expertise.

"You'd better get over there," said Rosolin, nodding downstream. "You might be needed."

The car had stopped at an angle to the crash barrier along the Seine. Its front right wing was crumpled. The driver's door on the opposite side had been thrown open and the driver was trying to extricate himself from the safety belt and the airbag that pinned him against his seat. Three of the homeless stood waiting for him, their fists clenched.

Franck strode over and waved them aside.

"He killed Vincent!" one of them protested.

"Vincent's not dead yet," insisted Franck, "despite doing his best to kill himself. This guy didn't have a chance. Let him out."

The driver, a man in his early fifties, dressed in a sober churchgoing suit, was making little progress.

"You OK?" asked Franck.

"I think so," said the driver, stopping in his struggle. "Nothing broken, as far as I can tell. Heart's racing though. How is he?"

"Doesn't look good."

"There was nothing I could do. He just stood there, like he was daring me. I wasn't even going particularly fast. I didn't see him until I was under the bridge." His explanation came in staccato bursts.

"You're right. There was nothing you could do. If it hadn't been you, it would have been somebody else. Today, tomorrow, in a week's time." Franck said this hoping that it would help, but knew that the driver would have to deal with his memories of this morning for a long, long time. "Stay there."

Franck headed back to Rosolin, who was on his knees over Vincent, talking to him calmly. He had added a few more surgical dressings, building a dam of clotted blood and cloth across his forehead.

"Got your knife?" asked Franck.

Rosolin pulled it from a sheath attached to his belt. An infantry knife with a nylon grip and a half-serrated blade. He shifted his hand instinctively to present it to Franck grip first. As Franck took it he could sense Rosolin's hand shaking. Maybe Vincent meant more to him than Franck imagined.

"Thanks," said Franck and returned to the car, where he punched it into the airbag and drew it downwards, opening a large gash and deflating it immediately. He stepped back and extended his other hand to help the driver out. The driver looked at it, frowned at the blood, and got out on his own.

"Take a seat over there," Franck suggested, pointing to the crash barrier, whose inner surface bore the scars of the car's passage. "The police will soon be here. They'll take your statement."

The driver mutely followed his instructions.

"Somebody get him a blanket and something hot to drink," Franck told the handful of homeless who were still hovering around the car. One of them nodded and headed back to the colony under the bridge.

Franck looked around for something on which he could wipe his bloody hand. Finding nothing, he sat on the crash barrier, a few metres away from the still-shaken driver. His fingers reached out to trace the scrape marks left by the car, a mixture of freshly revealed concrete and blue metallic paint.

He was still there twenty minutes later when Paul Rosolin brought him a plastic bucket whose handle was attached to a coil of rope.

An ambulance had been and gone. Vincent had been clamped into an external body frame and carried off. A police car was still on the scene. Traffic had been stopped further upstream.

"It's the Seine. It's all we've got," said Rosolin, handing him a worn and scarred bar of soap.

Franck began to wash his hands in the frigid water.

"Remember you told me about the car that picked Michel up?" asked Franck. "The one with the tinted windows?"

Rosolin looked puzzled for a moment, his mind presumably too involved with all that had just happened. "The BMW?"

"Yes, the BMW. Can you remember the paint job? Was it black?"

"No. Not black. Lighter. Much lighter. Kind of silvery. Why?"

The wrong colour. At least as far as Halphen's BMW was concerned, but the image of another chauffeur-driven car of the same make suddenly came to Franck.

"Doesn't matter. Not right now."

Franck pulled his freezing hands from the water. Rosolin carried the bucket to the crash barrier, tipped out its contents, and dropped it into the river, hauling it back up again with the rope.

"Again," he said.

Without asking why, Franck plunged his hands back into the bucket and began rubbing his palms against each other. Rosolin wandered away. As Franck was emptying the bucket back into the Seine he came back.

"Clean," announced Franck, holding up his hands for inspection.

"Not yet," said Rosolin.

He swung up a large white plastic canister and screwed off the top. He poured about five centimetres into the bucket.

"Steep your hand in that for at least five minutes. It'll burn your skin, but it won't kill you."

Franck did not move. He was studying the label on the canister. Industrial-strength bleach. Twelve percent.

"What's this for?" he asked.

"Vincent has hepatitis C," explained Rosolin. "Believe me, you don't want to catch it. Bleach is nasty, but it kills everything stone-dead. Anyhow, you've not got the prettiest of hands."

*

"What is it with you and early morning calls?"

Franck thought the charge a little unjust. Half a year had gone by since he had last called Sonia Delemazure unfashionably early, but her number was still hidden away in a corner of his phone.

She yawned at him.

"Sorry Sonia, I won't keep you long," he said.

It was now after eight, and the sun had begun to rise. He stood on top of the Alexandre III bridge, watching the light catch the gold on its statues and on the roofs of its near neighbours, the Invalides and the Grand Palais. Franck found himself unable to surrender to the beauty of the scene. He felt sure that there was little hope for Vincent, and Michel had still not turned up. A comfortless night had afforded him the spectacle of an inevitable accident and the discovery that Paul Rosolin had spent five years in the army before, with a little help from the bottle, switching ranks to join that of the homeless. The more information he gathered in this enquiry, the muddier the waters seemed to become.

"Want to join me for brunch in, let's see, five hours time?" suggested Sonia. "I'm meeting some friends. You'd add an exotic touch."

"I've just spent a night sleeping under a bridge. I'm not really presentable."

"You do lead an interesting life, captain. And five hours aren't enough to make you presentable? Actually, I take that back – five weeks wouldn't be enough to make you presentable. Particularly if you keep spurning others' attempts to make you so. Do you have any idea how much some people would pay for a one-off coat by Marco Chiriotti?"

"You would have been happy if I'd slept rough in a designer coat?"

"Good point. But I'm serious about brunch. Come as your scruffy self. I can introduce you to some nice girls. Or some nice men if you prefer. Put an end to that sad and single thing you've got going."

"Who said I was sad?"

"Your eyes, captain. You've got little abandoned puppy eyes."

"Right now my little puppy eyes are bleary and bloodshot and have just seen a homeless man broken into pieces by a car."

Sonia sighed petulantly. "You do like to share the misery around, don't you? What was it you wanted?"

"Do you know where Francesca Craveri lives?" he asked.

"You're planning on calling on Francesca Craveri at home, uninvited?" she asked, scandalised.

"I won't tell her you told me."

"You'd better not. Rue Guynemer, right against the Jardin du Luxembourg."

"What number?"

"You think she's ever invited me to dinner? I don't know."

"In which case, I'll tell you once I've found out. You can go back to sleep now."

"I'd better. Otherwise I'll just end up snacking, and you'll be responsible for destroying my promising career."

*

"You picked that up off the street?"

It was a fair question. With his rumpled clothes and messed-up hair, he probably looked like he had. At least his unwashed state was cloaked by the smell of bleach emanating from the red and raw left hand which held his police ID.

"There's a number on it you can call if you like," suggested Franck.

He was facing his fifth doorman: the one thing that had become abundantly clear over the past hour was that those who surveyed the comings and goings of the apartment buildings on rue Guynemer saw themselves as inhabiting a higher sphere than that of simple concierges. All thus far had been male. All wore shirts and jackets. Most had ties. Their general demeanour indicated that polishing shiny surfaces, cleaning stairs and taking out garbage were far beneath them.

"Well, captain Guerin – if that really is who you are – what do you want?"

"I'm trying to locate the residence of Francesca Craveri, managing director of the Ephémère group."

"And you think madame Craveri would like anyone and everyone to know where she lives?"

"Probably not. But if she knew someone from the Brigade Criminelle needed to talk to her, and it happened to be someone she has already invited several times to her office and private soirées, she might not be happy to discover he was turned away like a homeless tramp."

"Even if that's what the someone looks like?"

"Appearances can be deceptive."

"Not in rue Guynemer, believe me."

Their exchange was interrupted by a buzzing sound. Someone was standing outside the plate-glass door which sealed the privileged lives of the building's inhabitants from the public thoroughfare outside. A man in his early thirties in sharply creased black trousers, a black sweater and a long wool coat that hung open on his spare frame nodded familiarly to the doorman. He was carrying four large bouquets of freshly cut flowers and a paper carrier bag from which some *viennoiseries* could be seen to be peeking. Behind him, at the side of the kerb, sat a car whose engine was still running. It was a silver-grey BMW 520. Its windows were tinted.

The doorman abandoned Franck and walked to a marble-topped counter which was his customary vantage point over the entrance hall. He pressed a hidden switch. The outer door clicked open and the man stepped in.

"Just dropping these off. I'll move the car in two minutes. Promise."

Franck stepped in front of him, blocking his passage. He took out one of his cards and slipped it between the knuckles of the man's right hand, which was clenched around the stem of a bouquet.

"Give this to madame Craveri. Tell her I'd like to see her. Nice car, by the way."

He only had to wait four minutes. A phone rang on the doorman's counter.

Having listened silently the doorman said, "Very good, madame."

Franck raised his eyebrows, awaiting the verdict. The doorman pointed him towards the lift.

"Fifth floor on the right."

When he reached the fifth floor the driver was waiting to take his place.

"Here," said Franck, giving him a card for himself. "I may have to talk to you later."

"In which case," said the driver, reaching inside his coat, "have one of mine."

Franck glanced at his card. It bore the Ephémère logo, named him as Richard Louvel, and provided a mobile number and an email address.

"You've got email in the car?" he asked.

"It's the twenty-first century," commented the driver, stepping into the lift. "My car's more intelligent than me." A sliding door then hid him from sight.

There were only two doorways on the landing. Franck went to the one on the right, which was slightly ajar.

He knocked gently with a knuckle.

"Come in, Franck," came the voice of Francesca Craveri. "I'm just putting the flowers in water."

He stepped into a sizeable hall where he shrugged off his parka and hung it on one of the three coat stands to hand. He could hear a tap running off to his right, down a short corridor. It soon stopped and Francesca appeared, dressed in a black dress cinched at the waist with a silk ribbon and enlivened by a translucent purple scarf draped around her shoulders. Her flat ballerina shoes were the same shade. Her black hair was unbound. She smiled broadly at him.

"This is a surprise, Franck," she said, coming up and kissing him on each cheek. "You do look a little crumpled, if you don't mind me saying so. And what on earth is that smell?"

Franck held up his left hand.

"You don't want to know why, but I had to marinate this in bleach earlier on."

"You're absolutely right I don't want to know why, but let me see it."

She reached out and lightly took his wrist, teasing his hand towards her.

"Your skin will take some time to forgive you for this," she commented.

"It's seen worse."

"That's no excuse. You really ought to take more care of

yourself. Come with me."

She steered him into an enormous salon which looked out over the Jardin du Luxembourg. Large enough to have five sets of double windows dominating the park, the room also boasted a ceiling six metres high and a mezzanine reached by a twisting set of brushed aluminium stairs with no guardrail. This time the furnishings had nothing to do with Louis XV, but reflected the streamlined fashions and futuristic aspirations of the twenties and thirties. Francesca deposited Franck on one of the room's four three-seater leather canapés and briefly disappeared back the way she had come.

When she returned it was with a box of moisturising wipes and a small plastic tube. She sat beside him, placed his hand in her lap, and slowly cleaned its back, palm, wrist and five fingers with the wipes, depositing those she had used on a low-lying table that was built in the canapé's armrest. She then flipped the top off the tube and squirted a generous helping of a white cream onto the back of Franck's hand.

"Hold it up," she instructed.

Franck lifted his hand horizontally before her and she began to massage the cream into his skin, turning his hand as she did so.

"An Ephémère cream?" asked Franck.

"No. We do cosmetics, but we don't do skincare. Skincare is for scientists. It's a bit too clinical for us. But, if it reassures you, this is a very good product. I have trusted my skin to it for years."

"Not cheap, I take it?"

"No," she said, matter-of-factly. "I have the good fortune to be able to afford it."

When she had finished, she returned Franck's hand to him.

"Feel better?" she asked.

"That's certainly soothed it."

"Good."

She placed the now half-empty tube on the side table, crossed her legs, and let her hands fall into her lap.

"Would you like some coffee? I have a fine selection of croissants, *pains au chocolat* and brioches, as you might have noticed when you bumped into Richard. I have some friends coming over at eleven but there's more than enough, if you're tempted."

"I'm fine," said Franck. "Thank you."

"What brings you to my home on this day of rest? Assuming you have days of rest, which I somehow doubt, given your current condition."

"It's got something to do with Richard Louvel."

"My driver?"

"Not so much him, as the people he picks up for you."

"He does a lot of that," said Francesca. "He must spend half his life waiting at Roissy airport. We always make a point of sparing our visitors an encounter with Parisian taxi drivers."

"It's not Roissy that interests me. It the Alexandre III bridge. A certain Michel."

Francesca looked at him appraisingly.

"You know of Michel? You are quite a detective, Franck. I thought he was my little secret."

"Well, if you don't mind, could you share it with me?"

"How much do you know already?" she asked.

"I've talked to him twice. He's a homeless man. He's called Michel. He's never told me the rest of his name. He was in the André Citroen park the day Alain Perrin was killed..."

"He was?" interrupted Francesca. "He never told me that. What was he doing there?"

"Looking for something to eat apparently. He came back later to scavenge when the extension was being taken down."

Francesca shook her head. "What a waste," she said quietly, more to herself than to him.

"And your driver has picked him up at least three times, including last Thursday, since when he hasn't been back to the bridge."

"He hasn't? That's strange. I'm pretty sure he left early Thursday evening. But, now that you mention it, he said he didn't need a ride back to the bridge. We could try phoning him, if you like."

"He has a phone?"

"Of course."

Francesca crossed the room and retrieved a mobile phone from where it lay on a bookshelf. She keyed up a number and held the phone to her ear.

"He's on voice mail. He generally is. I'll leave him a message – Michel, this is Francesca. I'm with captain Franck Guerin of the Brigade Criminelle, who seems a bit worried about you. Do call me back if you can."

She replaced the phone on the shelf.

"I'm afraid Michel only turns his phone on when the fancy takes him. Which is not very often. I suppose the fact that he's got nowhere to charge it has something to do with it. In any case, I don't think I've ever succeeded in talking to him directly since we gave it to him."

"Francesca," said Franck. "I'm still a little lost – 'I'm pretty sure he left early Thursday evening' – left where?"

"I must ask you to use this information in confidence," she said.

"I'm investigating a double homicide. I don't have much leeway."

"Michel has nothing to do with these crimes. If there's anything we can be sure of, it's that. Let me explain, and I will trust you to use your discretion with what I tell you."

Franck nodded.

"The homeless man you know as Michel is called Michel Verdier. Six years ago he was the most promising Nose of his generation."

"I thought that was Halphen."

"More than twenty years separate them. Different generations. Louis Halphen already reigned supreme when Michel burst onto the scene in a big way. At twenty-eight he created several perfumes for major fashion houses, each one utterly original. Some said a little too original, and it's true that none of them managed to carve a niche. They were all pulled off the market within a year at most. But everybody who worked with him came out of it stunned at his talent – his olfactory sensitivity, the range of his palette, the imaginative leaps of which he was capable when creating new combinations. He was audacious. Recklessly so, said some. But in a profession where self-doubt lurks constantly in the background, creating a constant temptation to err on the side of prudence, he certainly stood out."

"I've not met many Noses," commented Franck. "But I can't say I've the impression that Louis Halphen is given to self-doubt."

"You are wrong. Louis' immense gifts have left him isolated, marooned on a pinnacle far above the rest of his profession. There is no one with whom he can confer, no one to whom he can look for confirmation that he is on the right track. Were his confidence never to waver, his trust in his own judgement never to falter, he would have to be insanely arrogant."

"He's not?"

"No, Franck, he is not. Take it from someone who worked with Louis for a long, long time. I could do only two things for him – give him all the resources he required – within reason, of course, which is why I lost him – and reassure him of his impeccable taste as and when necessary."

"So Halphen was no exception, but this Michel Verdier was?"

"What made Michel so different was that he was not afraid to be wrong. Or rather, that he refused the very notion of 'wrong'. The rest of us divide smells into two broad categories – attractive or repulsive, alluring or irritating, suggestive or offensive. We seek the delicate scent of a rose and flee that of the farmyard. To Michel this was absurd. For him there was no such thing as a good or bad smell. Every odour had a tale to tell."

"*Humani nihil a me alienum puto*?" offered Franck.

"More *naturae nihil a me alienum puto*," suggested Francesca in return. "It's nice to see that your literary knowledge is not limited to your own countrymen but extends to encompass mine."

"I'm not sure Terence would agree with that. Wasn't he Carthaginian?"

Francesca thought for an instant, her brow creased, and then smiled. "I do believe you're right, Franck. I stand corrected."

"So why is this avant-garde Nose sleeping under the Alexandre III bridge?"

"Why indeed? Because life is a cruel mistress. I tried to bring Michel to Ephémère. I persuaded him that, if there was one person from whom he could learn, it was Louis Halphen. I told him he had everything to gain from trying to assimilate Louis' sense of balance and harmony. He accepted. He agreed to work under his guidance on a project for us."

"I'm not sure I'd have volunteered to work under Halphen," said Franck. "And I've put up with some very unforgiving bosses. One in particular."

"Well, it didn't work out. They fought endlessly, pitilessly, a war of zealots. Admiration for the other's talents turned to contempt for the other's lack of judgement, or vision, or whatever it was they found to despise in each other. I had to separate them. I even had to separate Michel from Ephémère, otherwise Louis threatened to leave."

"So, when forced to choose, you preferred Halphen. I suppose that means that he was indeed the greater Nose?"

"At the time Louis was in his late forties. Michel in his late twenties. Both had astounding gifts. But Louis was a mature artist and had proved that he had staying power. Michel was a young rebel, and history has shown that rebels tend to burn bright and fast. The decision I had to make was a bit like choosing between Boileau and Rimbaud. I chose Boileau. Ephémère is, fundamentally, a classical fashion house. We have a century of tradition behind us, and we refuse to disown it. Louis Halphen was exactly right for us, and we for him."

"So you turned your back on Michel, and that sent him on a downward spiral?"

"Nothing of the sort. We set up a company for Michel."

"We, as in Ephémère?"

"Of course. But I hid the fact that we were behind it – from Louis, above all. With the new company I gave Michel *carte blanche*. I didn't give him much money, but I freed him from all constraints and waited to see what happened."

"What did?"

"Life got in the way." She paused. "I believe you've spent some time with Louis Halphen?"

"Yes."

"Louis is an anchorite. Acutely aware of the unique nature of his gift, he sees it as his duty to protect it from everything he perceives as a potential threat. He lives in isolation. He seeks total control over what he tastes, what he touches, what he sees, what he hears, what he smells. He is convinced that the only way he can exercise his art is by placing himself in the midst of a blank canvas. Outside of his laboratory, Louis takes no risks. He refuses to interact with the world in which you and I live because he believes that it will debase, blunt, or corrupt him."

"He might be right," observed Franck. "It's a pretty unforgiving place."

"But there is a difference between prudence and paranoia, and Louis has great difficulty making that distinction. Anyhow, I bring Louis up only because on this point the difference between him and Michel could not have been greater. Michel would have laughed at the idea that an artist's essence lay in his fragility, in the very delicacy of his talent. Michel believed that an artist's ambition and ability were both expressions of his vitality. Where Louis shut out the world, Michel plunged into it."

"There was nothing he would not smell, or taste," anticipated Franck, thinking of his two encounters with Michel.

"Or touch, or lend his ear to, or gaze upon," Francesca continued. "Michel lived as you would expect a young man in his twenties to live. He embraced every opportunity and refused few, if any, temptations. He immersed himself in the world."

"And destroyed himself in the process?"

"Not in the way you are thinking. Open as he was to every sensation, every feeling, it was inevitable that when Michel fell in love, he would fall as long and as hard as Satan did from heaven."

"So this is a tale of a broken heart?"

"This is a tale of a heart crushed underfoot. Michel's soulmate – for once the term is appropriate – was a photographer called Hughes, Hughes Tabard. Hughes was like Michel in every way – as adventurous in his life as he was in his profession. In a sense, it was as well Hughes lived so intensely, as he was given less time than the rest of us. He developed liver cancer, and fought with it for seven months. During that time Michel never left his side. He withdrew entirely from his professional commitments. He told me to wind up the firm we had created for him, as he couldn't say when or if he would be back."

"And when Hughes died?"

"When Hughes died, Michel disappeared. Utterly. Walked out of his apartment and into oblivion. Left his money – his bank accounts were never touched again – his clothes, his art collection, his friends, everything. The police were called in. Many people were convinced something must have happened to him. Or that he had committed suicide. Samples were even taken from his apartment to identify his genetic fingerprint in case his corpse turned up in some unimaginable state. Then the years went by and he was forgotten."

"It's not easy staying off the grid," commented Franck. "But if you're homeless, you never seek work, you stay out of trouble, and you live with whatever cash you can get your hands on, then it's doable. When did he resurface?"

"Three weeks ago. One morning I arrived at our offices and saw him standing on the other side of place François Premier."

"He was waiting for you?"

"Yes. I didn't pay much attention to him at first, but each time I looked out a window that day the same figure was there, like a statue that had sprouted on the spot. I began to study him. It was clear that he was watching our offices, and little by little I began to believe he was looking specifically for me. At one point in the afternoon a member of our security staff went over to chase him away. He refused to budge. And then, for some reason, I suddenly knew who it had to be. I called off security and went out myself. We talked there, in the middle of the street. He refused to come into the building, because he didn't want to be recognised and have everyone make a fuss of him."

"No killing of the fatted calf."

"Exactly. So we arranged that I would have him picked up one evening and brought to a place where we could talk."

"What did he want?" asked Franck.

"To help me. He knew that with Louis' departure, Eternal had been frozen in time. He offered to take over. To keep it evolving."

"Weren't you worried that he might have lost his touch?"

"No. And I was right. Michel had not lost his touch, he had improved it. His range was even greater than before. Much more importantly, he had found some kind of peace. He no longer sought to shock and astonish. He could finally be trusted with our crown jewels."

"And that's what he's doing now? He remains a homeless man living under a bridge while he works on Eternal?"

"I get the feeling he doesn't want to wrench himself away too quickly from the world that has been his these past years. Strangely enough, it seems to suit him. So thus far, all we've done is put a laboratory as his disposal. A secret laboratory. Right now, there are only four people in Ephémère who know about it. Sometimes he turns up there on his own, sometimes he arranges for Richard to pick him up. There have been no concrete results yet, but I know – I just know – that he will work wonders with Eternal."

She smiled to herself, ran a hand through her hair, and leant slightly towards him.

"So now you know my secret, Franck, and I think you'll agree it has nothing to do with your case."

"Has Michel been back in touch with Halphen since he reappeared?"

"I doubt it," said Francesca, showing surprise at the suggestion. "Why would he? They were at daggers drawn before. And I can't see Louis allowing a homeless man to come within a hundred metres of him. Or his ever-present Justin for that matter."

"You know this Justin?"

"I know of him. Justin Valens. Isabelle Arbaud wanted to hire him as a personal assistant when she was in charge of brand strategy. I blocked it."

"Why?"

"He seemed competent, intelligent, industrious and very ambitious. But he reminded me too much of Sire Fox. He was a sycophant. And I share La Fontaine's opinion that behind every sycophant lies a potential manipulator."

"You didn't think Isabelle Arbaud could handle him?"

Francesca laughed. "Of course Isabelle could handle him. She would have worked him night and day, bled him dry, and then tossed him aside. Justin Valens has no idea of the favour I did him by preventing her from hiring him. But I didn't want someone like that inside Ephémère. A fashion house is a fragile mix of talent, vocation, and prickly personalities. Inject the wrong element at any level – a board member or a receptionist – and you can destroy the perfect equilibrium that makes such a place work. I already had Isabelle to deal with. I wasn't going to multiply the risks."

"So you would never have hired Justin for Louis Halphen?"

"No doubt Isabelle knows what she is doing. She always does. Or at least, she always thinks she does, since she has not yet realised that her judgement – like mine – is not infallible.

And in many ways, Justin is the perfect major-domo for Louis. He will not cross him. He will protect him with jealous zeal. But he will also become his only link to the outside world. I wouldn't be inclined to trust him with that."

"Did he ever have anything to do with Michel Verdier?" asked Franck.

"Who?"

"Justin Valens."

"No. Michel had disappeared before Isabelle attempted to hire Justin. And I cannot imagine Michel tolerating such an individual. He hated being treated like someone special. He still does. After all, he's still sleeping under the Alexandre III bridge despite my offering him an apartment."

"I can't see why he's so keen on it," observed Franck. "I slept in his place under the bridge last night. It's a far cry from the Ritz."

"Well, at least that explains the crumpled, unshaven look. Why on earth did you do that?"

"I was hoping he might come back."

"But he didn't?"

"No. And nobody there has heard from him since he last disappeared in your BMW."

"As I said, I believe he was in our lab most of the day last Thursday. Since then, we haven't had any news. But that's Michel's way. He's a free spirit."

"Guillaume Thèves was killed on Thursday evening. Probably after Michel left your lab."

"Surely a coincidence."

"I don't like coincidences. They make me uneasy."

Monday, 4th February

"You've been busy. I sometimes wonder whether you know what weekends are for."

Yves de Chaumont looked at Franck with apparent disapproval. They sat in their accustomed places in his ever-tidy office, empty coffee cups and a plate bearing the crumbs of half a dozen madeleines before them. As this briefing had been scheduled in advance, madame Alba had foreseen some sustenance, since she trusted neither of them to make a serious attempt at eating breakfast before coming in.

Franck knew that Yves was half-serious and half-complicit in his criticism. Franck had seen the piles of dossiers that accompanied the *juge* when he left on a Friday evening, and on many occasions the two of them had met on a Saturday in the very building where they now sat. Neither of them was able to turn his back on his vocation for long. Yves, though, had a wife, three children, two grandchildren, a couple of dogs, a horse, and an eighteenth-century manor in the fertile plains around Chartres. He knew a thing or two about balance and harmony, and from time to time would chide Franck on his failings on this front. Franck's standard defence was that it was not entirely his own fault. He had, after all, spent years following the example of Catherine Vautrin.

"It was chivalrous of you to escort mademoiselle Arbaud on Friday evening," observed Yves, although not without little malice. "Would I be right in thinking she's a very attractive young woman?"

"I suppose she is."

"But you're not entirely sure?"

"It's the kind of thing that slips your mind when you're in her company. She's above all a very acerbic young woman."

"Be fair. She had good reason to feel a little on edge on that particular day. The last of her investors had just been gunned down, after all."

"She got over it quickly enough," Franck pointed out. "And

how fair should I be with someone who refuses to believe me when I tell her that the case is not about three, but two, dead investors?"

"She's supposed to find that reassuring? Only two out of three? Don't forget that the Arbaud connection is the only decent hypothesis we've got, even if it turns out to be a different version from the one Isabelle Arbaud herself imagines. If I've understood correctly, ours now involves a homeless Nose and maybe even a homeless soldier. We know this Michel was to hand when Perrin was shot, and nobody seems to know where he was when Thèves was killed – which just happened to take place on a stretch of the riverfront he must know well. If Michel is doing this to stop Louis Halphen achieve his masterpiece, then Isabelle Arbaud may well not be a target but she's still the unwitting victim of another's revenge."

"Except that the only source we have for any bad blood between Louis Halphen and Michel is Francesca Craveri. Maybe she was leading me astray when she told me Isabelle sought to be her nemesis. Maybe it's the other way round."

"I can see a tiny problem with that theory," said Yves.

"Which is?"

"We can be pretty sure that Francesca Craveri did not lure Thèves to his death. She does have an alibi, after all, since she happened to be in your company at the time."

"A remarkably convenient alibi, no? A last-minute invitation, and there I am, as and when required to ensure that Craveri is above suspicion."

"Don't you sometimes think you spent too long in the DST, Franck? Craveri has been remarkably cooperative since this whole thing started. If she's behind all that's going on, she's very good at concealing it."

"We've seen that before," observed Franck.

The pair of them nodded in unison and then sat silent for a while.

"What if we don't have two out of three?" asked Yves.

"What if Thèves and Perrin were not killed by the same hand?"

"It's the same weapon," Franck objected. "6.5mm slugs. Same kind of rifling marks on them."

"That indicates they were shot from a weapon with the same characteristics as the one used on Perrin. We may think it's the exact same pistol, but until we have it we won't know for sure. There are – what? – a hundred PI87s in circulation?"

"Two killers who just happen to use the same model? Which just happens to be one of the most expensive handguns in the world? That's stretching things a bit far."

"Not unless killer number two chose his gun in order to make us think of killer number one."

"Nobody knows about the bullets recovered from Perrin's body," insisted Franck. "Nobody knows about the bleach either."

"I know. You know. Georges Sternberg knows. Catherine Vautrin had someone tunnel into our network to find it out. I suspect a lot more people know about this than either of us would be comfortable with."

"So what's your theory?"

"What if the similarities between the Perrin and Thèves shootings are merely, and deliberately, superficial? It might even explain the over-eager use of bleach this time. What if the real link is between Thèves and Nathalie Chautard? What about that pamphlet you picked up outside IPS? Maybe somebody thought Thèves was an enemy of the planet."

"Agostini?" said Franck. "He wouldn't have tried to confuse us with the gun. If he'd done it, he'd have told me."

"That wasn't the pact," Yves reminded him. "He said that if you asked him a question, he'd answer it honestly, or not at all. He didn't say that he'd keep you up to date with all his deeds."

"So what are you suggesting I do?"

"Ask him the question."

Franck bit his lip, conscious that he had never seriously considered the notion that Gabriel might have had a hand in Thèves' death.

"Catherine thinks I've fallen under Agostini's spell," he confessed.

"She knows you well, Franck. She might be right."

*

"You know you're not welcome here, captain?"

The owner of Les Calanche stood at the side of the table where Franck was sitting, a menu flat on the red and white chequered tablecloth before him. They were in the middle of the restaurant, between a row of tables jammed against a window looking out onto rue des Orteaux and another nestled against a long counter. It was twelve twenty and a little under half of the tables in the place were taken.

"Are you going to deny me hospitality?" asked Franck.

The owner narrowed his eyes. Franck had just made it impossible for him to turn him away. He was from Porto, and had set up this little corner of Corsica in the twentieth arrondissement fifteen years ago. His file had been one of many Franck had read during his last assignment with the DST.

"What would you like?" he asked.

"I'll have the *cannellonis au brocciu.*"

"Some wine?"

"I'd better not. I'm carrying a weapon."

"You're a wise man," said the owner, retrieving the menu.

In the early days of the hunt for Agostini the DST had staked out Les Calanche. Several of its regulars were suspected of having links to Corsican nationalist groups and an informer had insisted that it was involved in channelling funds to Appoghiu Terra Corsa. When Agostini had escaped capture in the heights above Calvi, newspaper accounts of the incident had been pinned triumphantly to a cork board hung behind the bar. Given that several of these stories had featured photos of Franck in his injured state, it was not surprising that he had been recognised when he walked in. Indeed, he had been counting on it.

He was served quickly and wordlessly. He ate slowly, letting the restaurant fill up. He caught several glances aimed in his direction, and was pretty sure he was the object of more than a few conversations.

When his plate was taken away he turned down the suggestion of dessert, and contented himself with a coffee. It came accompanied by the bill. He placed fifteen euros on the table and stood up.

It was now ten minutes to one. Every table was taken, and there were people clustered around the door waiting for one to open up.

Without addressing anyone in particular, Franck announced in a clear voice, "My name is Franck Guerin. I need to talk to Gabriel."

The hubbub of conversation around him momentarily dipped and then returned to normal.

He gathered up his parka and his briefcase and left.

*

It took her twelve minutes to call him.

"Hello Catherine," he said. "Still got Les Calanche under surveillance then?"

"Never you mind," said Catherine Vautrin. "You never told me the pair of you had agreed on a channel of communication. Not the most discreet one, I have to say."

"We hadn't. And since we hadn't, I was forced to improvise."

"Why do you need to talk to Gabriel?"

"It's in the context of an ongoing investigation that's being conducted under the authority of Yves de Chaumont, *juge d'instruction*."

"Very funny," she said, flatly. "Tell me."

"I want to know if he killed Guillaume Thèves."

"I doubt it. It's a student group that's picketing IPS. They're from Nanterre university. They're naive, sincere and harmless."

"How can you be so sure?"

"We're running them."

Franck paused. "You could have told me that before."

"Maybe I would have if you'd asked me in the context of the ongoing investigation you're conducting under the authority of Yves de Chaumont, *juge d'instruction*. But you didn't."

"What about the charge of selling vast quantities of non-WFPA paper?"

"All that is true. You know our Research section. They're rarely wrong. They wrote the first draft of the IPS pamphlet with great gusto."

"What exactly are you playing at with this group?"

"They're bait. We're waiting to see who takes it."

"Maybe Agostini did."

"The group has never been contacted by anyone with even tenuous links to Appoghiu Terra."

"Doesn't mean Agostini hasn't read the leaflet and drawn his own conclusions."

"Oh, you don't have to read the leaflet. There's a really nice web site too."

"Catherine, you realise you could be the cause of Thèves being targeted, if that's what happened?"

"If we hadn't put the facts out, somebody else would have," she said, dismissively. "Anyhow, there's no reason to believe it was Agostini. Where would he get a PI87 from?"

"I'll be sure to ask him."

"Just be sure you let us know if he sets up a meeting."

Franck said nothing.

"We'll be watching you, Franck," she warned him.

"You think Agostini doesn't know that?"

*

A Peugeot 607 pulled up at the kerb on the south side of place de la Nation, between rue Jaucourt and rue Fabre d'Eglantine. Franck was sitting waiting on a nearby bench. The driver waved to him. Franck stood up, looked around, and got into the back of the car.

The DST had to be watching, and he would have liked to have told them not to waste their time following him. However, had he called Catherine, she would have assumed he was being duplicitous.

"Where are we going?" Franck asked the driver.

"The bar of the Meurice," he replied.

Franck sighed. It could have been worse. She could have chosen the Crillon.

Sylvie Thomas had called him just after he had hung up on Catherine Vautrin. She had insisted that she had to talk with him immediately and asked him where he was. Without thinking, he had revealed his location in the twentieth arrondissement before getting round to asking her why it was so urgent that they meet. He never got the chance to put his question. She cut across him, told him her driver would pick him up at place de la Nation, and rang off. He had tried calling back twice, and both times ended up with one of Lasry Frères' impeccably polite assistants who expressed heartfelt regret at the fact that mademoiselle Thomas was unavailable.

The trip was short and uneventful. With Bach doing his best to subdue him, Franck gazed at pedestrians and shops as the car headed down to place de la Bastille and then crawled along rue Saint Antoine and rue de Rivoli. A top-hatted groom stepped forward to open the passenger door as they came to a halt in front of the Meurice hotel.

"In the bar," the driver reminded him.

"Through the lobby and to your left, sir," said the groom.

Franck followed his directions and soon found himself surrounded by the dark wood, velvet and leather of the Meurice's largely empty bar. Sylvie was poised in one corner on a two-seater chaise longue. She wore a cream-coloured open-necked blouse with a wide collar, a dark pencil skirt that grazed her knees, and kitten heels. A jacket and a Burberry trenchcoat were tossed over a nearby chair. She rose as he approached and let him kiss her cheeks.

"Nice quiet bar," remarked Franck as he sat beside her.

"They Starcked it up for Christmas," she said. "That's why you won't be able to afford to drink anything."

Franck shrugged. "I'm sure they're happy to lend a little corner space to a police officer."

Sylvie raised an imperious finger and within seconds a waiter stood before them.

"A coffee for the captain and a dry martini for me."

"Difficult day?" asked Franck.

"You could say that." She swivelled to face him. "When were you going to call me?"

"About what?"

"About Guillaume Thèves, of course."

"Why should I have called you about Guillaume Thèves?"

"That way I wouldn't have found out in the middle of a meeting in the office this morning – when I was asked why three of my private wealth clients had all recently met violent ends, and whether this was likely to continue."

"Who was doing the asking?"

"Samuel Lasry, our president. The last of the Frères. He already thinks I'm losing my grip because I disagree with every other partner over where the market is heading. So he's delighted to have a new stick to beat me with."

"What does he think it's got to do with you?"

"That's what he was asking me. And I've got to come up with a convincing explanation."

"I really don't understand," admitted Franck, to whom the whole thing sounded absurd.

"That's because you don't know how superstitious bankers can be. Or – more to the point – how superstitious our clients can be. Particularly private clients. They're all looking for someone with the Midas touch. I was last year's golden girl. Now people are wondering whether I might be tainted with leprosy."

"What's the problem? Nothing's happened to their money."

"Precisely! Their money's tied up in testamentary disputes and is doing nothing. It's just sitting where it was. And soon – maybe even very soon – that's going to be a big problem. Then there's the inconvenient fact that all three of them are dead. You may hold a dim view of the super-rich, Franck, but even they prize their lives above their wealth. Three of my clients die, and the only thing they have in common is that they were all involved in a deal I brokered."

"What deal?"

"The Arbaud deal. Who do you think Isabelle Arbaud came to when she was seeking a few adventurous private investors? Who do you think was capable of persuading a pair of wise old foxes like Thèves and Chautard to even consider signing up for a convertible debenture rather than taking an equity stake straight away? Who other than Sylvie Thomas – the woman they'll soon be calling the kiss of death."

"I don't know what to say to you," said Franck. "Unless you're about to tell me you've just become a crack shot and own a PI87..."

"A what?"

"Never mind. Unless that's the case, then you personally have nothing to do with what's happened. If your clients are being killed, that doesn't make you guilty. Only unlucky."

"Only unlucky," echoed Sylvie, an edge to her voice. "You have no idea what that means. Napoleon wasn't the only one who preferred a lucky general to a talented general. Banking is dominated by the lucky – lucky in birth, lucky in friends, and lucky in business. All I've got's the latter, and right now it's turning sour. If I begin to develop a sinister reputation, you can bet anything you like I won't be senior partner much longer."

Their drinks arrived. Sylvie grabbed her martini and drained a third of it. Franck sat and watched her, bemused. She took a deep breath and nodded at his coffee.

"Drink it," she commanded. "I know it makes you think

faster."

Franck did as he was told.

"You can start by answering my original question," she said. "Why didn't you warn me?"

"I didn't know you had anything to do with Guillaume Thèves."

"Is that true?" she asked, sceptically.

"You told me you had dealings with Nathalie Chautard and Alain Perrin. I have no recollection of you bringing up Thèves."

"Well if I didn't, it's your fault. You made me drop the subject before I really got going. Anyhow, now you've got to help me."

"How?"

"By proving that their murders have nothing to do with the Arbaud deal, or with their links to Lasry Frères."

"I'm sure it's true for the Chautard case, but I don't have jurisdiction over it and so I can't prove anything."

"Why not?"

"Because."

"Because of what?"

"Because," Franck reiterated, this time more slowly.

Sylvie sipped her drink again, eyeing him.

"Because of the DST," she concluded.

"Because," he repeated, refusing to give her more.

"OK. But if Chautard's death has nothing to do with Arbaud, then presumably the two others don't either."

Franck shrugged. "Right now, your guess is a good as mine. There's a possible alternative explanation for Thèves, but it's a pretty twisted one. As for Perrin, we're still in the dark."

"You're not helping, Franck," she said, icily.

"I'm aware of that. But this thing is going to drag out some time longer. And in the end, it may well turn out that the Arbaud connection is indeed behind Perrin and Thèves."

Sylvie finished her drink and slammed it down on the low table in front of them.

"This is so unfair. I might have got them into Arbaud, but I did my level best to get them out."

Franck frowned and touched Sylvie lightly on the arm. "Say that again?"

"I told them to get out. Perrin and Thèves. First week in January. And several times afterwards."

"You have to tell me the whole story. From the beginning."

"Why?"

"Because right now you know more than I do, and I'm the one trying to solve the crime."

"If you insist." She tilted her head back and took a deep breath. Franck caught himself studying her neck and the tiny diamond studs in her ears, which he had always thought rather shapely.

"Stop admiring me," she said, frowning at him over her raised chin before she brought her face back parallel with his. "This is neither the time nor the place."

"That's for sure," he said. "Go."

"I met Isabelle Arbaud for the first time in May 2006. She sought me out. She was still in charge of brand strategy at Ephémère at the time. At first I thought she just wanted us to help her manage her money, and I was looking for a polite way to turn her down, as she hadn't amassed the kind of wealth Lasry Frères is interested in. But then she told me about her plan to create a fashion house from nothing, to construct it around herself, and to buy her way into the market. It was audacious, maybe even insanely so, but it was 2006, the Dow Jones was above 11 000 points, a lot of money was swishing around the system and bold ventures promising substantial gains were very much in the spirit of the times."

"So you found her some backers."

"She was very picky. She only wanted private investors whom she could deal with one-to-one, presumably so that she could seduce or browbeat them as required. And she didn't want to give up stock, so we came up with a ten year convertible debenture, with a three year amnesty on interest payments, a progressive lock-in and a guarantee of twice the going yield for ten year Treasury notes."

Franck looked at her blankly. She ploughed on regardless.

"We managed to pitch a high-risk investment without having to offer junk bond yields. The progressive lock-in helped, as did the fact that we allowed for redemption at any time. But above all it was because Isabelle was so convincing. I rounded up Chautard, Perrin and Thèves and she won them over. Perrin was an easy touch, but Chautard and Thèves were seasoned cynics, and yet they signed on the dotted line – despite the fact that, for once, they weren't playing with other peoples' money."

She paused.

"You still with me?"

"Not entirely," admitted Franck. "But I get the big picture."

"The debentures were signed and Arbaud was set up in September. We took our commission out of the first loan payment, but I always kept an eye on how things were going. Isabelle started weaving a myth around herself and in January 2007 proved to the market how serious a contender she was by poaching Louis Halphen and promising to launch her first product – a perfume to knock Chanel and Ephémère from their pedestals – that summer. Everybody was happy. I even had people come to me to see if I could get them a slice of the Arbaud cake. She could have gone public at that point and become a multi-millionaire. The Dow was over 12 000 points and the luxury goods market was exploding."

"But the perfume didn't come in on time."

"It didn't. In October Chautard and Thèves started kicking up a fuss, but Isabelle put them in their place. When they called me about it, I pointed out that I had a waiting list of people ready to buy their positions. The Dow was about to touch 14 000 points. Seventh heaven for us financial types. I told them they were sitting on a gold mine – although I think Chautard remained pretty sceptical."

"So what had changed by the beginning of this year?" asked

Franck. "I know the perfume was still running late, but what's a few months in a ten-year investment?"

"Nothing – you're quite right. When I advised Perrin and Thèves to call in the debenture and pull out what they could – which, including the hôtel Lambert, would have been maybe half of what they'd put in, given the rate at which Isabelle had been burning their cash – they thought I was crazy. The Dow had slipped, but was still above 12 000, and everybody knew that the big luxury brands would soon be reporting record profits for the previous financial year."

"So what made you change your mind?"

"You know how I spent last Christmas, Franck? After drinking a lot of champagne to celebrate my promotion, I went to New York. I met some very interesting people there. Most of them Wall Street stars, but the odd heretic too. And I came to realise something."

She paused for effect. Franck deliberately waited a few complicit seconds before prompting her.

"Yes?"

"I realised that the party will soon be over. That everybody is over-leveraged and up to their necks in risk. That it's all going to come crashing down, sooner rather than later. And when that day comes there's going to be a fire sale. Stocks, bonds, you name it, they'll be plummeting by the hour. Whoever has their pockets full of cash and has the courage to spend it when the bottom falls out of the market will be unthinkably rich twelve or twenty-four months later. As for Arbaud, Isabelle will find she has chosen the worst possible time to launch her new company. She doesn't know it yet, but she's heading for a brick wall. I told Perrin and Thèves to get their money out before it all disappeared down the drain. I would have done the same for Chautard, had it not been for her unfortunate accident."

"Did you tell all this to Isabelle Arbaud?"

"No. I told you. She's not one of our private wealth clients."

"Did they believe you? Perrin and Thèves?"

"I'll never know. I talked to each of them individually two or three times. They said they'd think about it."

"There's a theory that Perrin and Thèves were killed to cut the money supply to Arbaud and cause it to be stillborn," said Franck.

"In which case your murderer's been wasting his time and energy. The market will take Arbaud out. All he has to do is wait."

"He doesn't know that. And neither – frankly – do you. Didn't you say no one else in Lasry Frères shared your analysis of the situation?"

She smiled at him, admiringly. "Maybe I did. You do pay attention after all, Franck."

"In which case we may have a problem. As of three days ago, the last of Arbaud's sources of funds was frozen with the death of Guillaume Thèves. The killer may assume that Isabelle will now start looking for new ones."

"Well, she's not called me," said Sylvie.

"Maybe not, but what if whoever is behind this simply assumes that you're the person she'll call?"

"I think I know what you're about to say. I'm having another martini."

*

"Ask monsieur *le juge*. The need for protection arises in the context of an ongoing investigation you're conducting under his authority."

"Come on, Catherine," said Franck impatiently. "You know full well we don't have the resources to do it."

"OK. Let me put it another way. She's not my sweetheart, Franck. She's yours."

Franck closed his eyes and propped himself against the thin trunk of a leafless tree. He was in the Jardin des Tuileries, just across the road from the Meurice. Sylvie was in her chauffeur-driven car, heading back to La Défense.

"I'm not going to dignify that with a response. Look, I know it's an unlikely scenario, but Sylvie is a plausible next step for our killer."

"Your killer, Franck, not our killer. My killer took out Nathalie Chautard. He's called Gabriel Agostini. You might have heard of him. Apparently the pair of you are quite close."

Franck said nothing. He knew what was coming.

"Now maybe we could do a deal. If Agostini sets up a meeting with you, then you tell us about it. In advance, of course, not when it's all over. In return, I'll make sure a team is watching over Sylvie Thomas night and day. That way, at least we'll know if she goes back to her old habit of money-laundering."

"You know I can't do that."

"Because your word of honour to the leader of a terrorist group is worth more than your friend's life?"

"Because I wouldn't be worthy of anyone's friendship if I didn't keep my word."

"Should I take that personally?"

"You decide."

He rang off.

Tuesday, 5th February

"Where is he?"

Justin looked pale and diminished. The interior behind him was more brightly lit than the street outside. The sun had risen, but it was struggling to provide any cheer to a grey and overcast winter's morning.

"In the conservatory," said Justin.

"Is anyone else here?" asked Franck, offering a rapid handshake and moving past him.

"No. We gave the entire lab team the day off."

"We?" asked Franck, stopping and turning back to Justin.

"Sorry?"

"Who gave them the day off?"

"I did. On monsieur Halphen's instructions."

"OK. If anyone does turn up, you keep them out. Except the forensic team. They'll be here soon."

Justin nodded.

"How long have you been here?"

"I got here just before eight."

"Was the door locked?"

"No. It was shut, but it wasn't locked."

Franck looked at the rear of the door. There were two separate security locks and an inertia sensor.

"The alarm system was off too?" he asked.

"Yes. But it isn't the kind of thing monsieur Halphen gives much thought to."

"He wouldn't have locked the door behind him?"

"Not always. It's my job to look out for things like that."

Franck glanced at Justin's feet. He was wearing tennis shoes along with his lab coat. Just like the last time.

"Can you get me a clean pair of those? I'll have a coat too."

He tugged off his shoes and parka and dumped them in one of the nearby lockers. Justin brought him footwear, a cellophane-wrapped lab coat straight from the cleaners, and a box of disposable gloves.

"Thanks," said Franck, "Did you get changed as soon as you got here?"

"Yes. It's standard procedure."

"Good. At least that means the crime scene's largely uncontaminated."

Justin swallowed, apparently in reaction to the lab's new designation.

"Stay behind me, and stay in the building," instructed Franck.

He moved through the open space, skirting pillars, benches and desks in order to reach the airlock that led to the steel-framed conservatory.

"Is it freezing out there?" he asked.

"Not really," said Justin, a few paces behind him. "A heating system kicks in whenever it drops below fifteen degrees."

The inner pair of doors opened and Franck stepped through them. They shut behind him and the outer pair parted silently. He stepped into the conservatory. It was indeed warmer than the ambient temperature outside, but he was glad he had a thick sweatshirt under his lab coat.

He moved slowly, his eyes sweeping the plants, the low-lying tables that supported them, the flagged stone floor, and the glass panes. He spotted nothing out of the ordinary until he reached the wooden deck in the middle. Louis Halphen sat in the very same chair Franck had occupied the previous Saturday afternoon. He wasn't reading the press, however. He had draped a thin merino wool blanket around himself, pulling it over his shoulders but letting it slip off either side of the chair. He wore light-khaki trousers and a cotton sailor's jumper in blue and white, with dark espadrilles on his bare feet. His head was bent back as far as it could go over the top of the chair.

Franck inched closer across the surface of the deck, skirting round the chair until he was looking directly down into Halphen's blindly open eyes. The entry wound lay dead centre, bridging the gap between his eyebrows. A little lower than the previous victims, but effective enough. Particularly if it had followed the shot which had left a pool of congealed blood on his stomach.

Halphen was soaking wet, from his close-cropped hair to his feet. A damp patch spread in a rough circle on the decking around his chair. Franck did not have to bend any closer to recognise the smell.

"You were wrong," he murmured to the dead man. "His collection wasn't complete."

He retraced his steps back to the house, studying the glass doors of the airlock as they opened and shut around him. They didn't look smudged.

Georges Sternberg was coming through the front door with two of his team in tow.

"Out the back," said Franck. "You may have a sense of *déjà vu*."

Sternberg nodded and started kitting up. Franck beckoned to Justin, who stood listlessly by the front door, and led him to a pair of stools near a workbench in a far corner.

"You need something to drink?" he asked.

Justin shook his head.

"Well I do. Where's the coffee machine?"

This request seemed to reawaken something in Halphen's assistant. He strode off to a compact machine, inserted a foil-wrapped dose, and returned with an espresso in a square-sided ceramic cup.

"You pair stop touching everything!" yelled Sternberg from across the room.

Franck caught his lower lip in his teeth, shrugged a *mea culpa*, and tossed back his coffee.

"Won't do it again."

Sternberg shook his head and turned back to his team.

Franck eased himself onto a nearby stool, inviting Justin to do the same.

"When did you last see Halphen alive?"

"Yesterday evening. I left him here about eight."

"I thought the pair of you were inseparable."

"We didn't live together, captain," snapped Justin. "I may have been at monsieur Halphen's call day and night, but he didn't keep me on a leash. It just so happened that yesterday he told me I could leave him here alone."

"He didn't want you to drive him home?"

"No."

"He was going to take the metro? A common taxi? Walk? Louis Halphen?"

"We didn't discuss it. I assumed he was planning on staying here. There is a small bedroom on the third floor for his exclusive use."

"Does he often stay here?"

"Sometimes. We've worked through the night several times, but sometimes he does so on his own and sleeps in his room if he gets too tired."

"He was still working when you left at eight?"

"No."

"So why stay?"

"To savour his triumph, I suppose. To sleep next to his masterpiece."

"You mean he'd finished?"

Justin nodded. "Yesterday monsieur Halphen added the final touch to Night-Scented." He spoke with evident pride. "It's done. It's perfect."

"Is it still here?" asked Franck.

Justin leapt instantly from his stool and ran to the stairs that led up to the first floor.

"Slowly!" shouted Franck. "Don't disturb anything you don't have to."

Sternberg had gone out into the conservatory. In his absence, Franck let Justin have his way. It scarcely mattered – given the time Justin had spent alone before his arrival, if anything had required spiriting away, it had already been done.

Justin vanished up the stairs and reappeared five minutes later, rejoining Franck.

"Everything's there. The samples, the notes, the formula."

"Were they locked away?" asked Franck.

"They're kept in a secure room with a keypad and electronic lock."

"So either the killer wasn't interested in them, or he didn't know the code."

"People don't kill to steal formulas for perfume," protested Justin.

"They kill to steal industrial secrets. Given how much is riding on this particular perfume, I don't see why it couldn't be a target. Anyhow, let's get back to yesterday. Take me through the entire day."

"From when?"

"From when you got up."

"I arrived at monsieur Halphen's apartment at six o'clock in the morning. We had worked till after midnight on Sunday evening."

"Just the two of you?"

"No, the whole lab crew was here throughout the weekend."

"OK. Keep going." Franck waved him on.

"We had scarcely stopped since last Thursday. That was when we'd given our last sample to Isabelle Arbaud."

"The day I met you at the hôtel Lambert?"

"Yes. With that version we knew we were close. After that we only stopped for six hours or so every night. We were all exhausted, but not monsieur Halphen. I don't even think he was interested in going off to sleep. When he forced himself to stop it was to refresh his senses, to make himself pause and reflect. I'd drop him off at the church in the Institut Catholique once a day so that he could gather his thoughts. You could tell he felt that the prize was at his fingertips."

"Who knew about this?"

"He didn't say anything, but we could all feel it. The entire team."

"Anybody else? Isabelle Arbaud?"

"No. You wait until you've reached the summit before you

announce it to the world."

"Unless your investors are on your back," countered Franck. "But then, they weren't, were they – not any more. Not since last Thursday evening, when the last of them was gunned down. It's kind of ironic. A sudden burst of speed when the pressure was finally off."

Justin frowned at him. "What's your point?"

"I have no idea," admitted Franck. "Keep going."

"I picked him up at six, we were here by six thirty. The crew came in at eight. We worked non-stop until about half two in the afternoon."

"And then?"

"Monsieur Halphen told everyone to go out and have something to eat."

"Including you?"

"Including me."

"Where did you go and when did you get back?"

"I had a late lunch with the lab crew in a brasserie round the corner. We came back around four."

"And?"

"Monsieur Halphen was waiting for us. He was clearly very excited. He had us run a series of tests, checked the results, and by six told me to send someone out for champagne. Henriet – the best. He disappeared upstairs to write up his notes and clean up."

"Clean what up?"

"Himself. There are shower rooms upstairs. Monsieur Halphen showers when he reaches the lab, and showers when he stops working for the day." Justin paused, correcting himself. "Showered. That way his palette was neutral when he started, and he wasn't distracted or tormented by the fruits of his day's efforts when he chose to rest and refresh his senses."

"Makes sense, I suppose, given he was hypersensitive," said Franck.

"Particularly when dealing with Night-Scented, given the trace effect we were seeking."

"OK, so he showered, and changed I suppose, then what?"

"Around seven o'clock we toasted the birth of Night-Scented. By eight the lab crew had gone, and monsieur Halphen told me I could do so too. He said he wouldn't need me before eight thirty this morning, and that I was to come directly here, to the lab."

"What did you do?"

"When?"

"When you left here last night."

"I took the car, drove back to my flat, and caught up on my sleep. It's been like running a marathon this past week. I was dead on my feet."

"Was anyone with you?"

"When?"

"When you were sleeping."

"What is this, captain?" Justin leapt up. "Am I a suspect? After a year watching over Louis Halphen night and day, protecting him and his gifts from the world, I'm supposed to have shot him hours after he completed his masterpiece?"

Franck remained unperturbed. "Can you answer the question?"

Justin slid back onto his stool. "I was alone," he admitted, ill-temperedly. "Last I heard it's not a crime."

"Nor is it," agreed Franck. "I think you should sit down at one of the PCs in here and type out a statement of the events of the past week, putting in as much detail as you can remember. Where Halphen was and when. When you were with him and when he was alone. Who he saw or talked to on the phone. If you can provide names and contact numbers for the lab crew, that would help too. You OK with that?"

Justin nodded.

"Have you told anyone else about Halphen's death?" asked Franck.

"No. I phoned you as soon as I found the body."

"And you didn't call anyone while I was on my way?"

"No."

"Not even Isabelle Arbaud?"

"Certainly not," said Justin. "I don't want to be the one to break this to her."

"That I can understand," said Franck, turning and walking away from him.

He went through the airlock and called Georges Sternberg over.

"Anything I should know straight away?"

"No broken panes, so it's safe to assume the shot did not come from outside. There don't seem to be any lights in this conservatory. That means the only way to locate the victim was the secondary light leaking from the house. Not ideal conditions for such a precise shot. So once again we've got a close contact shooting and a victim who wasn't expecting it and didn't put up a fight. Can't see any cartridges, but one might have slipped through the decking, so when we get the chance we'll have a thorough sweep underneath."

"Found the bleach containers?"

"Not yet. They're probably in the house. Looks like a well-equipped chemical lab to me. I think we'll find all sorts of interesting solvents and solutions in there."

"I'll phone the local commissariat. Get them to send some uniforms to canvass the neighbours about last night."

"I tried that," said Sternberg. "I called from the van on the way here. They said they can't send anyone until tomorrow. They also asked why the Brigade Criminelle can't do it themselves."

"What, they're drowning in crime here in the sixteenth arrondissement?"

"Apparently the mayor is throwing some big event today. They're making sure the rich and respectable receive proper attention and protection. You know who you should try?"

"Who?"

"Lieutenant Blanchard. I bet he'll be delighted. He calls me regularly to ask for updates on the case."

"Good idea. I'll do that. Let me know what the medical

examiner says about time of death."

"You going somewhere?"

"I'll be back. First, though, I'm going to ruin someone's day."

*

"Turning up out of the blue in my office? You're catching some of my bad habits, Franck."

So today he was entitled to 'Franck'. He wondered how long it would last.

Although Franck had presented himself at the hôtel Lambert unannounced, the receptionist had greeted him like a treasured client, installed him comfortably in the oval vestibule, plied him with coffee, and promised to do her best to sneak him in to see mademoiselle Arbaud. Forty minutes later Isabelle had come to welcome him, accompanied by her customary hypnotic scent and an uncharacteristically complicit smile. They were now seated on opposite sides of her desk at the far end of the Hercules gallery.

"I'm sorry to barge in," said Franck. "But I have a very serious matter to discuss with you."

She laughed lightly. "A serious matter? Timing is everything, Franck, and yours is pretty poor, but at least you remain true to yourself. This is an auspicious day. One for celebration. But I suppose we can talk seriously if you insist."

"Celebration? Why?"

"Because Night-Scented finally exists. The definitive version. Not this." She raised her right arm alongside her face and grazed the inside of her wrist with her nose. "This was close to perfection as far as I was concerned, but Louis wanted to go one step further. Yesterday he did so. And although I haven't yet encountered the result, I know – because, in the end, even the insufferable Isabelle Arbaud bows before the greatest Nose of her time – that it will be sublime. Arbaud is finally up and running for real, Franck. I've kept the world on tenterhooks for a year with smoke and mirrors – promising, teasing, flattering, misleading, whatever it took. Now I will lay Night-Scented before them, step back and watch it conquer all in its path."

"When did you learn this?"

"Yesterday evening. Louis phoned me. He was ecstatic. Drained, but ecstatic. A Sisyphus who had found a way to make the boulder stay at the top of the hill. I was ready to rush over and discover the final version, but he just wanted to be left in peace. He's going to bring it here sometime this morning. That's why my schedule is clear. I'm waiting for him to arrive in triumph." She glanced at her watch. "He's probably still sleeping. He's been at it non-stop for weeks."

"When exactly did Halphen phone you?"

"Nine thirty? Around then."

Her smile faded.

"What's wrong? Why are you here?"

"Louis Halphen has been killed. His body was found this morning. In his lab."

Isabelle got up, turned her back on Franck, and walked behind her chair to the floor-to-ceiling windows that looked down at the Seine. She clenched a fist against her teeth and placed her brow against the glass. Franck could hear her take control of her breathing, slowing its rhythm. He could not see whether her eyes were open or shut. One of the fingers of her free hand, which hung by her side, began to tap slowly against the glass, as if she was conducting her heartbeat. To the rhythm of a funeral march.

"I'm sorry ..," began Franck.

"Shh!" The sound was short and sharp, both commanding and menacing.

Franck waited. Her body was rigid, the only movement coming from her finger and the rise and fall of her shoulders as she took deep, slow breaths.

Finally she turned slowly and returned to her chair, her eyes focused resolutely on his.

"How many bodies, captain? Will it take mine? Is that when you'll finally believe that someone is intent on destroying Arbaud?"

"Who, Isabelle? If you're so sure, tell me who. Don't just make dark suggestions about Ephémère and Francesca Craveri. Tell me who, and why and how."

"The why is pretty obvious. The millions of dollars in worldwide sales that I will take from those who currently have them. As for who and how, that's your job, captain. Isn't it about time you did it properly?"

"If you're right about the motive, why was Halphen killed after he had completed his task and not before?"

"To take his notes and his samples. Without Louis, I can't reconstruct that final step. All I've got is the last version he showed me. Am I going to market a perfume by announcing that it is Halphen's unfinished symphony, a priceless diamond with a flaw running through it?"

"What makes you think the notes and samples are gone?" asked Franck.

Her brow expressed puzzlement. "They're not?"

"As far as I'm aware nothing was stolen. All the work Halphen did yesterday is still locked away upstairs in his lab."

"They killed Louis but left his perfume?"

"So it seems. Which makes it look more of a personal than a corporate vendetta."

Isabelle ignored his last comment. "Spite. They killed him out of spite. Punishment for coming to me. Well, if they think I can't launch Night-Scented without Louis Halphen by my side, they've made a big mistake. I'll crush them with it. I'll do it for Louis."

She smoothed her hands over the surface of her desk. She then reached out towards a laptop that lay upon it, powering it on.

"Thank you for coming. But now I must work."

"I'm going to need a statement from you about yesterday evening," said Franck.

"I'll send one over."

"And I'll probably have other questions once we've processed the crime scene."

"You have my number. I will help in any way I can. You do your job, captain, and I'll do mine. Between us, Louis will have his revenge."

Isabelle tugged her laptop directly before her. Her fingers stabbed at the keyboard.

Franck kept his thoughts to himself. Revenge was cold comfort for the dead, and tended to be dangerously intoxicating for the living.

"I'll be in touch," he said.

She removed her eyes from the screen and shot him a brief nod. He was dismissed.

He had almost reached the door when she called out to him.

"Captain. When can we get at the data and the samples in the lab?"

"I'll let you know."

The wheels of commerce were grinding relentlessly on.

*

"I no longer think you've got anything to worry about."

"With all the things I have to worry about, that would be nothing short of a miracle," said Sylvie Thomas. "Particularly as I've now taken some very aggressive put options for the end of this year. So if you're telling me you found a way to save the stock markets from ruin, I'm not interested."

"Sylvie, I'm not talking about finance, I'm talking about your life."

"You can tell where one stops and the other begins? You must have very sharp eyes, Franck."

Franck lifted his phone from his ear just long enough to allow himself an exasperated sigh.

"The killer's moved on," he explained. "I think he's done with hitting at Arbaud's investors. It's more a frontal attack now."

"You mean I can stop asking my driver to accompany me to my front door when he takes me home? That's a relief. I do get the feeling he's dying to be asked in. And although he's the buff, handsome type, he's not for me. Never sleep with the staff, Franck. A tip from the top."

"Keep your eyes open, but I don't think you should be too worried. I just wanted to let you know."

"I'm touched. So what's happening at Arbaud? Don't tell me someone's taken a shot at Isabelle?"

"No, she's OK. It's her Nose."

"Somebody punched her? That's a brave soul. I wouldn't want to get into a fight with Isabelle Arbaud."

"Not her nose. Her Nose. With a capital 'n'."

"Halphen?" asked Sylvie. "The alchemist who's to turn Isabelle's promises into gold?"

"He's dead."

"She's screwed. She bet everything she had on Halphen. Without him, it's all over. Problem is, who's going to believe I told Perrin and Thèves to get out before this happened? Thanks, Franck, you've just added to my problems."

"The perfume's ready."

"It is?"

"Halphen finished it before he was killed."

"That is interesting," mused Sylvie. "I wonder if Isabelle's capable of running with it on her own?"

"If she's not?" asked Franck.

"She'll have to sell it to someone who can."

"Like?"

"Oh, I don't know. A little operation called Ephémère, perhaps?"

*

"I've already told the young lieutenant everything I saw. I have other things to do, you know!"

Franck forced a smile onto his face.

"I do realise that, I just wanted to go over one little detail," he said.

"Captain Guerin is from the Brigade Criminelle," added lieutenant Blanchard from where he stood just behind Franck. "It's normal procedure for him to verify essential information in an enquiry."

They were on the second floor of 51 rue Boileau. In front of them stood Jean-Pierre Loiseleur, 71 years old, owner and sole resident of a four room apartment: a semi-retired gastroenterologist and a widower with two children, both doctors. Blanchard had read all this to Franck from his customarily thorough notes just before they rang Loiseleur's doorbell.

"You'd better come in then," said the old man, who led them to a crammed salon overlooking the street. They both declined his offer to take a seat.

"You told the lieutenant you saw an unusual figure in the street last night," said Franck.

"Between nine o'clock and nine thirty," added Blanchard.

"That's right. One of those homeless types," said doctor Loiseleur.

"What made you think he was homeless?" asked Franck.

"He walked right past me. As close as you are. You could tell he was out of place. This is a rather select street in a rather select neighbourhood, lieutenant."

"Captain," corrected Blanchard. "I'm the lieutenant. Captain Guerin is the superior officer."

Loiseleur raised his eyebrows but, thankfully, just continued with his story.

"More to the point, it's a quiet side street. We don't get much, if any, passing traffic – be it cars or pedestrians. We get residents and their visitors and the odd tradesman, that's it. Of course, there are the pupils being dropped off for the Algerian school, and the queues for visas at the Vietnamese Embassy, but that's strictly daytime."

"So you don't get many homeless wandering through," said Franck.

"No homeless, no vagrants, no unsavoury elements. I've lived here eighteen years and, I'm glad to say, that's never changed."

"So this man you saw, can you describe him?"

"He was shabby. Not dirty, as such, but shabby. The kind of person you'd hesitate before sitting beside in the metro. His clothes were worn and crumpled. A stained mackintosh. Big boots like he was heading off into the mountains. One of those hats with a crease across the top, the kind that normally have a ribbon around them."

"But it didn't? The hat. No ribbon?"

"No. Like I said, everything he wore should have been replaced some time ago. Not so much his boots, but the rest, definitely."

"How old would you say he was?"

"Your age, perhaps. Not any older. Maybe a bit younger, even. He was certainly fit since he was walking along briskly. Quite polite too."

"Polite?"

"Yes. Said good evening and touched the brim of his hat."

"Are you sure he wasn't tugging it down over his eyes?" asked the lieutenant.

Loiseleur shrugged. "Maybe."

"Can you remember the colour of anything he was wearing?" asked Franck.

"It was dark, captain. Our paths crossed near a streetlamp, so I saw he had longish hair, but I can't say I noticed any colours."

"He seemed to be in a hurry?"

"Not necessarily. He was going at a good clip, like I said, but he certainly wasn't running."

"Was he heading in the direction of number 54 or away from it?"

"Towards it."

"Was he carrying anything?"

"He had a bag hanging from his shoulder. One of those flattish bags you can put large documents in."

"How big?"

Loiseleur separated his hands horizontally and then vertically to give an idea of the dimensions of the bag. It was big enough for a PI87.

They thanked him and left, returning to the street and then to number 54. Franck told lieutenant Blanchard how much he appreciated the fact that he had come over from the fifteenth with one of his men and worked the entire street in the course of the afternoon. He was particularly impressed by his attempts to interrogate the staff of the Vietnamese Embassy next door to Halphen's lab, and grateful that he had finally backed off before provoking a diplomatic incident.

The lieutenant promised he would send through his collated notes within twenty-four hours at the latest. Franck was tempted to tell him that forty-eight would do, but he did not want to deprive him of an opportunity to feel in the midst of things. They shook hands and parted.

Franck stepped inside the lab. Georges Sternberg and one of his technicians were sitting on stools drinking coffee.

"You want one?" asked Sternberg.

"I'll get it myself," said Franck.

"Put some gloves on first. You've mucked about with my crime scene enough already," said Sternberg, and tossed him one of the many boxes of disposable gloves they had found on site.

Franck followed his instructions, despite the fact that neither Sternberg nor his colleague were wearing any. A symbolic act of penance was a small price to pay for a coffee.

He selected a foil capsule, made an espresso, and knocked it back. He considered making another and toying with it a little longer this time, but managed to restrain himself.

"So?" prompted Sternberg.

"Lieutenant Blanchard was right. It was well worth having

another chat with doctor Loiseleur."

"Don't tell me we've finally got a viable suspect?"

"Don't get carried away. We've got an unexplained and suggestive presence near a crime scene."

"It's that homeless guy, isn't it?"

"Yes, it's that homeless guy."

"The one who was enigmatically present in the André Citroen park when Perrin was killed?" Sternberg had full access rights to Franck's case notes on the network. Since the DST was given to browsing them, Franck had seen no reason to deprive his allies of the same pleasure. "The one who was mysteriously absent from the Alexandre III bridge on the night Thèves was killed? The one whose whereabouts are currently unknown?"

Franck nodded. "That's the one. Michel Verdier – the recently anointed saviour of Ephémère. Absent when he should be present, and present when he should be absent."

"Well, let's hope he didn't put on a pair of these if he came in here." Sternberg tapped on the box of plastic gloves. "That's the problem with a lab – if you want to cover your traces, all you need is immediately to hand."

"Did you find the bleach canisters?"

"Yes we did. In the cupboards over there we found enough industrial-strength bleach to disinfect this entire place ten times over. There are three empty two-litre bottles."

"Any prints on them?"

"Doesn't look like it. Do we have any reference prints for this Michel?"

"Did you pull any off the wooden box we think the PI87 came in?"

"I treated it the evening you brought it in. Before you went off for your fancy dinner. There were plenty of prints, but I reckon they were all from the homeless woman you took it from. She'd been taking good care of it. It had recently been polished."

"I got Michel to handle it the next day. You could dust it

again."

"Sure, but if you can get any more objects he's handled, it would help."

"I can do that," said Franck. "You don't need me here, do you?"

"I can't think of anyone less useful."

*

"Hey, what the hell are you doing?"

Franck had reached the makeshift city underneath the Alexandre III bridge at around half five. As he waited for a break in the constant stream of traffic under the bridge he could see that it was almost deserted. Having dashed across the road, it took him little time to reach Michel's niche. He had done it often enough now to be able to navigate the web of steel beams without pausing to work out where to place his feet or hands. He had expected to be challenged when he started going through Michel's gear, having first gloved up. He was not mistaken.

"I'm a police officer," he shouted over his shoulder, not looking round to see who had spoken to him. "I'm taking a few things for testing."

"Has something happened to Michel?"

The voice was closer now. Franck turned to see a face that was vaguely familiar. So was his, it seemed.

"You were here when Vincent was hit by that car," he was told.

"That's right," said Franck. "I slept here that night, waiting for Michel. Have you seen him?"

"No. He's not been back. We're getting worried. That's why I asked if you knew something."

"I'm looking for things that might help us find him," Franck lied. He then changed the subject. "Any news about Vincent?"

"Dead."

"I'm sorry."

"It was going to happen, the way he carried on. It's a shame, but life's a shame."

The man wandered off.

Franck came upon Michel's cooking gear. He took an aluminium cooking pot, his camping stove, the gas canister to which it was attached, and a double-ended plastic fork and spoon. He put them in separate self-sealing clear plastic bags, wrote the date, time and location upon them, and carried them carefully back down to the roadway.

He watched the traffic hurtling heartlessly past, the drivers averting their eyes from the shelters perched under the bridge.

Little wonder Vincent had been driven to curse them.

"His prints are everywhere. He made no attempt to conceal himself when walking to the lab. It's almost as if he wanted us to know he was there."

"If this Michel wanted us to know he was there, why did he wash the body?" asked Yves de Chaumont, who was standing with his back to the window of his office. "Why get rid of the biological evidence that we're assuming will lead us straight to him?"

"Some kind of ritual?" suggested Franck.

"If so, you'd better work out what it means. Until you do, there's something important we're missing."

"The focus of the rite of cleaning may be Michel himself, and only incidentally the victim," suggested Franck. "Maybe the whole point is to purify himself, to ensure that no trace of the victim remains with him? Halphen showered every time he arrived in his lab and left it. Maybe this is Michel's equivalent. He is a Nose, after all."

"Like you say, Franck – maybe. If there's one thing this case doesn't lack, it's 'maybe's. What about Halphen's assistant – he's definitely out of the picture now?"

"I reckon so. Justin's got no one to back up his story about going home when he left Halphen alone, but on the Thursday evening when Thèves was killed he was in the lab until after midnight with six other people. Same thing for the previous hit – when Perrin was shot at the Ephémère *défilé* Justin was at the lab with Halphen and the rest of the staff."

Yves turned and let his gaze drift outside. He said nothing for a minute or so and then addressed himself to Franck without looking round at him.

"Last summer, whenever I came in here early – before seven – I'd pass a homeless man on the Pont Neuf. I assumed he was sleeping in one of the half-turrets that hang over the river. By the time I'd pass he'd be packing up, getting ready to move on. We'd wish each other a good morning. He never asked me for money, and I came to assume he'd feel insulted if I offered him anything. It was probably the only moment of normality in his day – two people whose paths and routines crossed, recognising each other as fellow early risers. I knew nothing about him, and he knew nothing about me – aside from what each of us could deduce from the way the other was dressed."

"And?" prompted Franck.

Yves abandoned the window and regained his place behind his desk.

"One day he was gone. Vanished. I've never seen him again."

"You think something happened to him?"

"No. I suspect he just decided to move on. So he disappeared – for me, and for anyone else who had got used to seeing him there. The homeless are very good at disappearing. Maybe that's what Michel has chosen to do. His job is finished, and he's moved on."

"Why leave us a calling card then? Why not just vanish without a trace? He'd done a pretty good job of staying invisible right up till now."

"Maybe those were his instructions. Keep a low profile until the job is done, then leave a visible signature to ensure that he got the credit – or, in this case, the blame – for it."

"Instructions?" echoed Franck.

"As a general rule, where there's a job, there's a boss."

*

"What if the crow had been too smart to sing?"

Franck stood before the La Fontaine tapestry. Francesca Craveri had just come through the room's double doors. He had been waiting for over an hour, having forced his way past the Japanese receptionist and imposed himself upon Craveri's assistant. She had warned him he might have to wait some time to see her boss. He had assured her he had nothing better to do.

"The fox would have gone hungry," said Francesca. She wore a pink blouse, a knee-length black skirt with a wide embroidered waistband and low heels. She smiled at Franck, but looked somewhat weary.

"He might have tried climbing up," suggested Franck.

"Have you ever seen a fox climb a tree?"

"He might have enlisted a squirrel to do it for him. Squirrels live in both worlds – up in the branches and down on the ground."

"Why would a squirrel do the bidding of a fox?"

"Ours is a very persuasive fox, don't forget."

"I get the feeling we're not talking about La Fontaine anymore," observed Francesca. "Or this is a version of the tale I've not heard before. Why don't you sit down, Franck?"

He followed her suggestion and she chose a chair immediately next to his.

"You're here because of Louis Halphen, aren't you?" she asked.

"Yes."

"His death has been a great shock to us."

"Unlike those of Alain Perrin and Guillaume Thèves?"

"That's unfair. Nobody grieves for every death, otherwise life would indeed be no more than a vale of tears. Perrin and Thèves are no doubt sadly missed by their friends and loved ones, but they were strangers to me. I worked with Louis for decades. I cannot say with confidence that I was his friend – his vision of his art stood between him and true friendship – but there was much affection in my esteem for him. The world – or at least the universe I inhabit – has become darker with his passing."

"Not his passing," insisted Franck. "His murder."

"His murder," said Francesca reluctantly, as if the word itself left a bitter taste in the mouth. "You believe it was the same person? Whoever was responsible for Perrin and Thèves?"

"Everything points that way."

Francesca nodded and folded her hands in her lap.

"Have you come to ask me for my alibi, Franck?"

"You had one for Thèves, I'm sure you have one for Halphen. Where were you on Monday evening?"

"I had dinner at Hélène Darroze with four Japanese guests, Jean-Pierre Doumenc, our head of Asian markets, and an interpreter. We were there from nine till some time after midnight. Jean-Pierre brought me home."

"You're covered," confirmed Franck. According to the coroner, Halphen had died before midnight.

"I must confess, I don't find your tone very reassuring."

"Michel Verdier is still missing. Not unless you've heard from him?"

"No, we've heard nothing from him since last Thursday. His phone's always off. But there's nothing sinister about that. Absence is Michel's default mode. It's his appearances that are unpredictable. Why do you persist in thinking of him as a suspect? His quarrel with Louis is over five years old."

"He was in the lab."

"Our lab?"

"Halphen's lab."

"Impossible," insisted Francesca. "Not only would Michel never go there, but Louis would never let him in."

"Given which, the fact that he definitely was in the lab – and I can prove it – moves us from the realm of the impossible to that of the highly suspicious."

"Are you sure about this?"

"I can be even more precise – he was there on the evening of the murder, about the same time you were wining and dining your Japanese. But let's assume you're right, and Michel would never go there of his own free will. What does that leave us?"

Francesca tipped her head back, her fingers slipping behind her neck as if to massage it, and breathed deeply.

"How about this," continued Franck. "I've pulled the records on the phone you gave Michel. The last time it was used was on the evening of Thursday the 31st. Just around the time we think Guillaume Thèves was shot. You know who he phoned?"

"I have no idea."

"You. But you didn't pick up, either because you were too smart, or because you were busy distracting me. Sounds a lot like someone checking in, though, doesn't it? Passing on information about a job well done."

"Were I intent on bringing Arbaud to its knees, wouldn't I choose a more promising agent of destruction than a homeless Nose? As squirrels go, Michel Verdier is a pretty unconvincing specimen. Wouldn't I choose someone like you, Franck? A man who lives with a gun on his hip? Don't you think Ephémère has the means to offer itself a real hitman, if we were so inclined, and if such creatures really do exist?"

"Use a mercenary, the only hold you have over him is money. You had other strings to pull with Michel."

Francesca sighed and sat back in her chair.

"It pains me to be forced to play this game with you, Franck, but let's do it. My reign at the head of Ephémère has been very successful. I'm not known for lapses of judgement. So would I have got involved in a criminal undertaking that is in the process of spectacularly backfiring?"

"Backfiring?" echoed Franck.

"Arbaud announced this morning that Night-Scented will be launched worldwide on the 24th of June. In order to whet the market's appetite there will be an *avant-première* this Saturday in their headquarters in the hôtel Lambert. Everybody who counts in fashion and luxury goods will be invited – with the exception of anyone from Ephémère or Chanel, of course. All those invited are certain to go, since they will all be in Paris this Friday in any case to pay their final respects to Louis, and no one will be able to resist the opportunity to discover his posthumous masterpiece. For an undertaking that is supposed to have been blown out of the water, Arbaud is going full steam ahead."

"Isabelle Arbaud's clearly a very adaptable young woman," commented Franck.

"That I don't deny, but don't forget that truly successful predators don't adapt to their environment, they sculpt it."

*

"What's this about a funeral on Friday?"

Franck stood on the opposite side of the place François Premier from the Ephémère offices, trying to zip up his parka with one hand while he held his phone with the other.

"I don't understand your question, captain," replied Isabelle Arbaud with her habitual calm.

"You've set a date for Halphen's funeral?"

"What on earth makes you think I have the power to decide when Louis will be buried? I'm not his next-of-kin. His mother, however, has requested that his body be released as soon as legally possible. Since the autopsy has already been carried out, that should take twenty-four hours maximum. Which means that her wish to bury her son this Friday can be respected."

"And you had nothing to do with this?"

"Louis Halphen died in my employment. We grew very close over the past year. I took it upon myself to contact his mother and offer to help in organising a burial service commensurate with her son's gifts and fame. She's a fragile woman in her eighties. Louis was the only family she had left. It was the least I could do."

"And who's managing the guest list? Madame Halphen or you?"

"I suggested that it would be fitting if Louis' funeral be an occasion for all those who had admired him to come and express their sorrow at his passing. His mother was in complete agreement with me. She recognised that she could scarcely organise such an event. I have taken that burden from her shoulders."

"You don't find it all indecently hasty?"

"It took six days to get Diana from the Alma tunnel to Westminster Abbey. It took seven to get Gianni Versace from Miami Beach to Milan Cathedral. Since we're projecting something a little more modest for Louis, we figured we could do it in half the time."

"Not to mention organising the launch party for Night-Scented the next day."

"It's an *avant-première*, not a launch. But don't worry, captain – I've made sure you're on the guest list."

*

"Do I look the part?"

Lieutenant Blanchard's jeans were ripped, his running shoes worn down, his jumper a few sizes too big, and his coat missing a sleeve. He had taken great care to assemble a motley collection of clothes. Franck refrained from pointing out that they were visibly clean and smelled of fabric conditioner.

"Sure," said Franck. "Anyhow, we're not going undercover. We just don't want those driving by to catch a glimpse of a homeless police officer. Are you armed?"

Blanchard patted the side of his coat.

"Is your phone charged?"

The lieutenant nodded.

"Good. I'll introduce you to your new neighbours then."

He led the way down the stairs from the Alexandre III bridge to the roadway beneath. It was late afternoon. There was no more than an hour of daylight left.

Having waited for a gap in the traffic, they dashed across to where the steel beams rose from the river bank. A woman wrapped in a large blanket, maybe in her thirties, eyed their approach warily.

"You're not from here," she said.

"We're friends of Michel," announced Franck. "Is Paul here?"

"Which Paul?"

"Paul Rosolin."

"He'll be back soon. Are you with the police?"

Blanchard moved to shake his head, but Franck said, "Yes."

"What kind of police?"

"I'm with the Brigade Criminelle. The lieutenant here's from the commissariat in the fifteenth arrondissement."

She looked at Blanchard.

"You want to do something about the dealers on the allée des Cygnes. They set up shop under the Grenelle bridge. The kids just stroll over from Beaugrenelle and the sixteenth arrondissement. There're empty crack vials everywhere."

"We know about it, madame," said Blanchard, glancing uncomfortably at Franck. "We're doing our best."

"Try harder, or you'll find yourselves dragging an overdosed adolescent from the Seine down there someday."

Blanchard nodded as earnestly as he could.

"Any other problems you'd like to point out?" asked Franck. "The lieutenant is very interested in liaising with all the local communities."

It took her about fifteen minutes to exhaust her list of complaints. Blanchard's head bobbed continually as he made a great show of listening intently. Franck allowed himself to wander off, clambering up the bridge's beams to see if Michel's encampment was as he had last seen it. Nothing had changed.

When Paul Rosolin turned up he had an empty flour sack over his shoulder. It was full of neatly sliced bits of baguette. Franck greeted him, introduced Blanchard and admired his catch. Rosolin explained that it came from the nearby ministerial office canteens, which pre-sliced bread for their customers every lunchtime and threw out whatever had not been eaten in the early afternoon.

"If you're still looking for Michel, he's not been back," said Rosolin.

"I know," said Franck. "But things are getting urgent. One

of us is going to stay here from now on so that we can talk to him as soon as he turns up. Is that OK?"

"Sure. That means I'll have a little help keeping the peace around here."

"That's your job?"

Rosolin laughed. "If you can call it a job. I don't see anyone paying me, though."

"Well, you are ex-army. You're a natural choice. You've stayed in good shape. Never think of going back?"

"No point," said Rosolin. "They wouldn't have me back. Not after a dishonourable discharge."

"The army always needs a good shot."

Rosolin shook his head unhappily. He held his hands up before Franck, flat out, fingers spread.

"See that?" he said. His hands trembled. The movement started at the wrists and became more pronounced as it reached the tips of his fingers. "Only goes away when I drink. Or at least I think it does. I rarely drink little enough to be sure."

Franck placed a consoling hand on his shoulder.

"Sorry," he said. "I didn't mean to ..."

"Don't worry about it," insisted Rosolin. "You didn't know."

"I'm going to leave lieutenant Blanchard with you. I'll be taking the night shift. I'll be back around eleven."

"I'll tell the night porter to watch out for you."

Thursday, 7th February

"She's a pretty one, that one."

Franck could only agree.

Adeline held the February issue of *Vogue* up high so that they could both admire the cover. It was a cloudy day and the temperature inside the glasshouse in the André Citroen park was far from Australian. It was, however, colder outside, and the glass walls at least held at bay the wind that was blowing across the Seine. All in all, it was a pretty miserable afternoon.

"Will this go in your archives?" he asked.

"I reckon so," she declared. "I've kept *Libération* for Alain Perrin's death, *Le Parisien* for Guillaume Thèves', and *Le Figaro* for Louis Halphen's. I thought I'd add this issue of *Vogue* for the overall context since all these deaths seem to have something to do with fashion, don't they?"

"Fashion, or the luxury goods market, depending on what you like to call it. But yes, that does seem to be one of the things linking them all."

"There's something else?" she asked.

"There might be. Not something, but someone."

"This Isabelle Arbaud?"

Adeline flicked open the copy of *Vogue*. An advert for Arbaud monopolised the inside front cover. It featured Isabelle and Louis Halphen standing in the gardens of the hôtel Lambert flanked by two tall young women resplendent in the pleated silk of Fortuny Delphos gowns. The only words it bore were 'Arbaud: the very essence of luxury'.

"You're right," admitted Franck. "All the victims are linked to Arbaud, but I'm thinking of someone else. Someone we both know."

Adeline shut the magazine and set it carefully beside her on the bench where they were sitting.

"Michel?" she suggested.

"Yes, Michel. He's disappeared. He's been absent from the Alexandre III bridge for a week. You wouldn't have seen him by any chance?"

"What's Michel got to do with all this killing?" she asked, ignoring his question.

"More than either of us would like to think, I fear."

"He's a suspect?"

"Right now, he's the prime suspect. And the longer he stays missing, the more suspicious he's going to seem."

"He didn't seem suspicious to me."

"Appearances can be deceptive, Adeline."

"Not to these eyes. I saw him yesterday. He may have had things on his mind, but it was still the old Michel, not some murderer on the run."

"You saw him yesterday? Where?"

"Here in the park. Not here." She pointed to the bench they were sitting upon. "Down there, on the banks of the Seine."

"When?"

"Early afternoon."

"What was he doing?"

"Watching the Seine flow past with its cargo of lost loves. Like Apollinaire."

"Did you speak to him?"

"No, I didn't like to. You could tell he was thinking, trying to take a decision. I didn't want to disturb him."

Franck pulled out one of his cards, and reached for his wallet.

"If you see him again, please phone me as soon as you can. It's really important."

Adeline took the card, but waved aside the money Franck had extracted from his wallet.

"I don't need your money, captain. That, on the other hand, does interest me."

She pointed to the cardboard cake box Franck had carefully deposited on the bench when he had arrived in the glasshouse. Franck handed it to her and she slipped off the narrow plastic ribbon that held it shut. Inside were a selection of *patisseries* from a local *boulangerie*.

"There's more," announced Franck. He opened his briefcase to reveal a sturdy thermos flask. "I'm afraid it's coffee. I know it's supposed to be teatime, but I didn't have any tea."

He had prepared the flask that morning, after regaining his apartment and standing in the shower for fifteen minutes, attempting to reheat himself from the outside in. He hoped the coffee was still warm. His flask had suffered some rough treatment in the course of a few stakeouts, and was not entirely reliable.

"Coffee will do fine," said Adeline, watching as Franck set the flask between them and added a pair of plastic goblets, "but I'm not drinking it out of those."

"It's all I've got."

"I have something better."

She got up and left Franck, lumbering out of the glasshouse to where her supermarket trolley was parked. She slowly untied one of the plastic bags that hung from its rim and carried it back in with her. Sitting down again, she extracted a pair of delicate bone china cups, complete with saucers and silver-plated spoons.

Franck reached for one of the cups and held it up. It was pale white, semi-transparent and in perfect condition.

"How do you keep them so clean?" he asked. "Bleach?"

"Certainly not."

"Ruins the taste?"

She shook her head. "The cup's not the problem. You can rinse bleach from porcelain easily enough, but not from your hands. You clean something with bleach, you stink of it all day. I hate that smell."

Friday, 8th February

"I'm afraid you can't come any closer, sir."

There was no such thing as an invitation-only event in the Père Lachaise cemetery. A municipal property, any member of the public was welcome to enter its gates during opening hours and wander, aimlessly or purposefully, amongst the innumerable tombs which had been constructed on its slopes. Deploying an army of dark-suited security men with earpieces and military-style haircuts in a wide perimeter around a freshly dug grave might erect a *de facto* barrier, but it was not going to hold Franck back.

He pulled out his ID and held it before the eyes of the man who had stopped him with an outstretched arm.

"I know you're just doing your job," said Franck. "But don't get in my way while I do mine."

The arm that had blocked his progress was withdrawn and Franck approached the crowd of mourners. Behind him a paparazzi endeavoured to follow his example. He did not get far.

Louis Halphen's final resting place lay at the centre of a series of concentric circles, ripples caused by his dramatic disappearance at the height of his fame. At the lip of the grave stood a priest and Isabelle Arbaud. Propped between her and Justin Valens was Halphen's elderly mother. They were accompanied by a guard of honour of Halphen's peers, eight men and three women who formed the elite of his profession and who had come to pay homage to the man who had outclassed them all. The second circle was made up of fashion and design professionals, executives of luxury brands, and celebrity peacocks addicted to the world the former created. They huddled in a tight mass, pressing in on the open grave, their ranks closed around one of their own and against the indifference of the mundane. Then came the security detail, the only ones facing outwards, scrutinising all who came too close. Beyond them paced lens-wielding predators: photographers and cameramen there to snatch as many portraits of the famous as their memory cards, tapes and hard drives could hold. Mixed amongst them was a miscellany of eager fans of one or other of the notable figures present, desperate moths who dreamed of burning their wings against the candle of unattainable fame.

Like all those within the secure perimeter, Franck had come from the church of Saint-Germain-l'Auxerrois, where Halphen's coffin had lain in state while a mass was celebrated and a clutch of international opera stars had sung. Isabelle Arbaud had offered a few words in praise and remembrance of a man whose vocation was to infuse the world with beauty and delight, and whose legacy would reveal that his genius had been at its mightiest mere hours before he was savagely torn from his family, friends and innumerable admirers. Standing alongside, rather than behind, the pulpit, clad in an unadorned black dress that clung to her with such grace that she may well have been sewn into it, her hair arranged in a perfect chignon, her face pale but majestic, she had played the church with the restrained mastery of a veteran tragedienne. Not a pause, not a stifled tear, not a hastily bitten lip, not a steady, indomitable regard, not a valedictory gaze raised to the vaulted ceiling, was out of place. Each arrived in perfect synchronisation with her simple, cadenced words. Franck had felt sure he was watching a performance that had cost hours of preparation and rehearsal.

It had distracted him from the real reason for his presence, which was to stand with his back to one of the pillars that ran down the church's nave and cast his eyes over the faces of those present. It was not that he expected Francesca Craveri to reveal her hidden thoughts while sitting in a nearby pew surrounded by what he assumed was Ephémère's entire board of Directors, but he was prepared to clutch at any straws that might come his way. Her reaction to Isabelle's defiant determination to carry on was subdued. Her head registered the tiniest of shakes at the spectacle of a funeral mass transformed, albeit with painstaking taste and decorum, into a marketing offensive. At one point Francesca had looked across at Franck, her eyes meeting and then slipping from this, as if unsure which of them ought to feel the more embarrassed.

Franck had arrived at the cemetery before the rest of the funeral party, since he had slipped into the metro while they jostled for access to the fleet of cars which suddenly converged on the church as the coffin was being carried out through its doors, creating traffic chaos in the immediate vicinity. He had observed Francesca Craveri once more when her BMW 520 dropped her off at Père Lachaise. Her coat and dress – which in her case descended to her calves, whereas Isabelle's stopped dead at her shapely knees – shared in the general colour scheme, but did not seem freshly minted, unlike so many of the costumes on show. This suggested that funerals were not a novelty in her life, but a regular occurrence, and that she chose to attend them in clothes which had become trusted friends.

Franck began to cut through the crowd of those privileged enough to have received an invitation to the cemetery. He had found one lying beside a pew in the church and returned it to its anxious owner, who was no doubt panicking at the thought of being denied access to the graveside. He had not failed to spot the Arbaud logo printed discreetly in the centre of the bottom margin. It was safe to assume that nobody else had either, nor failed to admire both its deliberate modesty and its confident presence as the sacred repository of Halphen's gifts and reputation.

The only one of the mourners moving with purpose, Franck was able to get halfway through the crowd before encountering an obstacle. A hand encircled his sleeve as he was edging his way forward and pulled him up short.

"How about lending me your coat, captain?" whispered Sonia Delemazure. "I'm freezing."

Franck turned to her. Her tall frame was draped in layers of dark silk tulle over a tight-waisted sleeveless black dress which did little to cover her thighs. It was down to the shifting transparency of the tulle, which extended to her wrists and ankles, to provide a semblance of modesty. A veiled pillbox hat completed the effect.

"Your mourning weeds?" whispered Franck in return.

Sonia rolled her eyes and teetered slightly on heels that were a little too ambitious for the uneven ground.

"Marco had a moment of inspiration yesterday. It looks great, but he said I couldn't wear anything over it."

It did look great, but as a means of retaining body heat it was a visible failure. On this dull, cold morning it was an open invitation to hypothermia. Franck shrugged his coat from his back and placed it across Sonia's shoulders.

"That's a far better suit than the last time," she observed.

He did not explain that he had made a hasty visit to the drycleaners that morning on his way home from another frigid night under the Alexandre III bridge. Sonia pinched his coat around her neck with one hand and used the other to pull him closer until they were leaning against each other.

"You stay there. It'll look like I'm really upset and you'll help to keep me warm."

Now close enough to hear what was being said at the graveside, Franck acquiesced, extending his arm and hugging Sonia against him.

The priest had finished speaking. Halphen's mother was lost in tears. Isabelle stepped forward and extracted something from her handbag which she placed delicately upon the coffin. Two photographers who were hovering close by, presumably working for Arbaud, caught every nuance of this gesture. Isabelle then stepped back and Justin nodded towards the perfumers arranged around the perimeter of the grave. They moved forward, picked up the ends of black ribbons that were looped under the coffin, and held them as an unseen mechanism lowered it slowly out of sight.

The priest made the sign of the cross and bowed his head. The crowd followed suit.

Two minutes later Isabelle looped her arm around Halphen's mother and led her away from the grave, parting the mourners before her with no less quiet authority than Moses walking confidently into the Red Sea. Justin, the Noses and the priest brought up the rear. The crowd's attention followed them, the grave itself now utterly forgotten. Moving together, all those present advanced sluggishly towards the cemetery road where cars and limousines were parked, the security detail advancing before them to clear the way.

Sonia slipped out from under Franck's coat, tugging at the layers of gauze around her shoulders to ensure they were perfectly positioned.

"You can keep it," offered Franck. "Get it back to me later."

"Are you kidding? The photographers are still here," said Sonia, beginning to stalk away from him. "You coming?"

Franck shook his head. Having come this far, he might as well pay his own respects to Halphen. And have a closer look at what Isabelle had laid on the coffin. He walked slowly to the edge of the grave and glanced down.

He could see a wax-sealed crystal vial. He had no doubt what was inside. Halphen had always insisted that Night-Scented would prove to be his masterpiece. Although he was tempted to find it all rather crass, Franck accepted that it was fitting that Louis' perfume accompany him to his final resting place.

Franck put his coat back on and sunk his hands into its pockets. He had actually remembered to dig out his gloves this morning, only to realise that their scuffed and torn state rendered them unfit to accompany him to the funeral service. He remained where he stood, staring down at the coffin, almost willing Halphen to provide some kind of explanation of his death and of those which had preceded it. How long he stayed there, he could not say. Long enough for a chill to take advantage of his immobility and wrap him in its embrace.

It took the arrival of another mourner to break his reverie.

The newcomer wore a dark overcoat which hung open, revealing a purple silk lining and a narrow-lapelled black suit. With his mint-condition white shirt, black tie, stiff black leather gloves and polished black shoes, he looked no different from the rest of the crowd which had just wandered off. His hair was cut close to his skull and his eyebrows narrow, as if they had been plucked. He stood alongside Franck and focused his eyes on exactly the same spot: the vial of perfume.

"You had an invitation?" he asked Franck, without turning to face him.

"No."

"Neither did I," said the man. "What a strange thing, to be coveted in death as this week's indispensable fashion accessory."

This seemed harsh, even to Franck. "He may have inhabited a superficial world, but that doesn't mean nobody in it felt anything for him."

"Superficial? Now it's you who's being unjust. Halphen was an artist. The sphere he occupied was one of fragile beauty pursued with discipline and tireless effort. Those who just trooped past here were his consumers, not his acolytes. At best, a handful of them might have understood what he was pursuing. To the rest he was just another exclusive product they could afford and others could not. They didn't live in the same world at all."

"Very few of us are lucky enough to be truly understood," offered Franck. "A handful's better than nothing."

He stepped back, not wishing to disturb the reflexions of what appeared to be one of Halphen's few genuine mourners.

Franck began to walk away.

"You really don't recognise me, captain?"

At that moment, hearing the voice dissociated from the man's physical presence, he did.

*

"Thank you."

Michel Verdier rubbed at his wrists where the cuffs had been.

Franck left them in the middle of the table and moved to the other side. They were in one of the basement interrogation rooms in 36 quai des Orfèvres, having caught a taxi from Père Lachaise. The taxi driver had spent much of the trip frowning in his rear view mirror at Verdier's cuffs, until Franck had suggested to him that the traffic around them posed more of a threat than the prisoner in his custody.

His hands free, Verdier took off his coat, folded it inside out, and laid it across the table. Franck did the same, getting rid of his jacket too. The basement rooms were notoriously overheated.

"Where's your phone?" asked Franck.

Michel extracted it from an inside pocket of his coat and handed it over. It was not switched on.

"Do you have any idea how many messages I've left on this?"

"No more than the people from Ephémère, I imagine," said Michel. "They gave me a phone so that I could arrange to get into their lab as and when I wanted, but I quickly realised that if I left it on I wouldn't have a moment's peace. I couldn't tell you when I last used it."

"I can," said Franck. He had abandoned Michel in the room when they first arrived and had picked up a dossier from his office. He opened it now. "Thursday 31st of January, ten thirty-two in the evening. You called Francesca Craveri. She didn't answer. You didn't leave a message."

"I wanted to tell her that I needed more time to think about what to do with Eternal. That I wouldn't go back to the lab in the immediate future."

"So why didn't you? Why not leave a message?"

"Because I realised what I was doing. I was checking in. I was reporting on my whereabouts and my intentions. I was going back to the way things used to be, before I walked away, before I became destitute and free. So I hung up and decided I really had to think through what I'd got myself into. Was I just doing Francesca Craveri a fleeting favour? Was I just providing a helping hand because I couldn't bear to think of

Eternal tumbling into obscurity after all these years? Was I just reassuring myself that I could still do what I had once been trained to do? Or was I turning my back on my new life for good, and going back to the old one?"

"You're not looking particularly destitute," observed Franck, gesturing at Michel's clothes. "I don't expect you're planning on sleeping under the Alexandre III bridge in those."

"These were for Louis. Ephémère had given me five thousand euros in cash the first time I went to their laboratory to tinker with Eternal. I'd kept them but not spent them. To do so would have been a definitive act – an end to my vow of poverty, if you like. But I couldn't turn up at Louis' grave dressed like a tramp. He would have hated that."

"I'm surprised you cared, given what I've heard of your past relations."

"Oh, I cared, Franck. There's what you've heard, and what you don't know ..."

"We'll get back to that," interrupted Franck. "So now you have a new suit, new coat, and new shoes. What's next?"

"Even this morning I couldn't have answered that question honestly. But now I know. I have to pick up the banner that slipped from between Louis' fingers. I have to go back. I'm going to accept Francesca's offer to be Ephémère's head perfumer."

"Slipped, or was torn from him?"

"Sorry?"

"The banner. Did it slip from Louis' fingers, or was it torn from his dying grasp?"

Michel laid his hands flat on the surface of the table and studied them for a while. He then raised his head.

"I have no idea what a murderer's hands look like. But I can assure you that they don't look like mine."

Franck reached across the table, seized the back of Michel's right hand, and turned it over.

"Your prints are all over Louis Halphen's lab. They are in the downstairs work area. They are on the banister of the stairway leading up to the first floor. They are on the furniture in the conservatory where Halphen's body was found. A witness saw you walking towards the laboratory on the evening Halphen was killed – after all his staff had departed and before the estimated time of death. Then there's the fact that no one knows where you were on the evening Guillaume Thèves died. As for Alain Perrin, you have admitted to being in the immediate vicinity of where he was shot. All of the victims were washed down to clear away all traces of DNA, suggesting the killer knew it would lead us right to him. Your DNA signature has been in the national database since you disappeared."

Michel's eyebrows shot up. "Really? I didn't know that."

"No kidding. Everything points towards you, Michel. The one thing we don't have is the location of the murder weapon. If you can tell me where you've hidden it, you'll save us all a lot of trouble."

"I'm supposed to know how to shoot a gun? Where would I have learned that?"

"You have some strange friends. Know who told me that? Paul Rosolin. Spent five years in the army. Was rated an excellent shot before he lost it to the drink."

Michel took a deep breath. "I like you, Franck. I enjoyed our little chats. You seemed to me a man with an open, curious mind. I hope you'll forgive what I'm about to say. This investigation must have gone desperately and frustratingly astray for you to have come to the conclusion that I am guilty."

"Or you did your level best to lead me astray, giving yourself the time to commit three murders."

"Why would I have done it? Don't you have to establish motive before accusing someone?"

"Jealousy of Halphen. Determination to stop him achieving his life's work. You start by trying to cut off the funds that allow him to develop Night-Scented. You probably got the idea by reading about the death of Nathalie Chautard and decide you can provide the other two. When that doesn't work, you go after the man himself. You finally take your revenge for the fact that Ephémère put him before you, after your brief attempt to work together." Franck gestured towards Michel with an open hand. "As motives goes, how does that strike you?"

"Creative. But misinformed."

"Then correct me, Michel. You know better than me. Tell me why you did it. Or, if you want to start with something simpler, tell me what you were doing in Halphen's lab on the night he died."

"I can tell you what I was doing in the lab. Why my last visit there coincided with his murder, that I cannot explain."

"Your last visit?"

"Yes," said Michel, calmly. "If fingerprints were date-stamped, you would have realised that there's a simple explanation for the fact that mine were everywhere. I've been to Louis' lab maybe five times over the past two months."

"That's hard to believe."

"Because of what you've been told of our old rivalry?"

"There's that. There's also the fact that you are – or were – homeless. It was hard enough for me to get to see Halphen, and I shower every day. I don't see him letting someone who sleeps under a bridge into his lab on a regular basis."

Michel smiled. "You're not wrong, Franck. He found that hard to cope with. I had to strip at the door and take a shower straight away. I had to use the staff shower, of course. He wouldn't let me anywhere near the one reserved for him."

"If your story's true, then Justin Valens would have known about you."

"Louis' little pet dog? He was sent away every time Louis asked me to come."

Franck raised a sceptical eyebrow. "Sounds a bit too convenient to me. Justin did everything for Halphen. He filtered the outside world for him."

"Once again, you're not wrong. But if Louis were to have any secrets, then the first person he'd have to hide them from was Justin."

"And you were Louis' secret?"

"I was," said Michel.

"His secret what? His lover?"

Michel burst out laughing. "Even when I'd washed, Louis avoided all physical contact with me. The life I was leading was anathema to him. In a sense, our differences of opinion hadn't changed at all. He remained an ascetic monk and I remained a Dionysian wanderer."

"So what had changed?"

"We were no longer at war. We had both lost the desire to claim victory for our way of seeing things. We had learned to tolerate that which we did not understand."

"Louis Halphen did not strike me as a very tolerant man," observed Franck.

"Believe me, you encountered a very mild version. You should have met him six years ago. He wouldn't have deigned to breathe the same air as you."

"Why would Halphen have wanted to see you?"

"Louis stood at the peak of his profession. His ability, his judgement and his instinct had gone unchallenged for as long as anyone could remember. For months he had laboured in solitude to create the greatest perfume of his time. But when he finally had a vision of what it should be, and began to work towards making that vision a reality, who could he turn to for confirmation? Not Isabelle Arbaud, who praised every sample he sent to her, and whose only wish was for a perfume – any perfume – that Louis would declare his masterpiece."

"Why should he care what anyone else thought?"

"Because Louis was no solipsist. Everyone was convinced he was self-absorbed and contemptuous of the rest of the world. Even I thought that when I first worked with him. But I was wrong. Louis was an example of utter self-abnegation, not self-absorption. He gave himself to the perfumer's art, but knew that he alone could not be the sole judge of what he produced. That is why he was for so long content to work on Eternal, to build upon a tradition that embodied the taste and desires of several generations. He distrusted his own olfactory sensitivity. Like a dog that hears sounds we cannot, Louis was afraid that he might produce a perfume whose individual notes and collective harmonies would go unnoticed by those who wore it."

"Night-Scented was never intended for the lowest common denominator," objected Franck.

"Night-Scented was intended for the rich. Whether or not they represent – in terms of taste – the lowest common denominator would be an interesting subject for debate. Louis didn't care about the average Arbaud customer who would covet his perfume simply because it bore his signature. But he did want to be sure that one in a hundred, or maybe one in a thousand, would be capable of understanding what made it genuinely special."

"So he had to have a second opinion."

"Exactly," confirmed Michel. "And Louis being Louis, it had to be the most demanding, the most unforgiving second opinion he could find. That – for better or for worse – was me."

"How did he find you?"

"He didn't. I found him."

"What, you walked up to the lab and knocked on the door?"

"No. I went for a more discreet approach. Before I decided to offer my services to Francesca Craveri, I first sought out Louis."

"Why?"

"To ask for his blessing, I suppose. He had worked on Eternal so long, it didn't seem right to think of touching it without his permission. So I went to the one place I knew he visited regularly and – more importantly – alone."

"The church," said Franck.

"That's right. Saint Joseph des Carmes. A place of martyrdom. Louis always felt he was in some way a martyr to his gifts. He found solace in the company of others who had borne a similar burden. I sat in the church for several days until he turned up."

"Must have been a strange reunion."

"Strange and surprising. He recognised me straight away. Maybe his former hatred of me had burned an indelible image in his mind's eye. He sat at the opposite end of a pew from me and said nothing for a long time. Then, when there was no one else in the church, I told him that I was going to approach Francesca. He just nodded, and then asked me if I would be prepared to do something for him."

"You agreed straight away?"

"Of course. I was deeply touched."

"And he never told Justin?"

"Confess that he had doubts about his own judgement? To someone like Justin, a worthless flatterer who would turn on him in a second if he thought there was something to be gained from it? Of course not. Louis was happy enough to have Justin at his beck and call, but he knew he couldn't entirely trust him."

"So he arranged for you to come to the lab at times when he would be alone?"

"That's right. I lent him my nose. I was proud to. Although, to tell the truth, he didn't need it. I don't think Louis ever set a foot wrong in his entire career. He had something I lack – an innate sense of what will enrapture the rest of the world. He wasn't the one who needed a second opinion. I was, and still am today. That's my challenge now. That's why I'm going to lose myself in Eternal before trying anything too individual."

"You're no longer the rebel you used to be?"

"I'm glad to say I'm not. Growing older has to have some advantages, after all."

"Halphen had asked you to come over last Monday?"

"Yes. I didn't stay long. I didn't have to. What he had made was perfect. It was astonishingly and elegantly magnificent. The definitive version of Night-Scented will enchant and seduce generations of women and men."

"How did you communicate? I've got the records for your mobile phone. All the calls are linked to Ephémère numbers."

"When he wanted to see me, he left me a note in Saint Joseph des Carmes. Behind a small statue of Saint Sebastian. I went there once a day to check."

Franck got up and paced back and forward, his eyes on the floor. Michel waited for him patiently. When Franck returned to the table it was to loom over it, his head low between his shoulders and his face close to Michel's.

"It's a great story, Michel. But the only person who can confirm it is dead."

*

"Prove to me he's innocent."

"Is that a challenge or a request?" asked Georges Sternberg.

Franck twisted his lips and said nothing.

"Seriously," insisted Sternberg. "You arrested him. Everything we have points towards him. What's he just told you?"

"Got any coffee?"

"Not here."

They left Sternberg's office, which was a glass-walled cubicle at one end of his forensic lab, and followed a long corridor to a coffee machine. Franck dug out some coins and bought them both black coffees. He drained his and grimaced. Sternberg preferred to sip, taking his medicine in small doses.

Franck recounted Michel Verdier's tale of working with Louis Halphen. Sternberg listened without interrupting. When Franck had finished, Sternberg tossed their empty plastic cups into a nearby bin.

"Come with me," he said.

"Where?"

"Ever been for a ride in a crime scene van?"

"No."

"You'll love it."

Forty-five minutes later they parked illegally in rue Boileau, jamming the van nose-first with its front wheels up on the pavement in a space between two cars. Sternberg took three large bags from the back of the van, gave two to Franck, and hooked the other over his shoulder.

"What if no one's in?" asked Franck.

"I kept the keys," said Sternberg.

Somebody was in. Halphen's lab had been handed back to Arbaud, its legal owner, the previous day. Franck was nonetheless surprised to recognise some of the faces milling about inside it. The same lab crew as before, although its ranks had swollen. All seemed very busy.

"Looks like business as usual," remarked Sternberg.

A young woman in a white lab coat came towards them.

"Can I help you? How did you get in?"

While Sternberg dangled a set of keys in the air Franck pulled out his ID.

"I thought the investigation was over," she said.

"We just want to take a look upstairs," said Sternberg.

"I'm not sure you can," she objected.

"Yes we can," stated Franck, moving past her.

The two of them walked briskly up the stairs. The young woman hesitated, and then set off in pursuit. She caught up with them outside the sealed room in which Halphen kept his notes and key samples.

"You know the code for this door?" Sternberg asked her.

"No," she said. "Alain Couret is the only one who has the code. He's the technical manager. You shouldn't be up here without him."

"Is he downstairs?" asked Sternberg.

"Never mind," interrupted Franck. He pulled out his mobile phone and called up a number from its memory. He got an answer within seconds.

"Justin? It's Franck Guerin. I need the code to the safe room upstairs in the lab. I'm standing in front of it. I need it now. You need to give it to me. Thank you."

He ended the call, reached over to a wall-mounted keypad, and tapped in an eight digit number. The door clicked and

Franck pushed it open. Sternberg stepped through.

"You know who Justin is?" Franck asked the young woman. She nodded. "He let us in. You don't need to worry about us."

Franck joined Sternberg inside the room, shutting the door behind him.

"What are we looking for?"

"What we can't see."

Georges Sternberg declared himself happy with his haul a little over two hours later. He had lifted fingerprints from every possible surface, including cabinet handles, the undersides of countertops, and the tinted windows that allowed a subdued light into the room. Franck had played the part of his diligent assistant: holding a UV torch; passing him brushes, jars of powder, wide rolls of tape and glossy blank cards; bagging the results and noting everything in an evidence log. In the process Franck had opened most of the cabinets and drawers in the place. They were all empty.

"Want to come back with me?" asked Sternberg when they left the room, stripping off their plastic gloves. "You could help scan the prints if you like. The computer does all the work after that."

"You go ahead," said Franck. "I'll ask a few questions downstairs."

As they descended the stairway from the first floor, the young woman who had tried to prevent them from entering pointed them out to a man in his forties with a trim beard and thick-rimmed glasses. Franck was vaguely aware of having seen him on a previous visit.

He intercepted them and introduced himself.

"Alain Couret. Technical manager."

They shook hands.

"I'm Franck Guerin from the Brigade Criminelle. This is Georges Sternberg, one of our forensic experts."

"Did you get what you wanted?" asked Couret. "I'm afraid we emptied out the safe room this morning. We had been told the site was no longer of interest to the police."

"That's OK," said Franck. "We weren't expecting to come back. You have to excuse my colleague, he's in a bit of a hurry." Sternberg nodded to both of them and headed towards the entrance. "You all seem very busy. What's up?"

"We're getting ready for the next step," said Couret.

"Which is?"

"We're moving to an industrial site to test batch production techniques. We know we can make Night-Scented by hand in tiny quantities in a place like this. We have to be able to reproduce it at far larger volumes. It's a complicated mix and there's some clever chemistry involved. It'll be an interesting challenge."

"Are you confident you can do it?"

"I don't like tempting the gods, but yes, I am. Anyway, if not, we'll just keep on doing it by hand."

"I'm sure Isabelle Arbaud could factor that into the price."

Couret offered a wary smile. "I'm sure she could. But that wouldn't be a niche market, that would be a fissure. It took ten of us working through the night to bottle two hundred five millilitre doses this morning. That's a very high cost per litre, particularly if you take into account the preparatory work on the individual components that had already been carried out over the past months."

"Is that why the safe room upstairs is empty?" asked Franck.

"No. The important stuff from the safe room has been moved elsewhere, to a secure location."

"Can you tell me where?"

"No. We just loaded it into an armoured truck. I've no idea where it went."

"And the rest? The unimportant stuff?"

"The archives, you mean?"

"The archives?"

"That room contained every single version of Night-Scented Louis Halphen had developed. All trace of them has now gone."

"Why?"

"It's easy to tell the difference between a painting in the Louvre and the artist's preparatory sketches. Distinguishing one subtly different perfume from another – unless you happen to be a professional, and one of Halphen's quality at that – is a lot harder. If Night-Scented is to be unique and safe from any confusion, then all memory of its elder siblings has to disappear. Orders from the very top."

"So how do you make a perfume disappear?"

"You shred and burn the experimental notes," explained Couret, walking Franck across to a sealed firebox, from which he lifted a bevelled lid to reveal a pile of ashes.

"Then you dilute and denature the liquids."

He led Franck to a ceramic-topped workbench containing three deep square-shaped sinks. A host of small glass vials lay, unstoppered, in a bath of clear liquid with a familiar smell.

Franck nodded at the plastic canisters aligned on the floor at one end of the bench.

"Bleach?" he asked.

"Twelve percent sodium hypochlorite. Wipes the slate clean every time. We do the same thing with the trace tests."

"The what?"

Couret guided Franck to another, identical workbench. This time the sinks contained a host of squares of fabric and paper suspended in an even deeper pool of bleach.

"One of Night-Scented's unique properties is its staying power. We tested each version on different surfaces to check to see how the scent evolved through time. Louis was particularly interested in fabric adhesion. He wanted Night-Scented to leave a ghost of itself in the clothes that it encountered."

"Is that a good thing?" asked Franck.

"So long as it's not permanent. It washes out. You don't have to do this to get rid of it," explained Couret, pointing towards the bleach-filled sinks. "If left alone, it becomes very subtle over time. After twenty-four hours you'd have to be a

Nose to notice it."

*

"We found your fingerprints in the safe room in Halphen's lab."

"So you believe me?" asked Michel Verdier, once more in the interrogation room, having spent the afternoon and the early evening in a nearby holding cell.

"Well, either you frightened Halphen into giving you the code, got into the safe room, searched for something, never found it, and killed him in retaliation."

"Or?"

"Or he invited you into it on several occasions and your story's true."

"Which do you prefer?"

Franck smiled. "I prefer stories where people are kind to each other and the good guys always win in the end."

"You sure you're in the right profession?"

"That's a good question. Hope you don't mind if I don't answer it."

"Fair enough. But what's your conclusion about my story?"

"I'm letting you go. You have a plausible explanation for your presence at Halphen's lab on the evening of the shooting, and your links to the two other murders are merely circumstantial. I can't connect you to a murder weapon. I've got no case." Franck gestured towards the door. "You're a free man."

Michel did not move.

"But do you believe me?"

"Does it matter?"

"It does to me."

"I believe you. Now, let's get out of here."

Franck opened the door and Michel followed him into a corridor lit with fluorescent tubes. They paused at a locker from which Franck extracted Michel's coat and the other personal possessions which had been taken from him. They then walked to a wooden staircase that took them up to the ground floor. A few minutes later they were standing outside on the quai des Orfèvres. It was dark and cold.

"Do you have somewhere to go?" asked Franck. "Other than the bridge, I mean."

"I've got enough money for a hotel. Don't worry about me. Next time I go to the bridge it will be to say goodbye."

"Do you have any plans for tomorrow?"

Michel paused, mulling over the question. "I had forgotten about that."

"About what?"

"About having plans. It's going to take some getting used to."

"Coming back to the real world?"

"Coming back to the conventional world. You were at Louis' funeral. Real is not the adjective that springs to mind."

"Want to go to a party?" asked Franck.

"A party?" echoed Michel.

"The Night-Scented launch party, although I think they're calling it an *avant-première*. Tomorrow evening. I'm invited. I can take a guest."

"You really want me to come?"

"I do. I actually need you to come."

"Well then, OK."

"Meet me here at eight."

"Should I dress up?" asked Michel.

"Not so much that you make me look bad."

"Not so long ago, you were better-dressed than me," said Michel. "You didn't hear me complaining."

They shook hands.

Michel buttoned his coat and pulled out his gloves. He looked at them and then glanced at Franck.

"Here," he said, handing them over. "You're badly in need of a pair of these."

*

"Who's left?"

Yves de Chaumont had four dossiers stacked on top of his desk, each in a bulging folder restrained by a strap. His coat was on and his scarf looped around his neck. Franck had interrupted his departure for the weekend with the news that he had just released Michel Verdier.

"You know who's left," said Franck.

"I also know we've got no proof."

"Then I'll just have to sniff some out."

It was almost as difficult to reach the main entrance of the hôtel Lambert as it was to pass through it. The street outside was blocked by camera-wielding paparazzi, several television crews, and a horde of well-dressed young men and women who seemed to be there on the off-chance that someone would have a spare invitation. Since the rue Saint Louis en l'Ile had been laid out in the seventeenth century to accommodate nothing wider than a horse-drawn carriage, those present had no option but to jostle up against each other and watch their footing, since any who slipped and fell would face a significant challenge reclaiming their previous breathing space.

The security staff, all muscles and unadorned black suits, were having a hard job clearing a route to the gates they held fast against the uninvited. They had, however, managed to open up a narrow protected corridor running along the hôtel's external wall to the corner of the boulevard Henri IV. Those who arrived by car were being dropped off there and ushered through this narrow lifeline to the evening's festivities.

Franck and Michel, having come by foot from the Ile de la Cité and followed the rue Saint Louis en l'Ile as the shortest route to their destination, had to squeeze and elbow their way through the scrum in the street to reach the entrance. Their angle of approach meant that their invitation attracted more careful scrutiny that those waved by guests emerging from limousines on the boulevard. In the end, however, they were waved through into the hôtel's inner courtyard.

Having been temporarily roofed over with some kind of transparent material decorated with glittering stars, the central courtyard had been heated so that guests could shed their outer garments and display their décolletés, bare shoulders and sculpted footwear to their best advantage when tackling the monumental staircase which ran up to the first, and principal, floor. Franck and Michel deposited their coats and followed the others' example.

As they climbed the stairs Franck noticed that Michel was hanging back, remaining one step behind him, as if using him as a shield.

"Are you OK?" he asked.

Michel shook his head from side to side in a non-committal fashion.

"I used to love this kind of thing," he said. "But it's been a long time."

"If you're going to be Ephémère's head perfumer, I suspect you're going to have to get used to it again pretty quickly," said Franck.

"Well, I've been sleeping under a bridge with alcoholics and drug addicts for years. This ought to be easy by comparison."

"Scratch the surface, I'm sure you'll find a fair number of alcoholics and addicts. They're just better-dressed and better-housed."

"How about better-behaved?"

"That, we're about to discover," said Franck, leading them up to the first floor.

Two young hostesses in matching pink dresses directed them towards a vestibule whose centre housed a round, compact bar in the midst of which three men in dress shirts juggled cocktails. A long gallery – a less spectacular twin of the Hercules gallery, one floor above – ran off one side of the room. It housed a myriad of tables piled with food and watched over by attentive staff in long-tailed formal wear. At the far end a chamber orchestra, complete with harpsichord, was running through the lighter side of its eighteenth-century repertory, concentrating for the moment on Albinoni.

They chose an alternative doorway which led to a series of panelled salons running perpendicular to the gallery, providing a different vista of the hôtel's geometrically ordered garden. Lights had been strung between the trees and heat-generating lamps installed at regular intervals along the garden's gravel paths so that guests could wander outside.

Isabelle Arbaud glided towards them in a tight-fitting silver gown that accentuated her slim figure, chastely hid her breasts and exposed long, delicate arms. Diamonds glittered from her ears, her right hand, and the hollow at the base of her neck. She smiled broadly at all she passed, exposing impeccably white teeth against the vivacious red of her lipstick. This was a version of Isabelle Franck had not yet encountered.

"Good evening, Franck," she said, her cheeks brushing against his. "I appreciate you coming. I imagine that this kind of evening is not really to your taste. But your presence helps remind those who did everything in their power to stop it happening that we stand unbowed."

"Let's just hope whoever was responsible isn't actually here," said Franck.

"I doubt that. Madame Craveri and the rest of the Éphémère board haven't been invited. Nor has anyone from Chanel, for that matter. It would have been cruel to force them to watch the fall of their *ancien régime*."

"May I introduce you to a friend? This is Michel."

Isabelle extended a hand for Michel to shake. He bowed slightly as he did so.

"You are the princess of this ball, mademoiselle," he said. "And you smell like very heaven."

Isabelle beamed at him.

"You are clearly a man of taste, and I am therefore greatly flattered. Please excuse me if I move on. It may be my ball, but I must dance for everyone."

She left them, only to halt a few paces further on with some other guests.

"Smell familiar?" asked Franck.

"The last time I encountered that scent Louis was hovering over me like an anxious mother presenting her daughter for an audition."

"You should have told him it wasn't ready. He might still be alive today."

"It would have been a difficult lie to pull off. A Nose is

trained to sniff and point. When it comes to what we sense, we've got about as much free will as your average gun dog. Anyhow, what makes you so sure that Louis' death was triggered by the final version of Night-Scented?"

"All this," declared Franck. "The trick is to prove it."

They moved on, slowly navigating around the other guests. Most had congregated into small, animated groups, their backs turned to passers-by, their conversation only for those admitted into their tight circle. Others hovered attentively, singly or in pairs, eyes shifting in their search for suitably prestigious prey. Franck and Michel attracted no one's attention.

The salons petered out in a library full of imposing, but clearly unread, leather-bound tomes. In a far corner a pair of double doors stood open, providing access to a short flight of stairs leading down to the garden.

"Mind if I step outside for a moment?" asked Michel. "It's all a bit crowded for me. A little fresh air and the gentle odours of the night are what I need right now."

"On you go," said Franck. "I'll do my rounds and check up on you later on."

Michel went out through the open doors and headed off to one of the less-frequented corners of the garden. Franck turned his attention to a conversation that was going on next to one of the towering bookshelves.

Justin stood with a drink in either hand listening attentively to a man in his early sixties who stood tall and proud, albeit rather stiffly, in a traditionally cut dark-blue suit. His hair was cropped close to his head and his shoes highly polished. His finger jabbed repeatedly at Justin as he talked.

Franck walked towards them and stopped at a respectful distance. The elderly man stopped talking momentarily and frowned at him.

Justin jumped in. "General, this is captain Franck Guerin. Captain, this is general Charles Arbaud."

"Captain?" echoed the general.

"Brigade Criminelle," said Franck. "I'm in charge of

investigating the murders that have troubled your daughter's project."

"You're taking your time solving them," observed the general, very much his daughter's father.

"It's a tricky case. But I have to express my admiration for the way Isabelle has handled it all. She's never allowed it to intimidate her or distract her from the task at hand."

"I should think not. Focus. Concentration. A calm head and a clear aim. I made sure she learned all that early on. She would have made a good soldier, Isabelle."

"Having served under her," interjected Justin, "I can assure you she makes an excellent commander-in-chief too."

The general condescended to offer Justin a brief smile. His attention remained with Franck, perhaps sensing that he had not yet finished with him.

"Can I ask what regiment you're with?" asked Franck.

"I was with the 35th, but now I spend most of my time parading around the corridors of the Ministry of Defence. The only really useful thing I've hung onto is a command at the Army Training Centre in Montpellier."

"In what field – if it's not indiscreet?" asked Franck.

"I'm the director of the sniper school. Marksmanship has always been one of my passions."

"Really? I could probably use a few lessons."

"What do you carry? A good old PA50?"

"No. In the Brigade Criminelle we're equipped with MR73s."

"You have a 73 Match?"

"No, just the standard model."

The general shook his head and patted Franck consolingly on the shoulder.

"Not much I could do for you then, captain. With a standard MR73 your best bet is to count on proximity, not on precision."

"I'll keep that in mind," said Franck. "I'm very glad to have made your acquaintance."

"Likewise," said the general. "It's reassuring to meet

someone serious amongst all these marionettes."

Justin smiled and moved back in to reclaim Isabelle's father.

Franck retraced his steps back to the vestibule. He glanced into the food-laden first floor gallery. He was looking for Isabelle Arbaud, but she was nowhere to be seen. He headed back to the main staircase and followed it up to the second floor, stepping into the familiar oval room where Isabelle's assistant normally guarded the door to her office. The assistant's desk had gone, but nothing had been set up in its place to attract guests, a handful of whom had nonetheless taken advantage of the room's collection of comfortable chairs. To his right, though, Franck could see that the second floor's suite of salons had also been given over to the evening's festivities.

As he walked into the first of them he was spotted by a familiar figure, who immediately detached herself from a group of three men and beckoned him over.

"I wouldn't have thought you'd get invited," said Franck.

Sylvie Thomas traced an arc in the air with a languid hand.

"None of this would exist without me," she proclaimed. "Sixty million or so for the hôtel, a few more to do it up, the development costs for the perfume, not to mention the price tag of the year-long marketing campaign that had the world's trendsetters straining at the leash to be here tonight. I think it's safe to say that if I hadn't found Isabelle her backers you wouldn't be sipping champagne in that rather tawdry suit."

"It's actually one of my better suits." It was the one he had worn to the funeral the previous day.

"Yes, but it's not your best suit, is it Franck? I know your best suit. It's a miraculous one, since it succeeds in making you look rather affluent. This one, though, you bought yourself. You really shouldn't go shopping without me."

Franck had no intention of getting caught up in a debate on this subject. He could only lose. Sylvie, for her part, wore a deep-red evening gown retained by a single strap over her right shoulder. Its hourglass bodice made her look lean and athletic: poised for the kill atop high-heeled sandals.

"Before you claim the credit for making this event possible, don't forget that you tried to pull the plug on Arbaud," Franck reminded her.

"True, but Isabelle doesn't know that, does she? Thankfully, neither Perrin nor Thèves are likely to tell her in the near future. My secret's safe with them. And I trust – unless the pair of you have become inexplicably close – that it's safe with you."

"But will it be safe with you?" asked Franck. "If your predictions are right, and Isabelle's fledgling fashion house is crushed as the world's markets teeter and fall, won't you want to tell everyone that you saw it coming? Won't your reputation depend on it?"

Sylvie tipped her head to one side and looked at him coquettishly.

"My secrets are mine to tell, Franck, as and when I like. Anyhow, a new variable has been introduced. I may have to revise my opinion."

"Which is?"

"Death does wonders for an artist's reputation and the value of what he leaves behind. Thanks to Halphen's untimely demise, Isabelle is launching Night-Scented from a platform even she couldn't have dared imagine twelve months ago. If she can convince those present tonight that Halphen's genius was unparalleled, and that Night-Scented is its very quintessence, then she might have the magic ingredient that will allow her to thrive where others will fail. If Ephémère pulled the trigger, then Francesca Craveri is a short-sighted fool."

"What if Isabelle pulled it?" asked Franck.

"If Isabelle did it then she's a visionary. A callous, cunning visionary."

"You'd invest in that?"

"I most certainly would."

"I have to talk to her. Have you seen her?" asked Franck.

Sylvie squared her shoulders and looked at him archly.

"Is it her charms or her potential crimes that interest you so much?"

"Whichever of the two she's trying the hardest to hide."

"Given the dress she's wearing tonight, I think that means you're about to ruin this party. I saw her go that way about ten minutes ago."

Franck followed the direction given by Sylvie's outstretched finger and moved into the next salon. Once through the doorway he stepped to the side, his back against the wall, and scanned the room.

"Good evening, captain," said a voice immediately to his left.

Franck turned his head. He was looking at a waiter in evening wear with a starched white dress shirt, a black bow tie, a long-tailed jacket, razor-creased trousers and a black silk cummerbund. Given his face, he ought to have been slimmer. He had either been on a crash diet of steroids, or the padding in his jacket was not limited to its thick shoulders. He was certainly bulkier and more muscular than when Franck had last seen him.

"Would you like some champagne?" asked the waiter, presenting a round tray bearing two glasses and holding it at shoulder height in front of Franck.

"What the hell are you doing here?"

The waiter tutted and shook his head slightly. "Not here, Franck. Follow me."

He stepped back, smiled, and inclined his body, inviting Franck to follow him. He then set off at a brisk pace, leading Franck back through the salon he had just left. Sylvie, who had been snared by a grey-haired man with a well-proportioned blonde half his age hanging on his arm, threw a curious glance in Franck's direction as he passed, but he ignored it.

When they reached the oval room the waiter walked directly up to the door to Isabelle's office and turned the handle, discovering it to be locked. There were three couples seated nearby, but all were paying more attention to each other than to the new arrivals.

"Never mind, sir," the waiter said to Franck. "I have the key."

Placing himself so that his back stood between the lock and anyone who might glance over, he slipped a set of skeleton keys from his pocket and opened the door in under a minute. He pushed it inwards and stood back, inviting Franck to go first. Franck momentarily hesitated and then crossed the threshold.

His new companion followed him in and shut the door behind them. The room's many windows let in some of the illumination from the garden and from the banks of the Seine, but remained dominated by shadow. Franck's hand explored the wall alongside the door and found the light switch. He turned it on.

"How did you know I'd be here?" asked Franck.

Gabriel Agostini shrugged his shoulders without disturbing the glasses of champagne still balanced on his right hand. "We found out."

"You have someone in Arbaud?"

"Would we have needed someone in Arbaud? Have you any idea how many different firms are involved in preparing a little soirée like this? Catering, security, lighting, hired help – like myself – cleaning, entertainment. Or how many guest lists circulate? You can bet all the celebrity magazines and gossipmongers have a copy, sent express by the organisers. It wasn't very hard for us to lay a hand on one when I began to wonder whether you'd be on it."

"You're under arrest, Gabriel," declared Franck.

Gabriel held up a finger, halting Franck's words, and bent at the knees to lay the tray he was carrying on the floor. When he rose again it was with a snub-nosed pistol in his hand, having slipped it from an ankle holster.

"Wide trouser cuffs," he remarked. "Very useful. I'm not

under arrest, Franck, because I have a gun and you don't – I am right about that?" Franck's expression had evolved into a hard stare, but he slowly nodded his head. "But more importantly, I'm not under arrest because I'm here at your request." With that, Gabriel lowered his gun and let it hang by his side.

Franck thought back to his visit to Les Calanche.

"That was five days ago," he said. "I assumed the message hadn't got through."

Gabriel chuckled. "Oh, it got through loud and clear. It's just I've been busy. And you've been under surveillance. You are aware of that?"

It was Franck's turn to shrug. "I never checked, but I always assumed so."

"I had to wait for an ideal opportunity to present itself. Thanks to Louis Halphen, this came up. I must say, it doesn't look like your case is getting any easier. You've got three bodies now. Still no closer?" There was no hint of mockery in his question. The tone could have been that of a concerned friend.

"You should have called me, Gabriel. Halphen's death made my question for you superfluous."

Gabriel took this news with stoic resignation. "I do have your number, but even if you manage to slip from the gaze of your DST watchers from time to time, I think we can be sure that your phone is tapped twenty-four seven. At best, we could have talked for a few minutes, and I didn't know if that would be enough. So here I am."

"Indeed you are. And the smartest thing you can now do is go. I'll give you five minutes before I call this in. It'll spoil the party, but that was going to happen anyway."

"So you'll have two women yelling at you before the night is out? Isabelle Arbaud for breaking the evening's enchanted spell and Catherine Vautrin for giving me five minutes to get away."

"She'll never know."

"Oh, she'll know. She knows you – that's enough. Anyhow,

since I'm here, what was the question?"

"I wanted to know whether you had a hand in the murder of Guillaume Thèves," explained Franck.

"And you're now sure I didn't?"

"Thèves was killed in the same way as Perrin and Halphen. You didn't do Perrin and I can't see Appoghiu Terra going after a Nose, particularly the greatest of his generation."

"Halphen was that?" asked Gabriel.

"Apparently so."

"Well, let's hope the next generation up has a suitable substitute." He seemed genuinely interested in the subject.

"He's out there somewhere," said Franck, hooking his thumb over his shoulder. "Mingling with his future admirers."

"That's reassuring. But before Halphen was killed, what made you think Thèves was an Appoghiu Terra operation?"

"Massive sales of non WFPA-certified paper."

Gabriel shook his head. "That's wholesalers for you. Think they can wash their hands because they don't tell their suppliers how to make things and they don't tell their customers what to buy. They're just the middlemen, and if they didn't make the deal someone else would. Thèves might not have been destroying the Amazon with his own hands, but he was definitely aiding and abetting."

"Hang on," interrupted Franck. "Did you have anything to do with Thèves?"

Gabriel's lips had only just parted when the door behind them opened. His attention shifted instantly. He stepped forward, shoving Franck brusquely aside and jamming the barrel of his pistol under the chin of the woman who had just walked in.

Not a sound escaped from Isabelle Arbaud.

Franck regained his balance and reached out towards her, but Gabriel slammed the edge of his free hand down on his outstretched arm.

"Back!" he warned with a low cry.

Franck took a few steps backwards, raising his hands.

"She's not here because of you," he said calmly. "Let her go."

Gabriel did not budge. Neither did Isabelle.

"Who are you?" he asked her.

"You don't know?" she replied, acidly. "You're at the *avant-première* of my perfume in the headquarters of my fashion house, not to mention standing in my private office, and you don't know who I am?"

"Isabelle Arbaud, I presume," said Gabriel. "Sorry I didn't recognise you. I don't get much time to read the fashion press these days."

He walked backwards, away from the door, one hand hooked on her arm to make her follow him. He stopped near a small canapé next to a low table.

"I'm sorry, but I have to do this," he said. Without moving his gun, he ran his free hand over the surface of her dress, skirting her breasts, smoothing her stomach and crossing her back. He then crouched down and lifted the hem of her dress, sliding his hand underneath it and up between her legs.

"You do this to every woman you meet?" she asked.

"I'm a wanted criminal. Ask the captain. The instinct for self-preservation doesn't sit well with refined manners. But I do apologise. Please sit down."

He stepped back and allowed her to sit gracefully on the canapé. He gestured towards Franck, who had followed them warily as they progressed across the room.

"Franck, could you move over there?"

He pointed to a spot three or four paces from where Isabelle was seated. Franck assumed he was placing them both within his arc of fire. He nonetheless followed Gabriel's directions.

"She's not armed. She's not a threat to you," said Franck.

"No she's not, but she's remarkably calm if she is who she says she is. I would have expected the real head of a fashion house to be hysterical on running unexpectedly into an armed man. A DST agent pretending to be the head of a fashion house, on the other hand, would probably be as steely."

"Ask me," said Franck.

"What?"

"Our pact. Ask me."

Gabriel smiled. "I knew that would come in handy. Franck, is this Isabelle Arbaud?"

"It is."

"Is she in some way connected to the DST or any other security or police organisation?"

"Not as far as I know, no. Like you said, she's just the head of a fashion house. She is, though, from a military family. You're not the first man with a gun she's seen in her life. She's also known for her icy self-control and formidable will. What you've just seen is in character, believe me."

"That's very flattering, captain," said Isabelle. They were back to 'captain'. Given the circumstances, Franck could not blame her. "Perhaps you can return the favour and introduce me to your friend?"

"Friend is not the term I would have chosen," said Franck.

"Not your friend? Just someone with whom you happen to have some kind of strange pact?"

"We have an understanding. It's a long story. This is Gabriel Agostini. You may have heard of him. He's the head of Appoghiu Terra Corsa, a Corsican terrorist group, recently rebranded as Appoghiu Terra, an ecological terrorist group."

Isabelle cast an appraising glance over Gabriel. "Why rebrand? It's a difficult exercise, and it rarely works."

"Our mission has changed," explained Gabriel. "Our audience too. While we're on the subject, I of course disagree with the captain's careless use of the adjective 'terrorist'."

"Gabriel's organisation killed Nathalie Chautard," interjected Franck. "I could have said 'homicidal', but I think 'terrorist' is an accurate description, given its wider goals."

"You killed Nathalie Chautard?" asked Isabelle, leaning forward and fixing Gabriel with an avid stare.

"I wasn't driving the truck that forced her off the road, but, yes, I had it done."

"What about Alain Perrin, Guillaume Thèves and Louis Halphen?" she demanded.

"He had nothing to do with them," intervened Franck, before turning his attention to Gabriel, "Not unless you've got something to tell me about Thèves?"

Gabriel shook his head.

This was not how Franck had planned to play his hand, but he decided that the unexpected presence of Agostini might even work to his advantage.

"He didn't have them killed," Franck resumed, "but I'm pretty sure you did."

Isabelle's eyes widened.

"Me?" she exclaimed. "I'm being held at gunpoint by a terrorist and you're accusing me of murder? Somebody's been drinking too much champagne, I think."

"Gabriel no doubt played an unwitting role in it all, as the killing of Chautard probably inspired the murder of the others. I'm prepared to bet that Nathalie Chautard was so angry about the delays over the development of Night-Scented that she finally threatened to pull out her loan unilaterally. It came to nothing because of her death and the chaos that her estate has been in ever since. That was a valuable lesson for you. When Perrin and Thèves suddenly started talking about redeeming their debentures a few weeks ago, you realised how convenient their sudden disappearance could be. You disposed of them before they could go through with it."

"And where am I supposed to have learned how to eradicate uncooperative investors? At the feet of the machiavellian Francesca Craveri?"

"At the hands of general Charles Arbaud, I suspect. What's the head of a sniper school to do when he finds himself with no offspring other than a disciplined young girl? I'd guess he either taught you to shoot himself or had you taught by someone under his command."

"And what am I supposed to have shot them with?" she protested.

"That's easy," continued Franck. "A Perrin Industries PI87, a weapon that can only be used by an accomplished marksman with a sense of style. A weapon that you talked Alain Perrin into giving you as a present. You lured him backstage during the Ephémère show, probably using the pretext of discussing his withdrawal from Arbaud. He showed you the PI87, maybe to soften the blow of his decision to pull out. You took it from its presentation box and used it to get rid of him."

"And you're confident I could do such a thing with the practised ease of a hardened killer like our monsieur Agostini here?"

"You're known for your cool head. You certainly proved it that day, because you realised that you had been close enough to Perrin for long enough to have impregnated him with the scent of Night-Scented – the very trace effect Halphen had spent so much time and money developing – a scent that could only lead back to you. So you bleached him, just as you subsequently ordered that all the test samples of the experimental versions of Night-Scented be bleached."

"Bleached? You've lost me." This came from Gabriel Agostini, whose eyes were on Franck, although his gun remained obdurately focused on Isabelle.

"She doused his body and clothes in bleach, washing away all other smells," explained Franck. "It was an inspired move, since when we discovered it we assumed it had been done to remove traces of foreign DNA."

"And I had smuggled all this bleach into the Ephémère show in my Louis Vuitton handbag?" mocked Isabelle.

"No, you found it at the back of the catering area where you shot Perrin. You were improvising with what was to hand. But that was the last time you had to do so. You now had a weapon and a *modus operandi*. A week later Thèves came to the same decision – he wanted his money back. You made sure it didn't happen."

"Can you enlighten me as to why all my investors were supposedly clamouring to get out of the deal? Look at what is going on around us tonight, captain. The evening is a resounding success. Arbaud isn't going to be big, it's going to be huge."

This was the moment to surprise her with his knowledge of Sylvie Thomas' role behind the scenes. But he could not. It was not his secret to tell. He could only forge ahead.

"Of course it is. With Louis Halphen's death you've become the custodian of his memory. Night-Scented is no longer just an upmarket perfume, it's the posthumous masterpiece of an artist who's now a tragic legend in his field. All thanks to you. When Halphen announced that he had finally perfected Night-Scented you hurried to the lab and killed him. Then you realised that he had showered and changed, and therefore shouldn't bear any trace of perfume, which you of course had carried there with you. More to the point, you were wearing the penultimate version, which would betray you even more clearly if someone with the right nose came by. So you covered your tracks again. The lab was a perfect crime scene. Everything you needed was there."

Isabelle still refused to react. She watched him with something akin to detached amusement. Agostini's eyes shuttled between the two of them, fascinated.

"Thèves was different, though," continued Franck. "That was the only time you had to take everything with you. But since you arranged to meet him under the Mirabeau bridge before your dinner appointment, you were able to bring the bleach in your car. Luckily for you, you brought a lot, since the pair of you sat and talked in Thèves' car before you got him to walk with you under the bridge – where you were both invisible to the traffic up above – and you finished him off. You then realised you had to treat not only the corpse but the interior of his car as well."

"It's a remarkable story, captain," said Isabelle. "But my lawyers will crucify you if you start telling it to anyone. It's just a web of supposition whose sole purpose is clearly to damage Arbaud and the launch of Night-Scented. I suspect you've been doing a little more than chatting with Francesca Craveri recently. Perhaps she's offered the odd gift? Ephémère has the means to be very generous with those who help make their problems disappear."

The Ephémère hypothesis once again – her favourite diversionary tactic. Franck decided to throw down his final card. He hoped it proved an ace.

"You missed something in Thèves' car," he declared. "A scarf that was lying in the compartment at the bottom of the driver's side door. I've had it analysed. It bears a trace of one of the experimental versions of Night-Scented. And, as we know, you're the only person who ever got to try them. You were in that car long enough to affect every textile surface inside it. Since you shut the doors after you'd poured the bleach and left, the scent managed to survive until we got there."

Isabelle raised a sceptical eyebrow. "You're telling me police labs are able to detect and classify traces of a unique perfume? Nobody's yet invented a machine or scientific procedure that's up to the challenge, captain. That's why the very best Noses still earn vast sums of money."

"I didn't use a police lab. I gave the scarf to a Nose. The best there is, now that Louis Halphen is dead."

"And who might that be?"

"Michel Verdier."

"Impossible!" exclaimed Isabelle. "Verdier went missing years ago."

"So he did," agreed Franck. "But he's back. I introduced you to him less than an hour ago. I'd like to be able to say that I found him, but I didn't. He came back in from the cold to help Louis Halphen perfect Night-Scented. They worked together secretly for almost two months. All the samples and test swatches may have disappeared from Halphen's lab, but Michel remembers what every version of Night-Scented smelled like. Olfactory memory – isn't that one of the things that makes a Nose a Nose?"

"Fiction upon fiction," declared Isabelle, dismissively.

"You'll see," said Franck calmly. "As soon as Gabriel has gone, I'm taking you to the quai des Orfèvres, and we'll talk about it there."

This was bravado. Isabelle was not for breaking. He sensed that he had lost the game, but he had gone too far to pull back. He was obliged to hold on grimly till the end, even if it meant the Brigade being humiliated and Isabelle walking free.

He turned to Agostini, who had followed the debate with equanimity, his gun never wavering in its scrutiny of Isabelle as he switched his gaze back and forward between the two protagonists.

"I thought you'd forgotten I was here," said Agostini. "But I think you're right, Franck, it's time for me to go."

"You're going to let a known terrorist, who's just confessed to having murdered Nathalie Chautard, walk out of here?" demanded Isabelle. "Just so that you can detain me on the basis of a fairy tale you spun out of nothing with Francesca Craveri? My lawyers will have a field day with this."

"He does have a gun," Franck pointed out. "And it's pointed directly at you. I'm acting under duress. But as soon as he walks out of here, I'll call in the DST." He waited until Isabelle's eyes had switched to Agostini's face, awaiting his reaction, before silently mouthing 'five'.

"I'd better go then," said Gabriel. "First, though, I'd like to thank you both for a remarkable evening."

"Wait," ordered Isabelle. "I can't have you leaving empty-handed. It's not every day I get to meet a notorious criminal, a terrorist even. May I?" She gestured towards the low table near to where she was sitting. Her handbag sat upright upon it. "At the very least, you deserve a sample of Night-Scented. Normally it's only for our female guests, but I'm sure you have someone who would appreciate it."

Gabriel smiled. "I really shouldn't. If I've understood correctly, it'll make it very easy for captain Guerin to track me down. But it would be discourteous to refuse." He indicated that Isabelle could recover the handbag. As she did so Gabriel looked over at Franck and shrugged, raising both hands in a gesture that told of his amusement at the situation in which he found himself. "That way I won't have gone to all this bother for nothing."

He then fell back violently, one hand homing in on his chest, his mouth thrown open, the noise of a gunshot covering whatever sound he had made. As Agostini hit the ground with a heavy thud, Isabelle turned a long, elegant barrel towards Franck with a flick of her wrist. She held the PI87 lightly, her arm outstretched, her grip perfect. Jean-Charles Velasque would have been proud of her. General Charles Arbaud too, no doubt.

"I wouldn't move if I were you, Franck," she said. They were back on first-name terms. "You know by now how good I am with this."

Franck did as he was told. He did not move. He did speak though.

"I have something to confess, Isabelle."

"And what might that be?" she asked, standing up from the canapé.

"I made up the bit about the scarf in Thèves' car. You were right. There was no proof that it was you."

"So you tugged my strings. Good for you. It's going to cost you dearly, though."

"You're going to shoot an officer of the Brigade Criminelle in your own office? You can bleach me all you want, you'll find this one a lot harder to deny."

"Your friend Agostini is going to shoot you," she said calmly. "I'm then going to wrestle the gun from him and kill him with a desperate but lucky shot at close range. You'll be a dead hero. I'll be a plucky heroine, traumatised but alive. Agostini will take the blame for all the unfortunate events leading up to today, since his prints will be on the PI87. And Arbaud's legend will be secure – a fashion house forged in adversity, a phoenix rising from others' ashes. Goodbye,

Franck."

Then she doubled over, her scream strong and painful enough to be heard above the shot. Franck leapt towards her, hooking one arm around her chest as she fell to her knees. With his other hand he tugged the PI87 from her now feeble grasp.

Agostini rolled over onto his side, groaning as he did so, his pistol still in his hand.

Isabelle was writhing in Franck's arms. He wrestled her to the ground and forced her folded knees away from her body. Blood was welling from beneath her ribcage. He glanced around at Agostini, who was unbuttoning his white shirt, which was torn but not stained.

"Kevlar over a ceramic plate," gasped Gabriel, studying the stiff breastplate that had been hidden by his shirt. The bullet from the PI87 was lodged in a spot near his heart. "Makes you look fat, but there are compensations." He took another painful breath. "Think I've lost a few ribs though."

Franck placed his hands flat across Isabelle's stomach and pushed down with all his weight, keeping the wound compressed.

"Call an ambulance," he said. "I have to maintain pressure."

Gabriel got to his knees and then to his feet. He walked unsteadily towards the door.

"She needs an ambulance!" Franck yelled.

Gabriel glanced back at him.

"Five minutes. Then you've got one."

He opened the door and disappeared.

Isabelle stared at Franck, her eyes wide with pain and disbelief. She no longer struggled against him. Her lips were forming a word. He leant as close as he could while maintaining the force behind his palms.

"Franck."

Then she said no more.

Monday, 11th February

"There's someone in your office."

So that was the new security protocol: the doors were still wide open, but at least he was being warned.

"Anyone I know?" asked Franck.

"It's not your pal Agostini. Not unless he's in drag. Then again, it seems he's a master of disguise."

Franck held his tongue and walked on into the inner labyrinth of 36 quai des Orfèvres. Isabelle Arbaud's death had been a gift to the media. The fatal shooting in the midst of the glitterati of the fashion world had sent every other story reeling. It had dominated Sunday's newscasts and grabbed the cover of every newspaper the next morning. A sensational story in and of itself, Agostini's presence had added extra zest. 'Killer perfume princess slain by Corsican terrorist' was one of the more restrained headlines Franck had spotted at a newsstand on his way in.

Franck navigated the stairs and corridors that took him to his office, whose door was slightly ajar. He knocked lightly on the doorframe.

"In you come," said a familiar voice, as insouciant as ever.

Sonia Delemazure stood by his desk in faded jeans, knee-high boots, a wide-necked jumper of thick, coarse wool, a long velvety scarf that trailed on the ground and a beret perched on her blonde hair. She had been writing something on a scrap of paper that lay beside a large stiff paper bag bearing the Ephémère logo.

"I was leaving you a note. I've got a shoot this morning. I'll soon be unfashionably late."

"What does it say?" asked Franck, moving into the room and kissing her on each cheek.

Sonia snatched up the piece of paper with a flourish and read, "To the hero of the hour. This should stop you catching a cold while you're catching the bad guys."

"Or bad girls," observed Franck.

Sonia thrust the bag at him. "You can't refuse it now. The investigation is over."

Franck pulled out the coat he had been offered nearly two weeks previously. At Sonia's prompting he took off his parka, tossed it onto the nearby coat stand, and slipped on Francesca Craveri's gift.

"Perfect," declared Sonia. She then stepped around him and grabbed his parka, emptied its pockets onto his desk and stuffed it into the now empty bag.

"Where's that going?" asked Franck.

"Where you can't wear it anymore," she said.

Franck frowned. His parka had been a loyal companion for some years.

"It's part of the deal," announced Sonia. "Francesca insisted."

"Fair enough," he conceded. "But leave it with me. I know some people who could use it."

"You promise? If I see you in it again, I'll shoot you. Right between the eyes."

"I promise," stated Franck.

"OK. I have to go."

She was reaching for her own coat when Franck pulled something out of his briefcase.

"It just so happens I've got a present for you," he said, holding a small crystal vial on the flat of his palm.

Sonia caught her breath and snatched the tiny bottle from Franck's hand, holding it up to catch the available light.

"Is this what I think it is?" she asked, her eyes shining.

"I fear it is."

She delicately broke the wax seal on the vial, teased out its glass stopper with her long fingernails, and deposited a single drop on her left wrist. She waited a few seconds and then held it to her nose. A slight moan escaped her.

"I'd kill for that."

www.nightscented.com

Check out the Night-Scented web site for:

Reading Group notes

Photos of all of the key locations in Paris featured in the story

More about the author

More about John Law Media

WASP-WAISTED

David Barrie

A young model is found dead in a luxury hotel in Paris. A stunning photo of the scene features on the cover of the country's top-selling scandal sheet. It was delivered before the police found the body. In a city obsessed with images of perfection, the murderer's artistic talents are the object of much admiration.

It's Franck Guerin's first criminal case. Used to the murky world of national security, he has to learn to play by the rules. Not so easy when your only clue is the *ultra-chic* lingerie in which the victim was draped.

The fashion trail takes him into a universe of desire, deceit, beauty and profit. As the victims mount and the images roll in, Franck has to train his eye to spot the killer's signature. Not to mention whoever is collecting photos of him...

The first of the Franck Guerin novels. Original, stylish and tightly-plotted, Wasp-Waisted recounts a murder enquiry born of a fatal encounter between fashion, art, business and desire.

ISBN 978 0 9562518 0 0

www.waspwaisted.com

Rimbaud, Arthur   A rising star in the firmament of French poetry in the 1870s, author of a famously tormented collection (*Une saison en Enfer*), Rimbaud abandoned poetry in his early twenties before moving on to a slightly more lucrative career as (amongst other things) an arms dealer in North Africa.

viennoiseries   A collective term for bread-like products which nonetheless aspire to the condition of cakes (croissants, *pains au chocolat*, *pains au raisins*, brioches, ...). Viennoiseries are generally consumed for breakfast. The name is a reference to Austria, the original home of the croissant.

WWD   Women's Wear Daily. The daily newspaper of the fashion industry, published in New York.

L'Officiel de la Mode	A monthly fashion magazine which is the oldest surviving French women's magazine (founded in 1921).
pétanque	A serious contender for the title of France's national sport, pétanque involves tossing steel balls (with a diameter of 7-8cm and weighing 650-800g) as near as possible to a small wooden target. Easy to play badly, it has the advantage of demanding very little physical fitness. A pastime whose roots lie historically in the south of France, the nearer you get to the Mediterranean the more it takes on the trappings of a religion (amongst male *pastis* drinkers, that is).
RER Réseau Express Régional	The suburban rail network, the RER links Paris with its dormitory towns and airports. Running north-south and east-west underneath the centre of Paris, the RER sometimes provides a quick way of moving about inside the capital. It makes fewer stops than the metro but has none of its charm.
RG Renseignements Généraux	Created in 1911, the Renseignments Généraux were a branch of the police charged with keeping an eye (some might say spying) on the citizens of the Republic and all others to be found within its frontiers. In July 2008 (as foreshadowed in this book) the RG merged with the DST to become the DCRI.

juge d'instruction	A *juge d'instruction* is an investigating magistrate whose job is to carry out preliminary investigations of crimes and misdeeds and judge whether they are ripe for prosecution. Once charged with an inquiry, a *juge* has complete autonomy to proceed as he wishes and is almost impossible to stop (only the nation's highest court – the *cour de Cassation* – can wrestle an affair from the hands of a *juge*, which makes it very difficult to do so discreetly).
	A *juge* neither prosecutes cases nor decides their outcome (he never announces that a party is innocent or guilty), but simply whether they merit to be tried before a court of law.
	The role of the *juges* is to handle very complex or sensitive cases deemed more suitable to elucidation by a powerful, independent and highly experienced judicial expert than by normal police and bureaucratic process.
	It is said that the *juges d'instruction* are the sole actors capable of keeping the nation's elite in check, as it is well-nigh impossible to pull their strings. It is also said that the current government is intent on abolishing them.
La Fontaine, Jean de	Another poet from the age of Louis XIV, but unlike Boileau one who stood warily on the sidelines as far from the burning rays of the Sun King as he could. Famous for his *Fables*, moral tales featuring a cast of animals and a wry (sometimes slightly subversive) sense of humour.

défilé   Literally, a parade. Used without qualification,
                     the term generally designates a fashion show.

Les Echos   One of France's two daily business papers (the
                     other being *La Tribune*).

flic   Widely-used slang for "cop".

gardiens de paix   The rank and file of the police force.

haute couture   A general term for the creation of luxury
                     garments.   To be officially recognised as a
                     leading fashion house you have to be a member
                     of the *Chambre Syndicale de la Haute Couture*.

Heurtaut,   A renowned furniture maker from the 18th
Nicolas   century.

humani nihil a   A shorthand form of a quotation from Terence, a
me alienum puto   playwright from the 2nd century BC: "as I am a
                     man, nothing that is human is alien to me".
                     Thought to have been born in Carthage (in
                     modern-day Tunisia), Terence was brought to
                     Rome as a slave, where he was later freed by his
                     owner.

Comité Colbert	A lobbying organisation created in 1954 to promote the interests of the leading lights of the French *industrie du luxe*. Its membership includes the most upmarket fashion houses, jewellers, perfumers, wine producers and luxury hotels.
commissariat	A police station.
DCRI Direction Centrale du Renseignement Intérieur	Officially created on the 1st of July 2008 (some months later than the events related in this book), the DCRI brought together the two feuding arms of the French national security apparatus, the DST and the RG.
DST Direction de la Surveillance du Territoire	Part of the nation's police structure created in 1944, the DST was a secretive organisation in charge of counter-espionage, counter-terrorism and protecting the French economy. It should not be confused with its sister organisation, the DGSE (Direction Générale de la Sécurité Extérieure), which carried out operations outside national borders. The DGSE was part of the Ministry of Defence whereas the DST was attached to the Ministry of the Interior. In July 2008 (as foreshadowed in this book) the DST merged with the RG to become the DCRI.
La Défense	A massive business district to the west of Paris. Born out of nothing in the late 1950s, it boasts a host of ever-changing skyscrapers built above a massive concrete plateau. Many French and overseas firms are headquartered here.

arrondissement
For administrative purposes Paris is divided into twenty arrondissements whose size and population varies widely (from 18 000 to 230 000 inhabitants). In the course of the city's history each one has evolved a distinct social character.

Boileau, Nicolas
Member of the Académie Française and royal historian to Louis XIV. An acclaimed poet and arbiter of literary style under the Sun King. His long poem *L'art poétique* is a manifesto for the refined and polite style of the 17th century.

Brigade Criminelle
Also known as "la Crim", the Brigade Criminelle investigates the city's murders and most serious crimes. Its offices are to be found at 36 quai des Orfèvres on the Ile de la Cité, an address well known to readers of Georges Simenon.

Citroen, André
An ambitious entrepreneur, André Citroen demonstrated his talent for industrial organisation by setting up a huge munitions factory in record time on the banks of the Seine during the First World War.

In 1919 Citroen turned to manufacturing automobiles and had the good sense to follow the example of Henry Ford in mass-producing standard vehicles for the popular market. Within ten years his firm had become the second most important manufacturer of cars in the world but ran into severe financial problems in the 1930s and was taken over by Michelin.

In the 1990s the riverside site which had been reused throughout Citroen's history was transformed to become the André Citroen park.

Glossary

Most of the French words, phrases and references in this book have long since been adopted into English usage. The following glossary attempts to cover those which might be less well known.

Apollinaire, Guillaume	An avant-garde French poet active in the first two decades of the 20th century, Apollinaire was one of the casualties of the flu epidemic which swept across Europe just after the First World War.

It is well-nigh impossible to avoid his poem *Le Pont Mirabeau* if processed as an adolescent by the highly prescriptive French educational system. For good measure, it is engraved on a plaque at one end of the bridge itself.

Sous le pont Mirabeau coule la Seine
Et nos amours
Faut-il qu'il m'en souvienne
La joie venait toujours après la peine
Vienne la nuit sonne l'heure
Les jours s'en vont je demeure

One possible reading (not quite a translation, strictly speaking) would be:

Beneath the Mirabeau bridge flows the Seine;
Our loves too.
A never-ceasing reminder
That pain is the prelude to joy.
Come the night, toll the bell,
The days pass, I remain.